Rev

'The majority of his work reflec~~ts his gift for~~ ... tales that are] exercises in fear.'
  – Mike Ashley, *Who's Who in Horror and Fantasy Fiction*

'Roger F. Dunkley is best known in Britain as the creator of elegant, blackly humorous, supernatural tales ... "Twisted Shadow", however, which Mike Ashley calls "his most chilling to date" is a grimmer work than most, conjuring up a horror both ancient and terribly modern – and one that touches us all.'
  – Ted Klein, *The Twilight Magazine*

'Roger F. Dunkley relates his ghost stories with tongue wedged firmly in his cheek and "The Ghost Machine" has us chuckling and shivering, whilst marvelling at the ingenuity of the plot.'
  – R. Chetwynd-Hayes, *Fontana Great Ghost Stories*

'He has many excellent short stories to his credit, most combining mystery and horror with memorable black humour.'
  – Richard Dalby, *Mystery For Christmas*

'I like ["Twisted Shadow"] very much. It is very good.'
  – Herbert Van Thal

'I read "Zazine Forsyth's Resurrection Affair" again the other day and was delighted once more by it.'
  – James Hale, Gollancz, Macmillan *inter alia*

'"The Man Who Sold Ghosts" diverted me very much ... "Miss Brood's Speciality" is a goodie ... "Surprise! Surprise!" is one of the funniest yet.'
  – Mary Danby, Fontana/Collins *inter alia*

THE MAN WHO SOLD GHOSTS
AND OTHER LIGHT TALES FROM THE DARK SIDE

THE MAN WHO SOLD GHOSTS
AND OTHER LIGHT TALES FROM THE DARK SIDE

ROGER F. DUNKLEY

GREENWICH EXCHANGE
LONDON

Greenwich Exchange, London

First published in Great Britain in 2017
All rights reserved

Roger F. Dunkley © 2017

Printed and bound by imprintdigital.com
Cover design: December Publications
Tel: 07951511275

Greenwich Exchange Website: www.greenex.co.uk

Cataloguing in Publication Data is available from the British Library

ISBN: 978-1-910996-09-6

For Ro, Olive, Ralph and Marshall

CONTENTS

Foreword

A FOREWORD SEEMS UNNECESSARY, FORWARD EVEN. Like saying grace before breaking into a box of chocolates. For this assortment which you are about to receive is indeed a very mixed confection of short stories, varied in style, content and publishing history. A number of them are emerging blinking into the light of publication for the first time, some purring, some with fangs bared; the majority have appeared in a range of different anthologies over three decades – *Pan Horror* (edited by the legendary Herbert Van Thal), *Fontana Horror* and *Ghost* (edited by the talented, generous and, of course, equally discerning Mary Danby and R. Chetwynd-Hayes), *Twilight Zone* and many others – but all are at last in this collection, thanks to James Hodgson, free to loosen their literary stays, and, released from the constraints of genre labelling, able to be themselves with comic, serious, gruesome, ghostly, ironical, SF ingredients often promiscuously intermingling in the same story. Their common aim: spectral shudders with chuckles, merriment mingling with the mysterious and macabre. Beneath the stylised, black comic surface run seams of more thought-provoking themes, exploring questions which tease the imagination and enhance our sense of wonder in the mysteries of the unseen universe – ideas of survival and reincarnation, prophecy and fate, time-slips and telepathy, extra-terrestrial hopes and Armageddon fears, as well as the phenomena of ghosts, remote viewing and

11

extra-sensory perception in general. And what of the sinister Tibetan tulpa, the thought-ghost, of *Mea Tulpa*, a tale, crowning this anthology, which descends into the grim vaults of the gothic imagination: what monsters and nightmares are lurking there in the dark pit of the collective racial unconscious waiting to be born ... ?

So I suggest you check your doors are safely locked and bolted, and look once more under the bed (you can never be too sure), before you settle down with a comforting bag of toffees and prepare to turn the first page and be toe-curlingly, knuckle-whiteningly ... entertained.

Roger F. Dunkley
2017

A Problem Called Albert

A CLEAR NIGHT, THE STARS RISING raw and sharp. In the prowling, howling wilderness of the dark, nature was roused and tense.

Pain – sudden and shrill. A tearing of tendons. Agony, sharp-toothed, biting into shrieking nerve fibres, ripping at still living muscle. Still living. Twenty-three slow, excruciating heartbeats to endure. That was the part Albert enjoyed most. Twenty-three, and then, for his victim, the stars would go out.

The body, still warm, its nerves refusing to die, was heavy and unhelpfully shaped for conveying up the path and into the house. But it had to be done. Some untidy, on the spot surgery got rid of the less convenient limbs and protrusions, and, glowing still with a profound exhilaration and pride, Albert negotiated the corpse upstairs, and pushed open the bathroom door. Its hinges squealed, as usual.

In the next room, Maud jerked awake and sat up in bed, trembling. Her eyes and ears strained after secrets in the darkness. Her heart pounded with unnecessary zeal.

'A burglar,' said her fear. Her calico-clad bosom rose and waited.

'The loose slate,' replied her reason. The bosom sank, expelled a sigh and resumed work. She plumped up her pillow and prepared herself again for sleep.

A scuffling noise, dim but distinct, reached her from the bathroom.

'Or a murderer!' suggested her fear, with a horrified, internal scream.

Appalled, she poked her husband in the ribs. Henry Wortle stirred, extended an arm gnarled with arthritis, upset the smiling tooth mug by the bed, and grunted loudly. She hissed for silence still more loudly and applied her elbow again to his side with the cruelty born of desperation and marital privilege.

Like many men, Henry Wortle was not at his best at two o'clock in the morning. He was disinclined for conversation just now. The words were not there. He tried.

'What –?'

His wife clapped a hand to his mouth.

'What — ?' he began again, less distinctly.

'The bathroom,' she whispered urgently.

A command? Had incontinence set in? He felt the sheets. A request, perhaps? Not, surely, after twenty years of competent married life? His comatose mind groped round the words without success.

'There's someone there. In the bathroom.'

Signals shivered along his brain; something clicked.

'It's probably Albert,' said Henry Wortle.

Nine stealthy strides later, Henry tugged dramatically on the cord of the bathroom light, flung the protesting door wide, turned to his wife and said, more in smugness than in anger: 'You see?'

Albert was sitting on the side of the bath. He blinked his yellow eyes and purred. Maud Wortle moved forward in a surge of affection and relief.

'Naughty Albert,' she began, 'frightening Mummy – '

Then she screamed. Her bare feet cringed. It was soft and warm and sticky. She looked down.

'What is it!' she gasped.

Albert looked proudly on.

'It would appear to be a rat, Maud,' said Henry Wortle. 'Without a head.'

Albert lifted a paw to his mouth, unfurled his tongue and with great dignity began to preen himself. Maud, her toes tightly curled, gazed at him with uncomprehending astonishment. A shudder of nausea passed through her, followed momentarily by hatred.

'Or a vole,' said Mr Wortle.

'Whatever it is – '

'Rats are different.' Henry, normally fastidious, was tired.

'Whatever it is, we ought to punish him.' Maud struggled to be firm. 'Naughty, horrid Albert.'

The yellow eyes narrowed. Albert inclined a furry head to be stroked.

'It's disgusting. It's savage.'

'It's nature,' observed Henry Wortle.

'I don't know what got into him. Oughtn't we to show him he's been a bad boy, Henry?'

Albert leapt elegantly to the floor, seized the treasured offering in his mouth and looked up, seeking approval and gratitude. The creature, which had been on the point of devouring some lesser creature at the moment of its demise, hung from between Albert's fangs, its blood staining the synthetic fur of the bathroom carpet.

'Henry! Do something.'

Henry did something. He seized Albert by the scruff of his neck in the very zenith of the cat's triumph and generosity – he had after all only eaten the head – and struck him.

'Nasty,' said Henry, and, moved by an impulse as wild as it was obscure, hit the animal again. 'Vicious,' said Henry, and delivered a third blow.

Maud flinched. She put out a restraining hand. But Henry was red and excited. Savagely he picked Albert up, carried him downstairs and flung him out back into the rustling, preying jungle of the night.

Maud was sitting on the edge of the bed when he returned.

'That's taught him a lesson he won't forget,' he pronounced.

In the darkened room he didn't notice his wife was crying.

*

After two days of mutual mistrust, Albert surrendered once more to Maud's maternal ministrations. He lay, large, black and furry in her arms and allowed her to rock him to and fro, making curious cooing noises, because it evidently gave her pleasure. He stretched back his head for his neck to be stroked because it gave him pleasure. He avoided Henry.

'Mummy's naughty boy,' murmured Maud meaninglessly.

Henry looked up from behind his paper where 'Languid Lulu, 38 – 23 – 38; hobbies: sunbathing and posing', was sunbathing and posing extravagantly across the centre pages, and observed, with a familiar hint of jealousy: 'That cat's spoiled. That's his trouble.'

Maud smiled, cooed and tickled the warm fur.

'Pisces,' she demanded suddenly.

'What?'

'Pisces. What does it say? The long-range forecast.'

Guiltily Henry forsook Languid Lulu and turned to the horoscopes. He lowered the page to find the correct focal length, wincing as arthritis creaked in his elbow.

'"Expect a young arrival in the house towards the end of the month",' he read.

'"A young arrival"'. Maud held the cat closer. The silence was burdened with hopes, long dead, with regrets and resignation. No children would run in the Wortle house now.

'It just shows,' said Henry Wortle darkly. He looked at Albert cradled tenderly in his wife's arms. 'Spoiled,' he thought. He spoke on impulse: 'That cat will have to be ... seen to.'

'Seen to?'

'You know – adjusted. At the vet's.'

He bit viciously into his toast. Marmalade spurted on to his paper. Maud was tense.

'It's either that or the voles,' he said, with more passion than logic.

Albert purred noisily.

'If it was a vole,' he added.

Maud gazed down into those half-closed, ecstatically enigmatic, yellow eyes and sighed. 'It's against nature,' she thought. But she remembered the savaged corpse of the vole.

'No time like the present,' said Henry. 'I'll get it done today.'

Maud stroked Albert, kissed his head and slowly nodded.

*

And thus was Albert, protesting eloquently, strapped ignominiously into a shopping bag and conveyed to the vet's for his 'adjustment'.

On his return he retired into dark corners, slunk in the shadows out of reach, his narrow eyes smouldering and sullen.

Maud was pale with worry.

'He's not the same,' she said to Henry once again.

'That's the whole point.' Henry's patience was ever threadbare.

'In himself, I mean. Not the same.'

'Different, yes. No voles, though.'

'No activity, no warmth, no nothing,' she said, her anxiety overriding her grammar. 'Just eating and sleeping.'

'He's certainly grown – even in a week. It's the operation.'

'Sleeping and eating,' she mused. 'He never used to have such an appetite.' She hoped Henry hadn't found the remains of the shoulder of mutton which Albert had seized and devoured last Sunday morning. Her husband had certainly complained at length about the corned beef which she had hastily served up as a last-minute alternative.

'It's just a phase.' Henry Wortle was not interested.

'But he doesn't – love us any more,' said Maud, infinitely sad. 'He always avoids us now.'

And the door opened to admit Albert.

He loomed large against a chair – Henry was right: he had grown remarkably – gazed at each of them in turn, crossed over to Henry, lowered his head, and bit him. He savoured the experience. Then, ignoring Henry's yelp and the invitation of Maud's outstretched arms, he sprang to the sill and disappeared through the open window.

'He bit me,' said Henry.

Albert   'Henry never bites,' said Maud.

'He bit me.' Henry was adamant and aggrieved. 'Hard.'

'His spirits are returning. At last!' said Maud, pleased.

That was the last they saw of Albert for a whole week.

*

Maud's grief at the cat's absence was as great as Henry's indifference. But both were profoundly affected by Albert's return. Henry, who had reversed the custom of a lifetime and gone downstairs to make his languishing wife an early morning cup of tea instead of waiting in bed for the tea to come to him, celebrated the event by dropping a saucer.

Maud, disturbed more by the ensuing silence, empty of expletives, than by the actual crash, came hurrying down, her curlers awry.

The sound of her descent had obviously stimulated Henry into an uncharacteristic flurry of activity. He stood up as she entered the kitchen, his features contriving successfully to be ashen and flushed simultaneously.

'Henry, whatever's the matter?' Maud Wortle was shocked. It was a new husband who stood before her, registering alien, incomprehensible emotions. Then her bewilderment surrendered instantly to delight.

'Albert!' she cried. 'Henry, it's Albert.' Henry knew. Her voice changed gear abruptly. It began to croon. 'Mummy's here, darling. Where's Mummy's naughty pussy been to then?' She reached out a hand to fondle him.

'Don't!' shouted Henry Wortle.

'Don't?'

Albert licked his lips, rose rather stiffly and heavily to his feet and stretched. His claws bit into the patterned linoleum. Maud stepped back, aghast.

'Henry! Look at him. Look at – the size of him!'

Henry looked, but his mind was elsewhere.

'Is it a disease?'

Shaking her head in a vain endeavour to dismiss her confusion and anxiety, and succeeding only in dislodging a precarious curler, Maud stooped to pick up the remaining fragments of the saucer. She crossed to the waste bin.

'No!'

Maud jumped. The curler clattered to the floor. 'Henry, you quite frightened me!'

He raised a hand to stop her and something dropped from his arthritic fingers. She picked it up.

'What is it? A cloth? A shawl! What are those stains?'

Henry snatched it back, stamped on the pedal of the bin and dropped it inside. As the lid fell shut, Maud gave a noiseless scream.

She could see the object with perfect clarity. It projected still from under the lid. The tiny fingers were clenched round a small blue and white plastic rattle.

'Henry,' she gasped, 'why is there a baby in our waste bin?'

'"Expect a young arrival in the house",' said Henry Wortle bitterly. 'Anyway, it's not a baby – exactly.'

'But I saw an arm ... '

'That,' said Mr Wortle, 'is all that appears to be – left.'

'There's the shawl,' said Mrs Wortle, and fainted.

Albert stalked magnificently towards them. Henry backed away and the cat moved on, contented and triumphant, into the next room where he curled up hugely in front of the television and slept the sleep proverbially reserved for the just.

*

'It isn't as if we didn't feed him.' Mrs Wortle was reinvigorated by three cups of tea and some unaccustomed sympathy. 'Nibblebisks and Pussomeat. He's always had as much as he wants.'

'He hasn't come home for a week,' Henry reminded her, lowering his voice quite irrationally lest his words should carry as far as the object of their deliberations in the next room. He paused. 'The question is,' he whispered, and stopped. His mind struggled to formulate the problem. 'The question is – what are we going to do?'

Maud's mind was dazed. 'The stars. What do the stars say?' she asked.

Pinioned between irritation and helplessness, Henry seized the paper and thrust it at her. She fumbled. 'Page three,' he said.

Maud scanned the columns.

'He'll have to be put down,' said Henry. 'And then there's the police ... ' His mind clouded over again.

'"A number of obstacles will stand in your path",' intoned Maud, disguising difficulty – she always refused to admit she needed spectacles – as drama. '"A death may provide some solution"'.

'There! He must be put down,' repeated Henry Wortle, decisively.

'But Henry ... '

'"A death". "Solution". It's in the stars!' Henry Wortle had scored his point. He folded his arms and closed his mind. His case rested.

'It's only a phase,' suggested Maud. 'You said yourself. He'll grow out of it ... '

The unhappy reference to growth won her little sympathy. They sank into a moody and unprofitable silence.

'The baby ... ' said Henry.

'Mummy's naughty, furry baby,' mused Maud.

'A mother somewhere has lost her child,' he asserted

aggressively. Couldn't she see the gravity of the event and the inconvenience for them when the police began their disbelieving inquiries into Albert's unfortunate new pastime?

His wife looked back down the barren, childless years of their marriage and was silent.

Then she put her cup down suddenly on the table. Tea surged to the brim. A dark stain materialized on the tablecloth.

'The men ... ' she said abruptly.

'Police ... ?'

'Dust. They come on Thursday. Tomorrow. They'll find that – thing.'

'Arm,' said Henry. They would have to act now. He wondered whether to tell her about the mauled torso, its ribs picked clean, as well. Then he wondered, uneasily, how they would manoeuvre Albert to the vet's; a trunk would be more appropriate than a shopping bag now. Finally he wondered, with growing alarm, how they would get Albert into the trunk in the first place.

Problems branched into tangling thickets of problems. Henry saw only trees. But Maud could see the wood clearly.

'You must bury the arm,' she said. 'Tonight. In the allotment.'

Henry thought fleetingly of his sweet peas. It was an ignoble objection. He imagined again the scornful laughter of the police. Principle fought, lost and surrendered to expediency. He agreed.

'I'll get the vet to – deal – with that cat as soon as he can send a van round,' he said, placating his conscience.

Maud blanched. There was a streak of cruelty in her husband which she had never been able to understand or condone. She tortured her handkerchief in her clenched palm, while her forefinger traced the dahlias of the tablecloth with savage intensity.

Henry strode to the phone. 'I'll call him now,' he said, his voice abandoning the hushed, conspiratorial tones he had maintained up to now.

The deed done – the vet would send an assistant over tomorrow

23

to collect Albert: Thursday was their day for difficult customers –
Henry replaced the receiver and turned back to his wife.

Framed in the doorway between them loomed the great bulk of
Albert. His eyes burned uncompromisingly in the gloom of the
hallway.

Henry stifled his report. 'They'll send those extra tins
tomorrow,' he announced, gesticulating rather wildly and
speaking with the exaggerated volume and clarity he reserved for
the deaf and foreigners. 'Cat food,' he explained in Albert's
direction. The absurdity of his impulse only intensified his
irrational sense of guilt.

The bright eyes narrowed.

'I thought you locked the door,' hissed Henry.

'I did,' said Maud.

She beamed maternally at Albert. 'Mummy's clever boy,' she
crooned.

Then they discovered the claw marks and primitive lacerations
round the lock.

*

Evening died. The shadows of night preyed stealthily about the
Wortle household. Henry, clutching a torch and clad in his ex-
army gardening coat and the checked cap, which always offended
Maud's social pretensions, came into the bedroom. Maud's chins
were slippery with cold cream.

'He's still in the cellar,' whispered Henry.

'Henry!'

Henry started dramatically.

'That cap! What would the neighbours say?'

Henry choked back his customary retort. 'He's still in the cellar,'
he repeated harshly. 'Asleep, I think. The dresser's across the
door.'

'But his food, Henry ... '

'He's had quite enough food for one day.' Henry had just

24

parcelled up the gnawed ribs in the kitchen and dropped the arm in a polythene bag. 'And he won't be needing any tomorrow.'

Maud's lip trembled.

'If you hear any noises, put on a coat and leave the house. Quickly. I'll be in the allotment. It shouldn't take long.'

Maud turned away, her eyes tightly shut, and Henry went out into the night. Awkward parcels bulged furtively beneath his coat.

Mrs Wortle's sleep was fitful. She tossed and thought about her husband. She turned and worried about Albert. No, she tried to reassure herself, Henry wouldn't be so cruel as to take Albert away from her. He wouldn't destroy his own family. It was against nature. Only half persuaded, she was just slipping back into the shallows of sleep when a harsh grating sounded deep in the house. She lay taut, listening.

A stair creaked. Then another. A heavy tread. Henry must have finished already. She sat up and put on the light as the footfalls reached the landing. They paused. The door swung open.

Albert's eyes confronted her, glaring fiercely. She gasped. Whatever *was* happening to him? Such a size!

He stood a moment in the doorway, flexing his enormous muscular shoulders and, before she could move, sprang on to the bed. The springs objected. Maud stifled a squeal and pressed herself back into the pillows. Albert's head approached. His yellow eyes narrowed to a fiery slit. Then he bared his teeth, yawned, and curled up beside her. Maud held out a tentative hand. Like a superannuated traction engine, Albert began to purr.

'There,' she murmured, affection displacing fear, 'Albert can sleep with Mummy. Just like he did in the old days – when Daddy was away on nights.'

And adjusting her position to accommodate Albert's hefty contours, she fell into a deep and contented sleep.

*

The sly light of dawn insinuated itself through the moth-corrupted shrouds of the bedroom curtains.

The mound in the bed stirred, shifted its position and Maud opened her eyes. She could not say for sure what it was that had awoken her. She extended an elbow instinctively towards Henry. There was no Henry to prod. She remembered Albert, looked, looked again and found only the rumpled sheets and a large depression in the bedclothes.

Concerned, she got out of bed, wrested her dressing gown from the hanger and cautiously tiptoed from the bedroom. She hesitated at the top of the stairs.

The sound of activity reached her from below. Her anxieties melted. Henry was downstairs, she realized, making a cup of tea. She was about to return to bed when she became aware of a different, more subtly pervasive sound. The noise, part rumble, part drone, teased her sleepy mind. It was something she felt as much as heard vibrating up the walls and along her nerve ends.

'Henry,' she called. No response. She became uneasy. The droning noise, insidious and uncanny, intensified her fears.

She made up her mind. She gripped the banisters firmly, descended the stairs and approached the kitchen. The sound increased. Maud pushed open the door with some difficulty. Glancing down, she realized why. That cap! Henry had dropped it and it had wedged under the door. Such an untidy man; his mother *had* warned her.

As she stepped back to tug it free, she skidded and nearly lost her balance. A marble? In the kitchen? She peered more closely. The round, glassy object peered back.

She reached down and picked it up. Perhaps reading glasses might be a good idea after all, she thought. The gelatinous sphere clicked into focus. Blood-encrusted ligaments trailed untidily from the displaced eyeball.

But Maud Wortle recognised that look. And she knew only too

26

well the ownership of the severed legs and arms, mutilated and reorganized in an unnatural and improbable heap about the central torso in the middle of the kitchen floor: the bleeding fingers – those that remained – were knotted with arthritis.

Even without the head, Maud knew the anatomical anarchy to constitute the greater part of her late husband, Henry Wortle. Her vision went grey at the edges. The room lurched. She turned.

Albert, serenely triumphant, bloated with Henry and pride in his nocturnal achievement, sat awaiting approval. Little bits of Henry adhered stickily to his whiskers.

'Naughty Albert ... ' she began.

Then she looked up. The noise had grown thunderous – an insistent, jungle drumming of pulses more ancient than man. Horror flared her nostrils.

Pressed against the windows of the kitchen were hundreds of pairs of green and yellow eyes, gleaming in the greyness, feasting on the dismembered carcass. Hundreds of furry throats vibrated with noisy anticipation. Maud heard, but could not understand, the death rattle which shook the fabric of the building and threatened to drown so many centuries of feline dependence and domesticity.

The reproaches died on her lips. Helpless, she tried to remember: what solution had the stars to offer?

'Mummy's clever boy,' she said, with difficulty. She stooped to pick up the blood-stained spade. 'The dustmen will be coming soon and Mummy's got a job to do. In the allotment. Albert must stand by his Mummy and help her now.'

Albert's purr rattled. He kneaded his crimson claws.

Out in the wild dawn a thousand animals did the same. The few stars that remained were far and cold, already fading back into the endless dark behind the coming day.

'It's only natural,' pleaded Maud Wortle.

Impatient claws started to rip at the kitchen door.

Miss Brood's Speciality

'DEREK WILL DIE,' PRONOUNCED MISS BROOD, and when Derek duly expired, in a flurry of feathers at the bottom of his cage, she was not surprised. Clairvoyance was her gift. Doom was her speciality.

'I shall never find a husband,' said Miss Brood.

'You're a pessimist,' said the cheerful, trainee social worker who came to see why she lived alone.

'No, I shall never find a husband.' Miss Brood expelled a withered sigh. Then she trembled, had one of her presentiments and added sadly, 'And you'll fail your exams.'

'You're a pessimist!' asserted the social worker.

But she failed her exams.

Disaster, in fact, registered on Miss Brood's psychic vision with all the regularity and comfort of frosts in spring. It was depressing. Her foresight seemed impervious to happiness. No consolatory glimpses of good fortune leaked through from the future.

Until the morning she dreamed her dream. She was still in bed. At first, so alien was optimistic precognition, she assumed she had been asleep. So she got up, concentrated, and dreamed it again. The vibrations were strong. There had been no mistake. It was a good dream. There was a man. Tall. With deep, smouldering eyes. Here in her house. Here – dare she dwell on it? – in her loveless bedroom.

Excitement fluttered her maidenly bosom as she turned from

clairvoyant intimation to the daily Press for confirmation. 'Virgo,' she murmured, ignoring for once the customary catastrophes on the front page – the daily rape, war looming somewhere oriental, axe killer on the loose – and fumbling for the horoscopes. Normally she mistrusted the bland, off-the-peg forecasts of the astrology columns, but today things felt different.

'A tall, dark, handsome stranger may enter your life at the end of the day. Be prepared for romance. An important day lies ahead.'

Proof from the stars. Miss Brood, simmering with unaccustomed anticipation, wasted much of her important day in excited confusion. Eventually, decisiveness returned. She would embrace fate with open arms. So she laid her plans and the table accordingly.

The new social worker returned her effusive welcome with uneasy delight. She noticed the flowers, the table set for two.

'Aha,' she said significantly. 'Supper party? Tonight?'

'Aha,' said Miss Brood disarmingly. 'Breakfast. Tomorrow.' And blushed.

The social worker wondered whether to say 'Aha' again, and was just turning it into a cough when Miss Brood announced:

'They've changed.'

The cough shifted into the interrogative.

'My vibrations. Changed. I expect you'll be able to close your file now.'

'Miss Brood – !'

'It may be *Mrs*,' said Miss Brood confidently, 'very soon.'

The evening ticked uneventfully away. At ten o'clock she went to bed. Her visitor would come later. She did not doubt it. But the unusual excitement had tired her, and besides, the bedside lamps suffused the upstairs room with a softer, more intimate warmth.

She tried to relax. Then she remembered. She went downstairs, put the door on the latch – there was no point in putting obstacles in the way of fate – and, leaving the bedroom door ajar, settled herself comfortably again between the crisp, virgin sheets.

Tall. Dark. With deep, passionate eyes ...

The latch clicked and the door downstairs scraped stealthily shut. A pause. Then footsteps crossing the lounge, the hall, ascending slowly. A board protested. The fifth stair. Miss Brood stirred. Adrenalin surged along dilated veins. 'Be prepared for romance.' But something wasn't right. The vibrations ... Suddenly pleasure surrendered to fear. She looked at the door. It was locked. She had left the door ajar. And now it was locked!

In a haze of unreality, she heard the footsteps reach the landing. They hesitated, and then – in three, loud strides – she knew the stranger was standing outside the door, breathing deeply. Her toes cringed. She wanted to call to him lightly, invitingly. Panic dried her throat. It was all going wrong.

The door handle moved slowly. Then it was twisted – violently, repeatedly. There were savage grunting sounds. The walls of the room lurched. Her clenched fingers tortured the bedclothes.

Silence.

Then a primitive yell, the ripping of wood and something glinted in the scar of the door. Miss Brood tried to shield herself behind the delicately embroidered sheets as the tall, dark visitor blundered into the tidy room, the heavy axe swinging playfully from his right hand ...

An arid scream found its way to the surface, the nightmare exploded, and Miss Brood woke up. She was trembling. Reality reassembled itself. She stared at the door; it was still ajar after all.

But she was hardly relieved. Because Miss Brood *knew. She* recognised a prophetic dream when she had one. Doom was her speciality.

Shivering, she slipped out of bed. The front door. She must lock the front door.

She pulled the flimsy nightdress more tightly about her and hurried across the room. But instead of going downstairs, she locked the bedroom door and fled to the temporary safety of her bed.

From downstairs she had heard the click of the latch and the familiar footsteps.

White faced, despairing, Miss Brood sat up in bed waiting for the door handle to turn ...

The Immortal Longings
of Geoffrey Wortle

GEOFFREY WORTLE LOWERED THE LARGE, LEATHER-bound volume and peered pensively over his spectacles.

'O Death, where is thy sting?' he said.

Mrs Wortle was polishing. 'I don't know, Geoffrey. Where did you put it?' she asked.

And went on polishing. 'Other wives,' Geoffrey had once told a friend, in the days when they had had friends, 'make treacle tarts, beds and love. My wife dusts.' The parlour proved his point; from fire-tongs to Coronation chinaware, it gleamed about them with the hygienic, futile brilliance of a desert carcass burnished by centuries of wind and sun.

'You broke the milk bottle on the doorstep,' said Henrietta Wortle. 'Again. It's becoming a habit. You're forever doing it.'

'It's forever there,' said her husband. He returned to less mundane realms of contemplation. 'Hmm,' he said. He pulled at his moustache. 'Bzz,' he added meditatively.

'That's becoming a habit too,' she said.

'What?' said Geoffrey.

'That,' said Henrietta. '"Bzz"'.

'I'm thinking.'

'Most people say Mm.'

'*I* say "Bzz",' said Geoffrey decisively. He lifted his feet dutifully to accommodate the energetic attentions of a feather duster fussing about his armchair's spotless mahogany feet.

'I'm thinking,' he said, 'about reincarnation.'

'Mm,' said Mrs Wortle, and quickly turned it into a cough. 'Already?' The duster feathered past his ear. 'Can you get it at the Co-op now?' she asked.

Her husband sighed. 'She never listens,' he thought. 'It'll be different when I'm dead.' He reached out and arrested the polishing arm by its busy wrist. His wife glared down at him. The pendulous wings of her dusting cap twitched indignantly. 'Life – after – death,' he said, enunciating the syllables with elaborate clarity and unnecessary volume. 'Heaven knows,' he thought, 'there's been precious little life *before* it in this household.'

Mrs Wortle pulled herself free. 'I was having a little joke,' she explained. 'Just this once. About the Co-op. That's your trouble: you never listen to what I say.'

'Hmm,' said Geoffrey Wortle. 'Bzz.'

His wife rubbed viciously at a porcelain shepherd frozen in the throes of some obscure act of animal husbandry with two of his flock. 'Life after death,' she said: 'that's all you think about. I can't see the point in it. Now Bicycle Maintenance, for instance ... '

Her husband watched her moving from figurine to photograph, picking up, polishing, replacing, with relentless zeal.

'I,' he said simply, 'can't see the point without it.'

The grandfather clock gave a dyspeptic wheeze as Mrs Wortle flicked a foolhardy spider from his glittering face, and continued, with ponderous deliberation, to tick away their lives.

'Reincarnation: fiddlesticks,' she said. 'Where's the evidence? Where's the proof?'

Geoffrey Wortle picked up his pipe. 'Just you wait,' he said darkly. The match hissed and flared. 'You'll see.'

The Wortle bosom drew itself up extravagantly to expel a lingering, incredulous sigh. 'Coming back for another turn.' She shook her head, nearly dislodging a precarious curler. 'Like

throwing a double-six.' The feathers paused, vibrated. 'Mind you'
– she inclined her head with a regal gesture, adjusting her cap with
an elegantly cupped palm – 'I sometimes wonder whether I wasn't
born to higher things. These hands belong by rights to noble stock.
A bronzed Egytian princess, perhaps, languishing in sultry
splendour on the banks of the Nile. I'm not devoid of drama either,
you know. *I* get the immortal inklings too ... '

'Longings,' said Geoffrey Wortle.

She straightened her Marks and Spencer's pinafore. 'Anyway,'
she said, 'so long as you don't come back as that dreadful man at
number thirty-seven.'

'Mr Thing with the whippets?'

'Mr Thing with the habits,' said Henrietta Wortle, pursing her
lips. She shivered delicately. 'And I don't want you back as the
postman either. Waking me up at all hours with next door's
parcels.' She paused to restore the latest *Wife and Woman* to its
appointed place in the rack. She gazed at the glossy cover, toying
momentarily with life. 'Why not,' she said, 'come back as Robert
Redford?'

'And wake you up at all hours, I suppose,' murmured her
husband, teeth clenched about his pipe-stem. 'Robert Redford's
already been done. Incarnated. He's it.' He frowned. 'It's him.' He
frowned again.

'Or Paul Newman,' said Mrs Wortle.

'Plenty more where they came from,' said Geoffrey. He
stretched his legs, extended a histrionic arm – 'Mind the spider-
plant,' said his wife, 'I've just dusted it' – and breathed out a
luxuriant cloud of St Bruno. 'There's the whole of creation waiting
for us next time round. Kings and prime-ministers ... '

'Film stars,' said his wife.

'Thinkers, parsons, poets; males and females ... '

'Men with habits.'

Smoke thickened in enthusiastic puffs about the balding Wortle
head. 'Eagles and anteaters ... The whole kingdom of creation,' he
coughed, 'waiting in the wings, ready for our souls to have another

go.' He tapped the leather covers of his book. 'It's all here,' he said. 'The endless procession of souls. Trailing clouds of glory ... '

Mrs Wortle could be blunt. 'Why?' she demanded. She waved a hand to dispel smoke and mystery. Her husband's face reappeared.

'Improvement,' he said. 'Nirvana,' he explained. 'Mankind's eternal climb towards perfection.' His face darkened. 'Of course, some souls have to go back a turn to do penance.' He thought back along the dismal corridors of their marriage and nodded slowly. 'Penance.'

'You make it sound like Snakes and Ladders,' said his wife. She sniffed. 'Anyway, don't you dare come back as a snake,' she said. 'You know what they do to me. The very thought ... ' She subsided on the settee with a reminiscent shudder. 'The doctor put me on those yellow tablets after I saw that programme. You only have to say the words David Attenborough ... Look.' She held out a shaking arm. 'It's starting again.'

Geoffrey Wortle saw. 'Other souls have to return to fulfil Unfinished Business,' he continued. 'To exact, for example, revenge.' He savoured the word.

'Stuff and fiddlesticks,' said his wife.

'The universal law of life,' he said. 'Survival. Life goes on.'

'Not beyond the grave, it doesn't,' she said, in the manner of one who would soon put right any universal law that decreed otherwise.

'You'll see,' he said, trying unsuccessfully to sound more knowledgeable than aggrieved.

'Prove it,' she said.

The moustache bristled at her complacent certainties. 'One day,' said Geoffrey Wortle, reddening, 'there'll be proof. A sign. One day.' He thumped the freshly laundered cover of the chair arm with a clenched fist. 'Just you wait.'

As it happened, Mrs Wortle did not have to wait long. Her husband rose and marched angrily from the room. 'You and your reincarnation, Geoffrey!' She shook her head, laughing. 'You'll be the death of me.' She reached for the hoover, and remembered. 'Mind the front step,' she called. 'I've just polished it ... Geoffrey!'

There was a brisk skid, a brief expletive, an untidy smear on the front path, a superfluous post-mortem, a tasteful if cursory service at the crematorium, and a period of emotional adjustment which Mrs Wortle planned to achieve by tidying under the stairs and treating herself and the house to a second Spring-cleaning.

She was girding her head for this very purpose, several weeks after Mr Wortle's funeral, when she found herself beset by a visitor.

She condensed her features into a defensive grimace, shook her head vigorously and flailed her arms. It did not help. 'Go away!' she said breathlessly.

The visitor was a wasp. It was a large creature, luridly marked, and possessed of a singular malevolence and persistency. It was a prize specimen and seemed bent on hovering noisily and constantly about her.

She backed across the lounge, flapping her elbows about her head in an energetic motion that only a Watusi could envy or emulate. 'Ugh,' she said, and, as it zoomed playfully about her nose, 'Agh'. Its attentions grew increasingly importunate, her antics increasingly desperate. Finally her angry helplessness found vent in a tremulous appeal, born of long habit: 'Geoffrey!' she cried.

The result was as unequivocal as it was unexpected. The wasp flew across the room and into the late Mr Wortle's study, droning still like a distant Stuka.

Much relieved, Henrietta Wortle searched quickly about the room, seized the heaviest and largest book she could find and, hunching her shoulders like a B-feature villain, and clenching her tongue between her teeth, tiptoed to the study door. She peered apprehensively inside. The drone had subsided to a faint, erratic buzzing noise. She stepped tentatively forward on pink-slippered feet – and saw the creature. Having fallen into her deceased husband's inkwell, the wasp was lurching laboriously about on his stationery. She raised the book with some difficulty over her head, fixing her gaze upon the inky trail and the furry insect, blackened but industrious.

She emitted a triumphant squeak. The book – *Reincarnation: a Study of Survival* – descended with a sticky thud.

The wasp twitched.

'Bzz,' it said. It twitched again and expired.

The dying intonation sparked a memory both domestic and familiar. Mrs Wortle looked more closely. The ink marks focused. She inhaled sharply.

'G.W.,' she read, deciphering the clumsy, vespine scrawl. 'I surv- '

An amorphous blot, indelible black, terminated life and message.

Henrietta Wortle subsided onto a chair, her fingers fluttering ineffectually over the tragic scene. Clarity of vision whelmed over her. Privileged was she among women. For her the veil had been momentarily twitched aside. For her the promised sign had been vouchsafed. Her husband had returned.

And here he lay, mute, stripey and inglorious. Spurned. Worse: bent and crushed beneath his favourite literature. By her own hand. 'O Geoffrey, O Death, O Wasp,' she thought, 'where is thy sting indeed?' Her reaction at first merely poignant, provoked, on reflection, comfort and, on further reflection, distress. 'His soul survives,' she told herself, and was comforted. 'He will return.' But darker understanding followed. 'Unfinished Business,' she reminded herself, and was distressed. 'I have just murdered him. He will return. And revenge.'

*

Three years elapsed, however, before she finally heard the tapping, soft and low, at the front door. She crossed the lounge and entered the hall. Here an habitual unease slowed her movements. Her hand paused on the door knob. With a sidelong squint through the stained-glass bambi porthole, she attempted to distinguish the identity of her visitor. She could see nothing. Encouraged, she started to turn the knob. The noise came again, surreptitious, impatient. She opened her mouth: apprehension dried her lips and heightened her voice an unexpected semitone. 'Is there anyone there?' she demanded, with more suspicion than originality. 'Who are you?'

She hesitated.

'*What* are you?'

Another susurration on the doorstep.

'Geoffrey?'

Silence.

Extended silence.

Her fingers fumbled at the knob; she pulled the door open a fraction, peered round, and gasped.

The door swung slowly open.

With a dark, sinuous splendour, the coils of the great viper rearranged themselves unsteadily on the glassily polished tiles. Its head reared, tongue flickering, in sinister greeting.

'Geoffrey?' repeated Mrs Wortle faintly. Her pulses fluttered. Was this more proof? Another sign? 'I believe you,' she said urgently. 'I believe it all: the progress of the soul, the purpose of life. Survival ... ' She seized her husband's umbrella from the stand and waved it about. 'I'm sorry about the accidents: the steps, the wasp. Isn't that enough?' She lunged with the umbrella and whimpered. 'What's done is done. What good is revenge?'

The coils bucked and, with deft deliberation, the viper flicked the milk bottle with its tail. The bottle toppled and exploded against the step.

Henrietta Wortle screamed.

The snake heaved.

'Geoffrey!' she said breathlessly. 'Don't waste any more of your lives. Think of all that penance. Think of your immortal soul.'

The sliding curves disentangled themselves from the debris of spilt milk and shattered glass, and lurched across the slippery step towards her, determination in every fold.

Mrs Wortle's eyes brightened with alarm and sudden inspiration. 'The whole of creation,' she babbled. 'Geoffrey, just think. If you – fulfil your – Unfinished Business, I shall return too.' She swallowed. 'For another go. The universal law.' She lowered her voice, attempting a tone of dreadful menace, and croaked hoarsely: 'I might return – as a snake. We would be together again. Think of it, Geoffrey.' She gazed threateningly into the beaded, alien eyes. Her grip tightened on the umbrella. 'You and me. United once more. Like another marriage. Slithering side by side into eternity ... '

She stood, her back against the wall, watching.

'Never, ever, to be parted,' she said.

Dripping with pasteurised milk and indignation, the viper rose magnificently, expelled a venomous hiss, arched his neck and, within striking distance of his goal, paused and agonized ...

Eternity was an awful long time.

The Man Who Sold Ghosts

IMPRISONED IN THEIR HEAVY FRAMES, CHILLY smiles frozen unconvincingly on their impassive features, the dead forebears of the ninth Earl of Snood watched his lordship far below in the echoing gloom of the dining chamber ineffectually juggling peas on his knife.

Lady Snood watched him too. A hint of regret stirred in the placid shallows of her apathy; it *was*, after all, the best silver. There would have been a time when the family crest gleaming dully on the blade would have been reproach enough for such plebeian table manners.

Her husband negotiated the knife unsteadily towards his mouth.

No wonder fashionable society was fashionable in their absence these days, she thought. An ancient admonition hesitated on her lips. The shrouds of resident silence braced themselves for her voice. But a distant peal forestalled her reproof.

Lady Snood waited.

Several peas fell back onto the Snood plate. They bounced.

Then she wiped a corner of her mouth with unnecessary exquisiteness, put down her napkin and sighed along the bleak expanse of the table.

'The door, Godfrey,' she said.

Lord Snood breathed in; spiders froze in dark crevices; the hall tensed.

'The door *bell*,' he corrected.

She stiffened. 'Tipton. What's the matter with Tipton?'

'Deafness,' said Lord Snood succinctly, and with unaccustomed alacrity, snared a quick mouthful of peas.

'He *never* hears it, Godfrey.'

'He's *always* deaf, Eleanor.' With equal accuracy he might have pointed out that it never rang.

Eleanor Snood wondered whether to embark on a routine enquiry about why they bothered to pay Tipton at all, remembered that they didn't, pursed her lips, heard a second chime, paused, rose disdainfully and left the dining hall.

Her husband, roused out of an habitual torpor only by his meals, proceeded to savage his steak with the family silver and was assisting the disposal of his dinner with copious, if clumsy, draughts of red wine, when she travelled back across the room.

The air was sluggish with bored expectancy.

'There's a man at the door,' announced Lady Snood.

'Send him away,' said her husband and reached out for a cigar. 'Pegs. It's probably pegs. Or onions. He's bound to be selling something. Unless,' he blanched, 'unless he's one of those Revenue chaps.'

'Ghosts,' said Eleanor Snood.

Her husband's teeth closed abruptly over the end of his cigar.

'He's selling ghosts ... '

The Earl of Snood spluttered, wiped the frayed ends from his lips. Shreds of tobacco embellished his moustache.

' ... So he says.'

*

'Ghosts?' demanded the Earl.

'Ghosts,' insisted the man, shooting his cuffs and thrusting his chin forward in a vain attempt to free his neck from the restrictions of his tight, brightly patterned collar.

'And crystal balls, horoscopes, love potions.' He paused quizzically. 'Ghosts a speciality, though.' He peered sharply at them. 'Warts?'

Lord Snood stared.

'Got any warts?'

Eleanor Snood studied her rings with uncharacteristic zeal, wondering where Tipton was and whether he would have the strength to remove this impertinent little man anyway.

'No warts? No matter. One of the privileges of having the blue blood, no doubt. But if you're ever troubled, I've got these charms. Most efficacious. Work a treat. Especially good with pigs.'

'These ghosts ... ' began the Earl, labouring under the alien challenges of doubt and bewilderment.

'Speciality of the House,' repeated the man.

'The House?' Lady Snood lifted a languid eyebrow.

'By Appointment. To the very best circles.'

Her Ladyship nodded. 'I see.' A glint of nostalgia and thoughts of emulation quickened in her tired eyes.

The man watched her closely. 'Don't tell me,' he said, with skilled casualness, 'you're like the rest. Already got them. The ghosts. Oozing out of the panelling. Materializing all over the breakfast table. Jumping out on the milkman. Haunted up to here.'

His eyes flashed.

'I knew it. Just like the Gore-Pendleshams.'

'*The* Gore-Pendleshams?' murmured Lady Snood.

'Right. Laughed in my face only yesterday. Didn't even fancy a mini blood stain. One of those ever-ready, self-renewing jobs. That's a very profitable line. Very popular with your American tourist. Gets them flocking.' He paused. 'And brings the money in,' he added nonchalantly. 'Spending dollars like water. But you hardly need me to tell you that, of course.'

The ninth Earl of Snood grunted. His mind lingered on his tax returns, fled to seductive tropical climes – the Bahamas once more would be nice – and lurched unhappily back to his overdraft and the deserting retainers. He conjured the myriad rustling of dollar notes in his otherwise stale imagination.

The man waited, affected to straighten a jaded crease in his right trouser leg, studied a moribund potted palm with suitable fascination and, with impeccable timing, rose abruptly as if to depart.

Eleanor Snood, unused to the exercise of communication, struggled to prompt her husband with a significant glance.

Puzzled, Lord Snood glanced over his shoulder, shrugged and began again: 'These ghosts ... ' He stopped, thinking of the queues for English teas, his trampled begonia beds, the potential horrors of a Safari Park ... '

The man nodded helpfully.

'*The* Gore-Pendleshams,' reminded Lady Snood.

'What sort of – ah – ghosts are particularly popular these days?'

The man glanced at his watch, compressed his lips to indicate politely that he had more profitable business to engage him elsewhere, and sat down again. The cuffs were adjusted.

'Anything you fancy. Made to measure – within limits. We do a very comprehensive range. It depends on the clientele really.' He narrowed his eyes, appraising them and the drab, funereal hall which daily entombed them.

'There's the chains,' he suggested. 'Your tourists like a nice rattle. A sinister hint of nocturnal clanking. No?'

'Noisy,' said Lady Snood.

'Ah. Then you won't care for our assorted night novelties; we offer a rich variety of things that go bump.'

Lady Snood shook her head.

'Something rather headless might be interesting,' mused the Earl. 'In a conventional sort of way, I suppose.'

The Countess stirred uneasily. 'I don't think we want anything – well, untidy, Godfrey. Spare heads lying around frightening Tipton ... That sort of thing. Something quieter, perhaps.' She searched the bleaker recesses of the room for inspiration.

'You name it,' said the man. 'Anything from your screaming nuns and thwarted lovers to your solitary hanged personage. He's popular, your guilty suicide. But it's your jealous lovers that really draw the crowds, we find. They come in a set, slightly reduced. Buy one, get one free. You can't beat jealousy and thwarted passion. Romantic, you see.'

He looked from one to the other, then elaborately consulted his watch.

Lady Snood cleared her throat, frowned. 'Aren't they at all – dangerous?' she enquired casually. 'For domestic purposes.'

'Lord, no!' the man chuckled. 'Tamed and house-trained, you might say. We've had no complaints.'

Her Ladyship's frown persisted. 'But they all sound a bit – extreme. Rather ostentatious. Rather, well, *vulgarly* emotional.'

'Ah.' The cuffs were briskly exposed. 'A perceptive customer, if I may make so bold with a compliment. That's *it*, isn't it? That's what the Spook Trade – pardon the jargon – is all about, isn't it? Emotions. Passions. You see?'

They looked. They didn't see.

'The two Ps. Passions and Places. Take your suicide. Despair. Guilt. Desperation. Noose tightened around the neck, right? Tension. Outflow of emotion, unusually intense emotion, quick burst of psychic waves – like electricity – ' he gestured vaguely – 'and there you are. Passions burned into the panelling. Misery, anger, fear imprinted in the walls. In living memory. A ghost is born! And no need for a death first. Death's not compulsory. All very tidy.'

His voice echoed triumphantly, eddying among the disembodied armour and rusty weaponry that eternally lined the sombre museum walls.

'Once made, it's like a record. Always playing the same tune. Same passion. Same place. With me?'

'Emotions,' pondered Lady Snood.

'Bit much,' said her husband. 'We don't really go in for that sort of thing here, you know. Emotions. Quiet, respectable house, this.'

Lady Snood thought of the barren years snubbed by the best society, remembered the extravagant social assets of the Gore-Pendleshams, caught a glimpse of light amid her encircling domestic gloom and, more to her surprise than the salesman's, announced: 'I'd like a man.'

The salesman took out his order book, glanced for authority at Lord Snood and licked his pencil. A blue streak appeared on his tongue. 'Any distinctive features?'

Lady Snood hesitated.

'Handsome?'

'Handsome, yes.'

'Rugged, hero type?'

'Rugged. Muscular.' Lady Snood's memory stirred and blossomed. 'Active. A man of action. Tall, dominant.' Her eyes appraised her husband, from a great distance. 'Yes, and rather arrogant too.' She remembered the tense droning of the cicadas, the violence crouched behind the balmy, sub-tropical, Bahamian night. 'Young. And passionate,' she said. 'He ought to be passionate, with a streak of ... '

She broke off; the man was staring at her. What remarkable impudence. She looked away. Such penetrating eyes. Staring right inside her.

'Cruelty, perhaps? That sort of streak,' he suggested, and scribbled on his pad.

Lady Snood flushed and lapsed into a sullen silence. She ripped a palm leaf and tortured it in her left hand.

'Lord Snood?'

The Earl emerged from his own reverie. 'Quite so,' he grunted. 'A young woman, yes. Absolutely. Pale, submissive type. Sort that knows a man when she sees one. Shy, inexperienced – but plenty of, you know, energy.' He surveyed his wife's figure, stooped over the palm, across a gulf, without seeing her. 'Lively. Know what I mean? Sort to get a man's blood up. Make him feel alive ... ' He sighed heavily, reminiscently. 'Why're you looking at me like that?'

The man rose briskly to his feet. 'Right, sir – my lord! – we'll see what we can do. Two ghosts, one of each gender, with the aforementioned attributes. I take it this is a firm order?'

'Two?' The high-born moustache twitched.

'Yes, Godfrey ... '

'Tell you what. Special customers. Personal friends – now – if I may take the liberty. Two for the price of one! How's that for a special offer?'

'Price?' The Earl tugged unhappily at his whiskers.

'Now you're talking,' said the man. 'Ghosts don't come cheap, of course. Not weighed and packaged like your supermarket commodities, naturally.'

'Naturally,' said Godfrey Snood. 'How much?'

The man coughed. 'Shall we say two thousand?'

The stillness was sepulchral while the Earl's face took on colours more appropriate to apoplexy.

'We shall not,' he growled.

'Shall we say one?' suggested the man more cautiously. 'Five hundred?' he tempted. 'Can't say fairer than that, now. I'm cutting my throat for you as it is. Well?'

Lady Eleanor patted her husband's arm encouragingly and the man exhorted his lordship to remember those Americans queueing twenty deep to view his haunted room and disburden themselves of innumerable surplus dollars, as the Earl, with some misgivings, wrote out the cheque.

The man held out his hand.

The Earl proffered the paper, retracted it abruptly. 'How do we know,' he demanded slyly, suspicions congealing in the slow but lordly brain, 'how do we know if we've got them? Ghosts! Damnit, they're invisible, aren't they?'

The man essayed an expression of hurt pride. 'You'll know,' he said, smiling and extending a hopeful hand.

'How?' The Earl was obstinate.

'Signs,' said the man. 'Usual signs. Room goes chilly. There's an atmosphere. Unaccountable noises. Pictures drop to the floor. Usual sorts of things.'

The Earl vacillated, preened his moustache, looked fondly at the cheque. 'Look,' he said, 'we're not fools, you know. Some people will believe anything. Tell me this: how do you deliver the goods? Make a spell? Some sort of crate arrive? When do we get it?'

'You'll take delivery soon enough.' He clicked his fingers impatiently. 'They'll materialize when you've handed over the cheque, and not before.'

The ninth Earl of Snood formally surrendered the money. My lady inclined her head.

'Don't you worry,' said the man, though they hadn't moved; 'I always find my own way out. Don't forget: if ever you need any love potions or get the warts ... ' And deftly pocketing the cheque, he disappeared with a shrill, cheerful laugh into the shadows thickening round the walls of the ancient hall.

Silence settled back, dark and brooding, over the room.

'A ball,' thought Lady Snood. 'We'll hold a ball.' She patted a stray curl with a limply elegant hand. 'Invite the Gore-Pendleshams.'

The Earl was counting dollars. 'Replenish the family coffers,' he mused, repressing just in time something akin to a baronial titter. 'No more hiding from the Revenue chaps. Or fobbing off Tipton and the rest.'

They smiled and nodded vacantly at one another.

The shades lengthened.

Slowly the corners of the Earl's mouth sagged back into more routine contours; his forehead puckered with heavy thought. A cumbersome sigh heaved itself out into the panelled gloom of the chamber.

'A man,' he pronounced, 'selling ghosts.'

'He just came to the door,' said Eleanor Snood.

'Then he went away again,' said the Earl ponderously.

'I didn't hear a car, Godfrey ... '

'With my cheque!'

'We did buy – ah – something, though.'

'Say it,' commanded his lordship. His wife noted a premonitory quivering of the hereditary moustache. 'Say it!'

'Ghosts, dear,' whispered his wife. 'Two ghosts,' she added. 'For the price of – '

Pain, anger and an obscure sense of shame rendered the Earl inarticulate. He paced the room with unaccustomed energy, making primitive growling noises into the worn carpet.

'Charlatan!' he exploded venomously, and ground his fist into his left palm.

'Rogue!' he hissed, and kicked the mahogany table, which was harder than he had calculated. 'Trickster! Taking advantage of our good natures ... Preying on the upper classes ... '

The spiders scuttled, the air grew vibrant with old tensions. Tremors of sadness and excitement began to pulse along my lady's slow veins.

'*Two* ghosts, damnit! Damnit, why *two*?'

'I ordered a man,' said Eleanor Snood simply. 'You weren't listening. You never do. You haven't listened for years.' Her eyes glittered in the darkness. 'And you! You ordered ... ' She remembered: young, submissive. A mere girl. Someone to make a man feel alive.

'Brute!' she said.

The Earl stopped, turned.

'A man, eh?' he said. 'Yes, by Jove. A youth, bristling with biceps and passion. I remember.' The moustache trembled, the Snood fingers bit into his clenched palms, the ninth pair of baronial eyes appealed to the judgement of his watching ancestors.

'Strumpet!' he roared.

The shadows cringed flat against the walls. The air sang about their heads.

'Lecher!' shouted Lady Eleanor Snood. 'Don't you dare lay hands on me, you vicious brute!'

The Earl grasped her slim arms again, felt them struggling in his rough grip once more. She wrenched herself free. Cicadas hummed exotically in his ears. With an excited cry she delivered an impressive blow to the Earl's astonished left cheek.

Godfrey Snood swayed unsteadily, rage and primal frenzy thundering strangely in his head. His chest expanded, his muscles flexed and with a roar, summoning the vestigial energies of his youth, he lowered his head, charged the solid dining table, seized the knife athwart his plate and, regardless of peas and family honour alike, pursued my lady in a primitive, headlong rush, as exhilarating as it was undignified, around the hall.

Panting, apoplectic with passion, he caught her up, seized her by the waist, brought his face close to her angry, protesting, yielding lips. Then she glimpsed the knife, flung back her head, emitted a scream that scorched the very air and set the armour ringing, and swooned appropriately in his arms.

The Earl, dropping the unused knife, tottered backwards with gathering momentum. Together they arrived with a bump at the wall and sank abruptly to the floor, where they were noisily joined, seconds later by the ancestral portrait which they had unexpectedly dislodged from his rest immediately above them.

His lordship blinked.

Dazed but undamaged, he reached up a tentative hand to investigate the soreness on his head where the picture had struck him. He glanced at his crumpled wife, first with guilt, then with guilt and relief.

Her ladyship stirred and blinked too.

*

As the room reassembled about her, the Countess found herself propped up in the fireplace in her customary chair. The Earl, having laboriously restored both his wife and the portrait to their respective and hallowed places, was sitting opposite her, as always. He reached for his bedtime cigar, muttering unhappy apologies.

'It won't ever happen again, old thing.'

'No,' thought Lady Snood, offering a mechanical smile, 'I don't suppose it will.' She rearranged the dusty folds of her dress and suppressed a sigh.

The shades settled comfortably down; the potted palm sagged steadily; the spiders relaxed. Aloft, the ancestors, their company complete again, resumed their cheerless vigil.

Lady Snood surveyed the room thoughtfully. 'Passion,' she murmured sadly, 'and places.'

'Mumbo,' said Lord Snood, 'and jumbo. Passion indeed!' His guilt fed his indignation. 'In the House of Snood!'

'A living memory.' The sigh slipped out. 'Like a record, he said. Perhaps he was some sort of gramophone salesman too, Godfrey.'

'The man was a simple charlatan,' muttered her husband. 'Didn't even leave his address.' He drummed his fingers morosely on the arm of his chair. 'Not that we really needed any ghosts anyway. Far too disruptive. And flamboyant.'

The Countess nodded. 'So energetic,' she said, 'in such a vulgar way.'

And they lapsed into an accustomed silence.

The Earl stirred. 'Ten o'clock. Time for the port.'

'Shall I ring,' asked his wife, as she asked every night, 'for Tipton?'

The Earl shook his head mechanically. 'He never hears,' he said.

'Deafness,' said Lady Snood. 'He's always deaf.'

With its nightly dyspeptic whirring, the aged grandfather clock launched into his announcement of the hour. On the final stroke, a door in the panelling opened and a dark figure moved towards them with a slow, familiar tread.

'Port, m'lord,' announced Tipton wearily. 'Port, m'lady.' He raised the decanter. Then he flung it, complete with tray and the Snood family crystal glasses, on to the floor in front of them.

'Tipton!' said my lord.

'Perhaps you should sit down,' said my lady.

The old retainer lifted his hands to his grey face. He covered his ears.

'Can't you hear it?' he demanded, his voice shrill with fright. 'That unearthly scream?'

He shuddered as if exposed to a sudden wintry draught.

'Look there!'

He pointed a palsied finger across the room.

'By the table. Chasing after each other. He's threatening her. Those whiskers! My lord! He's going for her – with a family knife!'

They turned to look. Lady Snood saw the yielding, helpless figure of the woman and shivered with a recent apprehension and pleasure. The Earl preened his moustache, and swelled, despite himself, with pride as he recognised that firm, aggressive, manly behaviour. Fascinated and appalled they watched the passionate display.

'Only ghosts, Tipton,' said Lord Snood.

'We ordered them,' explained Lady Snood vaguely.

As they spoke, one of the Snood forebears appeared to squirm in his frame and, without invitation or warning, plunged with resounding violence to the floor on to the fading figures for the second time that evening.

Myth Understood

LEANING TO ONE SIDE TO AVOID the rows of creamed rice and primly organized ranks of corned beef and spaghetti rings, Henry placed the tin carefully on the top shelf. And another.

'Beans,' said Henry Wortle. 'Two tins. That makes ... fifty-seven.'

Alice Wortle supported her now unpretentious bosom on folded arms and looked worried.

'Or fifty-eight,' said Henry. 'Anyway, there's still time. To collect the rest.'

'And money, dear? Look at the Mulligatawny.' They looked. 'It's gone up four pence since The Brothers sent out the first decree.'

'Rising prices. Inflation. We are told to expect these trials in the latter days, loved one.'

'The Book,' said Alice, 'tells us that the Lord will provide. Surely for the Chosen Ones ... '

'The Lord,' said Henry, 'helps those who help themselves. Besides, He'll doubtless be very busy when The Day comes. Where are the prunes?'

Alice looked vague, remembered, shook her head. The superstore rack had been barren of prunes this week.

Her husband turned, nearly dislodging the pyramid of Mulligatawny soup cans. 'It's a sign of the times,' said Henry Wortle.

*

Deep in the hinterlands of Mesopotamia, someone stirred. It was Professor Chalford. He leaned on his power shovel, wiped his forehead with the back of his hand and peered at Maisie Seameirs, resplendent in orange-blossomed Bermuda shorts, outsize spectacles and undersized T-shirt, on which the words 'University of Oregon' were provocatively distorted. The vast plain, ringed with mountains, busy with extensive excavations, simmered under the late afternoon sun.

'If this really is Paradise, Miss – Maisie – I can't understand why Adam didn't give up horticulture, pick up his fig leaf and leave for cooler climes long before he was turned out by the celestial bailiff with the flaming sword.'

Miss Seameirs lowered her glasses and blinked. 'Horticulture?'

'Adam delved.'

'Huh?'

'A fellow wielder of the spade. Gardening, Miss Seameirs. Like archaeology – only more profitable.'

'Oh.' Miss Seameirs made up in nubility what she lacked in perceptive facility. 'Weeding and pruning, you mean?'

'And planting out asparagus tips for the little woman when she was constructed. Damn it, the sooner I can get back to my own little corner of Eden and stop grubbing about in this benighted, sub-tropical valley for bits of myth and a few highly suspect holy relics, the happier I shall be. Who wants to see Adam's original garden shears anyway?'

His companion raised an eyebrow and replaced her glasses. If the professor chose to ignore the fruits of painstaking research and to find the possibility that they were excavating in the legendary site of the Garden of Eden laughable, he was welcome to laugh. He did so – frequently. And The Sect, which she had to agree was as eccentric as it was American, continued to pay him extravagantly. For his part it flattered his complacency to have his view of transatlantic folly confirmed and, at the same time, he *was* secretly intrigued; several of the aerial photoscans of this remote, over-heated inferno had suggested unusual formations which had initially whetted his archeological curiosity.

But enthusiasm tended to evaporate in this relentless heat. Especially when one was working at the bottom of an exploratory trench. Professor Chalford was about to become sullen. Maisie Seameirs knew the signs. To her surprise he yelped instead and sank down on all fours.

'He's having a fit,' she thought. 'Or a tantrum.'

'Brushes,' he said.

'Medics,' she thought.

'Quickly!'

With professional care they cleaned an area several feet square.

'It's impossible,' said Professor Chalford.

'It's beautiful,' said Miss Seameirs.

'A solid surface of pure crystal. I don't believe it. It's not natural.'

'If I was a dumb B-feature Hollywood blonde I'd say it looks like an enormous diamond.' The Seameirs jumper heaved enthusiastically.

'If I didn't know it was impossible, that's exactly what I'd say it was.'

They stared at one another. They stared at the ground again.

At their feet the exposed rock, eternal as adamant, infinitely polished, gleamed like a jewel in the dull earth.

*

The door whirred softly shut and Doctor Eugens was alone.

Reassured by the gentle hum and occasional click of electronic gadgetry going about its complex, laborious duties, he checked the readings before beginning another night's vigil. Outside the Observatory the aimless, endless chattering of cicadas serenaded the precise, purposeful motion of the radio telescopes as they gazed up into the deep, star-scattered spaces of the Peruvian sky.

The dials were constant; the computer purred imperturbably

through its routine program; the bank of oscilloscope screens, where any communication would first be perceived, showed their customary, uneventful signal. The doctor was disappointed, but the familiar excitement of apprehension which greeted him every time he set foot in the Receiver Room refused to fade. 'Tonight,' he thought, echoing, despite himself, his father's words before those compulsive visits to the Casino at Trieste, 'our luck may change.'

Patiently and inconspicuously the small team of international scientists at the World Centre for Extra-terrestrial Communication had gone about their unrewarding, often maligned job for many years now, beaming their message of interstellar goodwill into the far reaches of space. And awaiting whatever faint, regular radio pulses, sifted from the random murmurings of the circling galaxies, would carry the trademark of intelligent life – perhaps even a reply.

Doctor Eugens looked out into the transparent darkness of the summer sky and gritted his teeth. 'So many worlds; so much probability of life – and intelligent life; of civilizations technologically gigantic compared with our own,' he thought. 'What knowledge lies out there waiting for us?' He rose and crossed to the receiver screens. 'Why don't you answer? When are you going to get up off your backsides and give us a sign?'

Behind him the computer disks paused, clicked and whirred on as before.

Outside, powerful transmitters continued to send their message whispering towards strange worlds. And the great dishes of the radio telescopes searched patiently still among the stars.

*

Nearly a year later, the letter came.

It interrupted the compulsory breakfast-time Bible reading, which was probably just as well, Alice daringly thought, as the more apocalyptic passages of Revelation tended to give Henry heartburn. Henry hastened to open it, decorating the envelope with smears of ginger marmalade.

'Is it from The Brothers? Surely we've only just had the latest *Armageddon Advertiser*? It's marked "Urgent",' said Alice, and poured herself a third cup of tea.

Henry's voice rose a semitone. 'It looks very important.'

It was.

Henry read the letter slowly. Then he borrowed Alice's reading spectacles and read it again more clearly. Then he put the letter down. His eyes glistened. They embraced and gave thanks. Then they read the letter again, to make quite sure.

'Beloved Ones,

The hour has come for the Chosen Few to rejoice. The end of worldly things is nigh. Our Brother has dreamed a dream; the old order is expected to pass away on Friday, February 19th. Be diligent and watch for signs; understanding is only for those who have ears to hear and eyes to see. Be prepared, therefore, and always believe.'

'There will be rushing winds,' said Henry, 'on the last day.'

'We shall miss the daffodils,' murmured Alice. 'They would have made a fine show this year. I put some new ones in by the hedge. Cheap, dear, from the market.'

'And dire earthquakes. Fire in the heavens. And they say that stars will fall from the sky.'

'It will be a day of Dreadful Reckoning, dear,' agreed his wife. 'We mustn't forget to cancel the papers.'

'And get some more tablets.'

'Tablets?'

'Heartburn,' said Henry Wortle, and burped.

*

Adam, after his fall, must have begun admiring his wife much as Professor Chalford was admiring his assistant's busy hindquarters which their owner was negotiating into a seat in the cramped hoverjet. Some of her assets, he had to admit, were undeniable. He climbed into the seat beside her. Cries of 'Any news yet, Professor?' pursued him from gesticulating reporters, hurrying towards them across the dusty clearing. He ignored them with a deafness born of long practice.

'You can't stall them any longer, Professor. Reuters and Global News'll be arriving again within the hour as well as Our Man from The Sect, coming to view his New Jerusalem.'

'Vultures.'

Clouds of dust boiled around the small craft as it shuddered and lifted. Now that the initial excavations were virtually complete, the Professor himself, overcoming an instinctive mistrust of aviation, was taking a bird's eye view of the operations – massive in scale as they had turned out to be. Never before had he seen so much technology or so many bands of trained helpers in the service of archaeology.

'Anyway,' he turned to his companion, 'what do we tell them?'

'The facts, perhaps?'

'The facts, Miss Seameirs, are distressingly simple. We've dug something up, and we've no idea what it is. Headlines: "Bewitched, Bothered and Bewildered; Eminent Garden-of-Eden Archeologist Tells All – And Nothing."' He grimaced. '"The *Chicago Tribune* Reveals the Truth About Adam and Eve Secret Discovery – the Truth that Even a Professor Dare Not Tell"'. The minute we release The Facts they'll be interpreted, distorted, glamourised, garnished with thrills and journalistic fantasies, and, no doubt, served up as one of your true-life Hollywood epics in 3-D Super-Panorama-Vision.'

Maisie Seameirs ignored the laying of the American film industry's failings at her personal doorstep. 'Look!' She caught his arm. 'Look down there, John. There're your facts.'

He looked and, despite his expectations, found himself suddenly breathless.

Now that the protective coverings had been lifted from the workings, the full splendour of their discovery glittered below them. It was clearly enhanced by being viewed from above. Those walls, thirty metres high and nearly twenty thick, moulded – not, it seemed, built or chiselled – out of flawless, polished diamond, flashed with an unearthly brilliance in the glaring sun. The bewildering senselessness of it seized him again. Walls? Was that really what they were? In the middle of nowhere? Who had wanted to keep whom out? Or in?

'And look at the shape of it – the perfection of that curve,' he whispered, following the circling ribbon which unfolded like a dazzling rainbow beneath the hoverjet, whose tiny, squat shadow chased over the ground far below them. 'Such perfection – and yet, why not a perfect circle? Why the loop – the two tails, like a – a cartoon fish?'

'Or a letter Alpha,' suggested Miss Seameirs. 'Perhaps the tails form the entrance – the exit, sorry – where the angel stood when he turned the tenants out. Perhaps that's why the Brothers are suggesting quitting and refusing to finance further research: they're frightened the angel's still on guard.'

'Waiting to smite us with his flaming sword!' Chalford grunted. 'And doubtless there's a useful tree somewhere down there ripe for revelation. A few golden apples waiting to tempt us. A succulent bite of knowledge would be a great help just at this moment.'

The scene below reclaimed their fascinated attention. Chalford wrinkled his nose.

'But seriously, just look at the age of the thing,' he shouted. 'Primitive man was still groping after a hundred and one crude things to do with flint when this – monumental folly was built; when it *happened*. What civilisation, even ours, could produce anything so perfect – so colossal? Where did the material come from? What is it? What did it do? *Why* is it? And what the hell do I say to the world when we land?'

'Well, I suggest we land quickly, sir.' As the pilot spoke, the hoverjet lurched to one side. 'The air currents are getting vicious. There's quite a breeze blowing up from somewhere.'

*

At first it was only a barely audible buzz in the recesses of the reception amplifiers' circuits. And Doctor Eugens, who was standing in for a sick colleague that night, and who was engrossed in polishing the mathematical argument of his latest scientific paper, noticed nothing. Insidiously, however, the change in the familiar, soporific drone of the apparatus in the Receiver Room gnawed into his consciousness. He turned to check the screens. His pulses quickened.

The regular trace of the oscilloscopes was now dancing agitatedly.

A fault in the pre-circuitry? An atmospheric freak? Another false alarm caused by a malfunction in the filter controls? Or the climax of many years' faithful waiting?

The self-activation of the computer-decoder system brought him to his senses. With curiously stilted movements his limbs performed the emergency alert procedures which he had lived through so many times in imagination during the empty nights of the past, waiting years.

Soon his colleagues would arrive. Meanwhile, his muscles tense, an unaccustomed fluttering in the pit of his stomach, Doctor Eugens of The World Centre for Extraterrestrial Communication took up his position in front of the master control panel and receiver screen. Impatiently he waited for the stars to yield their secrets.

Despite the rapidity of the decoders processing, the data took some time to arrive. He heard the whine of the airbug's descent, followed by the chatter of excited voices. Within moments, three of his fellow researchers and a couple of press-men, their faces also flushed and expectant, were standing at his side.

'Is our space phone really ringing, Alex? If this is one of your hot-line hoaxes, I'll – '

'Ssh! Something's coming through.'

They held their breath.

A small pin-point of light, brilliant as a distant star, appeared on the screen. And another. Intelligence – alien, remote – was reaching out across the immensities of space to contact man in this little room. The watchers grew profoundly excited.

'The reception! It's unbelievable.'

Before their eyes, the picture slowly took shape. A visual symbol of a thought concept? A diagrammatic representation of an alien life form?

On the screen, etched with crystalline clarity, had appeared an inverted U, its stems curving slightly outwards and upwards like a hanging tulip. It seemed to be growing bigger as they watched.

Three of the world's leading research scientists looked at one another. They looked at the screen.

They were very bewildered.

*

Henry and Alice were up early the next day, Friday the nineteenth of February. As members of the Elect they had, they felt, a busy and momentous day ahead of them.

'We must be diligent and watch for signs,' said Henry Wortle. 'The hour,' he added unnecessarily, 'is nigh. Today fiery comets will blaze in the heavens.'

And Alice finished her spring cleaning whilst Henry checked the provisions and made his final preparations according to the instructions they had received. At the end of the afternoon they came together, sat down, prayed for the world, thought a little sadly about the unrighteous like Cousin Mabel, and waited for the old order to pass away.

'Is there time for a cup of tea?' asked Alice.

Henry Wortle was thirsty. 'There is,' he said. 'Then we must have the Bible reading.'

*

'Damn all interviewers!'

Professor Chalford winced as the beams of the arc lights were swung on to them. The man from Global News with the minimike gave him a reassuring wink from behind ostentatiously stylish glasses. They were standing at the intersection of the walls in the 'V' formed by the immense tail sections which Miss Seameirs had fancifully described as the 'exit'. There had been delays – desert sand had sabotaged two of the telescans – and now twilight was shading softly into night. Stars had risen in the clear dome above their heads and, despite the activities of swarms of unnecessary media men, an oppressive stillness had descended on the plain after the fitful gusts of yesterday's winds.

'Got the idea, Professor? We chat as we walk towards the – the structure, and the telescans'll track in on us. Okay?'

Professor Chalford had got the idea.

The telecast began. They dutifully walked and talked and before the watching world the electronic eyes pursued them up to the towering, diamantine walls, which spangled fiercely in the powerful lights and blazed with fiery stars.

'It's at this point that the myth spinners can really indulge their fantasies,' the Professor was saying. 'Inside these great walls, Genesis: the garden womb of Paradise. Outside, rising out of the wilderness of mortality, sin and decay, you have the glittering City of God – of Revelation, as The Brethren of The End Days would have us believe.' He raised his hand to demonstrate the crystalline texture of the rock, shielding his eyes as he did so. 'Here, where the walls come together before parting again, the Angel Gabriel supposedly ... What in heaven – ?'

Chalford stopped, gazing upwards. An estimated billion viewers watched an expression of stunned horror flare on his face. 'Good God!' he said, causing offence to an estimated five hundred million. The telescans abruptly left him, panning swiftly towards the source of his blasphemy.

There was only a curt, premonitory rumbling beneath the watchers' feet before the earth heaved, buckled and, with a deafening flash of flame, flung itself apart in a rage of dust and debris, forming a massive gash only yards from where they had been standing.

'Emergency! Take cover! Emergency!' A hundred loudspeakers blared into action amidst the howling of innumerable sirens.

The Professor, media crews and digging teams needed no second warning.

Behind them as they fled, an awesome blaze of white fire, like a gigantic sword forged from a blinding sun, leapt vertically from the exit – or entrance – of the great crystal Alpha.

*

Doctor Eugens was weary. He and his team, gathering around him in enthusiastic groups, had remained on duty at Communications Base all day and in consequence were unable, at first, to register the evidence of their eyes.

'Look! Look there, on all the screens!' His colleague's voice was shrill with excitement. '*Another* symbol!'

He leaned forward. The established tulip pattern, which now almost filled the screen, had been joined by a second image. It was quite distinct: a near circular loop with two crossing tails.

'Like a fish,' said the colleague.

'Or ... like an alpha,' whispered Doctor Eugens. 'A symbol from the Greek alphabet reaching us from another world! Life speaks to life across the stars ... ' The scientist's voice broke, with something approaching religious emotion.

He watched the two signs, the new one at the bottom of the screen seeming to centre itself beneath the much larger hanging tulip shape. 'If that's an alpha,' he said, 'then the other one ... ' His voice tailed away.

*

In the Wortle household, Alice activated the telescreen.

' ... And we can only apologise once again for this startling interruption to our live telecast from the Middle East, where amazing unfolding events have left eminent scientists unwilling or unable to comment. We're still waiting for some coherent explanation of the discovery – of the phenomena – which are already being described as apocalyptic. Joining us now in the studio is Global News commentator – '

With a dyspeptic swirl of colour, the screen went blank. Henry was pleased. 'Neither the eyes nor the ears of the Chosen Ones should taint themselves with telescreen trivia at such a time, loved one,' he announced reprovingly.

'No, dear,' said Alice.

Henry picked up his Bible. 'We reached the last chapter of Revelation,' he said.

'Did you get Puss in, Henry?' said Alice.

But Henry was already reading.

*

The wind seemed to rush howling from the pit, which had torn itself around the entire circumference of the walls. Through the blinding dust, Professor Chalford realised that the dishevelled form of Maisie Seameirs was stooping over him. She was sobbing with alarm and concern, and pulling at his sleeve.

'What's happening, John?' She was yelling above the roar of the sandstorm which had engulfed them all. 'I don't get it. Have you seen?' She pointed her arm, its sleeve torn, unsteadily. 'Look ... '

Through a hailstorm of stinging sand and rocks and a raging darkness, which had snatched the setting sun and first rising stars from the sky, they peered in disbelief at the abyss of a crater which appeared to have been ripped open beneath the walls.

'It's not possible,' said Professor Chalford.

'If Faith can move mountains ... ' said Maisie Seameirs, whimpering despite herself.

But it *was* happening.

The earth was boiling and shuddering as the colossal walls heaved out of the desert wastes and lifted slowly, in glittering majesty, up towards the heavens.

*

In Peru, Doctor Eugens, still mesmerised by the oscilloscope images, watched the alpha shape rising into the enclosing embrace of the waiting tulip.

His face was flushed, his pulses racing; he knew he was living the climactic scene of his career.

His team, however, was gathered excitedly round the telescreen, where Global News had resumed its telecast of the century. (Their aerial coverage of the docking of the Alpha Craft with the Mother Ship was to sweep the board at the World Telejournalism Awards that year.)

'So, you mean, it's been lying there, dormant, in the desert for – for millennia,' said an earnest girl with glasses. 'Perhaps it just crashed – you know – like that spacecraft in America – '

'Roswell,' said a student assistant, anxious to impress her.

'No, more likely it's a spy ship,' said another. 'I saw this movie. It's been watching us all these years. A sort of explorer – reconnaissance – craft. On a mission.'

'To monitor the Life on Planet Earth Experiment, perhaps. ... ?' said Doctor Eugens, joining them. 'To see how it developed.'

His voice could not conceal his excitement. 'So many years listening to the stars,' he thought. 'Now contact – at last!'

'But why is it leaving us, sir?' asked the girl. 'They seem to be abandoning us ... That's what they're saying, the commentators.'

Doctor Eugens allowed the question, which had already cast a nagging shadow over his own thoughts, to the front of his mind. 'Perhaps,' he said slowly, 'the Experiment failed.' A deep sadness weighed down his words. 'War, superstition, over-population. Perhaps we failed the test. Perhaps we're just not up to intergalactic standards. Who knows ... ?'

*

But Henry Wortle knew.

He joined Alice at the window, watching dusk settle on a richly glowing sunset. 'Such beauty,' he said. 'We have been waiting for signs. Now we must finish our reading.'

Henry Wortle always recited clearly from his Bible.

'And I saw a new heaven and a new earth: for the first heaven and the first earth were passed away.

'It is done. I am Alpha and Omega, the beginning, and the end, the first and the last.'

Then they embraced, gave thanks, and waited.

*

Abruptly, as Doctor Eugens and his team watched, the merged images on his screen, the Alpha within the Omega, flared and disappeared. The flat trace of the oscilloscope screens resumed their vigil and, outside on the Peruvian mountain top, the great dishes of the receiving aerials continued their yawns of hope towards the stars. He looked back down the long years of patient waiting, and felt a sudden access of joy and wonder.

'At last, we *know*,' he told himself. '*We are not alone.*'

*

Besieged by swarming reporters, and frankly delighted by Maisie Seameirs' enthusiastic embraces, Professor Chalford was lost for words. 'It's all – well ... '

' ... Something of a Revelation?' suggested Maisie Seameirs.

*

At the same time, across the globe, viewers were abandoning telescreens in their millions to stare up and witness the historic event being written on the night skies of Earth – an event which was to inspire a fresh extravagance of astrological prediction and the birth of several new religions.

The heavens were on fire. For an unforgettable moment, the starblaze of both the alien craft tore a gash of flame across the sky, turning night into day, before the infinite deeps of space folded over their departure.

*

Henry and Alice Wortle were not surprised when the comet of incandescent light burst above the neighbouring rooftops.

'Angels,' murmured Alice, 'from the realms of glory.'

'It's all beginning,' said Henry, 'as The Brothers promised.' He paused. 'Beans – or soup, dear one? We shall need all our strength for what is to come ... '

The Method and Madness
of George Strode

'PERHAPS,' PONDERED MR STRODE, 'THERE *is* "a providence that shapes our ends". But sometimes it needs a nudge.'

One small nudge later, when Mrs Strode discovered her husband pouring measured tablespoons of expensive weedkiller into the china teapot – the one with the floral pattern – she was justifiably surprised. Suspicion, however, had never tainted her nature.

'That's weedkiller,' she pointed out.

'With arsenic,' said George Strode.

'For killing weeds,' she explained, with more complacency than subtlety.

'Hence,' said George, 'its name.'

His wife's sense of decorum was offended. 'Why are you putting it in my teapot?' she enquired.

'Because I thought you were elsewhere, Emilia.'

Despite her lifelong habit of incurious acceptance, Mrs Strode found the answer vaguely unsatisfactory. Besides, the teapot had a sentimental value. 'Make sure you clean it afterwards, dear,' she said. 'We don't want accidents ... '

George smirked. The smirk turned into a muscular twitch. It spread to his left eyebrow. 'No, dear.'

' ... Those roses are hand-painted,' explained Mrs Strode, and went out.

George stared at the tray with the china neatly laid out and sighed. Resignedly he picked up the steaming pot to empty it.

'Ouch,' said Mr Strode, and dropped the Strode floral heirloom on to his left foot. He nursed his fingers.

Then he nursed his toes.

Then he nursed his fingers again.

*

But George's determination at least remained undamaged.

While his bandaged foot throbbed gently, his mind simmered with poisonous fantasies. He constructed lift shafts of improbable depth with solid iron cages that seized up between floors in impossibly remote places where no man could hear the dying cadences of his wife's screams. He gloated over unmentionable dramas staged with simple props – a stake, some rope, a tablespoon of honey and a swarm of inexorable bees. He prowled through these dreams, directing, dominating and wholly successful; his wife, shocked at last out of passivity into passion, winced and struggled through a hundred obedient deaths, always recognizing his true strength of personality, acknowledging with her final, excited gasp that he, George Strode, man and husband, existed.

It was then that George conceived his second plan.

The shop bell tinkled rustily as he strolled, legs interweaving awkwardly in an unsuccessful attempt to feign casualness, across to the counter.

'A snake,' he announced.

The lady's spectacles flashed. 'Pardon?'

'A snake,' he repeated more urgently.

The lady glanced down with sudden alarm, cringing her toes. 'Where?' Then realization spread like a hot flush.

'This is the Post Office,' she said. 'The Pet Shop is next door.'

His palms moist, George changed shops and tried again. The man heard his request and was zealously prolific with advice.

'But vipers are poisonous, sir.'

'I want a viper, then,' reiterated George. Excitement made his voice more shrill than either of them had expected.

The shopkeeper was placatory. 'Newts ... ' he began.

'Vipers,' insisted George.

'Owls have grown very popular lately,' the shopkeeper mused persuasively. 'Tawny, Screech ... '

George glared at him. The man's sentence ebbed back into his throat, uncompleted.

'A viper, sir. With or without the poison? It's a question of glands ... '

'With,' said George, and brought his parcel triumphantly home. He went upstairs.

Having remade the bed with infinite care, George spent the evening urging the hands of his watch on to Horlicks time. At eleven o'clock Mrs Strode politely suppressed a furtive yawn with the back of her hand. It was promising. George fidgeted. At last Mrs Strode put down her empty cup and broke the customary silence of their marriage routine with the customary announcement:

'Bedtime, George.'

'Bedtime, dear.'

Immunized by habit and temperament from even noticing the unusual enthusiasm of his response, she made her way upstairs.

George delayed for a few minutes. He traced sinuously sinister curves in the carpet with his toe, still slightly sore, whilst his ears strained to catch every movement from the bedroom above. His pulse pounded and his chest swelled as the momentous minutes passed.

Then he allowed himself to go upstairs.

As he entered, he saw Mrs Strode sit down heavily on the edge of the bed and rearrange her hair-net. George winced in horror. Then his wife climbed into the far side of the bed, gave the other pillow a peremptory pat – '*This* side tonight, George: my lumbago' – and prepared herself for sleep.

George waited.

And continued to wait.

Finally and tentatively, he reached a hand under the bedclothes and groped. His fingers closed on the coils of a viper, crushed and bent in the middle of an otherwise warm and invigorating slumber. The coils heaved and slithered in a final spasm of life.

'What is it, George?' asked Mrs Strode sleepily.

'Nothing, dear.' His voice was breathless. He groped again, urging the moribund viper towards the calico-clad, supine form of his wife.

The viper twitched, expired and, with a posthumous muscular reflex, clamped its jaws shut on Mr Strode's hand.

'Ooh,' he said. 'It bit me. Help,' he added, in a whisper.

'Yes, dear,' said his wife, and fell asleep.

He made his way to the telephone, the snake still trailing, limp and lethal, from his left hand.

*

When he came out of hospital, George submitted in silent frenzy to the dutiful ministrations of his wife. The unthinking routine, the murmured platitudes and the silences alternately oppressed and enraged him.

'Talk to me,' he demanded.

'What about, dear?'

'About what you feel ... '

'Don't talk too much, dear.'

'About what you think ... '

'It's not good for you. Not with your heart.'

She handed him a glass. He knocked it on a wild impulse from her hand. The medicine splashed over his face and trickled down inside his pyjama collar.

'Temper,' remonstrated Emilia Strode blandly.

George bit his lip. A savage silence settled in.

'There, that's better.'

The silence prolonged itself. George, medicine trickling like blood from lip to chin, was planning again.

Several weeks later, he slipped furtively out into the dusk and did obscure things with a ladder and a saw at the bottom of the garden.

He enticed his wife, on the following day, to abandon the daily dusting and come outside to enjoy the sunshine. Duty fought hard before surrendering to pleasure. As they rounded the rose beds and entered the shadows of the orchard, George pointed casually to the clumsy, antique swing that hung from the heavily wrinkled branch of an elderly oak.

'The old swing,' he said invitingly.

'For the children,' she mused. 'So many plans ... ' She looked back down the empty, childless years. Even her nostalgia had become an empty habit, thought George.

He patted the seat. Emilia was tempted, moved forward and remembered the neighbours. She retreated.

George seized her impatiently by the shoulders. 'They're out – dearest.'

And Emilia Strode found herself seated on the old swing. A woodpecker tapped out a drumroll from the safety of a neighbouring tree.

George took hold of the seat and Mrs Strode's horizons began to lurch and sway with a rhythm that was as ancient as it was exhilarating.

'Ah!' she cried, as her childhood blossomed through the atrophied layers of adult experience.

'Ah!' responded George, as numberless marital frustrations evaporated and he inhaled invigorating gusts of clean, free air. Incipient triumph surged along his veins, rose to his cheeks and set his left eye twitching. He peered up at the overhanging branch.

The oak groaned. Its senile limb, already defiled by George's saw, swayed dangerously. Doom susurrated through the trembling leaves.

Mrs Strode laughed gaily.

George laughed too. A wild, exultant effusion that rose seething and bubbling hysterically into his throat. His face purpled.

His wife's disappointment was audible as the horizon abruptly steadied, slowed down and settled itself again. She turned her head, almost giggling.

She turned again.

'George!'

She brought the swing to an awkward halt and clambered off the splintery seat. The branch creaked, agonized.

Mrs Strode ran to her husband who lay, impotent and enraged, amid a clump of rhubarb, in the throes of an elaborate heart attack. He writhed.

'Keep still, George. Everything's all right, dear,' she murmured and went off to call the doctor.

George opened his eyes and the branch finally plunged down, acorns scattering, across his helpless body.

*

'I'm dangerous,' complained George.

The psychiatrist looked up.

'Very dangerous.' He bared his teeth in a rather unconvincing grimace. 'I expect I'm nearly certifiable.'

The doctor's eyes glazed over; they roamed aimlessly round the room. He fought down a familiar, hysterical fear that the walls were advancing in on him by doodling revealing analogues of his subconscious on his desk pad.

'And I keep feeling ignored,' said George Strode.

'Pardon?'

'Ignored,' repeated George.

The doctor absent-mindedly fondled the rubber plant that overhung his desk. 'I know.'

'It's a question of communication.'

'Yes,' agreed the psychiatrist.

'I can't get through to her. My wife. Her feelings ... '

'Quite.'

'She never notices things. Especially me. I might just as well be dead.' He sighed. 'And so might she. Especially her ... '

'Mm.' The psychiatrist swivelled in his chair to suppress an internal scream and drive back the walls. When he came to rest, George leaned forward.

'I have these desires.'

The doctor looked hopeful. 'Marital?' he whispered. His teeth bit into his pencil.

'My wife,' affirmed George.

'Ah.' The doctor nodded wisely.

'Dead,' repeated George.

Their heads nodded confidently in a unison of mutual misunderstanding.

Suddenly the doctor's eyes glinted. 'Do you like dressing up?'

'No.'

'*I* do.'

'Does it help?' asked George.

'Not very much. But it's such fun making the costumes. I've got a trunk. There's Madame de Pompadour ... '

'Doctor Crippen,' suggested George.

'The White Rabbit. With movable ears ... '

'The Marquis de Sade,' said George.

They paused. Pencil lead blackened the doctor's lips.

'Are we getting anywhere?' asked George.

The man shook his head sadly. 'I'm not.'

'I demand to be certified,' said George. 'It's the only solution. I'm a failure. Take me away from her ... '

The psychiatrist pressed a button and told his intercom to summon Mrs Strode.

Mrs Strode entered.

George Strode backed away. 'Certify me. At once,' he shouted. He leaned conspiratorially across the desk. 'I'm dangerous. I've tried to murder my wife!'

The doctor tutted. 'Really?' He smiled at Mrs Strode.

'Three times! I'm a failure. And it's bad for my health.'

'Nonsense, dear,' said Emilia Strode. 'Now come along home, and we'll have a nice cup of tea.'

*

It was over the cup of tea that George Strode conceived his master-plan. There was to be no room for error, chemical, animal or mechanical, and as little exertion as possible. They would have a picnic.

'By the seaside,' thought George. 'On a very high cliff.'

'It's windy,' complained Emilia Strode, when the day and the event finally materialized.

'Nearly at the top,' said George cheerfully.

'And this hamper's heavy.'

'Now you wouldn't want me to have another heart attack would you, dearest ... ? Here we are.'

They spread out the cloth, unloaded the hamper and, as the dilating sun turned the edge of the world into appropriately apocalyptic colours, they enjoyed the lavish picnic together.

Mrs Strode pointed to the reddening horizon.

'It's going to be a lovely day tomorrow, dear,' she remarked.

George secreted a sly grin in his cup and inadvertently inhaled tea. Choking, he was helped to his feet by his wife.

'The sunset,' he spluttered nasally. 'Let's go and look at it.'

'I'm looking, dear. Lovely.'

'A little closer, dearest.'

Cautiously, Mrs Strode supported her husband nearer to the cliff edge.

'That's quite far enough, George.'

George looked down. The greyness of the wrinkled sea frayed into bleeding foam on the rocky edges far below. The old ecstasy seeped into his brain again and his body reeled.

'Careful, dear. It's dangerous.' She pulled him back.

He fastened his grip on her arm.

'That's right, dear,' she said. 'Hold on to me if you feel unsteady. There. Isn't it splendid?'

'Dangerous!' shouted George. The wild look flared in his eyes. '*I'm* dangerous as well, you know. Very dangerous. Look at me.'

Emilia Strode looked.

Hard.

Emilia Strode saw. 'Weedkiller,' she said. 'The snake business. That tree ... '

'And now the picnic,' said George, dancing from foot to foot, exuberantly impatient.

'George!' Pride in her husband's strength of ambition battled with indignation. 'You tried to kill me, George.' She surveyed the discarded chicken bones and mayonnaise jars of the picnic idyll. 'You brought me up here to try again.'

'Not to try,' said George.

His wife, relieved, looked into his staring eyes. The eyebrow twitched.

'To *succeed*,' said George.

He pulled her a step nearer to the precipitous overhang. Space yawned dizzily around them.

'Don't squeeze my arm like that, dear. It hurts.' She looked at this assertive, aggressive man before her and, deep inside, for the first time, curiosity stirred, awoke and stretched her understanding. 'Why, George? Why?'

George hesitated. The inventory was a long one.

'You're naïve, cruel and complacent,' he began.

'It's not complacency. It's manners,' interrupted his wife.

'That's another thing,' he said. 'Your eternal, bloody politeness.'

'Don't swear, dear,' said Emilia Strode. 'I *am* your wife.'

'That's another thing,' said George, and pushed.

Mrs Strode pulled.

The sea heaved and waited. The rocks bared their wet, red teeth.

'George, be sensible,' panted Mrs Strode. 'You'll bring on an attack.' She pulled him to the ground.

'Shan't,' he retorted and pulled her to her feet.

A seagull dived screeching past her left ear. She jumped, skidded and accidentally knocked her husband and man, George Strode, over the edge of the cliff.

'George!' she screamed unhelpfully.

A white-knuckled, bleeding hand was tearing ignominiously at the gorse root by her feet. She grabbed at it and tried to pull.

'George,' she said, '*my* George.'

His voice came, thin with anguish. 'Let me go. I'm a failure.'

The root ripped further. The whole gorse bush quivered.

'You're a man, George,' screamed Mrs Strode. In a frenzy of passion and desperation she flung social and verbal decorum to the snatching winds. 'With guts,' she yelled. 'George, let's talk. I want you.'

She stooped uncomfortably and kissed the hand.

It slithered, with the rest of Mr Strode beneath it, another few inches closer to destruction.

There was a breathless and primitive tussle with the cliff edge, much panting, and a supreme effort of cooperation quite alien to the previous history of their marriage, and George was reunited with his wife. They clung together, red-faced, on the cliff top.

'George,' said Emilia Strode.

'Emilia,' said George Strode. 'I've discovered something after all. There *is*,' he announced, '"a providence that shapes our ends."'

Neither they nor the remote sun noticed the warning groan as the scarred edge of the cliff lurched, dropped and, with a terrible wrenching of earth, stones and roots, plunged down, turning through the screaming air, on to the uncaring rocks beneath.

It was the edge on which they were standing.

Broken parts of their bodies were later found 'locked together in an eternal embrace' that brought tears to the eyes of all who relished the coroner's style of oratory.

Virgin Territory

SLIGHTLY BREATHLESS AFTER THE LONG WALK up the desolate hillside, Andy sat down, gratefully leaning against one of the ancient stones. He patted the ground beside him invitingly.

Eve remained standing. The car, the road were out of sight. The stones, thrusting massively out of the moorland, misshapen by slow centuries of gnawing winds, were no consolation for the civilisation they had left behind.

'"Brooded",' said Andy.

'Pardon?'

'"Brooded". That's what they say. "The sombre sky *brooded* menacingly over the grim, jagged sentinels of the Stone Age temple where the two lovers were locked – "'

'Objection. "Lovers": it's inaccurate, presumptuous and – indelicate.'

'Overruled,' said Andy. 'Poetic licence.'

'More licence than poetry,' corrected Eve.

'" – Where the two lovers were fully interlocked in an embrace as old as – "'

'Time itself, perhaps?'

'Ah, a fellow lover of literature! We were made for each other. Come here, love.'

He tugged at her sleeve. She withdrew her hand instinctively, recognizing his mood. Andy, in a familiar surge of resentment, tugged again and, caught off balance, she found herself abruptly on the ground beside him. Then in his arms.

They were both surprised. Andy, braced against the rearing stone, tightened his embrace, roughly.

'Andy! Your hand. Please!' There was an undignified struggle. The gaunt rocks stood impassive guard.

Eve pulled herself away and straightened her blouse. Indignation fought with bewilderment.

'Why?' she demanded.

'Why not?' Andy's cheeks were flushed.

'Is that why you brought me here?' She looked beyond the lonely, circling stones to the far, empty horizon. 'The party. Even *that* isn't till tonight. Our engagement. Remember?'

Andy winced at her high-school decorum. 'Propriety, decency and chastity,' he thought, and pulled angrily at the grass, fertile, ageless, beneath his right hand.

'Mere formality,' he said. 'Ritual. Anyway, it's spring.'

'So?'

'Time for an honest, down-to-earth, sap-rising fertility ritual!'

'Sex, you mean.'

'Love, I mean.' He wondered whether he did. 'Love!' he repeated, throwing out a histrionic arm. 'The Primordial Urge. The Biological Imperative. How many lithe young maidens have sacrificed themselves on this very spot ... ?'

'To satisfy the lusts of some dirty old Druids,' said Eve.

Andy shrugged. 'They called it Agriculture then,' he said.

Eve pulled her jacket more tightly about her. 'Times change,' she said. 'I'm not sacrificing myself to get the crops going ... '

Andy stood up, looking and feeling aggressive. Eve backed against the moss-crusted stone. She tried evasion tactics. 'Let's ... count them,' she suggested. 'See how many ... '

'We're alone,' he said. 'No one here.' His hand pressed against the stone. The passion returned. 'Virgin territory. Isn't it time for a maiden voyage?'

His eyes were growing wild. She tensed, apprehensively. Then his head turned sharply. Eve followed his gaze. 'What is it?'

He strode across the edge of the inner ring, to the dominating, central monolith. He walked round it. 'Strange.' The wind? The edge of a cloak? Someone watching?

Eve came warily across to him. 'I want to leave,' she said. She stood beneath the great stone and shivered, feeling hemmed in by the waiting rocks.

'No. Not yet.' Andy was puzzled. The wind? 'Let's stay. Yes, we'll count them, if you like.'

They set off in opposite directions, counted and met again ten minutes later at the central stone.

'Seventy-five,' said Andy.

'Seventy-seven,' said Eve.

'Give or take a stone or two?' suggested Andy. But she was adamant. So they counted them again.

When he got to forty-four – or was it forty-five? – Andy felt the mists clouding his mind. He leaned against a granite column, oppressed by the futility of the exercise. What did it matter how many stones there were anyway? He watched Eve disappear behind the distant outer ring. Such determination. Such misplaced, sublimated energy! He called to her and suddenly, alarmingly, there she was almost behind him. Impossible. But there was certainly someone. *Surely* there had been someone. He looked across to see Eve reappearing in the distance, methodically starting on the inner circle ...

Andy investigated the nearby stones with growing unease. He found himself fighting an increasing fear, as foolish as it was irrational, of finishing the counting. A figure? The wind? A warning?

Eve was waiting for him at the first stone. 'Well?'

'Seventy-eight,' he confessed.

She smiled triumphantly. 'Seventy-seven! Again.' Andy bristled. He resented her grinning complacency, the way she fed on his error. 'Want to check?' she taunted.

He didn't. 'All right.' No, he definitely didn't. And she knew it. 'What's the matter? Frightened?'

'Why the hell should I be frightened?'

She had caught him off guard. 'It's the third count. You know what the locals say. I thought you'd grown too old for village superstitions.'

The locals. What did the locals say? Why was she so aggressive? 'I said "All right",' he asserted. And they began the third count.

'Third time lucky!' she called.

'Now who's superstitious!' he retorted.

He watched her go, marking off the stones one by one. Such method. Such madness! Perhaps there *were* seventy-seven stones. Why did it matter? And yet he felt increasingly, disturbingly, that it *did* matter. Why couldn't they agree? Why couldn't *he* arrive at the same number each time? Why was she so consistent? And if she was so sure she was right, what obscure mathematical zeal was driving her, step by rational step, to make a third count?

Thirty-nine. His pace was flagging. He forced himself doggedly to go on counting. The Third Count. What was it the locals said? A superstition. He struggled with the mists that blurred his memory, the mists that were starting to blur and warp the crouching stones. On impulse he whirled round.

There! By the centre stone. A tunic tugged by the wind. He peered through the haze. A farmer? A priest? One of the villagers? He ran gesticulating towards the figure. 'Wait!' he called. 'I must know ... '

And then his mind cleared. A profound sense of dread settled darkly inside him. He stared at the monolith. The figure was no longer there. But now he knew ... He knew that Eve must be stopped. She must not complete the third count.

He ran, bruising his shoulder against the raw, looming stones, trying to catch sight of the white jacket moving in and out of the stunted columns of the primitive temple. She was nearing the end of the circuit.

Red-faced, gasping for breath, he caught up with her and gripped her by the shoulders.

'Seventy-four,' she said. 'Andy, that hurts.'

'You've got to stop,' he said, trying not to shout. 'You mustn't finish the count.'

'Seventy-five. Who says?' She looked at him. Annoyance and scorn joined the determination which glared in her eyes.

'You know why. The locals. Tell me what they say about this place.'

'Country bumpkins.' She laughed.

His grip tightened. 'Tell me.'

Eve recited the words dully, mechanically, as to a child. '"The man will never live who thrice shall count the Stones and thrice shall count aright." There! And it doesn't even rhyme.' She tried to wrench herself free. She pointed at the next stone. 'Seventy-six,' she said.

'For heaven's sake, Eve.'

'You *are* scared,' she mocked. 'Why?'

'For my sake, then,' he protested.

'Give me one reason.'

'What's got into you? Do you love me or not? Isn't love a reason?' His voice rose. 'Can't you sacrifice anything for me?'

Eve struggled in his arms. 'Same old reason,' she said bitterly. 'Primitive man. Lusting after his virgin sacrifice ... '

She tore herself free and ran to the final stone, the centre stone. She raised her arms in a mock theatrical gesture. The surrounding stones stabbed silently into the blind, cold sky.

'Behold,' said Eve.

Andy fought through the sudden mists to where she stood; a shudder of passion and rage ripped like lightning out of the earth through his body.

'Don't do it!' He raised an angry fist.

'The seventy-seventh stone!'

Andy never found out precisely what he had done.

The fit ebbed away and he found himself leaning against the

Maid Stone with his intended bride cradled at last in his arms. As he watched the life-blood seeping down through the matted hair and trickling from the ancient rock into the grateful earth, he knew – as the silent watcher knew – that the locals would be assured of a fertile harvest that year.

A Question of Taste

THE MARRIAGE OF DENNIS AND MYRTLE Snipe was as predictable in its crises as it was insipid in between.

'What d'you call this?' demanded Mrs Snipe one evening. She flourished a diaphanous, lace handkerchief, heavily perfumed, under her husband's nose. He inhaled luxuriantly and felt a reminiscent smile glow within. All the perfumes of Peabody ...

'I'd call it a handkerchief,' said Dennis Snipe, 'dearest. No doubt you have a more subtle word for it.'

'Infidelity,' said Mrs Snipe. '*And* meanness. That's what I call it. The Peabody widow. Poor woman. Is that all you give her? You're as miserly to your mistress as you are to me. On your salary too!'

Mr Snipe denied neither charge. 'Equality,' he murmured, 'in all things, beloved.'

'Enough!' said Myrtle Snipe. 'You're heartless, selfish, arrogant, penny-pinching ... '

Mr Snipe nodded. 'And if I see that woman again or fail to increase the housekeeping ... ' he recited drily.

Mrs Snipe opened her mouth several times. 'Brute!' she cried. 'I'll – I'll – I'll – ' Words lost themselves in frustration; she turned puce instead.

' – Have a tantrum? Drink weedkiller?' Dennis Snipe helpfully ticked off the usual options for her on his fingers. 'Go home to mother?'

He saw the widow Peabody again.

And failed to increase the housekeeping.

So the morning he received the letter, Dennis Snipe was not surprised to find his wife had departed. Another holiday with Mother would be beneficial to them both – if not for the old lady. He sliced the top off his egg with satisfying precision, licked a smear of yolk from his fingers, savoured it, and found himself humming as he picked up the type-written envelope.

The message was both brief and anonymous.

'Mrs M. Snipe has been kidnapped. If you inform the police or fail to pay the sum of fifty thousand pounds immediately for her release, by the procedure described below, we will not be answerable for the consequences. The choice is yours – your money or your wife.'

Dennis Snipe stopped humming. The letter offended him. Its humour was trite, its tone operatic, its style clichéd, its demand outrageous. He took a slow spoonful of egg and digested the situation thoughtfully. Indignation battled with indecision, then surrendered to disappointment. He realised how much he'd been in need of a break from marital malignity. A couple of days of peace to regather his strength, cherish the inner man, put his feet up and enjoy television programmes of his own choice, free from the traditional uninvited satirical commentary from the other chair, offered a most tempting prospect. And his wife's absence – however enforced and, of course, unfortunate – would also give him a chance to practise a little of the haute cuisine of yesteryear and his stomach a hard-earned respite from the humbler culinary endeavours, serviceable but uninspired, of Myrtle Snipe.

He began to hum again.

Then an unhappy thought visited him. He made a discreet phone call to his mother-in-law. It was no hoax. Myrtle had definitely not gone back to her mother's.

He folded the note and replaced it decisively in its envelope. No, he would not be blackmailed by importunate strangers – especially when they resorted to such B-feature melodramatics. The more he thought, the more morally repugnant the whole business became. To surrender one's hard-earned wealth in such a squalid manner would be unthinkable, would show a lack of moral fibre. What sort of society was one living in? Moral decay. Everywhere. It was a sign of the times. He shook his head and wiped the corners of his mouth fastidiously with his napkin. The police? No, it would be unwise to contact them – just yet, at any rate. The police would precipitate action, disturb his domestic tranquillity ... and freedom.

He furled his napkin, and considered his wife – for the first time. She was clearly in a most regrettable plight.

But Dennis Snipe was still humming when he drove off to work.

*

The second letter arrived the following day. Mr Snipe frowned. It was cogent and, from its reckless typing, evidently despatched with some impatience.

'Pay up or your wife suffers. She'd write herself but her eyesight isn't what it was. See what we mean? Proof enclosed.'

Dennis Snipe reached for the envelope. He sighed. Would such people never learn? With a soft thud, quiet as fate, something rolled onto the table.

He peered at it. He prodded it with a tentative finger. Something gelatinous. Something globular. Something now sticky with marmalade.

The object clicked into focus.

Light glanced off the eyeball. Its dead stare glittered into sudden, piercing blue life.

Dennis Snipe recoiled, inhaling sharply. He knew that look only too well. 'Myrtle!' he said uneasily.

He had an extra spoonful of sugar in his tea that morning.

*

After this initial alarm, Mr Snipe felt able to face the next day's post with more resilience. He read and destroyed the simple note, written – with uncharacteristic clumsiness – in Myrtle's own hand ('Dennis, help'), averted his eyes to remove the wedding ring (after all, he'd paid good money for those diamonds), and threw the severed finger without further examination into the waste-bin.

*

The postman summoned him to the door the following morning to sign for the registered parcel. It was long, bulky and surprisingly weighty. He glanced over the accompanying note:

'All members of one body. *Arm* yourself for further meaty matters – or pay up IMMEDIATELY.'

He winced. It was too distasteful to contemplate. Especially so early in the day when one was never at one's best. He lifted the waste-bin lid. On the other hand, the smallest joints were inordinately expensive these days, even from the Co-op butcher's, and waste was such an affront to the moral core. He hesitated, then placed the parcel, still unwrapped, for decency's sake, in the freezer.

The sight of food – though the freezer was now sadly depleted of stocks – stirred revitalizing thoughts. It reminded him of Pamela Peabody, evoking visions of an intimate dinner party at which – now that fate seemed to be taking its dark and, naturally, painful course – they would inaugurate a new era of honesty and openness in their relationship. No more grubby secrecy and suspicion. No more pressing thigh to furtive thigh while pretending to pore over the less tempting appetisers in that Italian restaurant. He felt strangely renewed, purified. The Snipe cheeks glowed with rectitude and anticipatory fervour as he dialled her number, but Mrs Peabody was not at home. A written invitation would have to suffice.

'Dennis Snipe takes great pleasure – '

He paused and relished the words. Great pleasure indeed! He suppressed an undignified snigger, completed and sealed the note.

A celebration. At eight o'clock the following evening, joy, in the curviform shape of Pamela Peabody, would come again to the troubled House of Snipe. After all, damnit, a man deserved something to look forward to in these depraved and depressing times.

*

When the doorbell chimed its melodious imperative at the appointed hour, it caught Dennis Snipe in some confusion. Saucepans throbbed and simmered in the kitchen, candles were still unlit in the lounge, and unmatched socks lay strewn about the bedroom in angry disarray.

It had been that sort of day.

Preparing and staging his dinner party had put an unexpected strain on Mr Snipe's organizational energies. He began to remember the manifold uses a wife could be put to on such occasions. They planned, shopped, peeled potatoes, handed one the little chopping knife with the ivory handle when one had had it in one's hand only a moment ago, replenished the salt cellar, made sure that that Burgundy stain had been laundered out of the best tablecloth before now of all times, put finishing touches to things, knew where one's other sock was, and – above all – they *remembered*.

Dennis Snipe, to his chagrin, had *forgotten*. The most vital purchase of all. The *pièce de résistance* of the evening. By the time he had realised his oversight, the butcher's had closed. Provencale Roast Lamb – and even the freezer was devoid of meat. More or less. His fingers had hesitated over the parcel. The solution lay within his grasp – obvious, audacious, and unsettling. But the idea, once seeded, took dark root. Though it perhaps lacked propriety, it certainly did not want for ingenuity. Inspiration and flair: they were the hallmarks of the highest cuisine – as he had frequently had to remind the mundane Myrtle, rest her soul, soon, if not already, alas. He prodded the joint, weighed it pensively. It *was* very tender. Tenderness and Myrtle: deep in his mind the two alien concepts merged and far-off memories stirred ...

But not for long. He had carried the meat into the kitchen – how reassuringly, if fortuitously, it resembled a pedestrian leg of lamb – garnished it with garlic, rosemary and butter, and slipped it into the oven and out of sight. The deed, once done, had felt curiously satisfying, even spiritually uplifting. It was a propitiatory gesture. And it seemed, in a strange way, appropriate. It accorded with one's deepest sense of right that his former wife should be included, however unconventionally, in his new happiness.

And – less noble thought – it disposed of the evidence. If some person or persons unknown had been generous enough to resolve his marital problem piece by piece in this way, it would surely be churlish not to cooperate with destiny – and thus ensure that the inquisitive nose of the law would find no rats to smell.

The doorbell chimed again.

Dennis Snipe inhaled the seductive aroma from the kitchen as he hurried downstairs on forgetfully slippered feet. He kissed his finger-tips with satisfaction. 'Incroyable!' he murmured. Deftly he pressed a switch and languid airs lingered about the lounge. Then he sleeked back his hair and, somewhat breathlessly, opened the front door.

'Dennis ... dearest. I hope I'm not late.'

The simple greeting struck him like a bullet. Disbelief distorted the Snipe features. They went white. He felt an uprush of fear. He had expected airs from heaven, not blasts from hell. His voice, when it arrived, was unexpectedly shrill.

'Myrtle!' he said.

'Dennis,' said Myrtle Snipe. 'Home again, dear. Aren't you pleased to see me?' She contrived to pout winsomely.

'Yes,' he said. 'No,' he said. 'Myrtle,' he repeated. 'What – what are you doing here?'

'I'm being your wife,' explained Mrs Snipe. 'It's not unusual – even in these days. Wives and husbands, one of each, living together. In the happy home. Till death them do part.'

Both eyes shining – for she was clearly possessed of the full complement of eyes and limbs – she stepped forward.

Dennis Snipe stepped back.

'What a delicious smell!' said his wife. 'Doing one of your specials, dear?' She watched him wince. 'A little party to celebrate my return, perhaps?'

She entered the lounge and beheld the candelabra, the best silver placings, the room murmuring with soft music.

'Or am I intruding?' She paused and turned her gaze full upon him. 'Who are you having for dinner then?' She savoured the visible weakening of his knees, though she wasn't sure she wholly understood the cause. 'Have I said something I shouldn't?'

Dennis Snipe felt his joyous evening crumbling about him. 'You were kidnapped,' he said.

'No,' said Mrs Snipe. She sat down at the table and beamed comfortably. 'I kidnapped myself, dear. I thought it might help to clarify our marriage. It did. For both of us. Did you enjoy my letters?'

Mr Snipe's wits struggled to regroup themselves. 'But the parcel ... ' he said.

'I know how you love surprises, dear.'

'I cooked it ... ' said Dennis Snipe.

His wife stared at him.

'I had to ... ' He moistened his lips. 'Then who – what ... ?' Dark intimations dried his voice to a croak.

'I think the question that – um – sticks in your throat a little, dear, is: "*Whom* are we having for dinner after all?"'

Dennis Snipe nodded miserably. He heard the chatter and hiss of the stove; he smelt the pungent aroma of Snipe Special. He repressed an obscure urge to rush to the oven and baste the joint – a culinary caress, a libation of love.

'Peabody Provencale,' said his wife. 'Quite a dish, dear – you've always thought it.'

Mr Snipe's fists tightened. '*You* kidnapped *her*,' he said bitterly.

'And *you* cooked her! Eating People is Wrong, Dennis.' Mrs Snipe's tone was sadly reproving. 'We're partners,' she said, and touched his arm gently, 'in crime, at least, dear.' She paused. 'Until the police arrive, of course. They disapprove of murder, you know. But at least the press enjoy it. "Husband eats mistress who threatened to reveal secret passion to devoted wife." The *Telegraph* will be particularly salacious, as usual.' Her blue eyes surveyed him regretfully. 'But let's not think of painful matters – just yet. It's not your way, is it? And it'll spoil your cuisine. Let's enjoy our last supper together. Does Pamela – Mrs Peabody – make a pleasing sauce? Sharp, piquant – and plenty of it, I expect.'

'The police,' said Dennis Snipe. 'Murder.'

'Murder by cooking,' confirmed Mrs Snipe. 'Death by degrees: just like our marriage, dear. By the way' – she fumbled in her handbag and produced a typewritten document – 'have you got a pen? I'd like you to sign this.' She pointed. 'Just there. It's the allowance you're going to give me – and a very generous one too, dear. Thank you.'

Mr Snipe reddened. His fist struck the table. Candles quivered. 'It's shameful. It's immoral!' he exploded. 'It's – it's not fair!'

Myrtle Snipe gave a sharp laugh. She probed him with fierce blue eyes. 'You speak to me of fairness, Dennis Snipe. Was it fair to ignore my pleas for rescue? Was it fair to sit back while I was daily dismembered, limb by limb? Was it fair to serve me up, gaily garnished, to your mistress?' She stabbed the paper with an indignant finger. 'The dotted line,' she said. 'I'm entitled to compensation.'

'Never,' said Dennis Snipe.

'We'll see.'

Mrs Snipe left the room, busied herself noisily in the kitchen and returned bearing the dish of the evening with appropriate ceremony. Vegetable accompaniments swiftly followed.

Dennis Snipe regarded the roast with silent respect. It was an awesome and moving experience. The uniqueness of the moment cast its spell upon him. Such complete synchronicity of culinary perfection and personal disappointment is rare in any life – and Dennis Snipe knew himself privileged among men. Despite himself, he licked his lips. Pamela Peabody, it seemed, was as tempting on the dinner table as she had promised to be in bed.

'Done to a turn,' said his wife. 'It seemed such a shame to waste it.' She held up the sacrificial knife. 'Will you carve, dear, or shall I? It's *your* little treat after all.' She pressed the knife into his hesitant hand. 'What's the matter? Surely you're not losing your appetite for infidelity ... ?'

The knife hovered over the bronzed, succulent crust. It bit into the delicate flesh. And abruptly the front doorbell pealed.

The knife clattered on to the table and Dennis Snipe started to his feet. 'The police?' he said. 'You didn't really ... ?' He shot a glance, murderously compounded of accusation, malice and fear, at his wife, who responded with a wry, forgiving smile, and made his way unsteadily to the door.

He opened it and, for the second time that evening, Mr Snipe felt himself the plaything of amateur furies, the victim in some manic theatrical plot. He passed a hand over his brow, closing his eyes to the sight, but when he opened them again, she was still there, resplendent in every ample curve, upon his doorstep.

'Dennis,' said Pamela Peabody. 'Is Myrtle here yet?' She carried her magnificently distributed body towards him, past him, into the lounge.

'No! Please! What? Yes. How – ?' His world fragmented into monosyllables.

He watched his wife, his mistress, their embrace.

'Treachery,' he murmured. 'In league ... '

'From the start,' said Mrs Peabody. 'Poor Myrtle. I came straight round to see her after that first disgraceful episode in the Italian restaurant. If there's one thing I cannot condone, it's unfaithfulness.' The Peabody bosom heaved indignant disapproval. 'We found an immediate rapport, didn't we, dear? The late Mr Peabody, rest his wicked soul, had also been quite unrelenting in his lechery.'

Dennis Snipe groaned at past extravagances. 'All those meals. All those little gifts ... '

The widow's gaze fell upon the paper on the table. 'Has he signed yet?'

Mr Snipe looked up. 'What have you two – ?'

'Been cooking up, dear?' said Myrtle Snipe.

'Your goose,' said Pamela Peabody obscurely. She cast a longing, predatory glance over the table. 'Lamb Provencale!' she said. 'What a treat!'

'It arrived by post,' said Mrs Snipe. 'That leg of lamb you got from Sainsbury's.'

'The brute!' said Mrs Peabody. The two women chuckled in treacherous unison.

Dennis stared at his mistress. He stared at his wife. 'Leg of lamb!' he moaned. He sank onto a chair. 'What more do you want from me?'

'Money,' said Mrs Snipe.

'Regularly,' said Mrs Peabody. 'We're going into business together. A restaurant. Haute cuisine.'

'Or your life,' added his wife, 'if necessary. Cutlets *au Dennis* would take pride of place on the menu. In loving memory. Naturally.'

Dennis Snipe was appalled. 'Blackmail!' he exclaimed. 'Demanding money with menaces. Your moral standards were never impeccable, as Mother constantly warned, but *this* –!' His wild eyes focused on the phone. 'I shall call the police ... '

'That makes a change,' murmured his wife.

'Look at the evidence,' he blustered. 'The eyeball, that severed finger ... '

'Theatrical props,' smiled Mrs Snipe. 'Pamela knows a little man in Kensington. *Titus Andronicus* is his speciality. He's terribly proud of his wax fingers ... '

Together they placed the document before the speechless Mr Snipe.

Music faded and died; the tape clicked. Silence chilled the room. The atmosphere grew taut.

'The choice is yours, dear,' said Myrtle Snipe. 'Pay now ... ' She picked up the pen.

'Or pay now,' said Pamela Peabody. She picked up the best silver carving knife. The blade flashed.

Mr Snipe flinched.

'My savings!' he said. 'You wouldn't ... '

Determination glittered in their eyes. They loomed over him vengefully on either side, pen poised, knife poised. He turned from one to the other.

'Cutlets,' said Mrs Peabody. She gripped his arm with an appraising squeeze and bared her teeth in a smile. 'I'm hungry,' she said. Her words resonated ominously.

'Are you completely devoid of feeling, of moral scruple?' said Dennis Snipe.

'*Touché*!' chorused the two ladies.

'Do as you would be done by,' said his wife.

They gazed down at him. He whimpered helplessly.

'You carve, dear,' said Myrtle. 'Leg or breast: help yourself. But don't take all the choice cuts.'

They giggled.

'He's got nice thighs,' mused Pamela Peabody hungrily. 'Strong and meaty.'

'Save me some of the – you know – marital bits and pieces,' said Mrs Snipe. 'A souvenir. For old times' sake.' She sighed, recalling the vigorous ecstasies of their wedding night on that creaking antique bed. 'It does seem a bit of a waste,' she said.

Pamela Peabody nodded.

Dennis Snipe nodded too. 'Mind that knife!' he said.

'He's quite – well-built, isn't he?' said the mistress, running a tongue across her moistening lips.

'And plenty of energy,' said the wife. 'Firing on all cylinders. The beast!' They appraised him thoughtfully. 'Enough for two healthy appetites ... '

Their eyes met. Their thoughts focused.

'He'd need to be tamed, of course,' she continued. 'Kept in his place ... If he swore vows. Obedience – '

'Silence – '

'But not Chastity, dear.' The Peabody teeth gleamed. Appetite flushed her cheeks. She reached down and ran a lingering hand along his thighs. 'He could be quite – entertaining,' she said. 'Share and share alike, of course, dearest.'

The whimper shifted into a sigh. Passion stirred, then pounded, in their victim's veins. Dennis Snipe contemplated his newly charted destiny – and began to chuckle.

He put an embracing arm about each of the women in his life and pulled them close.

'At your service, ladies,' he said. 'As soon as you tear up this immoral document, we can begin.'

Sharp red fingernails seized the paper. There was a moment of agonized hesitation.

'Blackmail's so ugly. Besides, the lamb's getting cold,' warned Mr Snipe. He flexed his muscles.

'And I'm getting hotter,' he said.

The paper tore decisively.

Twisted Shadow

MRS HURSE, KNEELING UNCOMFORTABLY AT THE edge of the top lawn, was weeding.

Then she saw the shadow, black and crooked against the earth of the delphinium bed, and jumped.

'Bernard! Frightening me like that. I nearly made a kebab of that worm.'

She rose, smoothed a wayward curl with her arm and turned.

But the lawns were deserted. Puzzled, she stood, hand on hip, scanning the paddock and the enclosing hills where the famous caverns were just closing for the day. She listened.

'Bernard ... ?'

She shrugged and resumed her offensive against the weeds. Her fork stabbed into the damp soil and she coughed drily, wrinkling her nose. She smelled the odours of earth and decay, and shivered, a momentary prey to ancient fears. A worm squirmed its moist length out of the light down into the dead darkness of the clogging earth. She watched it, half expecting to feel the shadow fall across the ground in front of her again. Or – she shuddered at the thought – to see its twisted outlines rising darkly out of the soil.

'What nonsense,' she told herself and shook her head to dispel the threatening shades of her old depression.

The crunch of tyres on gravel and the plaintive peal of the door-bell pulled her back to immediate reality. Distantly she heard the customary curse as the office key was inserted by customary error in the front door. She winced, automatically, at the scrape of shoes on her newly polished conservatory floor. Climbing unsteadily to her feet, she felt the Saint Bruno flavoured moustache brushing her cheek as her husband's daily greeting was duly delivered.

Bernard had arrived home. He was carrying his latest camera and the new tripod.

'That's funny ... ' Isobel Hurse had gone pale. 'The car. You've just arrived – now, dear.'

'That,' said Bernard Hurse, 'is because I live here.'

'But it's funny ... '

'It's quite legal. They call it marriage. Now,' he announced, grimacing doubtfully at the light as he erected the stand and rotated the time exposure to its maximum setting, 'a portrait: the new Deputy Director of the Cavesham Experimental Nuclear Energy Station returns in triumph after a day of gruelling interviews to greet his lady wife! Smile!'

'Bernard!' protested the lady wife. 'My dress. My hair ... !'

'Other wives say predictable things like "Congratulations".'

Isobel laughed, kissed him and waved the hand fork menacingly under his nose. 'No pictures, dear,' she said. 'You can't.'

'Can,' he said, hastily joining her by the delphiniums and enfolding her in a suitably photogenic embrace. They grinned at the camera. The grins atrophied. The shutter clicked. 'And another,' he said, 'to finish the reel.'

The reel was finished.

'Brute,' said his wife, smoothing the folds of her grubbiest gardening smock. 'First you frighten me to death; then you take pictures when I look as though rigor mortis has set in. Hardly action becoming a Deputy Director, dear ... '

He smiled, shaking his head.

'Frighten you? When?'

'By coming home twice!' she said. 'Someone's playing tricks. I saw your shadow just before you arrived. Here. Across the border. Well, I thought it was yours.'

Her husband chuckled.

'He thinks I'm being neurotic again,' she thought. 'There *was* a shadow,' she asserted, the uneasiness creeping back, prickling at the base of her skull; 'here. From here to the hedge.'

'Nonsense.'

'I saw it!'

'Imagination,' said Mr Hurse, softening his voice as he noticed for the first time that day the all too familiar strained expression haunting his wife's eyes.

She compressed her lips and remained silent.

'The sun,' he explained. 'Look, Isobel.' He spoke quietly. 'The sun's throwing the shadows *the other way!*'

She looked at their feet, saw their shadows stretched out across the lawn towards the house and knew that he was right. Involuntarily she shivered again. She watched Bernard pick up the spade, heard him planning the new rockery.

'This is where we agreed, isn't it? Just,' he thrust the spade deep into the earth of the delphinium bed, 'here.'

His wife breathed in sharply.

'Blacklock's delivering the stones at the weekend. It'll mean shifting quite a lot of earth.'

He enlarged the hole he'd just started with one or two token gestures with the spade and turned to his wife for approval.

'Isobel?' Anxiety unexpectedly sharpened his voice. 'What's the matter?'

Mrs Hurse was trembling. 'That smell.' She coughed. 'No, not a smell exactly ... It's something in the soil ... '

Mr Hurse drove the spade home with his right foot.

'No!' said his wife. Apprehension seized her. 'Not there.' She put her hand to her head. The pain was throbbing behind her eyes. Decay. Mortality. An obscure panic dried her throat. An awareness of despair and unbearable suffering welled up, suffocating her senses. With a dry sob she repeated faintly, 'Not there', and felt the greyness reaching up to her, making her dizzy ...

'Look.' Her husband stooped over the border. 'Look what's here!'

But Isobel Hurse had fainted.

*

The decayed object lay before them on an old newspaper, grimy with dirt and age.

'Animal,' said Bernard Hurse. 'Probably a pig.'

'Too big,' objected his wife pithily.

'A horse, then.'

'Too small.'

'Well, it's hardly likely to be human, is it, dear?'

'No,' she said, without conviction, 'hardly.'

*

'Cheese, dear,' muttered Bernard wearily on being abruptly awoken by a particularly painful dig in the ribs during the first disturbed night. 'Too much Stilton for supper.'

Mr Hurse had preferred to ignore the implications of his wife's obscure insistence that the new rockery should remain unexcavated; it was a minor neurotic foible that was to be expected, perhaps, in someone of her age and temperament. The phase would pass.

But it was more difficult to ignore her when she started having the dreams.

He rubbed his side, winced and turned cautiously over again. Isobel, however, remained stiffly upright beside him, her face drawn and pale.

'Can you – smell anything?' she asked. 'Bernard?'

A gentle snore rose as the bedclothes sank. Instinctively she extended an elbow towards her husband's back – then resisted the temptation. What good would it serve? It wouldn't alter the simple, irrational fact: a smell of loam hung in the room, close, stifling, infecting the air ...

And what if Bernard couldn't smell it? Angry with herself for such neurotic imaginings, she turned out the light and, with difficulty, finally went back to sleep.

Immediately the nightmare was upon her again.

The setting was indistinct but it felt familiar. A bird calling, song soaring up through shimmering blue skies, up into the sun. Flowers, plump with scents, humming with bees and colour, open to the sun, grass new-mown breathing the sun. She bathed in sensations of relief, of release after pain. Elation.

Then, true to a fatal inevitability, the darkness crept in like a black plague and contaminated: the dream turned sour. Always things followed the same depressing direction. Always things decayed.

The bird song sharpened into stridency, a shrill of fear. A gust of stinging wind and stillness; the sun expanding, white. Then the first of the moans, low, insisting through the bending corn; and a dull pounding along the arteries of the earth promising panic and pain. Pain and panic pounding closer. The air heavy now with sobbing wails, the approach of some unnameable grief. Howls breaking deafeningly about her. A glimpse of stunted trees reaching black arms into a sky heaving with horrors she feared but could not understand. A face – dear heaven, the travesty of a face – lurched into hers, twisted and bubbled into sores and shapelessness. A weight of blistered misery, rotting into meaninglessness. Earth falling. At her feet earth, on her face earth, and between her fingers, writhing, the first of the worms. And everywhere that smell, unbearably familiar, suffocating. Struggling, she opened her mouth to protest, to scream. Why couldn't she scream? Her lungs. Her mouth. Something was clogging her tongue ...

And abruptly the bedroom walls reassembled themselves around her. There was Bernard bending over her, looking anxious.

Had she actually screamed? He was saying something. Holding out a glass of water.

'Sorry, dear,' she said. 'I seem to have been dreaming again ... '

Bernard Hurse smiled wanly. After a succession of similarly disrupted nights he began to find even *that* faint encouragement difficult.

*

'You're through.'

Doctor Bill Mark's voice was slightly harassed at first, but he shifted into more friendly gear on identifying his speaker.

'Bernard! How's things? How's the job? Coping with these Anti-pollutionists and their rally? They're all over the village again drumming up support for their annual knees-up next week.'

Bernard sighed. 'Don't I know it! Keep Britain free from Nuclear Contamination. Keep Britain back in the Stone Age. Anyone would think we'd planned to bring back the plague!'

'It's all right for you, you old rogue: moving out of the village out of sight of your beastly Reactor domes; cutting your old, less elevated friends. Only bishops and royalty now, By Appointment, eh? How's the Lady of the Manor? Keeping – you know – on top of things?'

Bernard caught sight of his wife – who seemed to have overcome her recent phobia and indulged in some gardening at last – advancing from the potting shed and lowered his voice. 'Bill, it's Isobel ... Isobel! I can't speak now ... Yes, it could be the old trouble ... Heavens no, not a surgery consultation. You know what she's like ... '

He heard the french windows opening in the next room.

'Look, how about dinner next week ... ? Yes, Laura of course. A delayed house-luke-warming. That sort of thing ... Wednesday ... ? Fine. Sorry to be so abrupt. Tell Laura tiaras will, of course, be worn. Carry on butchering ... Yes. 'Bye.'

He replaced the receiver, looked up and saw Isobel in the

doorway. He straightened his tie, smiled awkwardly and rose to his feet, scattering a sheaf of letters.

'Bill Mark?' she said. Her gaze was penetrating. 'What did he want?'

'Feeding. Good Lord! Where did you get those from?'

His wife subsided into a chair, looking suddenly fragile and exhausted. 'The border. They seem to be everywhere.'

Absently, Bernard brushed the sprinkling of soil into his wastepaper basket. Then he picked up the two earth-crusted fragments of bone and studied them, the creases deepening in his brow.

*

'Human,' pronounced Doctor Mark; 'not a doubt of it. As human as you or me – give or take a few hundred years of decomposition.'

He put down the bones, brushed the fine powder from his sleeve, nodded and held out his glass for a second offering from the port decanter.

'How exciting,' said Laura Mark, patting Isobel's arm. 'How does it feel, dear, living in a cemetery? Just think of the vibrations! What the old dears at my circle would say ... !'

'Circle?' asked Isobel.

'A sad case.' The doctor looked at his wife with compassionate resignation. 'She's joined a spectral branch of the W.I. – a sort of Psychic Sewing Circle. They spend their evenings waiting to be possessed by strange men.'

'Spiritualists,' explained his wife with a withering glare. 'They're a bit dotty but great fun. Especially Miss Friend. Like a militant Brown Owl who failed to make it as a witch. You ought to join us, dear. You're the receptive sort. Sensitive.'

'Neurotic,' thought Isobel Hurse. 'That's what she means.'

'Take this house,' said Mrs Mark. 'It must be a mine of rich vibrations!'

'Ah: if walls could talk ... ' murmured Bernard Hurse.

'Perhaps they can,' said Isobel. 'And Laura's old ladies – '

'Quivering with vibrations like superannuated psychic harps,' chuckled Bill.

' – Are picking up memories of vivid emotions, say, embedded in places.'

'Like recordings, you mean,' said Bernard.

'What about your garden, then? All those bones. Your lupins should be positively throbbing with messages,' mocked Doctor Mark. 'You'll have to practise communing with your herbaceous border sometimes, Isobel.'

Mrs Hurse gnawed her lower lip. Her husband glanced at her anxiously. A slight flush betrayed her excitement. She hesitated. 'Haven't you ever come to a place, indoors or out, and found it instantly, you know, depressing? Over-shadowed. Only certain spots; they seem to draw and repel you, as if there was something terribly important ... '

Her voice faltered. She became aware that the two men were studying her and Bill suggested rather too vigorously: 'Did you mention slides, Bernard?'

Her husband needed no encouragement. Pictures were duly splashed colourfully across the screen; the noises of admiration, proper on such occasions, were in full progress.

'I say, that *is* good, Bernard: *another* sunset,' said Bill.

Bernard, pleased, pressed the projector control. 'Oh,' he said.

They peered doubtfully at the screen.

'This week's mystery picture,' said Bill. 'Give us a clue.'

'Damn. I thought I'd thrown these away,' said Bernard. 'The exposure went haywire. There were two shots at the end of the reel. The wretched camera had a fit.'

'What's it supposed to be?' asked Laura, with more politeness than interest.

'The Deputy Director returning in triumph to greet his lady wife,' quoted Isobel.

'In the middle of a blazing June snowstorm?' murmured Bill.

'The other one's just as bad, only ... It's strange. This one seems hopelessly over-exposed and the other's quite the reverse – absurdly dark. Yet I didn't alter the setting at all in between.'

'Wait a minute,' said Isobel. Her voice was tremulous. 'You can see *something* ... Vague outlines. The edge of the border ... ' They craned their necks towards the screen. 'There's a faint sort of figure.'

Bill rose, put on his reading glasses and approached the screen crabwise, ducking from the beam. 'Good Lord,' he said. 'Who did you say this was supposed to be? God. What a face! It makes *The Night Of The Thousand Vampires* look like something out of Enid Blyton. I wouldn't like to meet that face on a dark night. Can you see? Look.' He pointed. 'All distorted and yelling. And covered in stains: see? Stains or – ugh! – they look like huge, festering blisters.'

He made his way back to his seat. 'What a ghastly sight! No – don't try and look, Isobel. I mean it. It's horrific ... Change it, Bernard, for heaven's sake.'

But Isobel did not need to look. That face had loomed at her, howling, out of each of her recent dreams. Every grotesque feature was distressingly familiar. She swallowed back her fright and bewilderment:

'There's something else, too,' she whispered. 'I don't understand. We *both* stood there. Bernard, why is there only one figure in the picture ... ?'

But the next slide had already clicked on to the screen. 'Damn,' said Bernard. 'Disaster slide, number two.'

Shaken but curious, the audience strained to identify the blurred and darkened image before them.

'I thought this was the rejoicing couple,' said Bill. 'Where are they? Hiding behind the hollyhocks?'

'You can see the edge of the lawn clearly enough,' observed his wife encouragingly. 'What's that thing lying across the garden by the hedge? That black stain?'

'A mark on the film,' said Bernard. 'I shall complain.'

'No.' Isobel's voice was hoarse. 'It's a shadow,' she said

unsteadily, the sobs rising in her throat. 'I've seen it once before. It's a twisted, black shadow!'

And as much to her own surprise and embarrassment as that of her guests, Mrs Hurse began to cry. They were angry, bewildered tears, releasing the tensions of weeks of fear and repression.

'Oh, Bernard, what's happening to us – to me? Is something haunting us? Is that it?'

Doctor Mark stooped professionally towards her. 'Isobel,' he said. 'Perhaps we could have a chat about it some time ... '

The sobbing rose helplessly and Isobel Hurse buried her face in the cushions to stifle her misery. 'Not, please not, that clinic again,' she thought.

The doctor and his wife took their leave in the hallway. 'Phone me again – if there are any developments, Bernard.'

The door opened and Doctor Mark tiptoed back in. 'Bones,' he said. 'I nearly forgot. I promised Bernard I'd let one of our forensic blokes loose on them.' He picked up the parcel and grimaced. 'The sooner I get them outside the better. They're beginning to smell quite – musty.'

*

Bernard Hurse slept fitfully that night. When he jerked from the shallows of sleep back into consciousness for the third time, he put on his bedside lamp and squinted at the alarm clock. It was three o'clock. He groaned, thinking of the working day ahead. He rolled over as cautiously as twenty years of marriage required to see whether his wife was faring any better than himself.

The bed was empty.

His heart fluttered, and settled again as memory returned and reproved his fears. She had, of course, been sleeping in the next room for several weeks now. He stretched, lay back on the pillows and closed his eyes.

The distant sound – an erratic, solitary clatter – which had been nagging at him subliminally, focused in his consciousness. It insisted, teasing his mind. It seemed to be coming from downstairs. Perhaps he'd left a window ajar, and the breeze was rattling it against the frame.

He pulled on his dressing-gown with a sigh, tiptoed past his wife's open door, retraced a couple of steps, peered inside the room, peered again, switched on the light and saw the crumpled sheets as clearly as the empty bed.

'Isobel,' he called. The bathroom was equally empty. He hurried to the head of the stairs. His voice was louder; it quavered. 'Isobel!' He listened, his teeth pressed together. The clattering noise came again. He hastened downstairs, looked about him, seized a walking stick from the hallstand which he immediately remembered was splintered and particularly fragile, and advanced cautiously through the house, flinging open doors and brandishing his stick into every deserted room.

Warily he prowled across the lounge. The noise clattered suddenly in front of him. He thrashed the air violently in an involuntary response, knocking an ashtray to the floor and further jarring his nerves. He strode forward, found the french windows open and entered the conservatory.

The door which opened on to the garden banged noisily against its frame at the whim of the low wind.

Bernard stood in the doorway, distinctly remembering how he'd locked the door only three hours before. He stepped on to the patio and pulled his dressing gown more tightly across his chest. His eyes explored the garden, which scraped and rustled with furtive, nocturnal activity.

He started. A low moan alerted his hearing. He moved forward, gasped. A shape, grey in the moonlight, stirred across the lawn. Over by the borders.

'Isobel?'

The figure rose to meet him.

Bernard hurried across the wet grass, his arms open. 'Isobel!' he exclaimed. 'What are you doing here? What – what's the matter with your face? Those – blotches?'

His wife's movements were vague, curiously detached. Had she even heard him? he wondered. She wiped a nervous hand across her face and he realised that the blotches were smears of earth. Her nightdress and hair were matted with damp soil. Her eyes were staring vacantly.

She was pointing to his feet, wet in the glistening grass.

'It's everywhere.'

'It's dew,' he said, comprehension suddenly dawning that she was walking in her sleep. 'You'll catch your death ... '

She shook her head. 'Blood. The ground is soaked with it. Here. And here. Feel it.' She fell on her knees, stretching out her hands over the border, kneading the soil between her fingers. Bernard tried to pull her away, but she wrenched herself free with a low scream.

'Can you hear them?' she groaned. She laid her head against the ground, eyes dilated, her ear pressed against the soil. 'Bernard, can they talk? Can the dead call to us out of the earth? Listen! Those cries. All that agony. Here. Buried in the soil.'

Bernard crouched and cajoled her into a sitting position. Grief numbed his responses.

His wife's hands clutched at her face. She scratched at the earth on her cheeks and, spluttering, wiped her hand again and again over her lips. 'Something happened here,' she said. 'Something terrible. The bones, the photographs. We must find out what it was. Look!' Her eyes opened wide. Bernard followed her pointing hand.

'Look there. That shadow again. Can't you see it?' She gave a choked scream. 'And there. Another one.' Her head turned in horror. 'Shadows, writhing. Bernard, the black shapes. What are we going to do? They're everywhere!'

She fell back in his arms. 'The phone,' Bernard told himself.

When Isobel Hurse woke up from a heavily sedated sleep, she was resting in the white, sterilized comfort of the clinic thirty miles away.

Returning, six days later, from an early evening visit to his wife – a rather strained emotional encounter – Bernard arrived home to find a motley gathering of people seated round his mahogany table, breathing with histrionic deliberation. Presiding over them, her ample bosom heaving impressively, was a colourfully clad female, surmounted by an excessively bushy plumed hat.

'Sorry about this,' said a voice, and Laura Mark materialized at his elbow. 'You sounded so desperate on the phone. I told Miss Friend about your – problem and she insisted on coming round at once.'

Bernard grappled with annoyance and curiosity. 'Frankly I'd rather trust to local history and science than mumbo-jumbo. I say, is she all right ... ?'

'She's in trance,' whispered Laura.

Suddenly, emitting a wild grunt, Miss Friend lurched to her feet, announced, 'The garden – she wants to show me the garden', and headed out, through the conservatory and across the lawn. The Circle straggled untidily after her. She came to rest by the new rockery, completed by Mr Blacklock the previous day, and already brimming with flowers.

'Ah yes.' Miss Friend gave a deep, withering sigh and lifted up her arms. 'I'm getting a sense of great unhappiness, great pain. Yes, it's someone from the village, she says. She *used* to live in the village once.' The medium began to shake her head. Her voice quickened, came in staccato rushes. 'Death. Many deaths. It must be disease, a rapid one.' She turned, her head on one side, feathers quivering. 'Was there a plague here? A sudden disaster like a plague? She's worrying about a burial. I think perhaps *she* was buried here. It shouldn't happen like that, she says. Being buried with all the others.'

Miss Friend's features tightened into creases of pain. Bernard's concern for her welfare struggled with his disbelief.

'I'm feeling great anguish of spirit. She's concerned about a warning. There's not enough warning, she says. And physical pain – in my throat – I – ' Miss Friend swayed on her feet in evident distress, her breathing laboured. Suddenly her hands flew to her throat; her face contorted. She uttered a tortured scream that ripped at the dusk and appalled her listeners.

'Suffocation!' she gasped. There was an agonized pause. 'Yes, I see it now: desolation; earth open to the sky; sudden death.' She heaved a sigh that made Laura whimper. 'Rest now, rest, perturbed spirit. We understand your grief. She tells me, yes, she tells me she is being buried in open ground. Rest; your agony is over now. No, there's something more.' Miss Friend drew her breath sharply. 'She is being buried – heaven protect her! – *alive!*'

The medium, relieved of her message, subsided rather heavily on to the grass. The Circle closed round her prostrate form.

Bernard felt dazed and confused. From the start he had been uneasy about the easy, instant assumption that the clinic was the best place for his wife – an unhappiness sharpened by his own guilty role in assisting her admission. Now Miss Friend's precise location of the trouble spot in the garden and the similarities between Isobel's breakdown and the medium's faltering, barely intelligible words, distressed him deeply. His uncertainty grew.

He felt someone tugging at his elbow. It was Laura. 'The phone,' she said. 'In the study. It's Ray – Bill's historian friend from the labs. The bone man.' She indicated the dishevelled Circle. 'I'll take care of this lot.'

The earpiece vibrated with Ray's enthusiasm. Bernard listened, his attention riveted.

'Again,' he said. 'Tell me again, please, slowly. How old are the bones?'

'At least five to six hundred years, it seems,' squeaked the excited telephone voice. 'Marvellously preserved. I don't think there's any doubt, Mr Hurse. You've stumbled on something we've been searching for for years. You're living over a medieval burial pit. One of the open mass graves they dug outside the village – 1348 or thereabouts – to fling in the bodies. It was the only way they could deal with so many victims. The population was decimated. Plague victims, you know. Very unpleasant. Swollen sores, speedy agonizing death. It polluted the whole of Europe, of course ... Are you still there ... ? No wonder they called it the Black Death!'

When Bernard Hurse replaced the receiver, his face was white.

'I must go to Isobel,' he said. 'Now. There's been some sort of confusion. I don't understand but it's not just another of her depressions. There's something more. I don't think they can help her at that place. She must get right away for a bit. A holiday. Capri again, perhaps. As soon as I can take a break.' He tried to explain his doubts to Laura. 'You remember what we suggested that night? About passions being somehow stamped on places ... ?'

Laura interrupted him. 'Well, you can't go now. At this time? In this state? Don't be ridiculous, Bernard. One night won't make any difference. Go tomorrow.'

Mrs Mark was adamant.

*

The following morning, Bernard Hurse, Deputy Director of Cavesham Nuclear Energy Plant, was faced with a crisis of conscience. With the Director himself on holiday and his Head of Reactor Control off sick, his sense of responsibility was challenged, his loyalties divided. He reduced the dilemma to its simplest terms – wife or work? – and made his decision.

After her discharge, achieved with maximum bureaucracy and minimum understanding from the authorities, he drove a bewildered and delighted Isobel back home, widely skirting the village to avoid the noisy crowds of protesters assembling in force for the day's Anti-pollution Rally, only to find a police road-block across the lane just round the corner from the house.

'Security. Can't be too careful, sir,' said the policeman who let them through.

'What about the caves?' said Bernard.

'Can't see anyone wanting to visit them today, sir. But there's always the bridle path over the fields, isn't there, if they're really keen!'

Isobel Hurse was home.

'But only for as long as it takes to pack for Capri,' her husband reassured her.

Together they strolled into the garden. The summer air was heavy with the scent of flowers and an occasional admixture from the Westons' cowsheds. A lark rose singing towards the sun. Isobel saw the new rockery, a yellow-blue mist of alyssum and aubretia, with delight. 'Look how they're growing. So fertile already. Like they did at the cottage. D'you remember?' she said. 'And no weeds!'

'Happy, dear?'

Isobel smiled. Of course she was happy now, wasn't she? As Bernard had told her in the car, her fears and dreams had been exposed and explained more or less satisfactorily. The Black Death and its attendant tragedy was played out long ago. Only its shadow had fallen over them from the past.

Her eyes lingered over the garden, basking and humming in the sun. Why, then, did that small, ungrateful voice remind her that shadows could fall before as well as behind? From the future, perhaps, as well as the past. The bones were possibly a warning as much as a sad reminder of human tragedy, unhappily disturbed. No. She must pull herself together.

So Isobel Hurse smiled and embraced her husband.

'One drink – to the future,' said Bernard, staring absently at the rockery, 'and then I must stop playing truant.'

He disappeared into the house, prepared the drinks and paused at the cassette loaded with his latest slides. Something was pricking at his memory. On impulse he hunted through the transparencies and found the two failures that had caused so much distress. He held them up to the light, scrutinizing them carefully.

The telephone bell jarred against his growing amazement.

He picked up the receiver.

On each of the slides, hazy but distinctly detectable, was a detail they hadn't consciously noticed before. It didn't make any sense, but it was there, a simple visual fact: there, complete with a suggestion of tumbling flowers, was the dim outline of the new rockery. Photographed *before* it had been constructed ...

He had no time to contemplate the significance.

'Yes, sorry, Hurse speaking,' he said.

He listened. His eyes widened.

When he rushed out to Isobel on the lawn, she too was tense. She plucked at his arm. 'Listen!'

A low, wailing moan rose in the distance, familiar as nightmare.

'I know,' said Bernard. 'Police cars. It's nothing. I've just had young Collingwood on the phone. Responsibility's gone to his head. It's probably only a minor emergency, some routine malfunction, but the fool's gone and alerted the police. Today of all days!' He pecked her on the cheek. 'Back soon,' he said.

Isobel watched his retreating back. 'He's leaving me,' she thought. She felt the black wings of nightmare beating close. 'I've got to face it alone after all.'

A gust of wind brought the cries of people, hundreds of them, raised in a confusion of fear and anger, across the fields. How well she knew those sounds! Unable to move, she stood where the border rose into the rockery looking out across the bridle path beyond the hedge, and felt a shudder along the earth like the pounding of stampeding cattle. The cries grew louder, wilder, the pulsing of the ground more threatening, and, as the first wave of frightened demonstrators – some still clutching their Anti-pollution placards – stumbled blindly through the corn, she knew that familiar surge of panic in her blood.

She turned, starting to run towards the house. At the conservatory she stopped. From the hubbub of hysterical wails an audible cry detached itself: 'The caves. To the caves!' Loud-hailers added to the chaos. Was that where the police were directing them? Was the only safety deep inside the hills? Confused, she turned again, and advanced uncertainly across the lawn. Her pulse raced.

Now people were rioting through their orchard. With a yell, a man with a beard came crashing through the hedge and raced down the lawn. She cowered back. Several more tumbled after, one with blood dripping from his hair, shrieking madly. Their howls rang about her head. She saw a woman, stout, with extravagant plumes in her hat, stumble and fall out of sight while the mob raged on.

She covered her face with her hands. 'Bernard,' she groaned, helplessly. The garden was a nightmare of yelling faces. She felt sick, knowing she had lived through these despairing moments many times before. She looked up towards the house. Bernard? Yes, there was Bernard, hurrying towards her.

A still moment. Sun, white, expanding.

Then, a gust of stinging wind. The earth heaved, the sky buckled and burst into blinding flame.

Scene over-exposed.

Isobel caught a glimpse of stunted trees, and of Bernard's face – was that scorched mass of blisters *Bernard's* face? – lurching into hers, before she was knocked to the ground and her peeling face trampled by demented, blackened figures into the polluted earth. It was wet with blood.

She tried to scream, to draw breath, but the soil, reeking with ancient secrets of mortality and unnumbered deaths, filled her mouth – dear God, was she to be buried still conscious? – and took her down, down into itself.

Beyond the hill, where the world's largest nuclear reactors had once stood, a mushroom cloud flowered and climbed the darkening sky.

Then the delayed arrival of the full, nuclear blast reduced the fallen bodies in the Hurses' back garden to instant shadows, twisted where they lay.

The Ghost Machine

THE PROFESSOR MADE A FINAL CHECK on the circuitry. Repressing an unscientific and jubilant giggle, he threw the switch. Power pulsed in a thousand sensor beams, scanning the room. The air hummed and vibrated softly like a finely tuned web.

The world's first 'ghost machine', as the press, ever facile, had labelled it, was ready.

He glanced at the screen. It glowed reassuringly but no image had materialized there. He was neither surprised nor disappointed. There had been no deaths in the room – so far as he knew: how, then, could one expect to snare and record a ghost? No, his research was only just beginning. But proof, scientific evidence of which he, nay mankind, had dreamed, was finally, he was sure, at hand. His cheeks flushed. Ultimate mysteries – he patted the control panel – would shortly be revealed. The unseen would be seen at last.

He sat, triumphantly expectant, at the console in the centre of the room. He adjusted the scanners.

A finely tuned web ...

Abruptly there came a low knocking sound. He jumped, scattering papers, recomposed himself and opened the door.

'Puddle,' said the man. 'Jeremiah Puddle. I've come about the advertisement.'

'Ah,' said the professor. He scrutinized the newcomer and winced.

The man was small and thin and had spots. It was not a promising start. The pale face lengthened.

'You *said* you could help,' the man said despondently. He flourished a newspaper at the professor, then peered at the columns, prodding them with a reproachful forefinger. '"Do *You* Want To end It All?"' he recited. '"For Help, Contact Professor Hamnet ... "' His sad eyes essayed a fierce glare. 'Well – I do.'

The professor hesitated, thought of his forthcoming paper, 'Death, The Last Frontier: a Psychic Breakthrough', heard the applause echoing round the Science Academies of the world, glanced at Mr Jeremiah Puddle, and closed his eyes. 'Splendid,' he said unconvincingly. 'So: you've come to take your place in the annals of History.'

Mr Puddle looked doubtful. 'I've come,' he said, 'for the suicide.' He gazed round anxiously. 'You do *do* suicides, don't you?'

The professor took his arm reassuringly. 'Under scientific compulsion. I am a mere servant,' he remarked humbly, 'it is Science herself who dictates the means which must be used to achieve her ends.'

'I see,' said the man, though he probably didn't. He glanced uneasily at his watch. 'When can we begin?' he said. 'It's my wife ... ' His meek eyes strayed apprehensively towards the door.

'She knows you're here?'

Mr Puddle shuddered. 'She'll find out. She finds out everything,' he whispered darkly. He picked nervously at a spot. The spot flared. 'That's why I've come to you,' he said, and launched forthwith into a despairing catalogue of marital misadventures.

Mrs Puddle, it transpired, was loud and somewhat encumbered with large limbs. She talked incessantly. She had, it seemed, talked her way steadily through their marriage, pausing only at statutory intervals to eat and sleep. Her words were as numerous as her themes were limited. She talked about Jeremiah's faults, his failures and his passivity.

'She's right,' he concluded. 'I'm a failure. I need help. I tried the weedkiller, but it went wrong.'

The professor raised an eyebrow and readjusted his face to blend a hint of curiosity with patient sympathy.

'Home-made wine,' said the man called Puddle. 'Parsnip. I drank from the wrong container.' The ghost of a smile scuttered across his sallow features and was gone. 'I was nearly happy then,' he reminisced. 'Just the once.'

He sank into silence. Pathos hovered about him. The machine murmured, probed the still spaces of the room, and waited. The professor seized the silence.

'Yes,' he said. 'Well,' he added. He attempted to rub his hands briskly, but he knew he was wringing them – now that the moment had come to assist his first subject. 'So ... Down to business, eh?' He unlocked and pulled open a drawer. 'How – ah – would you like it. ... ? Your death,' he prompted.

Something approaching life stirred in Mr Puddle's eyes. He watched the professor draw forth a length of rope. The eyes dulled. He shook his head.

'Tried it,' he said. 'The noose came undone. I slipped off the chair and sprained my wrist.' The memory welled up unhappily. 'It *hurt. And* she made me go without dinner for two days.'

The spots throbbed pink with indignation.

'It was the same when I jumped out of the bedroom window.'

The professor tried to turn his yawn into a cough; he succeeded in a hiccup. 'What happened?' he asked brightly.

'I fell on top of her,' said Jeremiah Puddle. The old ignominy shook his unambitious frame. 'She caught me. In her arms. And carried me back into the house.'

The professor reached into the drawer. 'Gun?'

'No bullets. She locked them away.'

'Bullets!' The professor loaded the gun and waved it at him encouragingly.

'Too loud,' said Mr Puddle. 'I was deaf for a week after I first tried it.' He shuffled miserably. 'And I shot the budgie,' he added, 'by mistake.'

The professor's hand twitched temptingly on the trigger. 'Too untidy,' he thought and laid the revolver on the desk. He dismissed the razor blade for the same reason. His hand hesitated over the hypodermic and came to rest on the tablets. He held the phial aloft. The purple pills gave a low rattle. Speedy, silent, painless and tidy, he thought.

Enthusiasm flirted with doubt on Mr Puddle's yellow face. 'I'm not very good at swallowing tablets,' he said. 'I bought five hundred aspirin once ... '

Professor Hamnet hastily curtailed the reminiscence. 'One capsule will do the trick,' he said. He filled a glass with water and offered it temptingly. 'Perhaps you'd like to lie down.' He ushered the man towards the couch strategically placed for maximum exposure to the detector field.

The centre of the web.

'Make yourself comfortable,' he said, his voice as soothing and concerned as an over-fastidious nanny's. 'Rest,' he said.

'In peace,' said Mr Puddle. 'That was a sort of joke,' he explained. 'I don't often make jokes.'

Submissively he received the glass in one hand, the pill in the other.

'Is this – it?' he asked.

The professor's pulse changed into higher gear. This was it, indeed. The spirit of Jeremiah Puddle was poised for flight; the psychic detectors were trained on the corporeal Puddle awaiting the release. It was an auspicious moment. The professor paused. A speech, he felt, was appropriate to so historical an event. He cleared his throat. Words, however, eluded him.

'We are gathered here ... ' he began. 'Today ... '

'Excuse me.' The watery eyes turned hopefully upwards. 'Do I swallow it now?'

The professor shook his head. 'Today,' he repeated, 'you

embark on a momentous voyage, a voyage of discovery into that "undiscovered country", as Shakespeare so movingly described it, "from whose – thingy – no traveller returns ... "'

'"No traveller returns",' echoed the man. He closed his eyes and an alien look of peace and ecstasy settled over his pimpled features.

The professor stretched out his arms; it seemed the right thing to do. His voice was tremulous with excitement and a touch of indigestion. 'Go forth, Jeremiah Puddle,' he pronounced. 'Go forth into Death and History!'

The man raised his glass. Eternity waited.

'Hold on a sec.' Professor Hamnet caught his arm. 'Don't go yet. Your suicide note. Sign here. Thanks. Indemnity,' he murmured. 'The law. Right. As you were. Bully off. Cheers.'

Mr Puddle placed the tablet carefully in his mouth, raised his glass and gulped.

He gulped again.

A seraphic contentment suffused his face. The Puddle pimples seemed to fade and assume an otherworldly hue.

The professor watched the screen with eager concentration.

Downstairs an angry door banged; the building trembled.

The white glow of the screen remained obstinately unblemished. The professor re-tuned the scanners. He turned the gain control to maximum. The circuits hummed industriously.

He peered more closely, attempting to pierce beyond the veil.

But nothing registered on the screen.

The veil refused to part.

Then light cleft his brain. The professor rose abruptly, choking back an exultant laugh. He saw it all: *there was nothing to see! That* was the point. Puddle had gone. Death was final. No traveller returned because nothing survived. Oblivion not Survival: that was The Answer.

He paced the room in pursuit of ultimate truths, completing several circuits of the recumbent Puddle. His mind raced on.

Eliminate the spirit, the soul. What, then, was a ghost, doomed endlessly to walk the same walks, groan the same groans, rattle the same chains? What else, he reassured himself, but a psychic recording, a dead memory vibrating eternally in the ether. But where then, if there was no living surviving spirit, he demanded of himself, was the *recording* of the deceased Puddle? The screen was conspicuously empty. Puddle had escaped without registering a trace of *his* passing.

He glanced at the face on the couch, glowing with serenity. There lay his answer! *Jeremiah Puddle was happy. Too happy.* Whoever heard of a placid, contented ghost? The professor found himself standing excitedly on tip-toe. The man – the truth had to be told – had been a failure even in his dying. He had been completely devoid of the passion, the energy, the misery needed to blaze the waves of his dying moments on to the surrounding air and become a successful ghost – the first ghost in Professor Hamnet's machine.

Startled, and then annoyed, the professor heard a second door slam at the end of the corridor.

He looked down reproachfully at Puddle and shook his head. Evidence. The world required proof, pictures.

What he really needed, he realized, was a research assistant who could be relied upon to die a lively, passionate, violent sort of death ...

'What ... !'

The door had crashed open and hung crookedly on its splintered hinges.

The figure was large and awesome. She seemed about to roar. Her glittering eyes lit on the body on the couch and she strode across to it. The room trembled. The roar escaped.

'What have you done with my man?'

The professor retreated. Mrs Puddle advanced. He opened his mouth but only an emaciated squeak got out. He lunged forward and seized the revolver.

'Aha,' he said. He waved it, suddenly triumphant. A violent death! It was self-defence. And it meant a place in the annals of history.

But Mrs Puddle was an ardent admirer of Hollywood movies of

the more criminal kind. Her ungainly limbs moved with improbable but lethal dexterity. The professor staggered to his feet in the corner and found himself staring at Mrs Puddle's arm. At the end of the arm was the single, black eye of his revolver.

'My poor little husband,' she said. 'You killed him.'

Panic surged through the professor. His nerves screamed and he gave vent to a resounding hiccup.

'My research ... !' he blurted.

'Murderer!' she said and pulled the trigger.

Eyes dilated, arms flung upwards, the professor, protesting, made his earthly exit. He was right. It was an untidy way to die.

Mrs Puddle turned, seized her late husband and flung him over her shoulder. She thumped his back vigorously.

He coughed.

'There, there,' she said.

Then he choked.

Then a purple capsule hit the floor with a clatter.

Jeremiah Puddle's eyes opened sadly on the world once more. He beheld his wife. His face sagged. She put him down, embraced him, straightened his tie, and took his hand.

She noticed the screen for the first time and stared at him disdainfully. 'What a time to be watching television!' she said. She cast only a cursory glance at the sequence of images which now haunted the glowing screen: the cornered man cowering with upraised arms, his mouth opened wide in indignant terror – an eternal psychic action replay.

'And a gangster film at that!' She tugged his arm. 'Time to go home,' she said. 'Success. We won. You're safe now.'

Jeremiah Puddle's spots flushed crimson.

'Yes, dear,' he said. 'Success ... '

The machine purred.

Zazine Forsyth's Resurrection Affair

IT WAS THE DAY SHE TRIED to buy Stonehenge that they said Mrs Zazine Forsyth III had gone too far.

They were always saying things about the third Mrs Forsyth, ever since she had been swept to stardom on the first great wave of holovision. Her friends applauded her for her wealth, ambition and snobbery, and her enemies condemned her for the same reasons. As her aim in life was to be the focus of the world's constant attention, Mrs Forsyth encouraged both friend and foe undiscriminatingly into her circle to witness her latest excesses and thus ensure that all flattery and slander were firmly centred where they rightly belonged – on herself. Never again need she stoop to the mundane rigours of actually making another holothrill movie; never again need she risk that Unspeakable Experience, at which she always hinted only in appalled whispers, which had almost – but not quite, thank Hollywood – befallen her in her more vulnerable starlet youth.

Being first was her forte. Long before the era of lunar package tours, she appeared on a balcony in Bavaria in jewels of deepest moon silver and quite outshone the centenary celebrations of the Republic of Europe. She it was who first beamed in style around the world in her private lasercar, and made holoview headlines again by owning a sky villa in Earth orbit *and* the most luxurious mansion on the Pacific ocean bed at the same time. Rumour reported her the possessor of the world's largest holoview chamber, and spoke of her private weather-screens as sophisticated beyond belief. If ever exotic pets arrived on Earth from the far reaches of the galaxy, one of Zazine Forsyth's thirty goddamned butlers, they muttered enviously, would be there, in Harrods or in Bloomingdale's, ahead of them in the queue.

It was Mr George Forsyth, the fifth and, therefore, the richest of her husbands, who provided her with her latest fortune and title, followed her dutifully making money and signing cheques across every continent from villa to villa, party to party, extravagance to extravagance, and contrived incessantly to achieve personal anonymity. He winced, however, at the stare of the world's fascination with more resentment than success.

Over the hectic years of their marriage – 'the ideal ordeal', as George, wordy with whisky, had once described it to himself – a more serious resentment grew; this, mined from deeper veins, burgeoned into darker bitterness. Only his four predecessors in his wife's marital bed would have divined his private, nightly anguish in the silk-spun sleeping chambers of 'the world's most voluptuous woman' – and they too were either shamed to silence or dead.

That Mrs Zazine Forsyth lived life to the full, no one else had any doubt. Lavishly she gave parties, glamour, excitement, everything – except herself. Playboys and princes, freshly optimistic, and roués, resigned but addicted, pressed for glimpses of the subtly heaving harmonies of her latest gown, clinging with skilful intimacy to the most holoviewed contours of the highest society. Women raised their eyebrows; men lowered their voices. 'Lucky devil!' they exclaimed to her husband's back when wonder and desire found words out of less articulate approval. 'It's a miracle he survives. Night after night. Give me half a chance ... !' Even his closest friends, their eyes bright with *savoir-faire* and honest envy, toasted his wife's unrelenting elegance and desirability with the standard refrain: 'You're a lucky man, George!' The lucky man sustained their comfortless praises with the wan smile so familiar to the features of her former husbands. Little did friends guess the secret of his wife's success: Mrs Zazine Forsyth, now as ever, preserved her energies by preserving herself. The world's most worshipped woman was as accessible, George fancifully told himself, as a vestal virgin in solitary orbit round ice-bound Pluto.

He tried. Argument, at first as frequent as it was futile, waned with the years. Cajolery and blandishment fared no better. Even now, when Mrs Forsyth summoned the marriage divan and it arose and unfolded, shimmering with softness and shifting pastoral hues, he made desultory use of gentle reproach. 'I am your husband,' he reminded her, 'dearest.' His wife deftly switched the bed into Sleeping Mode. Their legal partnership was a fact of which she was already fully aware, she said, and naturally was a continuing source of pleasure and a cause for undying gratitude to her, darling one. There: was that what he wanted to hear? But really, how could he be so insensitive as to press his attentions thus? Did he actually need reminding again of that unspeakable experience of her early years? Of those scars. Of the cloaked phantom from Planet Karlos and his horrendous importunities both on and off the set. Of course not. And anyway, sleep – here the eyelids that disturbed men's dreams across the planet, flickered drowsily – was so essential right now to preserve herself for her public tomorrow ...

'Damn the public!' was George Forsyth's unoriginal but heartfelt retort. 'What about me? I've given you everything.'

The divan, modulating into ever subtler colours, took his wife gently into its silken warmths. 'And *I*'ve brought *you* the admiration of the world – darling. Isn't that enough?'

Mr Forsyth watched his wife receding into her customary sumptuous tranquillity. His blood rose. He toyed savagely with his pyjama cord. 'No,' he said, 'it is not enough!'

Fragrant airs played about the bed. Her voice, delicious as ever, was softening into slumber. 'What more can you possibly want?'

George Forsyth grew frenzied. '*You*! I want you. I'll stop your allowance. I'll divorce you.' But he knew, as she did, how many wealthy suitors waited in the wings of her life and he shuddered at the scale of public incredulity and humiliation. His voice was tremulous with indignation and lust. 'I'm a man, you know ... ' He reached out, the cord snapped, his wife slipped languorously into the heavy torpor of sleep, and, clutching his nightclothes about him, he hobbled ignominiously away for his usual fitful and frustrated rest in the palatial ante-chamber to which he had long since been relegated but not yet grown fully resigned.

Thus, decently veiled from an unsuspicious public, private anguish flourished, while Mrs Zazine Forsyth, undeterred, sought ever new ways of fulfilling her mission to enthral society with unexpected wonders.

But being 'the first lady of the world', as that gifted and perceptive young man in the latest holoview chat had labelled her, was not without strains. Fresh wonders were hard to find; competition was ever more glamorous and treacherous; youth and beauty, even in these days, even for Zazine Forsyth's wealth, were not quite eternal; and Mrs Forsyth III felt, in bleaker moments, a nagging sense – no more than a pale shadow beneath the delicately brushed eye-silver – that glories passed, life passed, and surely there was more to be relished in both than this. Fearing, for the first time, social eclipse, she found herself posing the unpalatable question: might her gift for conjuring the spectacular and keeping the world in awe be slipping from her?

It was then that she conceived the idea of purchasing Stonehenge. Of course she had gone too far this time, they said. But Zazine was determined to regain her former glories: she had neolithic intimations. This party would dim the legendary lights of Las Vegas. The originality of its centrepiece, if it worked, would seize the imagination of the globe.

But the English authorities proved as primitive and inscrutable as their monuments. Stonehenge could not be bought. Nor could it even, in that revitalized land of technocratic wealth, be hired for the evening – though, as Mrs Forsyth confided to her closest and only friend, the Ministry official had blenched at the cheque she had proffered him.

'But my dear,' purred the friend, whose devoted amity was in fact focused more on Mr Forsyth than his wife, 'who needs Stonehenge for a party? What about those quaint old stone rings and temple things they're just digging up in the wilds of wherever it is? It was on the holonews the other day. All jungles and mountains. South America? Mexico, maybe? Somewhere quite unpronounceable and deliciously barbaric. My dear, how exotic: it would be the party to end all parties. *And* one in the eye for that Wyndsor woman.'

Zazine's eyes glittered behind the calm elegance she habitually wore. She nodded with casual complacence, smiled a dismissal, and went off to consult and instruct her husband in his capacity as Chairman of Laser Technocrafts, World Division. The screen located him on a consultation visit in Zanzibar and called him across the room with a discreetly triumphant bleep.

'Darling,' she said, her voice low, thrilling, and suspect. 'I want to help you.'

His features rearranged themselves several times as he contrived to remain simultaneously aloof and wary. He was more accustomed these days to receiving statements of fate accomplished than offers of assistance.

'I've had an idea,' she said.

Despite himself, he inched closer to the beamscreen, and cleared his throat.

'It's a promotion idea,' she said.

He paused.

'Another party?' he asked.

She hesitated.

'Another party,' he said.

She was piqued at his predictability and prescience. 'It's that new laserscan thing,' she said, overplaying the role of the big tycoon's little wife which so ill became her and always put her husbands back on their guard. 'What did your advertising people call it? The History Machine? You brought the prototype home, remember, and we put a pebble in it.'

'The Resurrection Machine,' he said glumly. 'We cancelled the project. A no-go market situation, they said.'

Her eyebrows arched. 'But we were there! Back in those prehistoric swamps. All in our own holoview chamber. With those ghosts and memories alive all round us.' Passion and persuasion raised her voice a seductive semitone. 'We even heard those strange beasts howling.'

'You were frightened,' he said.

She smiled faintly, repressing a reminiscent shudder. 'It was so' – words eluded her – 'so appallingly primitive, darling.'

George Forsyth glanced at the time, sent a secretary scurrying. 'Marketing were quite definite,' he said. 'They had the figures.' He recalled the director's smiling incredulity. 'A device for decoding the oscillations imprinted in natural materials and recreating them in holovisual playback! Try creating a demand for *that*, sir!'

'The project was shelved, dear,' he told the screen. 'Definitely. Indefinitely.'

Zazine Forsyth was undeterred. She always got her way. She knew it. All her husbands knew it – eventually. 'We'll make plans over supper, dear,' she said. 'And this time we won't use pebbles for playback.'

Her husband sighed. He knew his stars. 'At least you've given up this Stonehenge party nonsense,' he said.

'Of course, darling.' Her smile was saccharine. 'Mexico is always so much more – evocative. Especially with next month's solar eclipse.'

The Forsyth face froze abruptly. 'Mexico?'

'Quantahatapotec,' said his wife, 'actually.'

*

Thus, with the aid of Forsyth Laser Technocrafts, World Division, the Forsyth party of the decade – some said of the century – was conceived, planned, and on the verge of execution. In scale and opulence it would reduce the grandiose visions of Roman Emperors and the moguls of Old Hollywood alike into whimsical charades.

Thousands of invitations were despatched; even more were sought. Fervent enemies were converted into fervent hypocrites, and hypocrites matured overnight into fully-fledged sycophants. From Bombay to Biloxi the Best Society hastened to cancel prior engagements for the fourteenth, lest it be thought they had failed to receive invitations to the great event. In some cases the excuses were genuine, and exploited to the full. 'Actually we've been invited to the Forsyth "do" in Mexico next month. *The* Forsyth "do", yes. We're just beaming across for a drink or two to show our faces and see what she's cooked up for us all this time. Well, it would be so *unfair* not to drop in ... '

The media, with their hundred eyes already trained on Mexico, averted their gaze from the sun to wonder at Mrs Zazine Forsyth in all her daring splendour. 'Her proposed extravagances on the sacred mountain tops of Ancient Mexico,' enthused one reporter, 'threaten to eclipse the Eclipse itself.' Rumour reawoke and wagged her thousand tongues. Mrs Forsyth III had undoubtedly overreached herself this time, they said, more in envy than in mischief. The great lady herself presided over all, discreetly preening herself at the prospect of her restored pre-eminence in the world's esteem.

In the shadow at her side, Mr Forsyth dutifully prepared his party smiles.

*

The sun rose over the sacred monoliths of Quantahatapotec on the fourteenth of July. For a while. The jungle valleys murmured, crepitated, steamed; mists hung about improbable cliffs reluctant to depart. Ancient mysteries stirred just out of sight.

Then came man.

Lasercars beamed in the celebrants from every continent in their chosen thousands. The sacred site pulsed with synthetic airs, shrill and sweet by turns, secreted from a hundred hidden, electronic pores, by courtesy of Forsyth World Sound, Music Division. Perfumed guests eddied amongst the stones glittering expensively at one another. Relentlessly they were plied with pleasures of every kind. Caterers, human and robotic, dispensed extravagant delicacies to challenge the most exquisite and most jaded palates. Bronzed and bangled dancers of every sex performed, mingling with and delighting the company, who were all, they prided themselves, far too sophisticated to succumb to jealousy, envy or offence – even at some of the more adventurous audacities. Glasses were chinked, emptied and chinked again less certainly but more vigorously than before. People found themselves growing more amusing and, sometimes, more amused. Polite smiles surrendered to ruder laughter, and blasé repartee graduated, at length, into honest admiration.

One had to hand it to Zazi Forsyth; she really had excelled herself this time. Just when she had seemed to be losing her touch. What an inspiration to have chosen such a spot. Where was one, by the way? Was it Mexico or Peru? One forgot so easily these days. Anyway, somewhere so gorgeously remote and uncivilised as this. And such efficient weatherscreening too. One just hoped Mrs F.'s party surprise would live up to the location. One knew it wasn't fair, but there were those – one wasn't one of them, naturally – who said openly that Lady Wyndsor had quite overtaken her in the party stakes, that Our Zazi had run out of surprise novelties, that even the eclipse idea was hardly original for a party. No doubt one would find out later. Ah, there she was in person, there, over there, behind that girl, if she was a girl, with the three bracelets and the quite implausible chiffon dress; one had to admit it, she, Zazi of course, was looking as fresh and stunning as ever, and as voluptuous too, yes, in that strangely innocent way she had, didn't one think? And there was George, just behind her. Was he smiling

ZAZINE FORSYTH'S RESURRECTION AFFAIR

or glowering? One found it hard to say, but one wasn't one to talk and one knew, everyone knew, what a blissfully happy pair they were – didn't one!

'Lucky devil!' said a man to George Forsyth's retreating back.

'Is this a Mayan or an Aztec temple?' asked a young woman in ostentatiously serious glasses. 'You know: fertility rites, sun worship, human sacrifice and all that.'

'Why?' asked a laconic companion.

'Perhaps,' said another, guardedly, keeping his options as open as the questions. 'Perhaps not.'

A girl in her mid-twenties, diaphanously dressed, sat down abruptly on a massive stone, rough-hewn, eroded, centuries old. 'Sacred temple!' she squealed. 'It's all just divine!' She laughed a little too loudly. 'Did you hear what I just said, Wilbur?' She hiccoughed. The world's rarest wine splashed from her glass. Wilbur smirked apologetically at the encircling throng. 'They *all* heard,' he said.

The sun climbed the sky.

Beyond the weatherscreen the ancient jungle hummed and chattered; in its moist darkness unseen creatures prowled and slithered.

Within the weatherscreen, cocooned in civilized elegance on the mountain top, the rainbow crowds drifted. Immaculate in whitest silks and infinitely alluring, Zazine Forsyth shone enraptured and enrapturing in their midst. She was in her heaven. Her zenith approached.

George Forsyth watched her, hungrily attended by a dozen fawning suitors. He watched her lips pouting invitations they denied, her languid arm reaching out in a caress that never touched, her eyes, dark and heavy-lidded, taunting with infinite promises and betrayals. He shuddered. Unnumbered resentments and regrets thickened in his soul.

She turned and summoned him.

'George,' she said, scattering stars, studs and princelings with a winning laugh, 'it's time. Is everything ready? George, you're not working yourself into one of your moods again, I trust. Like Wallace. Not here. Not now.'

George Forsyth III struggled to reassemble his smile. It eluded him. He succeeded in a growling, satirical whimper. 'Everything's ready. Your slightest whim, dearest.' He made his way to the control centre to join the battery of technicians and holoengineers.

His wife exposed just too many teeth in an otherwise adroit, light laugh, for public reassurance and the holonews cameras, and mounted, through the parting crowd, towards the sun. The flight of carved steps culminated in the vast central platform. There, ringed by grey monoliths, she turned, and stood resplendent. Her presence drew applause; her arm uplifted stilled the multitudes. Music ebbed discreetly into silence.

Zazine Forsyth spoke.

The cameras closed in. Families in holoview chambers around the world fought over channel selectors – the eclipse or the Forsyth woman – and hushed each other into attention.

'The Resurrection Machine,' she said. 'A landmark in technotronics,' she said. 'A thrilling moment of history.' Her words gathered momentum. Enthusiasm disguised rhetorical unevenness. 'When, in a moment, the switch is thrown, it will activate an intricate network of laserscans to decode and recreate the memories etched into every stone of this awesome place. No one, not even the scientific wizards of Forsyth Laser Technocrafts, World Division, can know what you are about to witness here today ... ' She paused. 'Never has the Forsyth Resurrection Machine, shortly to go into production, been tested on so vast a scale.'

People shivered in the crowd. There were ripples of doubt and uncertain reassurance. 'Tampering with nature,' opined Wilbur's wife uneasily and unsteadily. 'Listen. Even the forest's going quiet.' 'The eclipse is coming,' said Wilbur. He rolled his eyes. 'Don't you know *anything*?' 'She's gone too far this time,' said someone. Murmurs of scepticism and disbelief foundered in the consensus of excited anticipation.

The Forsyth oratory rolled in closing cadences. 'We can be

certain only of this: what you will experience is simply the place's memory, a ghostly replay of the past – as three-dimensional and convincing as any holovision entertainment.' She extended an elegant arm. 'Let us now activate the Resurrection Machine and step forward together into the past.' The other arm joined the first, adding benediction to invitation. 'May you all enjoy our little party treat to the full, enhanced – as we hope you will find it – by Nature's very own spectacle: a total eclipse of the sun.'

'Courtesy of Forsyth International too?' murmured a party dissident to no one in particular. No one in particular listened.

Mrs Zazine Forsyth bowed, pre-eminence regained. She savoured the moment. She glanced at the sky, considerately veiled by a refinement of the weatherscreening to permit guests to outstare nature with ocular impunity, and turned to the control console far below her. She inclined her head. Her timing was impeccable. Nature, too, it seemed, had stayed her hand till Mrs Forsyth was ready.

'Look: the eclipse. It's started!' Excited fingers stabbed the air. Darkness had taken the first bite; the sun was disappearing from the sky.

George, obedient, followed her signal.

The switch was thrown.

Ten thousand complex circuits hummed; the air grew vibrant within the huge, charmed circle of the mountain top. Moments crawled. And then the gaunt, impassive stones, probed by the rigorous sensorbeams, awoke and began to yield their secrets. Centuries rolled back. Crumbled stones renewed themselves; pillars and plinths, massively sculpted, reappeared. An old glory came again.

The crowd drew its collective breath.

Distant cries, the throbbing of drums, a low chanting, resonated strangely in the listeners' ears. People instinctively drew closer, sophisticated proprieties forgotten. 'Over there!' cried a voice. Necks craned. Guests stood on tiptoe, on other guests' toes. Elbows elbowed.

The first hologhosts formed and thickened into life.

Initial suspicions gave way to uneasy delight.

'My dear, how gorgeous. A procession.'

'Just look at those robes. Isn't it *too* picturesque!'

'Hollywood alive!' exclaimed a Harvard youth. 'The whole thing: it's so unbelievably, you know, *ethnic*.'

Enchanted, the party-goers experienced history. They watched the procession mounting to the central plateau, lining the stairs, and marvelled bewilderedly. Who were those black-robed figures, their garments heavy with bands of gold? ('My dear, the cost!') And those troops of girls and youths, all so young and pretty: why were they so solemn? Not a party smile among them! And just look up there. A phalanx of trumpeters ranged itself in a huge arc behind and above the transformed columns; their burnished horns flashed in a sun that was slowly retreating from the sky. As of old, so now. The heavens revolved. The eclipse was at once ancient and modern.

The crowds clustered more thickly on the sacred mountain. Wilbur's wife clutched his Cardin sleeve. 'Behind you!' she hissed. Wilbur turned. His sangfroid abandoned him with a gasp. 'Is it *them*?' she demanded, cowering at his back. 'The Others?'

'Hologhosts!' said a man next to her whom she suddenly found terribly distinguished. 'More of them. Peasant folk, by their dress. They're all among us now. They've come to watch this sun ceremony, I guess. Don't worry. They can't see you, any more than you can feel them. See? Try it. We're not born yet!'

Wilbur disengaged his admiring spouse. 'That's what *I* was trying to tell you,' he muttered, aggrieved.

'Aztecs!'

'Bless you!'

'Aztecs,' repeated the earnest young woman in the sombre spectacles. 'Or was it the Mayas? It's all coming back to me. The sacrifice of the virgins.'

Her first companion snickered. '*You*'ll be safe enough then.'

She ignored him, lifting shining eyes towards the dimming

ZAZINE FORSYTH'S RESURRECTION AFFAIR

stone plateau. 'That's it: the eclipse! They went in for human sacrifice on a grand scale. That's what we're watching. It's a ritual slaughter. My God, those poor kids. And these priests are doing it to keep the sun in the sky!'

Her other companion roused himself from thought. 'Or the Incas,' he suggested.

But the explanation, once spoken, was abroad. Murmurs of shock and distress thrilled through the crowd, human and ghostly. They arrived, amplified by excitement, at the ears of Mrs Forsyth herself, reigning over the spectacle from her centre stone, beset by worshippers, some young and all too familiar, but the majority quaintly garbed and centuries old.

She looked up. The eclipse was impressively advanced. She looked down. Premature dusk was settling unnaturally about the slopes and peaks of the enclosing jungle. The shades of twilight and history were thickening, pressing closer. 'Ritual slaughter,' they were saying. An unfamiliar stillness seemed to chill the mountain top. 'A thousand virgins,' they were saying. She pulled her white stole more tightly against those unequivocal curves, which heaved now with unwonted agitation. The half-light, the drums, these spectral ancestors so real and unreal, replaying their barbarous rituals: everything was so alien. So uncivilized. It must be stopped. She peered through the gloom. Was George still at the Resurrection console? She shivered. For the first time in her life, Mrs Forsyth knew her essential isolation. She rose to her feet.

The drums rolled. All about her horns blazed forth a wild and primitive music; it echoed from cliff to neighbouring cliff, calling down the centuries.

The ring of black-robed priests, swarthy and bearded, advanced.

Zazine Forsyth shrank back, seeking the comfort of her courtiers, against the Virgin Stone.

There was an outbreak of scattered, slightly anxious applause from the hundreds of party-goers who were still close enough to distinguish events. One had to admit, it was a magnificent party show. One guessed it was all stage-managed, all done by mirrors no doubt, but one had to hand it to her: it was brilliantly conceived. Such an inspired blend of civilized splendour and barbarism. Really, the Wyndsor woman would have to look to her laurels after this!

Mrs Forsyth raised her arms. She gestured.

More applause.

'George,' she whimpered.

From the console far below, George Forsyth watched his wife. There, through a light that was neither day nor night, he saw guests and ghosts, shadows all, crowding up the steps towards her, the white goddess, supreme focus of her spectacle. He saw her reclining on that damned stone, surrounded, adored, caressed, whimpering even. All an empty charade. All for her public. All for those spectral priests and pampered playboys. The chief engineer, a personal friend, nudged him. 'Looks like a fertility rite after all, George. Virgin sacrifice indeed! Your Zazine'll take care of that little lot, eh? She'll sort out the men from the ghosts! Look at her!'

George looked. His life focused.

He saw his wife flattered and fulfilled; he saw himself eclipsed and barren, eroded by the bitterness of repeated frustration, pointless servitude and endless public posturing.

'Take charge,' he said, and made for the stairs.

Across the valleys of the earth, the moon's vast shadow raced east towards the sacred place of Quantahatapotec. Hedonist and heathen: two ages met beneath a single, dying sun.

Appalled and prostrate upon a peak in Mexico, Zazine Forsyth heard the cloaks rustling about her. She opened her eyes a fraction. The arch-priest, his golden robes sullen in the grey light, lifted his outstretched palms towards the crescent in the sky. That dreadful chanting broke out again. And those drums. She stared. She flinched. The man in gold had turned and was standing over her. His fingers closed round a handle vulgar with precious stones. From the handle sprang a curving blade.

How dare he? Overdressed upstart. At *her* party! Stealing *her* thunder with his primitive theatricals. That knife, that costume jewellery, would not intimidate her. She had no intention of playing the helpless heroine in his tawdry, B-feature, historical holothrill.

'Hologhosts,' she said, 'you're all hologhosts! Empty and harmless as air.'

Shades shifted and swirled. Rude hands gripped her. Shock stole her scream. Strong arms encircled her waist, lifted her, lowered her. She felt the rock hard against her back. The drums beat on. Her pulses fluttered. The man's chest pressed against hers. Unspeakable. The drums insisted.

'Stop the machine,' she meant to say. 'George, where are you?' she meant to say. But the pounding was in her blood, in her body. Barbaric. It was pain. It was pleasure. It was quite, quite unspeakable.

On the stairway, the procession of youths and maidens stirred, moved ceremoniously forward. The charade played on.

A sudden hush. All nature held her breath.

Total eclipse.

Zazine Forsyth was seized by an ancient ecstasy.

The halo of the dark sun blazed, glorious.

The watching crowds broke into awed applause.

The world's first lady, oblivious for the first time in her life of her public, sighed briefly at the banished ghosts of her long-cherished innocence, and smiled. She opened her eyes, more radiant than ever before, but her assailant was gone, another shade among the performing ghosts.

The Forsyth smile fractured, dissolved into an unfamiliar chuckle. 'The Resurrection Machine,' thought Mrs Zazine Forsyth; 'how true!'

Then someone threw the switch.

The parade of troubled ghosts melted into a second death and the party of the decade, conscious of witnessing and making history, watched the sun restored to brilliance, celebrated and congratulated themselves far into the tropical night, and beamed home to boast of and to deprecate, after plausible delay and with as much worldly ennui as they could muster, the Forsyths' little 'do' in Mexico.

*

The Forsyths themselves had only one more disagreement in their marriage. It happened that night in the sumptuous bedroom of the skyvilla, somewhere over the Indian ocean.

'It was a *sun* ritual,' repeated George. 'They were slaughtering the innocent to placate the gods. They wanted their sun back.'

'Well, it *felt* more like a fertility ritual,' insisted his wife, brushing her hair with a thoroughness unusual even for her.

'Virgin sacrifice,' murmured George Forsyth.

His wife frowned. 'The Machine,' she said. 'I've been wondering. Could there have been some – malfunction?' She tossed her hair. 'Could it – inadvertently – bring a ghost to life? Real life?'

Mr Forsyth laughed shortly, hollowly. He turned towards the ante-chamber.

'George,' said Zazine softly. The divan, though perfumed and enticing as ever, was not yet, he noticed, locked into Sleeping Mode.

'Stay, dear,' she said. 'Your black sleep-robe: leave it on. Just a little whim, dearest ... No, draped. Over your shoulders. Like a cloak.' She hesitated. 'And lower the lights ... '

'George!' she exclaimed, for her husband had seized her in hard, muscled arms and lowered her roughly – or was it tenderly? – on to the bed. She looked first quizzically, then suspiciously, into his eyes.

He chuckled. 'Much more comfortable than that wretched Aztec altar,' he said.

So George Forsyth III donned the robe of the cloaked phantom every night of his real married life, and lived, as people expected, happily thereafter. The world-wide craze for Resurrection

Machines did nothing to diminish his felicity, which surprised no one. And he was, after all, married to the world's most voluptuous woman, who seemed, after those excesses on that Mexican hilltop, to have discovered eternal youth. It was probably, they said, the result of some fabulously expensive treatment from that dubious little man in California, of course. Mind you, they said, even *her* eternal youth couldn't last forever ...

But they were always saying things about Mrs Zazine Forsyth.

Second Coming

CORRIDORS OF DARKNESS RUSHING UP INTO twilight deserts, bursting into the fire-dropping horizons of space-time.

They had arrived.

Xar's faculties reconstituted themselves as they emerged from the time gate, and he marvelled again, despite the familiarity of the experience, at the disturbing beauty of the star-hung spaces of the physical universe which now enclosed their craft. Xar tuned in to feel young Vartek's excitement and share his exhilaration.

The return. But for them, as individuals, a new galaxy, a new sun, new satellite worlds.

*

Night slumbered about the ivy-shrouded vicarage. Mary's bedroom windows were open but the curtains barely stirred in the hushed, oppressive summer air. The timbers of the old house creaked and settled about her.

'What nameless terror stalks the night?' The question had remained unanswered. Sleep had overtaken curiosity and Mary's book of horror tales with the tantalisingly lurid cover, 'guaranteed to thrill and chill' (and, satisfyingly, to appal her father), lay on the pillow, its open pages crumpled where her sleeping hand rested heavily upon it. Her 'History of the Decline of Faith in the Modern Age – Volume Two', which Daddy had insisted she take to bed with her, stood on the bedside table, uninviting and – apart from the page where Tommy's photo was secreted – unopened. Anyway, Daddy couldn't *make* her do extra reading. And what right had he to forbid her to go to the Vincents' party? Why should she always have to do her duty? *She* wasn't a vicar like him. Why couldn't *her* father be rich like Tommy's, and lead an adventurous, exciting life, with yachts and things, instead of stagnating in this mouldering ruin of a vicarage? It was, as she had just confided to her diary, all so boring, all so unfair.

*

Downstairs, immured in his study, the Reverend Clairview wrestled with the heat and the subject of next Sunday's sermon. Surrounded by menacing newspaper clippings of assorted global disasters and home-grown horrors – 'The Ripper Rips Again!' – he scribbled: 'The Devil – Still at Work in the Modern World!' and called Rose. His wife, ever patient, was always useful as a sounding board when inspiration faltered, though he rarely followed her advice.

Rose Clairview knocked, came quietly to his side, considered, and hesitated. 'The Devil again ... It's more of your dwelling on the dark side, George,' she said gently. 'Like Lady Otterdale at the W.I. Christmas bash said: "There's always a smell of brimstone about you in the pulpit".'

George grimaced with irritation.

'Why not give us something more – uplifting?' she suggested. '"Love: The Universal Need",' she thought. Aloud she said, 'Well, "Love Thy Neighbour" always cheers them up.' 'And thy family too,' she added to herself.

George grunted.

But he tore up his notes on 'Demonic Possession. Christ casting out devils from the Gadarene swine. The evils of Modern

Psychology', and reached, with a heavy sigh and furrowed brows, for a fresh sheet of paper.

Rose was, she assumed, dismissed.

*

Upstairs in the airless bedroom, young Mary stirred in her sleep, mumbled, freed her whole arm instinctively from the duvet, and dislodged her book. It slid further down the pillow. She did not wake.

As usual, the night voices murmured busily in the meadows around the neighbouring church. As usual that summer, flickers of sultry lightning flared in the sky beyond her half open window. As usual, the ancient stones, between which they had used to play hide-and-seek after school until Daddy had forbidden it, stood vigil, silent, circular, on the hillside.

His prohibition still upset and angered her. 'Pagan gods, pagan rituals. Devil worship. Stay away from them, Mary. You'll understand – when you're older.' She hated him in this mood, his Old Testament voice, his bushy eyebrows shadowing the steely glare. And his strictures had only fed her resentment. 'Why can't I play with the others – be *free* to have a bit of fun?' she had complained to her diary. 'He *says* he loves me – but he's robbing me of my life!' She'd crossed it out. 'Of my childhood.'

But now sleep had soothed her earlier indignation.

She turned over in bed, unaware of the insidious changes creeping across her room. Imperceptibly at first, the still darkness began to shimmer. By degrees, a new coolness, refreshing at first, developed a more wintry edge until, at last, the vibrant, icy atmosphere penetrated the consciousness of the sleeper. Drowsily she pulled at the bedclothes. The book slid to the floor with a sharp thud. The last threads of sleep snapped and Mary was awake, and shivering.

She tensed. Then she opened her eyes.

Then she opened her mouth. But it was some moments before her screams, breathless, half strangled by panic, could sound.

It was Mummy who finally managed to calm her down. Daddy, picking up her book and frowning at the worm-crawling skull on its cover, was no help at all. 'Just a young girl's nightmare. If she will insist on reading such ungodly nonsense ... '

Mary, trembling, crying, shook her head. He could never understand. She knew her mother was flashing a reproachful glance at Daddy. The hand was soft on her forehead. 'Tell us what you were dreaming, dear, if it helps. Tell Mummy.'

But it hadn't been a dream. The ice-cold whirlpool about her bed; the prickly, whispering feeling at the nape of her neck, over her scalp; that dreadful tugging of the bedding away from her shoulders. How could she explain, communicate? How could they understand?

And there was the rest.

'I saw – sort of saw – I *felt* a sort of white shadow. Growing. Just there. All blurry – but coming closer. Then' – she sobbed convulsively again at the recollection – 'then something happened right here – to the pillow. It went down. Sank into a hollow.' She made to touch it, but her fingers recoiled. She shuddered. 'As if there was a head next to mine, pressing down on my pillow!'

*

'Do something?'

'Yes, dear, *do* something. About the – the ghost. Perhaps the Psychical Research people – '

'Do what, for heaven's sake?' The Reverend Clairview bit savagely into his toast, ashamed of his inadvertent blasphemy. Marmalade spurted richly onto the clerical black of his suit. He sighed, his eyes appealing to heaven: penance enough. How could he conduct the funeral – a county, Hurst-Bramley funeral – with a sticky knee? Rose came to his side brandishing a napkin, dabbing it on her tongue.

'I suppose you'll be expecting me to go into the pulpit and announce to the entire parish – Lady Otterdale and all – that their vicar's house is haunted; that his daughter is being pursued by a love-sick phantom that tries to – ' he lowered his voice – 'to clamber into bed with her.' Rose pursed her lips, puckered her brow, glanced round. The voice dropped lower. 'Where is the child now?'

'Outside, dear. Playing. But – '

'Not with the Vincent boy, I hope. You don't have to look further than him for the cause of your "haunting". Encouraging my daughter's adolescent fantasies. She'll grow up and learn the paths of love and righteousness in the Lord's good time.'

Rose stood up and sighed. She couldn't go over all those arguments again. Yet something must be done. Neither she nor Mary could live with these present fears and tensions. She bit her upper lip, drew in her breath through flared nostrils, and waved the butter knife tentatively in her husband's direction. 'I know what you used to think about dear Mother – all those conversations with Ethelred the Unready ... '

The Reverend grunted irreverently into his teacup. 'And communing on cookery with Alfred the Great.'

'Yes, well, I know what you think about these things, George, but if we were to call in the Psychical Research people, for instance ... '

'Once and for all, Rose, this house is not haunted.' He gripped the sides of the breakfast table as he did the pulpit – an all-too-familiar gesture. Rose braced herself. 'Have teacups flown through the air?' He waved his cup, and Rose applied her napkin to the tablecloth. 'Have tables rapped out messages; marmalade jars crashed to the floor?' He paused to assess the impact on his imaginary congregation. Then leaned forward. 'Haunting is a serious and terrible business: a manifestation of the devil and his agents. This is a vicarage – a godly home. There is no evil here. Are you listening, Rose? Our daughter is possessed not by evil spirits but by nightmares brought on by wilful disobedience and adolescent hysteria. The cure is simple. She must return to her own bedroom tonight.'

Rose's knuckles went white as her grip on the butter knife tightened. But her retort was forestalled by the running steps and abrupt arrival of Mary, skipping rope trailing, at the breakfast room door.

'Daddy, there's an old lady coming round the side of the church. Looking for the vicar, she said. She's terribly funny. She's – '

Mary's voice broke off with a gasp, betraying as much fascination as fear. The butter knife clattered to the floor. 'What the devil ... ?' said the Reverend Clairview, despite himself.

And together they watched the jar of thick-cut, Seville orange marmalade rise from the breakfast table, hover uncertainly for a moment, and then travel unsteadily towards the brass-hung, inglenook fireplace.

A shiver of cold air eddied about them, Rose screamed, the doorbell rang, and the jar of marmalade paused, wavered and exploded in a thousand sticky fragments.

In the shocked silence the doorbell sounded again. The Reverend removed a shred of orange peel from his turn-up. He rose. He went into the hallway. He opened the door.

'I,' announced the lady, 'am Friend. Miss Friend. And this' – she tugged vigorously at a length of clothes-line which stretched tautly from her right hand – 'is Goat.' A pair of horns appeared from behind the lupins, closely followed by an entire goat. 'It's all right. He's a billy. Mascot. Army. Retired. I was just taking him for his morning walk and he brought me straight here. I'll be with you in a jiffy; it's just a question of tethering ... '

The Reverend George Clairview watched, still dazed, as the colourfully clothed figure, with ostrich feathers sprouting from her large felt hat, busied herself tying the rope to his rambler trellis-work.

'Nasturtiums,' said the lady. 'He's rather partial. There. That should keep them apart. Righto!' She advanced, plumes quivering, across the porch.

Clairview came to, stood firm. 'Look, I don't know who you are ... '

'Friend. Miss Friend.'

' ... But we have more than enough pegs and onions for our needs. And our requirements certainly don't run to goats, ex-Army or otherwise. I'm a busy man. And it's most inconvenient now. A family crisis ... '

'I knew it! Goat was right.' Miss Friend was delighted. She fixed him with gleaming eyes and swept skilfully past into the hall, nose twitching, palms uplifted.

The vicar followed her angrily into the breakfast room, skidding briskly on a patch of marmalade. Miss Friend beamed at the distressed, bewildered family. 'How rude of me,' she said, 'I haven't introduced myself. I represent the Beethorpe Road Open Circle. We got the vibrations. First from the old stone circle. Then yours. You need me!'

Outside, Goat was joyfully discovering a new predilection for the vicarage lupins.

*

It was, nevertheless, two weeks, three poltergeist outbreaks, seven levitations and innumerable scrapings and tappings, nocturnal and diurnal, before the séance finally transpired. As the web of disturbing and unexplained events closed in upon the family, the parents had become more frightened and more voluble. Argument had been continuous and heated; George had been assertive and adamant.

'Seeking forbidden knowledge. Trafficking with the devil. Remember Eve – the tree of knowledge. Remember Faustus ... '

'But we're not trying to sell our souls, George. We're trying to save them; to understand; to find out; to lay an unquiet spirit to rest.'

Mary, growing quieter and more reserved of late, suggested: 'Perhaps it wants to be friends; perhaps it needs friends.' George Clairview ignored the child.

Rose pressed on with her offensive. 'Well, something must be done, dear. The séance that Miss Thing mentioned ... '

142

'There will be no séances in this house in my presence.'

'In your absence, then,' decided Rose.

'I shall mention the matter to the Bishop next Thursday evening when I drive into town.'

'Next Thursday evening, then,' decided Rose.

'And that is all there is to be said on the matter.'

His wife said no more.

And now Thursday had arrived, along, rather furtively, with Miss Friend, a few colleagues from the Circle – 'to help with the vibrations, my dear' – and Goat, suitably tethered. They were standing together in an awkward but enthusiastic huddle in the middle of the oak-beamed lounge, and Rose was trying hard not to feel guilty and whisper.

Miss Friend was not so inhibited. She introduced her companions, told them to feel at home, distributed them around the polished mahogany table, beamed upon them all and wrung her hands with joyous approval. 'Such lovely vibrations, my dear.' Her eyes closed. She undulated ecstatically. 'And growing more exhilarating every minute. We've been trying to work up psychic waves like this at Beethorpe Road for years!' Her eyes opened wide. 'Well, to business!' Wider. 'Is the young gel staying with us?'

Rose turned and realized that Mary had crept into the room.

'Yes, Mummy. Let me stay. Please.'

Rose shook her head firmly. 'To bed, madam. At once.'

'But it's so early. Besides – '

'To your bedroom, then. Read for a bit. Go to bed when you're ready. But we're not to be disturbed.' She planted a farewell kiss, tender but decisive, on her daughter's forehead. 'And don't be frightened any more, dear.' Mary knew her mother's hands were trembling. 'Everything's going to be all right.'

'Everything?' Mary smiled, suddenly hopeful of new horizons.

'Everything. Just as it was before.'

'Oh.' Her shoulders sagged; her smile faded.

And Mary quietly left the room.

'Right, team. Ready for ops?' Miss Friend put out a large hand on either side and grasped her neighbours' upturned palms. A tall, wispy woman, with a beaded hairnet and long, improbable earrings, nodded meekly and wished she had gone to the lavatory before they started.

'Want the loo again, Lily? Hurry up then.' Miss Friend leaned confidentially towards Rose and whispered loudly, 'Bladder trouble. But a bloody good clairvoyant. Off you go, Lily. Can't keep them waiting on the other side.'

Lily hovered vaguely in the doorway. 'Second one on the left,' smiled Rose.

Around the table the sitters composed themselves, breathing, Rose thought, with rather histrionic deliberation.

'Pull up a chair. Join us, my dear.'

Rose hesitated, fingering the chain, with its small silver cross, that hung round her neck.

'It'll help. All shoulders to the grindstone. Just hold Herbert's hand. Herbert!' The gentleman's moustache twitched in a shy smile. 'And Lily'll complete the circle on the other side ... Here she is now.' Lily slipped into her seat with a sidelong smirk. Her limp fingers closed on Rose's left hand. 'There!'

Rose's features were taut with anxiety and apprehension. What if the exercise didn't work? What if George found out? How could she explain to him, make him understand her motives? What exactly was Miss Friend expecting to happen? Would the restless spirit that had been disrupting their lives declare itself and its posthumous complaints, and then return satisfied to its astral abode? Perhaps George was right? Perhaps they were interfering with dark and potent forces which, once unleashed, they might not be able to control. Perhaps she'd better cancel –

'Don't be surprised,' boomed Miss Friend, surprising them all, 'if there are a few manifestations, Mrs Clairview. Knocks, rattles, moving lights, vases and so forth. Reception's good tonight. Exceptionally good. It's going to be a trance job, team. A real snorter. Control's already warning me of that. Probably a Direct Voice or even a materialization if we're lucky. Right, bully off!'

Rose opened her mouth to voice a tentative objection but, to her surprise, the Beethorpe Road Open Circle sitters had launched into a rendering of 'Christians Awake' which was as lusty as it was unexpected.

'Sound waves. Shakes up the ether a bit,' explained Miss Friend. 'Now, give me your thoughts. Concentrate your energies.'

She closed her eyes, raised her head.

Rose sat tense on the edge of her seat and wondered how one concentrated one's energies. In the expectant silence she felt she could almost hear air vibrating around her head. She wanted to scratch her nose.

'Yes, dear, I'm coming,' Miss Friend murmured to her left shoulder. 'Gosh, the air's positively tingling tonight.' Rose shivered. 'It's beginning to work. We're going to make contact.'

And within seconds Miss Friend was slumbering in deep trance.

None of the sitters, anxiously watching the heavy rise and fall of the medium's ample bosom, was aware that Mary had been standing outside the door for the past five minutes.

*

'It's beginning to work. We're going to make contact.'

Vartek's renewed excitement was infectious if misguided. Xar remembered his own feelings on *his* first major reconnaissance assignment, even though the life forms on that planet had proved to be purely nominal. Nevertheless, his younger colleague's hopes still found an echo in himself, tempered by the sobering experience of so many profitless life-intelligence communication probes, and the disappointingly negative results of the past few days on Planet Three. Regrettably for their mission, Vartek's well-meaning but ill-focused attempts to make empathy-contact with the beings in the house seemed only to have caused physical dislocations and emotional distress instead of encouraging mutual psi-understanding.

The strange world of Planet Three, its surface shimmering in shifting veils of pastel coloured light, had revolved many thousands of times about its sun since their previous scout probe had landed. Even Xar had homed in on the original teleport site – marked by the makeshift, stone circle so characteristic of the earlier missions, and which they were now using as their centre of operations – with unusual optimism. The records from the earlier probe had reported the existence of a primitive form of intelligent, sentient life, 'with potential for development'. How many times had he heard *that*, thought Xar. But – another well-worn thought – perhaps Planet Three would prove to be different. Perhaps, even in this obscure corner of the universe, they would now make psi-contact with life forms as intelligent and civilized as they prided themselves on being.

'But,' Xar wondered, 'have I allowed myself to be over influenced by too much thought-sharing of Vartek's youthful dreams?' Sixteen planet-days, their scheduled withdrawal to the Fourth Planet already overdue, and they had still been unable to master the natural laws and essential character of this curious alien, whose mental and spiritual potential seemed strangely fused with, and somehow dependent on, the gross, molecular matter of which the planet itself was composed. Psi-consciousness embedded in physical matter! Mind locked in, constrained by the animal body. Xar's thoughts strained after understanding. Probably it was merely a quirk of early evolutionary development, but they could not, as responsible cosmic researchers, dismiss the possibility that this might conceivably constitute some hitherto unknown form of advanced, civilized life, perhaps superior to their own. The exhilarating idea alerted young Vartek's mind to share his excitement.

'We made a promising start,' Xar's thoughts told his colleague. 'In the upstairs space, with the small Mary individual.'

But after that, they had to admit, their experiments, utilising the most sophisticated, telekinetic conversion procedures, had been strangely unproductive. They had only succeeded – somewhat clumsily and briefly – in fracturing the dimension barriers. 'At least *you* managed to draw attention to your presence,' Xar sympathised encouragingly. 'But we can't claim an understanding of the essential native mind or make any scientific assessment of the quality and degree of the race's psi-development, can we? Not yet. Not one that will stand up to intergalactic standards of scrutiny.'

Xar's doubts were abruptly interrupted by Vartek's alert. 'The psi-energies are growing! Feel them! Especially now the being with the inaccessible mind has left. Let's try to manifest ourselves in *their* physical form one more time, make mind-to-mind contact.'

Xar acquiesced. But he was still uneasy. There were, he felt, darker, more primitive mental forces inhibiting them, blocking communication.

He waited. Vartek's concentration was intense.

*

Miss Friend's plumes stirred; she struggled momentarily in her chair, shook her head with increasing vehemence from side to side, moaned loudly, and lapsed back into trance.

Rose was frightened and relieved. Anxiously she glanced at the faces of the sitters, impassive, concentrating. Even more anxiously she glanced at the clock ...

None of them heard the faint gasp outside the door as Mary felt the familiar prickling sensation return; familiar – but with what burning, exciting, immanent intensity ...

*

They had failed with the Friend being. 'Why?' wondered Xar. But now, utilising the energy in the dimension-gate while it was still strong, they had turned their attention again to the small individual.

This time, as their sensor scans confirmed, there was a radical difference. While Vartek focused himself to materialize in the alien

147

dimension, Xar's mind reached out carefully from base to home in on the young being's mind, now exposed, now open and receptive.

The mists began to clear. 'It's beginning. We're going to make contact ... '

But in the background, unaccountably, the negative forces were nagging again, threatening to return.

*

Mary's actions were stilted but precise. She opened the front door, walked slowly out into the dusk, past the moss-crusted stones of the church wall and up the open hillside, where a fresh wind was blowing, towards the ancient monoliths.

She was not aware of being caught, for a glaring instant, in the beam of the headlights as the vicar's car swung into Rectory Lane.

But Rose had already heard the ominously familiar grumbling of the old engine, the crunching of tyres on gravel, the protesting brakes.

She leaped up, rushed to the window, saw 'George! And the bishop!' and turned back to Miss Friend. The medium was snoring in noisy contentment.

Lily had blanched. 'You can't break the Circle, Mrs Clairview. You'll snap Miss Friend's astral cord. You might damage her psyche. Permanently ... '

*

Mary walked on.

The excitement was flaring in her head. Vast shining horizons of freedom opened before her. This was being deeply alive. The stars burned, whirled, sang inside her mind. She was going out to experience, to share, something immense and important.

She looked ahead. There, shimmering in the rushing, calling fires that grew brighter, unendurably more brilliant, was the figure of a man. A tall white ghost of a man transfigured, radiant. She ran forward, trying to shield her mind, but the waves of dazzling light continued to crash and flow into her soul ...

*

The voices rose in volume, anger and incoherence as the small party, alarmed, bewildered, bickering, hurried up the hillside, its torches flashing erratically and unhelpfully in the twilight.

'I *knew* something had happened. I knew it!' Miss Friend, her psyche thoroughly intact, struggled to keep up with the rest of the party. 'Was there a materialization? A message?'

Rose felt sick. Her husband's loud, incessant accusations were superfluous. Why couldn't he think of the child – as she should have done? The bishop was soothing, placatory. He was also praying.

Behind them, Goat, unconcerned, moved on to sample the delphiniums.

Ahead of them, within the circle of stones, their torches picked out the prostrate figure of the young girl. Her arms were extended. Her expression was serenely ecstatic.

'Mary ... ? Mary!' Rose rushed forward and knelt to embrace her daughter. But she seemed unable to make the child hear or see her.

George stood over them. 'Look at her. Her eyes ... She's not with us.' His voice was harsh, frightened.

Rose stroked Mary's forehead. 'Her breathing, it's all strange ... What are you staring at, dear ... ? What is it? What do you see?'

'She's in a trance,' said George, directing a look of angry accusation at Miss Friend. He made futile passes with his hand before Mary's unblinking gaze. 'It's this pagan place, Bishop. Unholy rites. I told her never, ever ... Mary, wake up, Mary!' He shook his head. 'She's been – taken over.' His voice betrayed the pit of primitive horror opening in his mind. 'My daughter's possessed.'

Miss Friend pushed her way forward. 'Nonsense,' she

pronounced. The Reverend turned on her. She stepped hastily back.

'Perhaps she's having a sort of vision,' said Rose gently. 'Like those girls in France ... '

George turned to the bishop. 'This is an ungodly place, m'Lord.' He pointed a shaking finger. 'They call this The Slaughter Stone. Who knows what evils ... ? Perhaps a cleansing ritual ... ? The rite of exorcism? Drive the old gods out ... '

The bishop demurred. 'The Church moves with the times, George. Besides, look at your daughter's face. Is that the face of the Evil One?'

'Bishop, I beg of you. Something has cut us off from our child, snatched her from us. Is that not the work of evil forces? The devil takes many forms ... '

'And many that man makes for him, my dear George.' The bishop appraised his distressed colleague with sympathy and concern. 'Irrational fear and superstition, for instance,' he thought. 'The closed mind of prejudice. Intolerance, the failure to love and understand ... '

But George's passions were in turmoil. Fear flared his zeal into frustrated anger.

'I want my child returned. Forgive me, but to refuse would be evil. I demand' – he paused, apologized – 'I urgently request, my Lord – the sacred rite of exorcism. To set my daughter *free*. Now. Before it's too late.'

The bishop looked down at Rose. She was cradling Mary's head in the crook of her arm. Compassion for his anguished vicar overcame his doubts. He stretched out his arms and laid his hands with gentle reverence on Mary's head.

Miss Friend pursed her lips, resisted an incipient snort and withdrew into the darkness. Her party followed.

The bishop frowned, raised his crucifix, prayed, and started to recite.

*

The mists closed over again. The psi-energies faded.

And Xar's mind clouded. Contact had been established, but it had been too brief to qualify as 'intelligent communication' by universal protocols. Those negative forces, the gross barriers of primitive, racial characteristics, had closed in on them again. That was what had happened. 'Fear, superstition, prejudice, failure to love and understand.' The alien concepts began to clarify themselves as novel, disturbing insights in Xar's mind, though the words were strange.

'We've made a breakthrough discovery,' he thought; 'we've found an exception to the universal law of mind-sharing and empathy!'

His mind raced. Selfhood and hostility: that was the primal law, the basic instinct, of these creatures. They were condemned to mental separateness by their physical independence, and this was the result – a reversal of the accepted assumptions about the nature, and hence the cooperative survival, of all intelligent communities throughout the galaxies!

The concept was difficult for him to fully grasp and share with Vartek, but *there* clearly lay the inhibiting factor. It had been the same on the first mission so long ago. The gulf between their civilizations was fundamental, possibly even – for future generations – dangerous, in its inherent aggression.

Yet the fact remained: they had started to make a bridge.

Vartek's disappointment suffused Xar. He sympathised, consoled and erased. Other waves interrupted his consciousness. Xeta Base was calling on the telepath.

Xar tuned himself in. Mind reached mind across the stars.

'Mission monitoring station. All information has been collated and assessed. Despite presence of minimal psi-empathy in creatures called "Mary" and "Goat", alien life forms register as still in primitive, infantile stage. No appreciable development since earlier probe, though racial self-annihilation now seems more probable. Further communication attempts in current program are deemed futile. Immediate withdrawal to next phase is recommended.'

Thus, with a silent shiver of space-time, the reconnaissance craft and its disappointed crew slipped back towards the stars.

*

The air around the standing stones was suddenly electric with violent, unseen energy.

George was triumphant. 'It's leaving her, thank God!'

'*No!*'

Mary leaped to her feet and reached out her hands to the circling galaxies. Her mind was brilliant with a cosmic fire that cried along her blood. 'Don't leave me! Teach me. *I* can understand.' Her spirit soared and yearned. 'I want to share, to love ... '

Rose breathed a shuddering sigh of relief.

'Victory!' The Reverend was moving to claim his daughter. 'The powers of darkness are vanquished. Innocence is preserved.'

Mary whirled round. A last flicker of extra-terrestrial energy seared across her brain, surged through her uplifted arm ...

'You drove them away. You devil!'

Her ancient, savage scream, tore at the tranquil, summer night, echoed emptily from the dark, listening stones of her ancestors, rippled momentary regrets across Xar's distant consciousness.

As from a great distance, she studied them. The activity in the agitated group was remote, insignificant. They were bending over the man's body which had fallen from the force of the blow against the central monolith. They were making gestures.

Blood pulsed from the father's skull, its steely eyes set in an eternally uncomprehending stare at the heavens, and returned, drop by drop, to the receiving earth of Planet Three.

The mother wept.

*

Young Mary Clairview never spoke again.

At the trial her curiously detached silence concerned and confused the law and the psychoanalysts. The years of imprisonment brought her the freedom and boundless opportunity for study. She read avidly, feeding her mind with rich, new worlds of knowledge and ideas. Above all, she read Shakespeare. *He* knew. 'There are more things in heaven and earth ... ' *He* understood. At the bedside of her small, austerely furnished cell, her well-worn copy of *Hamlet* always lay open at the same page, the words repeatedly underlined: 'God, I could be bounded in a nutshell, and count myself a king of infinite space ... '

And thus the child murderer who, to the outraged delight of the popular press, finally entered a convent, profoundly impressed the nuns with her saintly tranquillity and inner radiance as she passed the rest of her days watching the stars, waiting for the second coming.

Typing Error

SHORT THIS MAY BE. STORY IT is not. Call it an investigation of a mystery. By a frightened man.

So forget fiction. Leave your Gothic ghouls to grope and gibber in the technicolor slime of their comfortable Hollywood graves. Let Gremlins tease and terrify in the reassuring gloom of the cinema's safe night. This is for real – whatever that may mean. I smell darker realities below, and I fear them: my senses are acute. No matter.

Facts. They must be our anchor. Investigation must not drift from the solid quayside of this world. First, then, the evidence. State the mystery. Bring on the fact – this simple, basic fact:

My typewriter is typing to itself. Words have appeared spontaneously typed onto blank pages left on this machine – without known human agency.

That is the mystery. Do you wonder I am a frightened man? I have the pages to prove it. See. Better: we will conduct an experiment. Here. Now. Scientific method. You must look for your bedtime terror tale elsewhere. There are spinners of yarns enough to flap bats across your face; they'll chill your spine and stake your Transylvanian heart while you sip your cosy nightcap and curl your toes. Our Business lies elsewhere. Our inquiry is open. Our destination uncontrived, uncharted and unknown. Hell is murky. Shakespeare knew a thing or two, Horatio ...

Bear with me; I'm a sensitive man. The experiment begins.

I've double-checked the house. The doors are locked and bolted, the windows fastened tight. Access is impossible. The whole building, I assure you, is empty. I've even looked – what obscure atavistic fear prompted this? – beneath the beds! Dust, spiders, childhood shadows: nothing more. There are no intruders in the place, human – or otherwise. I am alone. One sheet of paper, blank, please note, is wound into the machine – so. Our *tabula rasa.* All is set. I shall leave the study – let's say for half an hour. It's six-thirty. My nerves begin to jar. My headache nags again.

The scene is set. The trap is sprung.

Watch this space.

ALL DIE

SAVE THEM

SAVE YOURSELF

END

There! Q.E.D. Seven o'clock. The experiment succeeds. But why rejoice? The shadows of my fear blacken. We must check the facts, not slip our moorings. Check: one empty study. Nothing disturbed. No footprints, finger marks. No noises.

Yet, again, words have appeared on that blank sheet in my absence from the room. Words signifying – what? A moral exhortation to make amends before The End? A *memento mori*? All die. A sinister banality. Who needs reminders of death? I hear the lapping of that dark sea whenever dusk descends. Don't we all? The lighthouse flickers briefly but the night is vast. I am to die as all men must. Is that the message?

I digress.

Words. The evidence. Our anchor. What can explain this phenomenon? Let us consider the alternatives, rationally.

(Without reason we run adrift.) Scientifically, then:

(a) I have become the victim of a practical joker. Some manic typist, deprived perhaps by theft or poverty of his own typewriter, breaks silently into my house at irregular – but carefully chosen – intervals, leaving no trace of his passing, and taps out enigmatic warnings for the doubtful benefit of the householder. Purpose? To disturb and mystify. (Full marks for total success!)

Absurd, of course. But what alternatives are left?

(b) My typewriter is haunted. Some dark intelligence, obsessed with death, periodically possesses the keys. There's a ghost in my machine. Does it wish to drive me mad?

A quaint idea. Gothick with a k. Staple diet for Late Night Movie buffs, but not a tenable hypothesis in the real quayside world of light and reason. (Dusk, incidentally, is slanting down. Shadows bunch and thicken in my study. Switch on more lights ...)

Eliminate the joker's jolly jape. Eliminate the spectral tapper from Beyond The Veil. (Flippancy betrays my rising fear.) Is there any other 'explanation' for the inexplicable?

It must be faced. It must be written.

(c) The Psychological Hypothesis. I am going mad. I am trying to tell myself something, signalling from behind my own back. Unbeknown to my conscious self, I am writing automatic messages – or causing them to be written – on this faithful old machine!

Ingenious – but bizarre. Typewritten memos from the unconscious to the rational mind! Where are you now, Herr Jung? And – grant the suggestion for one moment – what then? What does this devious, thrusting voice from the Shadow Self need so urgently to communicate?

'Save yourself'?

The Shadow. The dark side of the soul. Not that. There's the rub: those darker realities. I'm a sensitive man: have I said that? I suffer for it. These headaches.

Press on. To our investigation. How do we advance the experiment?

Must I explore The Shadow? Is that it? Let it free? Make it speak clearly. I think the least we can ask of it is that it should state its business clearly – if it must speak at all.

I shall switch on another light. Shadows feed my fears. They cluster there in the curtain folds.

Yes, clarity is what is needed next. A clear communication. Why do I begin to dread an end to the mystery?

My headache gnaws and throbs. I shall go and take that extra dose of aspirin.

I COME HERE TONIGHT

Seven-thirty. See! So brief an absence.

My fears rush in.

The message grows clearer!

Me signalling to me behind my back? Forget it! The dark voice urging me to kill? Or be killed? A death threat. From me to myself! *'Man Plots to Kill Self in Bizarre Murder Mystery.'* The ultimate news story!

Laughable.

Who's laughing?

My pulses race. There's a snake pit of associations here. They slither and sting my brain. Slowly, now. Carefully. Pick them out one by one.

News story.

Murder plots.

Death threat.

The typed warning.

I must rest and clear my mind. Calmly now.

The still, small voice insists. I cannot erase those headlines! For weeks now they've been haunting the nation. You must know it. You've read them too. See: I have the newspapers here by my desk.

'Ripper Warned Victims With Messages.'

'Death Threat Ripper Kills Again.'

The plot thickens! It sickens. And now it centres on me!

Be still, my jangling nerves. I must take stock of this unexpected development.

The time is seven-fifty this dark – this black – October evening. Alone in my empty home I have become the unwitting (and, let it be said, terrified) recipient, by agency or agencies unknown, of a laconic and cryptic message: I am, it seems, the next intended victim of the lunatic killer who's been stalking the nation since September. The murder is planned for tonight. He intends it to take place *here*, he says.

Stay calm.

So much for Option (c): The Psychological Explanation! So much for canting theories of the Shadow Self, the furtive, subterranean plotting of the alter ego! Psychiatrists, analysts, therapists – the whole damned coven – they put your soul on the rack, not the couch, and wrench their hollow hypotheses out of your private dark; they ransack and romp in your dreams to plunder symbols – oh so meaningful! But do they 'come here tonight' to lend a practical hand when you're threatened with murder? Do they hell. They leave you stranded with the headaches still.

I escape into irrelevances. I must focus my mind. Stay lucid.

I am to be a victim. Therefore I must alert the police. That is clearly the next step. But the phone is out in the hall, and the hallway is dark. Is the front door properly secured? Listen! I hear it rattle now. The killer is cunning. He moves in mysterious ways. His messages, scorning locked doors and windows, already mock me cowering in my study. Can bolts and padlocks prevent his coming in person now?

Thoughts crowd and cramp my brain. I need more light.

These news stories taunt me yet. Murder disturbs me. Especially my own.

Look here – today's paper!

'Police are taking seriously the suggestion that the killer murders by fear. Yesterday's victim, like the rest, is thought to have died of fright before the bizarre mutilations, characteristic of these

*killings, took place. The latest weapon, its nature as yet
undisclosed, was found beside the body and is undergoing
forensic tests ... '*

Enough! I will phone the police.

SCREWDRIVER

END

NOW

So there it is. The truth at last. Blood will have blood. The pains in my head have gone. September was a bad month.

It is as I feared when I feared the worst. Look at this page. Defiled. These are the words of the damned. They come from the pit. They stink with the evil of the black soul that festers in my body.

The screwdriver.

Weapon undisclosed? Implement unknown? *Not to me. Not now.* The memories, the horrors have not stayed drowned for long. They've roared to the surface *now*. They crash black breakers in my consciousness, the dark fusing the light. O, the terror of self-knowledge.

Now I remember it all. It scalds and rips at my brain. The tearing and the gouging. The unmaking of that lovely face, those scarred and lifeless bodies ... Death, that killer of beauty, is my ancient enemy. Why else would I avenge it, disfigure it, except in rage? A protest. Would I hack and maim the living? No, where is the reason in that? I am no madman! No, it is the final, cruel ugliness of death that maddens and appals ...

So – *I know now who I am.*

'*The Ripper Reveals Himself To Himself.*' (Journalists, do your worst.)

He has come even as he promised. Here. Tonight.

And already sirens hoot and shriek outside the house. Voices, lights.

Is there time to savour the irony? – I have called the police to *save* the Ripper!

Stay cool. How easy it is to think clearly now the headaches have lifted.

How is our investigation coming along? Most satisfactorily. I think we have resolved the mystery. You can finish your nightcap now.

More voices. Shouting and banging. Glass smashing in the back yard. They're surrounding the house.

There's no need to hurry. The locks are strong. They'll hold. I know exactly what I must do. There's plenty of rope in the cupboard beneath the stairs. (The children's swing was never made.) The beams in the attic are stout.

Carry on hammering, gentlemen. Really there's no need to worry now. The danger is past. I'm sorry to have troubled you this bleak October night. I can handle this.

A final, simple fact: our inquiry ends here.

I will kill the killer myself.

Hot-Pot For Hubert

HOW DID ONE REMOVE THE EYE from one's toad? Abbie Darkthorn glared at the dark, gnarled creature. The creature stared back.

She prodded its tough, mottled skin pensively with her knife and tried to forget the untidy tussle she had just endured persuading the 'lusty, plump-bodied' rat to surrender its liver and a number of more dispensable organs for the recipe. A quick medicinal draught from the brandy bottle – (she had long ceased to question Dr Heartsease's epicurean prescriptions) – and a horrified glance at the clock provided her with the necessary impetus: it would never do for Hubert to arrive before she was ready. She gripped the slippery hind-quarters firmly, inserted the blade and with a skilful twist extruded the glutinous ingredient with an ease which surprised and pleased her. But there was no time for self-congratulation. The object lay glossy and baleful on the plate before her. She wondered what to do about the gristly bits that were still resolutely attached. Brother Martynne, the renegade monk who, according to legend, had rediscovered the ancient recipe and inscribed it in the gloom of the cloisters between his last Vespers and everlasting excommunication, hadn't foreseen such domestic details as recalcitrant optical ligaments. 'It all makes for a richer stock,' she decided, chasing the jelly, which still glared up with an impotent, green malevolence, around the plate with a fork. Finally she speared it, held it glowing like a rainbow in the dying rays of the autumn sun, and dropped it triumphantly into the pot. It sank below the steaming surface of the stew, which winked and chuckled like a primeval crater.

Abbie Darkthorn wiped her hands thoroughly and absent-mindedly on the voluminous folds of her red velvet dress, draped like an ambitious Victorian lampshade about her fuller figure, realized, hastily unearthed an apron from the bottom of an obstinate drawer (the pine dresser was another of Hubert's 'wholesome, rustic *objets d'art*), and wondered where she had secreted the phial of bat's blood. The 'phial' was, in fact, only an anachronistic approximation but she felt sure the monk would have condoned the use of a Marmite jar. Then a sudden alarm assailed her. Had Hubert tidied the jar away into the dustbin last weekend with all those assorted bottles in the alcove? 'Can't lead the wholesome, simple life, old thing, with all these things cluttering up the noble peasant household, eh?'

The alcove, on inspection, presented a rustic bareness which testified well to Hubert's zeal. The Marmite jar was no longer there.

The Marmite jar was in the dustbin.

Abbie recalled with angry frustration the trouble she had had collecting her bat's blood. Knowledge of such arcane skills seemed scanty. She had tried writing to *Woman and Home* after reading an article, 'How I was reborn into the Old Religion: a Lancashire Midwife tells All.' But the sortie had proved unrewarding. The witch was adamantly of the purist White School and in answer to her query had sent a sheaf of literature in stencilled type generously informing her how she could cure any pig afflicted with warts, 'except in cases where the affliction is hereditary'; how she could 'tune herself in to the music of the spheres – in her own sitting room!'; and how she could banish the hobgoblin that was 'breeding mischiefs' (unspecified) 'in her hen coop'. She was even offered a bangle of genuine pixie gold ('at a specially reduced, bargain price for readers of *Woman and Home*') guaranteed ('or money refunded') to ward off rheumatism, frost-bite and cabbage blight, whilst giving 'encouragement to faint-hearted bridegrooms' – or pessimistic brides.

But in the matter of bat's blood, Lancashire, home of the hot-pot and the black pudding, had proved no help.

Accordingly, Abbie had stalked the wet-grassed fields of the neighbourhood for several evenings at dusk furtively flailing an improvised butterfly net ('There's nothing you can't do with a bean-pole and calico cast-offs,' she told herself with pride.) But without success. At length, weary of dew-damp stockings and unnecessary exercise, she screwed her courage to a Burke-and-Hare effrontery, raided a nearby barn by day, and carried off in a tightly clenched shopping bag, after a quick struggle, one of the leathery inhabitants, who had been hanging from a rafter unawares in a deep slumber – and who had evidently viewed the whole operation with as much disgust as Mrs Darkthorn herself.

The memory of how she had divested the creature of its blood by a rather gruesome drip-dry process was overwhelmed by the realization that the trouble which she and the bat had been through together to obtain the precious ingredient was now, in all probability, bleeding away from a cracked Marmite jar at the bottom of the dustbin. Screwing up her features, she delved into the slimier regions of the household waste.

And salvaged the jar – intact.

She dripped the dark, rich juice – making a mental note that she was getting very low on gravy browning – into the simmering casserole, stirring each drop counter-clockwise and muttering portentous syllables from the faded recipe. A black, shining lump rose gulping to the surface. She prodded it under and held it down, vexed to find it still recognisable as the 'bladder of an ageing sowe' for which last week she had had to enlist the services of a veterinary surgeon of more ambition than principle.

She replaced the lid and set the kitchen timer for forty-five minutes hence. Just time to race through enough of today's routine to avert Hubert's suspicions.

Today was Wednesday. Wednesday was Hot-pot Day. It was also dusting, vaccing and putting-things-straight day. 'Cleanliness is the essence of the simple life, old gel.' And Wednesday was, in addition, weeding-and-trimming-the-borders day. 'Get some pure, fresh, wholesome country air into your lungs,' Hubert would say – every Wednesday at seven fifty-four as he left for the office, extravagantly inhaling the pungent morning air, redolent of Weston's pig farm, and patting the briar pipe and tobacco tin that bulged with manly promise in his rough tweed pocket. A threadbare laugh, a glance to check the brief-case clasp, a quick squeeze, a practised peck – how familiar was each routine gesture – and off he went, hearty and efficient, healthy and good humoured, as fit to run an office as a wife and home. Washing up the breakfast things on Wednesday mornings, as on other days, Abbie dreamed of the bright streets of Hubert's distant city, thronged with glamorous and glittering shops and people, doubted that Hubert even registered them, noticed the sadly balding mop in her hand, vowed yet again to do something about it, and contemplated the barren routines of the rural week: tomorrow – Shepherd's Pie and the Travelling Library; and tomorrow – Stew, Dumplings and Helping Out for the Over-seventies; and tomorrow ...

She flicked the duster with an unaccustomed and bitter energy over the table, pianola and china cabinet, wrinkled her nose defensively to blow dust from obscurer corners but decided to leave untouched the foliage of the potted palm where it loitered, palely optimistic. ('I always say' – and he always did – 'there's nothing like simple plants to nourish a room, give it a wholesome, natural charm'). There was no time this Wednesday to chase the spiders out of the bathroom and scullery from the safe end of a long-handled brush. She returned, rubbing her hands together in an attitude of business-like prayer, to the kitchen, and fell into a dilemma of priorities: should she set the table first; or had she time to pursue the hoover round the dining-room; or, now she came to think of it, hadn't she better discourage the weeds in the Michaelmas border with a hasty hoe? ... Then, abruptly, she remembered the Shark's Tooth! That should have gone in with the raven's wing and desiccated hoof of one-eyed goat! Suppressing a colourful curse, she reached for the spice jars – 'Nutmeg', with the corollary, scribbled in Abbie's hand, 'specially ground'. She shook the jar and watched the restless, heaving fluid hiss, spit, and then suck the powdered shark's tooth greedily into its molten, savoury deeps.

She sat down with a relieved sigh. Collecting that small jar of powder had required much patience and initiative. She passed the back of her hand over her lips and smirked reminiscently into her knuckles as she saw again the little man in the chemist's shop bristle out of a boredom of bath cubes and bicarbonate of soda when he heard her request. And then halt on the reflex turn towards the shelves, deciding that he couldn't have.

' ... Sharp's ... tooth-powder?' he suggested apologetically.

Abbie reassured him that aids to dental hygiene in whatever form – and personally she always preferred the paste – were not what she had in mind.

'Powdered Shark's Tooth,' she repeated, enunciating each syllable with the exaggerated clarity and volume that one reserved for the hard of hearing, and foreigners.

Bewilderment met, fought and surrendered to professional pride in the chemist's features. Excited by such a pharmaceutical challenge, he decided to bluff this one out.

'Dyspepsia ... ' he began.

'What?' said Abbie.

'Flatulence ... ' he pursued.

'No,' said Abbie.

'Leonard's Liver salts,' he announced, weakly defiant, producing a large bottle with an unconvincing flourish. His eyebrows lifted hopefully.

'No' – Abbie ground his hopes under her heel – 'thank you. You see ... ' She lowered her voice, glanced at the door and inclined herself conspiratorially towards the chemist. Intrigued, he mirrored her actions. Their eyes locked.

'It's for my husband,' she confided.

They nodded in sage unison.

'Sadly common,' he murmured. 'Any number of quack remedies, of course.' Repressing a polite chuckle: 'I know what you're thinking of, madam ... '

Abbie withdrew slightly, surprised.

' ... And you shouldn't be. Old wives' tale. Powdered rhinoceros' horn!'

'Powdered Shark's Tooth,' remonstrated Abigail Darkthorn aggressively.

'Beef steak – rare – plenty of it,' retorted the chemist. 'That's the answer. I'm not a young man myself any more either, but ... '

Abbie had not stayed for the reminiscence.

Discouraged by this sortie into pharmacy, Abbie tried a fresh line of attack, visited the local Natural History Museum and, while the attendant was engaged in an impromptu post-prandial snooze over his desk, executed a brisk and skillful piece of tactical dentistry on the gaping mouth of an ancient shark exhibit, whose need for teeth had long expired. The precious plunder, which from its scarred appearance, had exhaustively served the voracious appetites of its owner in life, was fed to the Darkthorn coffee grinder and enthusiastically reduced to the required powder within minutes.

Bemused by her recollections, she was alerted to present reality by the insistent, fruity murmur of the dish. She consulted the kitchen clock whose heavy, inexorable tick had so patterned itself on her mind that she had long ceased to hear it. It informed her bluntly that the vacuum cleaner must remain under the stairs for today and that even the cursory hoeing must give way to more important gardening matters. There remained one ingredient to be 'brief y-brewed', a root whose virtues were so potent, according to the manuscript, that only the last moment would serve for its uprooting and immersing. But the last moment was almost upon her. If she didn't hurry, the front door would slam, the china pig over the range – donated by Hubert's mother – would rattle sympathetically; there would be the familiar grunt at the barometer, elevated or depressed according to the reading, the usual cry, 'How's Wednesday's child, then?' from the hall, a pedestrian pat with the brief-case, a St Bruno-flavoured moustache grazing her upraised left cheek, and Hubert would have arrived and be disappearing into the dining room murmuring Wednesday's inevitable question, 'Hot-pot potted, old thing?' as he prepared to knock his pipe out over the comatose cat on the hearth and await the arrival of today's 'wholesome fare'.

Abbie hurried out into the garden, skirts swinging busily. She made her way past the lawns, which would still need mowing again before the winter came, and remembered to call in at the out-house lean-to. ('One day,' Hubert had said, his quaking chins foreboding mirth as his elbow prodded the right response, 'this shed'll stop leaning and lie down altogether.') She disentangled a fork from the confusion of garden ironmongery and abandoned stone toadstools, and followed a well-trodden path into the remoter regions of the garden.

Here, in a special plot of her own, hidden between the succulent compost heap and the hybrid hedge, Abigail Darkthorn had planted and nurtured her crop of hemlock. Tended with concern and plenty of straw through the bitter frosts of the previous winter, and with pride and plenty of water in the opulent months of spring and summer, the plants had amply repaid her loving husbandry. They were magnificent specimens, though she said it herself, expanding her bosom with admiration and satisfaction once again as she looked on the sturdy plants for the last time. She leaned sadly on the fork. Wrenching those great roots from the earth which had cherished and secured them for so many anxious months seemed almost a sacrilege.

But it had to be done. The hemlock was the heart and soul, the very essence, of Brother Martynne's recipe. His spidery script, from the moment Phyllida Ossibore, the local historian's wife, had produced it – to divert attention from her sister's fruit cake, as rich and durable as mahogany – in the tea break of the Broxthorpe Bee-Keepers' Annual General Swarm, had planted seeds of hope in her mind which had blossomed wildly against all reason, transforming the monotonous landscape of her life. She tasted the elaborately inscribed words of the title again, the words which had whispered with suppressed excitement through her dreams above Hubert's rhythmic snoring for so long:

'An olde receipt contayninge a cure infallible,' it said, beginning with an earnest of success, 'for the bringynge of relief to thilke huswyfe that to a booring husbande y-holden is.'

Her life, sunk into the aimlessness of petty, daily routine, had developed purpose again. This ancient dish offered the possibility of transforming Hubert (and he could certainly do with it); it guaranteed 'relief' (of which she felt much in need); it was undoubtedly worth a try (since nothing else had ever worked); and it could surely do no harm (given the monastic credentials of its authorship).

Inspired anew, she drove the prongs of the fork into the earth, working with brisk determination in the chill light of the dying October sun, which hung like a blood orange on the horizon, filtering its rays through the black, dripping leaves and hidden thorns of the hedge. Tangled roots rose to the surface and twisted at her feet. She was relieved to hear no shriek but more than a little repelled by the gnarled limbs and taproot, wrenched from a dark agony of underground growth, their hairy offshoots matted with damp soil.

Doubt flickered in her mind: what sort of 'relief' could be expected from such unpromising material? Yet Brother Martynne had laid much stress on the hemlock. It was, he said, the essential ingredient; the others functioned only in 'a magicale capacitie' to conceal the 'savoure of the roote', which 'though it be efficacious, pleaseth not', and to render it 'subtile and desyrable' to the husband's palate. In any case, Abbie dimly remembered that hemlock had been much in use among the Greeks; the wife of the history master had once distinctly said so. It had something to do with Socrates, with all those plays of his, or was it chariot racing? If carrots were good for the eyesight, as Hubert repeatedly said, why should not hemlock be good for Hubert? Socrates reincarnate in Broxthorpe! A vision of the new Hubert delighting his wife and their constant stream of sophisticated visitors with his sage and coruscating conversation, his whole understanding of life deepened by this miraculous root, brought the excited anticipation of months to simmering point.

In quiet elation, she followed the long path back to the house.

Threads of mist were whispering among the primly trimmed privet hedges and dying chrysanthemum beds of the garden, obscuring in a slow soft shroud the late roses which even Hubert had noticed and admired. Shapes old and familiar had already become new and strange. She saw the garden as it had been that May evening when she and Hubert, newly-weds on an excursion from the two-roomed Finchley flat, had first viewed it and converted it, in a brief evening's stroll, from a wilderness of yellow ragwort to a landscaped paradise, brimming with azaleas and wisteria, a rural retreat complete with antique timbered sun house, matching dove-cot (that was her inspiration), and rainbowing pools of angel fish or, if Hubert insisted, trout. As for the dangers of water with a growing family of playful children, Hubert had pointed out – he had no pipe then to stab home his remarks with – that one or two missing youngsters here or there would hardly be noticed once the 'breeding season' was under way.

She smiled sadly into the damp, autumn air. They had abandoned Finchley, the 'strident voices of traffic and telephone', as Hubert had once termed it and, pleased with the alliteration, had thus labelled it ever since; and they had retired 'to be nobly savage in the bosom of Mother Nature.' By degrees, theatre trips, dining out and house guests had dwindled and receded from view.

Settling to 'the plain and simple life', Hubert too had grown plain and simple; nobility had escaped him; nature's bosom had nurtured cabbages and ragwort but not children or azaleas; a dove or two had died, others had proved pigeons. And the garden now lay dying under the seeping pall of evening mist. Yes, Hubert needed to be socratised and their old dream revitalised as quickly as possible, before age overtook them both.

Like dirty, hirsute snakes, stiffened in the spasms of violent death, the hemlock roots sprawled on the kitchen table. Hoping vainly that they would look more appetising when they were cleaned and chopped, Abbie cleaned and chopped them – and then, with as much anxiety as triumph, committed them to the stew. It gave a plangent burp of gratified desire. Bubbles groped their way upwards from the depths, grew pregnant, burst their membranes, collapsed with a steaming slap, subsided. Abbie took heart. This was a sure sign, according to the culinary Brother, that the casserole had achieved full potency. Another few minutes at Regulo Five and a foreign word or two from the manuscript, and the dish would be 'ful tempting' and ready for service.

Hastily she laid the table with the country linen cloth which Hubert had provided for their house-warming twenty years before, remembered that it had a stain (also provided by Hubert ten years later when a noble or savage gesture had unexpectedly encountered a cup of nettle tea), wondered if she could hide it beneath the sugar bowl, saw Hubert reaching for the sugar and finding the guilty mark ('I always say, if a thing's worth doing, old gel ... '), and then re-laid the table with the blue-check cloth instead. She was just wondering whether to withhold the salt and pepper lest Hubert's customary and liberal use of both might disturb the delicate balance, 'magickale and chymickale', of the casserole when the reverberations of the china pig announced that her husband had arrived.

A surge of excitement brought a flush to her cheeks and she found her voice had grown rather breathless when it was required to deliver the expected response that Wednesday's child was 'busy but well, thank you, dear.'

Abbie braced herself for the pat.

The pat followed.

She inclined a rudely healthy cheek to be kissed.

The kiss was delivered.

The tabby twitched apprehensively on the hearth as Hubert entered the dining-room and took out his pipe.

In the kitchen Abbie removed the casserole from the oven and placed it reverently on the table. It heaved and gulped like an impatient quagmire. She tip-toed to the door and, tongue clenched between her teeth to suppress the groan of the hinge, pushed it to. After a hurried, and wholly superfluous, consultation of the manuscript, she raised her hands above her head and paced solemnly around the kitchen three times, stirring the stew with ritualistic deliberation at the end of each circuit. Still keeping a wary eye on the door – for the idea of explaining her ceremonial actions to a bewildered Hubert did not appeal – she was just beginning to pronounce the carefully rehearsed words (Latin she guessed they were) of the incantation, when Hubert's voice from the other room broke the spell. She started guiltily, flailing the air wildly with the spoon.

'Hot-pot potted, old thing?'

'Just coming, dear,' said Abigail Darkthorn, and launched, with difficulty, into the alien polysyllables.

'*Potentissimus*...' she intoned. '*Sacrificio*...'

'Hungry as a hunter.' Hubert's voice was raised with impatience.

'... *Damnatium*... *horrendum*...'

'Come on, old gel! Punctuality. Could eat a horse, y'know.'

' ... *Infernum* ... *necessitatem* ... *atrociter*.' Abbie stumbled through the words with a wild urgency, passing her hands over the dish like a manic conjuror.

There was an abrupt scraping of a chair, angry footsteps and Hubert flung open the kitchen door.

' ... *Fecit!*' shouted his wife triumphantly. And then, to be doubly sure, 'Abracadabra!' she added, eyes wide and staring, arms raised, dishevelled hair tumbling across her face. Her red velvet dress was streaked with grease and mud, and there was bat's blood on her face.

'Language, old thing!' said Hubert, lifting the lid of the casserole, 'and cleanliness, y'know.' He took a sip from the ladle, puckered his mouth, backed rapidly to the door, exited with a choke, and turned the key in the lock.

Abbie sat down on the kitchen stool and rocked contentedly. He had eaten! He had tasted transformation! He had ingested magic! The sound of retching and flushing from the bathroom and, presently, of the telephone did not disturb her. Already she felt the onset of fulfilment. A new life was beginning. Words indistinctly mumbling in the corridor (' ... change of life I shouldn't wonder ... poor old gel ... pretty damn quick, yes') had a distant and soothing sound. Placidly, she awaited Brother Martynne's promised 'relief' from a 'booring husbande'.

When, by and by, it came, she was surprised but undistressed. The two young men were cheerful and friendly, the ambulance warm and the drive exciting. Even a month later, sitting in her clean, tidy room and making a little pincushion in the shape of Hubert, she felt that Brother Martynne had proved not merely 'infallyble' but miraculous. Her life had, indeed, been transformed. The house was large and comfortable but required no housework; the guests were a little strange, especially when they wore white coats, but mainly kind; and Hubert, when he dropped in for a minute or two from time to time, hardly spoke at all and sounded as impressively unintelligible as Socrates when he did.

But above all it was the nice man from Occupational Therapy who pleased her most when he came with his clipboard to find out what her favourite fulfilling pastime was.

Abbie didn't hesitate. 'Cooking,' she said.

The man delivered a smile of professional encouragement.

'Lovely,' he said. 'You must make me supper one day. It would make a welcome change from boring old routine ... '

She looked into his kind, brown eyes. 'Boring,' she repeated, nodding sympathetically. 'Yes. Actually, I know just the thing for you,' said Abigail Darkthorn. 'I've got a very special recipe ... '

Eye to Eye

THE MOMENT HE PULLED THE CAR door shut, Myers knew something was not right with his latest acquisition. Had the garage delivered the wrong car? Did the cool leatherwork of twenty-year-old Daimlers always induce that strange flicker of unease? He straightened his tie, felt for the courtesy light, and clicked the switch. Nothing happened. Myers frowned in the darkness. The headache that had nagged at him all day returned. He was already late for the party; he was tempted to abandon the idea altogether. At least he wouldn't run the risk of colliding with the daunting Felicity Farr again. Ignoble and unprofitable thought. He dismissed it. Besides, he wanted to try out the car.

He placed the cigars and road maps on the seat beside him as if to establish his identity in, his ownership of, the new vehicle, then fumbled with the keys, cursed, fumbled again, and inserted the right one in the ignition switch.

But the sensation persisted, redoubled. The distant street light slanted cold shadows across the car's interior, leaving the back seat a wall of darkness. Myers wanted to turn round and check, but an obscure, a distinct misgiving held him back. Check what, for heaven's sake? He sat stiffly, staring ahead into the winter's night, angry and bewildered by this sudden foolishness. He recalled lying in bed as a child, cringing his toes in dreadful expectation of those gnarled, chilling fingers reaching up for him under the blankets. Why the hell should he be afraid to turn around *now*, afraid even to glance into the driving mirror? What atavistic impulse restrained him? Who – or what – was he scared of seeing? A masked hi-jacker, perhaps, sitting, silent and alone on the back seat, waiting? The glint of a knife? The eye of a gun?

The pain in Myers' head grew worse. He held his breath and listened. The air in the car seemed thick and oppressive, but he could hear nothing beyond the pounding of his own pulse; nothing stirred or breathed in the stillness behind him.

He put down his right hand to feel for the seat belt, which had evidently dropped to his side and, despite himself, hesitated before reaching behind him into the blackness of the rear seat. His fingers tentatively groped along the leatherwork, encountered a patch on the seat that was moist and tacky, and abruptly closed around something hard and cold. With a gasp he snatched back his hand. Then laughed drily. The seat buckle! He muttered to himself out loud to dispel his anger and to break the tense silence of the car. 'Afraid of groping the alien shoe now, are we? Afraid of a smear of oil?'

Darkness swallowed the words.

He fired the engine, revved aggressively, lurched forward onto the road with a roar, and drove out of town into the winding lanes of the Surrey countryside. 'There,' he told himself, 'confront a fear and it evaporates!' He descended the hill and swept round the yawning bend lined with towering oaks.

Abruptly, without warning, an access of fear rushed in upon him.

In that moment Myers Bainton *knew*. He knew he was not alone in the car. He knew what he would see if he were to lift his eyes to his driving mirror.

He could feel them quite distinctly: a pair of eyes, shining wide and wild. They were glaring into the back of his head out of the darkness of his new car.

Appalled, desperate for company, he held the car on the road and drove the last mile through the howling night into Gibbet's Corner.

The heart of the party was the lounge, which throbbed with noise, lights and people. Myers was thrust into it, introduced cursorily to several people who required him to repeat the pronunciation of his name, then to spell it, and then forgot both it and him, all with much merriment. A bottle of tonic and a glass were pressed into his hands and he was propelled towards a girl in blue feathers and tight, sequined pants who was hugging the last bottle of gin between her knees. She raised her head and stared into his eyes. 'I'm looking,' she said, 'for love.'

'I'm looking for gin,' confessed Myers. He reached out a hand.

'Don't touch me,' said the girl. 'Men!' Her feathers nodded savagely. 'One thing: that's all you're after.'

'Gin, actually,' said Myers. He introduced the tonic bottle into her line of vision and waved it about. She screamed. Myers retreated to a corner and wondered where Ronnie and Angela hid their bottle opener.

He watched the party.

It was loud and in high spirits; so was Felicity Farr. He pressed himself flat against the wall. But she found him. 'It's Myers!' she said.

'So it is,' said Myers. 'Still.'

'You're hiding again.'

'Yes,' said Myers.

People looked up curiously.

'Everyone's having fun,' giggled Felicity.

'Or having someone else.'

'Especially those two by the foliage. No-one likes to ask who they are – but what a floor show! It's all happening. Ronnie and Angela and Geoff are battling it out as usual in the kitchen. Come out and play.' Felicity tugged at his arm and saw his face in the light for the first time. 'Are you all right?' she exclaimed. 'My dear, you look positively grey. It's so unfashionable. Has something happened?'

'No,' he said. But he felt the warmth of human contact and saw concern in her look. He realized he was still trembling. 'Yes,' he said. 'Well, yes and no. Actually, it's the car.'

'Big end or tiny tappets, darling?' said Felicity. 'Sit down. Move that hand; she's not using it. Have a sip of this. That dreadful girl with the feathers – she looks like something predatory that just escaped from a zoo – is hoarding the gin. Now, tell Felicity all about it.' She beamed comfortingly and wove curls of his hair around her forefinger.

Myers sat back and began to unwind. 'It's a new car,' he said. 'I picked it up only tonight.'

'New-old or new-new?'

'Daimler; nineteen-sixty,' said Myers.

'Nearly vintage,' said Felicity, delight emerging in a squeal. 'How gorgeous! Bags of atmosphere.'

Myers shuddered. 'That's the problem,' he whispered. He felt himself back in the car, felt a dark shadow moving in the blackness behind him. He sensed those eyes. 'Bags of atmosphere,' he said. And relaxing in the attentive warmth of Felicity's caresses, he confessed to her, blundering through words in his attempts to convey experiences at once so intangible and so distressing, what he had felt earlier in the car.

'A tall, dark stranger in your back seat. You should be so lucky,' she interpolated. But by the end of the story she was hugging her knees, rapt with attention.

'And when you stopped there was really no one there?' Felicity was enthralled.

'No one,' said Myers. 'Nothing.'

'My dear Myers,' said Felicity Farr, her voice tremulous with excitement, 'how simply awful!' Her dramatic whisper penetrated the farthest reaches of the room. 'Your car's *haunted*! Something Very Nasty's happened in that back seat. What a pity Lucy isn't here.'

'Haunted,' said Myers gloomily. He drained the glass with a gulp. 'A ghost in my machine!'

'Something very sinister.' Felicity's eyes gleamed. 'We'll put ads in the paper,' she said. 'Won't it be fun finding out!'

*

But after the second owner had been traced, visited and found depressingly uninformed and uninformative, her enthusiasm evaporated. Myers' zeal correspondingly increased.

'You're obsessed,' said Felicity.

'I want to know,' said Myers.

'It's an obsession,' said Felicity.

Myers supposed she was right. But *she* had never actually experienced those eyes staring over her shoulder. Certainly their researches had produced little profit. One owner, a man with five children, a small wife and a large sheep dog, had used the Daimler to tow them all repeatedly in a caravan across Europe and back; he showed Felicity endless slides to verify these feats. An old lady with no children and a parrot called Piers had never allowed her chauffeur to let the car out of its garage in eight years of proud but stationary ownership. It was unpromising material, not redolent of the spectral nastiness that Felicity had set her heart on. The only sinister item they uncovered, as Felicity remarked, was 'that bloody parrot' – but that was because she was prejudiced; the bird, out of obscure motives of envy or revenge, had dismembered with its beak a rather chic hat she was sporting, concocted, they surmised, from parrot plumage.

'If you insist on pursuing this ghost hunt,' said Felicity, 'there's only one solution: Lucy.'

'Lucy,' said Myers.

Felicity tutted, and reminded him. 'Lucy has the vibrations.'

Thus Lucy was invited to Myers' house, flattered, dined, rested, and then taken outside to be sat in the Daimler.

'I'm not very good at this,' she repeated.

'Nonsense – darling.' Felicity's impatience sometimes travelled ahead of her manners.

'Honestly.' Lucy subsided tentatively into the driver's seat. They watched. She pressed a palm to her forehead.

Felicity leaned forward. 'What is it?' she said.

'My head ... aches.'

'So does mine,' said Myers. He closed his eyes, swaying unsteadily.

When he opened them again, he saw Lucy, her head thrown back, shaking helplessly. A distraught Felicity stooped over her attempting simultaneously to soothe her and extricate her from the car. 'Help me, for heaven's sake,' she was saying. Lucy's voice was choked with sobs, but her words were as clear as her distress.

'Blood,' she moaned. 'Blood. I see rope, a knife.' Her body writhed in the seat. Her voice dropped to a frightened whisper. 'There's death in the car ... It's black and twisted. A tree, a tree ... !'

Her voice rose shrilly. She raised a finger and pointed at the driving mirror, shielding her eyes from the sight.

'Look. Look there ... !' she gasped.

They manoeuvred her body back into the house.

'Brandy!' said Felicity urgently.

But Lucy opened her eyes, sat up, straightened her dress and gave an embarrassed giggle.

'Honestly, I told you. I'm not very good at this,' she said. 'Did anything happen?'

*

'The police,' said Felicity, when they met over a hurried lunch the following day. 'We should go to the police and leave it all to them.'

Myers sipped morosely. 'To tell them what? That my car's haunted by a murderer who strangled or stabbed his victim with a rope or a knife under some unspecified arboreal abortion that passes for a tree! Can you see their faces?' He essayed a wry chuckle and inadvertently blew bubbles in his coffee.

'I can see *your* face,' said Felicity, offering him a handkerchief.

179

Myers erased the coffee moustache. 'Evidence,' he said. 'We've got no proof.'

Felicity picked up her handbag, smiled brightly, said: 'Well, you've got only one option, haven't you? Sell the wretched car and forget the whole squalid business. Must rush, darling. I'm having a plumber at two. Delicious. 'Bye,' pecked him on the cheek, dropped the bill on his plate, and headed for the door.

Mysteries teased Myers; he could no more heed Felicity's advice than leave a crossword or jigsaw puzzle unfinished. As he watched her departing with her customary panache, he resolved to hunt down and confront for himself the one previous owner who had failed to respond to their advert.

He had formulated a plan.

Felicity reappeared at the table. 'No plans, Myers dear,' she said. 'Give up the Hercule Poirot bit. It'll only bring on your headaches.' She tinkled her fingers in farewell. At the door she turned and called, 'I meant to ask: are you coming to Whatsit's Corner tonight? Ronnie and Angela seem to do nothing but throw parties. I promise not to ravish you ... without due warning.'

Myers hunched his shoulders over his coffee, groaned, and tried to look as anonymous as possible.

*

The plan worked.

Myers visited the local police, spun an increasingly elaborate yarn to a variety of increasingly mystified officers about his claim to have a valuable item left in his car by a previous owner, and finally managed to take note of a computer print-out of their names and addresses before slipping out of the room. He popped his head round the door. 'I may be returning,' he told an officer at the desk. 'Citizen's Arrest.' He tapped his nose, nodding sagely. The officer gazed quizzically at Myers' retreating back. He shook his head. Then he picked up a phone.

Myers climbed into the car, smiling inwardly at his skill and cunning. He decided not to contact Felicity but, overcoming his reluctance to use the Daimler, drove across the town to seek out Mr Sidney Mortimer of 13A, Beaumont Buildings. He climbed the stairs, ignoring, after the first flight, the graffiti that, he decided, were more colourful than witty, and resorting to the rusted railings to help him up the fourth flight. He had even rapped briskly on the dolphin door knocker before realizing that he had no clear idea of how he intended to tackle his most promising suspect. He pressed a hand against his forehead to dispel a lurking headache, and had a sudden nightmarish glimpse of a large, dark shadow of a man appearing in the doorway looming over him, winding a rope round simian knuckles and gazing down at him out of lunatic eyes. He turned to flee, and at that moment, after much clanking and shunting of bolts, the door opened. Myers hesitated, and turned back.

'Yes?'

'Ah, yes,' said Myers.

'Yes?' repeated the man. He peered to his left and right into the gloom of the corridor.

'Mr Mortimer?' Myers said, confidence returning, for the man was built on a human scale after all and was, furthermore, balding. 'Mr *Sidney* Mortimer,' he added. It felt the right thing to add.

'Police?' said Sidney Mortimer.

Myers stepped forward. 'Might I be?' he asked.

'Or you might be the owner of my old Daimler,' said the man. He investigated Myers' face more closely. 'I've been expecting you.'

Myers stepped back, his face pale.

'You look like a man in need of a chair,' said Sidney Mortimer, gripping his arm and guiding him firmly through a narrow hallway into a small, crowded room. 'Turf the cat and those newspapers off that settee. And the thriller. Do you like murder mysteries? Agatha Christie? I'm a fanatic myself.' He waved an arm vaguely. 'Tea? I would offer you whisky but – you understand, Mr – er – . The days of Daimlers and roses are over. Times change ... ' An unconvincing chuckle failed to escape his throat.

'No tea,' said Myers.

'Still we keep cheerful,' said the man, 'back in the old trade.'

'Trade?' said Myers.

'Butchering,' said Sidney Mortimer.

Myers leaned forward. His eye twitched.

'With the Co-op,' added the man. 'Life's not all bad, is it?' He sighed. 'And we keep fit. Work-outs down the gym every night. It all helps.' He clenched his fist under Myers' nose and flexed his biceps.

Myers withdrew his nose, impressed.

'Helps you forget things.'

Myers' eyebrows lifted.

'The past.' The man stared ahead, lapped about with melancholy.

Myers cleared his throat – a brisk, business-like noise. 'About the car ... ' he began.

'She had a thing about that car,' said Sidney Mortimer. 'You married?'

Myers shook his head. The man echoed the movement sadly.

'My wife,' he said, 'of blessed memory ... '

'Ah,' said Myers.

'Down under,' said the man.

'How did it happen?' said Myers.

'Painful. Very sudden. Very cruel.'

'Was it – natural?' said Myers. He pictured the car, the rope, the helpless victim.

'Never,' said Sidney Mortimer. He tore at the arm of his chair and thumped it with a savage fist. Beads of sweat stood upon his forehead. 'Never!'

'Murder?' whispered Myers.

'Wagga Wagga,' said the man.

'Pardon?' said Myers.

'Australia. Down Under. She wanted to leave me. Just like that. One morning. My best mate and her. Start life again, they said. Painful, Mr – er – . It hurts still.'

'Yes,' said Myers. 'But they went? To Wagga Whatsit?'

'Never. She stayed with me. Died last winter. With her kidneys.'

'Ah,' said Myers. 'I'm sorry. And her mate – your mate – the other man ... ?'

Sidney stared abstractedly into the empty fireplace.

'You – dealt with him, I imagine.'

'I dealt with him all right.' He continued to stir amongst the embers of memory.

Myers stood up. He had heard enough. His suspicions congealed into a decision.

'Yes. That old Daimler. She developed quite a thing about it, the wife,' said the man. 'It reached the point where she wouldn't get in it. Even talked about it with Father Mulkerrins. Exorcism and such! Once she got an idea in her head ... well!'

Myers stared at him. 'Well?'

'One of her fancies. One of her ways of getting at me, I suppose. After. It's just – she always said there was a smell of death about that car. Do you believe in ghosts, Mr – ?'

Myers drew himself up. 'I believe in justice,' he said. He jingled his car keys. 'I was wondering, Mr Mortimer, whether you'd enjoy a ride in the Daimler – for old time's sake?'

The man's eyes brightened. 'Are you serious? I was trying to think of a way of asking – without causing offence. Just lead the way. Tell you what. Take me to The Oak – Gibbet's Oak. It's not far.'

'Half my friends live there,' murmured Myers.

'There's something there that might interest us both ... '

Myers turned in the doorway. He looked at the man sharply.

'A drink!' said Sidney Mortimer.

*

'If you're sitting up front being chauffeur, I'll sit in the rear: Lord Muck, eh?'

Myers, quietly triumphant, pulled away from the kerb with his prime suspect safely ensconced on the back seat. The car purred comfortably.

Then the man tapped him on the shoulder. Hard. 'Hey,' said Myers, 'that hurt.'

'It was meant to,' said the man. 'OK. Where is it?'

Myers shot a grimace of bewilderment over his shoulder.

'This valuable you told them you'd found left in the car.'

The Daimler swerved.

'Don't worry. The police got in touch. Told me to expect a nutter. I didn't realize I was in for a three-star loony. Why the excuses? Why the prying? What are you really after? What's the mystery?'

Myers kept his head. 'It's a murder mystery, isn't it, Mr Mortimer? You're the Agatha Christie fanatic. Self-confessed.' He glanced in the driving mirror, repressing a brief resonance of unease. The man's eyes were half-closed, averted.

'Murder?'

'The man you "dealt with" so efficiently,' said Myers.

Amused indignation flushed the man's face. 'Jim?' he laughed. 'Jim's all set up in Bermondsey. Or was, last we heard. Car repairs. After he got repaired himself. This car was his first customer ... '

Myers negotiated a bend, and drove on. 'Ghosts,' he said, 'talk. They leave memories. This car's like a travelling recorder, waiting for full playback.'

Sidney Mortimer produced a hybrid of snort and grunt, eloquent of disgust and incredulity.

'It's haunted with your crime, Mr Mortimer. We know it all. The knife, the smear of blood down the leatherwork, the rope for trussing up your victim, the staring eyes of the fanatic. It's all here. Vibrations. Printed into the fabric of the car.'

The Daimler veered dangerously into the side of the road as Myers' voice rose breathlessly.

'Stop the car,' said the man. Fingers dug into Myers' shoulders.

Myers slowed down. 'We've got your address now,' he said. 'It's too late to run.' He drew into a mud-furrowed lay-by. The late grey afternoon filled the car with thickening shadows. 'You're frightened,' he said.

'You're bloody right,' said the man. 'I've never been on a joy ride with a lunatic before. Get out.'

'I don't see ... ' said Myers.

The knife flicked close to his ear.

'I see,' said Myers.

'Keys!'

Myers flung them to the ground. The man retrieved them and led Myers at knife-point to the back of the car. He unlocked the boot, wrenched at the spare wheel, groped about in the dark interior muttering angrily, gave a muffled cry and hauled forth his trophy, like a triumphant midwife.

Myers' temple pulsed with pain.

'The rope!' he said.

'Tow rope,' said Sidney Mortimer. 'Still here! I always kept a length handy. After we broke down. Just in case. Come here.'

'There's blood on the rope,' said Myers, still struggling as the man coiled it round his arms and shoulders for the fifth time.

'Oil,' said Sidney Mortimer. 'Grease. You're obsessed, aren't you?'

'I want to know,' said Myers.

'Obsessed. And scared.'

A car, its headlights splashing a nightmare kaleidoscope of branches and shadows, swept past them into the twilight of country lanes. Myers shivered. He wished he'd phoned Felicity. Phoned anyone. The blind folly of his scheme began to oppress him.

The man trussed his feet.

'The police have got your number,' said Myers, staggering against the car.

'And yours, mate.'

'They're expecting me at the station. Citizen's Arrest.'

'I'm saving them a ride,' said the man. 'And a dangerous loony hunt.'

Deftly, he flexed his arms, picked Myers up and moved to deposit him in the back seat.

'No!' Myers panicked. The vein throbbed painfully in his forehead. Intimations threatened at the back of his mind. His scalp prickled. Not there, dear heaven!

A tracery of trees flickered into light ahead of an oncoming car. The vehicle roared into sight down the hill. 'Help!' yelled Myers. The car rushed past. 'Felicity! Lucy!' he groaned into the gathering night.

Roughly he was thrust into the back of the car. He struck out with his legs; he crashed his shoulders against the doorway. Then, lungs straining for air, he subsided onto the seat.

Blood dripped from a cut in his hand. The leatherwork by his feet grew moist and sticky.

The driver's door slammed, and with a skid and a guttural roar, the car pulled out into the night.

In the rear where Myers sat, hunched upright, trussed and helpless, the shadows closed about him.

*

'Lucy!' said Felicity, pouting her lips to breathe on freshly painted nails. She grimaced at the receiver. 'Look, I'm just off to the party ... '

'Pick me up,' said Lucy.

'Darling ... Are you all right?'

'No,' said Lucy. 'It's Myers. We got it wrong. I – feel it. You know that tree ... The tree I saw. I've just realized; I recognise it. It's down the road. We pass it every day ... '

'Give me two minutes,' said Felicity.

'Make it one. We've got to change things ... '

*

Myers struggled ineffectually. The rope bit into his arms, coiled about him as tight and implacable as fate.

He leaned forward. 'Listen!' he said.

186

His eyes grew wide in the darkness. He peered across the man's shoulder and caught a glimpse in the driving mirror.

His lips parted. Shivers of ice played at the base of his skull. Those eyes! Once before he had felt them, glaring into the back of his head. Now he saw them, shining wide and wild with fear, face to face.

Déjà vu – the moment of horror, its shadow cast before it, was locking into focus, now. Time was ticking inevitably towards place.

Myers stared at the reflection of his own terrified eyes, his mind tangling with impossible mysteries.

'Listen!' he repeated. His voice was choked by the shades that hung thick and stifling about the car. An awareness of mortality whelmed over him.

'Everything's changed,' he said. 'No, nothing's changed,' he said. 'But ... '

'Save it for the shrink,' said the man.

'For heaven's sake. It's not too late, after all,' shouted Myers. 'I was wrong. Accusing you.' He wrenched himself to the edge of the seat. 'The whole business: *it hasn't happened yet.*'

His eyes opened wide.

'No one need be killed,' he said.

The man gave a dry laugh.

Myers butted the driver's shoulders with his head. 'Stop the car,' he growled. 'For Christ's sake.'

'Maniac!' The man regained control of the car. He hurled obscenities over his back.

The shadows pressed closer. Myers' head throbbed. The car tyres squealed. Trees rose up, flared into momentary light, and hurtled into the blackness of the past.

Then, in the distance, Myers saw the tree, picked out in the headlights of an approaching car. Its black branches were distinctively gaunt and twisted in the shifting light.

Panic seized him.

'Gibbet's Oak!' he said hoarsely. 'Death. Of course: all those hangings.'

'Black spot,' said Sidney Mortimer drily. 'That's as far as friend Jim got. When he ran off in my Daimler. The bastard. I rearranged the steering for him. Very untidy. An experience he's never forgotten ... '

'Stop, now. Stop the car before it's too late!' cried Myers. Powerless, enraged and terrified, he launched himself against the driving seat.

Eyes dilated with horror, he watched the oncoming car sweep down the hill and approach the bend.

*

'Save Myers? Save him from what?' said Felicity to her distressed passenger.

Lucy pointed. 'There's the tree. Just ahead.' Then she screamed and pressed herself back in her seat. 'That car. It's gone crazy. Look out! Felicity – '

'The Daimler! It's Myers!' gasped Felicity.

*

The Daimler's wheel spun from the man's grip. There was a shrieking of tyres, the world revolved impossibly about Myers, time and the darkness of the shadow conjoined in one howling moment, and the ancient oak jarred at the twofold impact. Beneath its black boughs, the surrounding earth took the seeping blood and the pain and mystery of death deep into itself.

*

'Bottoms,' said Felicity, 'up! Have some more champers, darling. Matron's eating people somewhere else. Besides, she's signed your release. Here's to the future!'

'I'm sticking to the present,' said Myers, 'in future.'

188

'Perhaps one day we'll see eye to eye over something,' said Felicity.

Myers winced.

' ... If you'll pardon the expression.'

'Never!' Myers scanned the hospital drive. 'Cab's coming,' he said. 'Good old Lucy. Rescue at last. I hope she's done what I asked; I'm not setting one disabled foot in that taxi until I know it's been recently and comprehensively exorcised by the Archbishop of Canterbury himself.'

Felicity took his glass, giggling.

'Poor old Mortimer,' said Myers. '*He* can't just drive away from all this. Promoted to the ghosthood. Locked away in the past with all the rest.'

Felicity held out a supporting arm. 'What did you mean when you said it was all decided? That the accident, the events, were just there waiting for us to set them going? Did the poor man *have* to die?'

Myers shrugged. 'Ouch,' he said.

'But Lucy's warning? Your last-minute realization? Didn't we change anything, then?'

'What happened, happened,' said Myers. 'Who knows?'

Cross Talk

SILENCE SETTLED ITSELF COSILY AROUND the small, over-decorated cottage parlour.

'Buzz,' said Winifred Petherbridge.

Maud sighed. Was Winifred going to have another of her turns? Immunized from surprise by long experience of her companion, she continued to do battle with her daily crossword, and hoped that it would pass.

'A buzzing noise,' elaborated Winifred. 'More of a hiss, really.' Pensively she snared a loop with her crochet hook. 'A gargling sort of hiss. With clicks.'

'Perhaps you hold it wrong,' said Maud. 'The receiver. You know what you were like with the new tin opener.'

'Then it goes dead. The line. Only you can tell it's not. It's as if there's someone at the other end. Listening in. Someone waiting.'

Maud abandoned her abortive grappling with eight across. 'Win, they took us off the party line last year. After you complained.'

'This,' said Winifred decisively, 'is different.'

She smoothed out the colourful folds of her handiwork and, arms outstretched, held it up to be admired. Maud glanced up, sucking her pencil. She saw. The pencil splintered between her teeth. She remembered she must consult the dentist about the loose top plate.

'Like it?' prompted Winifred. The words emerged as a challenge.

Maud pursed her lips and tried to temper impatience with anxiety. 'You *must* try and do something about it, Winifred. Control, dear. Moderation. Common sense. Like that nice Doctor Keen said. When he came last time. The psychiatrist one. With the noisy car ... '

'And the leather trousers,' said Winifred. 'Also noisy.'

Maud's indignation fanned itself hotter. 'Anyway, I thought you promised. No larger than a doily this time.'

With an instinctive, guilty air, Winifred appraised the voluminous results of her recent labours with the crochet hook. 'I like making things,' she said. 'That's what time's for. Making things.' She followed Maud's exasperated gaze as it travelled round the doily-infested room. She paled into momentary penitence. 'Anyway, I forgot. My mind wandered. And it sort of grew.'

Maud slipped into her accusatory mode. 'You've been watching that Midnight Horror Movie again.'

Winifred confessed. '*The Torments of the Hell Sisters*'. She luxuriated in a brief reminiscence. 'About some poor old witches,' she said. 'The things they did to make them talk. Poor souls. In Technicolor, too!'

Maud reached across and seized the overgrown doily. She stretched it out on the floor, walked round it, sat down again and shook her head despairingly.

Winifred tried to be sympathetic. She pointed to her handiwork. 'I thought, perhaps, for the bathroom ... ' she suggested brightly.

Maud's eyes glittered dangerously. 'Winifred, I'm not having the man in to raise the bathroom door again. Over the other two rugs.'

'They match the seat covers,' objected Winifred, 'for the lavatory.'

'Seven covers is quite enough for one – bathroom,' said Maud.

'Lavatory,' said Winifred.

A tense silence of mutual mistrust and resentment hovered between them.

'There's always the dustbin,' said Winifred slowly. 'In cerise and magenta,' she tempted. 'It *is* an eyesore; you said so yourself ... '

Maud turned away, pained and disturbed. Dustbin covers indeed! This was developing into one of her more serious turns. Just like her cousin Albert. Before Flo got him into that home. *His* imagination had overtaken *him* too. Dressing up as the Angel Gabriel, bringing the Good News twice daily to Cousin Flo. All those Annunciations! No wonder they never had any children. There was an – unfortunate streak in the family.

She glanced round at Winifred suspiciously.

Winifred beamed back disarmingly. 'So,' she said, 'what are we going to do?'

'Do?'

'About the buzz, dear. In the telephone.' Poor Maud. Age was taking its toll of her memory as well as her imagination!

Maud rose, wincing with sciatica. A more serious turn indeed! First, this obsession with the phone, then the alarming extravagances with the crochet needle. Losing control. Where might it all end? Win ought to have one of the tablets Doctor Keen had given her. Or perhaps she, Maud, ought to phone him up. He said to give him a ring if there were any developments ... Yes, it was her duty. She thought of Cousin Flo putting Albert in the home. Did Flo suffer any self-reproaches? Well, it couldn't do any harm ... phoning.

She went into the hall, closed the door carefully behind her and searched on the pad for the number. Her hand hovered over the receiver.

Abruptly the door opened. Winifred hurried in. She stabbed an urgent finger at the telephone.

'Don't!' she said.

Maud's arm recoiled, her fingers fluttering. Was the phone electrified? 'What? Why not?' she demanded, guilt and shock feeding her annoyance.

'It's going to ring,' said Winifred.

Now she was going into one of her psychic phases! Maud prepared her features for a pitying look, but leapt painfully to her feet instead.

At her elbow the telephone erupted into a shrill, imperative ringing.

Seeing Maud evidently reduced to inaction, Winifred touched her arm comfortingly and approached the telephone herself. Nonetheless, she was visibly uneasy.

Her fingers closed over the receiver. She lifted it to her ear. Then, with a wry grimace at Maud, she reversed it so that the earpiece was not against her mouth.

She listened.

Maud watched.

'It's buzzing again,' said Winifred.

'Who is it?'

'Hallo?' said Winifred. 'Hallo?'

'Well?'

'The clicks. It's clicking. Now there's a sort of gurgle.'

Maud's impatience returned, became aggressive. 'Let me speak.' She reached out a hand. 'Perhaps it's one of those dreadful breathers.'

'Ssh!' Winifred pressed her forefinger dramatically to her lips. 'Wait ... Hallo? Can I help you ... ?' She listened. 'That's funny ... '

'Who – ?'

Winifred's eyebrows puckered; her nostrils flared in the effort to concentrate. 'Please, don't do that,' she said, her rising voice betraying her sudden distress. 'Yes, of course you can speak ... I'm listening ... We *will* listen ... No, please don't ... Can you hear me? Hallo?'

Winifred's face had gone moist and pale. Maud took the phone from her unsteady hands. She listened a moment, shrugged and replaced the receiver.

Winifred stood up, agitated.

Maud made her sit down.

'What did you hear?' she demanded.

'There was a voice,' said Winifred. And got up again. 'A strange voice.'

'It *is* a phone,' said Maud. 'That's what they're for. Hearing voices.'

'This one was sort of sobbing,' said Winifred. 'Only worse. She was desperate, whoever she was. Could hardly speak. Such terrible sobs.'

'Crossed lines,' said Maud. 'Probably someone for the Samaritans. Obviously it wasn't anyone we know.'

'She wanted me to hear something. Something important.'

'Wrong number,' said Maud. 'That's what it was. Like it was on the old number – when we had all those gentlemen asking for the French lady. For the lessons. With discipline. You remember.' She was concerned. Why was such a minor event distressing Winifred so much? She must find those tablets at once. And mention this to Doctor Keen.

'We'll get the phone men in tomorrow,' she said.

'It was very – distant,' said Winifred, struggling to find words for the indescribable. 'Sort of echoing. Alien.'

Maud raised a grim eyebrow. 'You'll be telling us the phone's haunted next,' she said.

Winifred's eyes narrowed. She said nothing.

*

It was two days before the telephone engineer arrived.

'We're getting the voices,' Winifred told him.

'Crossed lines,' said Maud.

'It's all right from our end,' said the man.

'Not from ours,' said Winifred.

And the engineer went away again.

He returned two days later with a colleague and a variety of picks and shovels.

'Spades?' said Maud.

'Spades,' agreed the man. 'Investigation. It's a digging job.' He pointed out of the parlour window to the bottom of the garden where, beyond the fence, beneath the ancient elm that dominated the scene, the telephone wires descended earthwards and were lost to sight. 'Buried,' he said. 'No fuss. No flowers. That's the easy part. It's what you might call the exhumation that's tricky. Roots of that tree've probably grown and snarled the cable up, see. Powerful things, roots. Often takes quite a bit of wrenching and tearing to get things free.'

'What about our border?' said Maud. 'And the poor tree?'

'What about your phone?' said the man.

And they went off to the far end of the garden.

Maud left them and wondered when Winifred would return from her Thursday Circle. *That* was another matter that was becoming unhealthy. These psychic goings-on. All these vibrations and miracle cures. Hobnobbing with deceased Red Indian guides. Allowing herself to be possessed by strange men from beyond the veil. At Winifred's age. True, she had to admit, Win had achieved some remarkable results. And not just with the warts. That little boy with the convulsions *had* improved surprisingly after one of her herbal concoctions and some sort of spiritualistic mumbo-jumbo, despite that dreadful fuss between the parents and the hospital. Win really couldn't afford to antagonize the medical profession that way. Anyway, it was all a question of psychology. Doctor Keen had explained it to her. Mind over matter. And of course this psychic business ran in Win's family too. But it was becoming obsessive. Unreasonable. Perhaps Doctor Keen would know how to cure it. Science always knew a way ...

A noisy scraping of boots interrupted her anxious meditations. The two engineers had returned.

'We'll be off now,' said the first man.

Maud peered through the french windows. 'You haven't started!' she objected.

'No.'

'No.'

'It's Harold.'

Harold shuffled uncomfortably. Maud winced at the mud compressed into her Axminster.

'He's a local lad, y'see. He doesn't want to dig there. Not so near.'

'Not so near what?'

'These yokels! Frightened, Harold? Frightened you might disturb the fairies at the bottom of the lady's garden?'

He gave Harold a good-natured cuff on the arm and, with a promise to return shortly with a fully operative team, they were gone.

Mystified and annoyed, Maud sought mechanical comfort in routine. She put the kettle on. Mystery upset her. She knew there was a reason for everything and she wanted the explanation for this. She was just pouring out a cup of tea and trying to remember whether she had sugared it when Winifred returned.

She poured out another. Winifred's high spirits didn't ameliorate Maud's frame of mind. It had apparently been quite a morning at the Circle. Another cure was in the offing. A young girl with some sort of paralysis. Already responding to the hands and prayers treatment. All that was needed were some obscure weeds from the end of the garden ...

Maud put out a restraining arm.

'Control, Win. You're getting excited again.' She thrust the cup of tea into her friend's hands.

'It *is* exciting.' Winifred leaned forward conspiratorially. Instinctively Maud did the same. Their eyes locked. '*And* we had a message,' said Winifred.

Maud put down her cup of unsugared tea, folded her arms across her meagre bosom and sighed. 'Another bunch of roses? From Reginald with love?'

'No: this was important. From Floating Cloud himself.'

'In person?'

'In *spirit,* dear.'

Winifred lapsed into one of the hurt silences with which she customarily defended herself against Maud's more persecutory moods.

'Well?'

'Well ... ' Winifred's enthusiasm had wilted. 'Well, it was rather vague, dear,'

'As usual.'

'He says we have "an eventful day" ahead of us, Maud.'

'We don't need a defunct Indian brave to tell us that.' Maud was lining up her heavy artillery.

'Tuesday the eleventh,' said Winifred quickly. 'He told us the date, too. That's next Tuesday.'

Maud frowned dangerously. 'Winifred, I'm not preparing for the end of the world again. All that fuss about cancelling the milk and the papers. And not a scrap of food in the place.'

'There *was* a bad storm that day,' countered Winifred defensively. 'Anyway, even Floating Cloud has his off days, I admit. But he seemed very sure about this one. He was only – reticent about the details ... '

'Perhaps,' suggested Maud with frozen levity, 'he could tell us what's wrong with our telephone. If there *is* anything wrong.'

Winifred, her cup poised at her lips, made a gargling noise into her tea. 'Bother!' she exclaimed. 'I forgot to ask him. Did they fix it? The men?'

Maud explained.

Winifred showed appropriate bewilderment. The behaviour of the man called Harold evidently intrigued her still more. She started to open her mouth, but her question remained unspoken.

The ticking quiet of the parlour was torn by a violent ringing.

'The telephone,' said Winifred superfluously. She shuddered. 'It's another of those calls, Maud. I don't want to answer it.'

Maud went into the hall.

'It must've been a wrong number,' she said on her return.

But Winifred shook her head. 'I'm not so sure ... '

*

Andy replacing Harold, the engineering team returned on the following Monday. Before Winifred could consult with them they had disappeared down the garden and proceeded to uproot the newly-mown border beyond the bottom lawn.

It was a sultry, overcast day. Winifred had one of her headaches. As the gash progressed across the end of the garden, her restlessness increased.

Maud noticed her agitation and was even more concerned to learn about the headache. She had promised to phone Doctor Keen immediately if the headaches recurred.

From the parlour window Winifred watched the men working beneath the outstretched, sagging branches of the old tree.

'I don't like it,' she confessed.

'Have a tablet, dear,' said Maud. 'Doctor Keen said ... '

'Bother Doctor Keen. It's not a question of tablets,' said Winifred. 'It's a question of vibrations.'

She pressed a hand to her forehead to steady a flicker of pain. Then: 'I'm going out,' she announced.

'Oh,' said Maud.

'To the library.'

'But your head – '

'It aches.'

And Winifred Petherbridge departed.

Maud took advantage of her absence to phone Doctor Keen.

'Hearing voices, yes, Doctor ... Erratic behaviour, that's it. And the doilies, of course. For the dustbin, if you please ... Yes, and now the headaches again ... Losing her hold on reality? Well, yes. It's like this phone business: I sometimes wonder, frankly, whether she knows what's real any more ... Or what isn't, as you say, Doctor ... Dangerous? Good heavens, no. At least, I hope not ... I'm sorry? Fits! She's quite harmless, Doctor. Quite harmless ... I just thought you ought to ... Coming round? Oh, I see ... Yes, if you're sure that's necessary. I don't want to upset – anyone. Yes, goodbye, Doctor.'

There. She had done her duty. Just, she realized, as Flo had done her duty for Cousin Albert. But this was all in Win's best interests. Maud seized a duster and started polishing the mantelpiece viciously in an obscure attempt to erase some dark and quite irrational emotions. She was still rubbing energetically at the sideboard, picking up and replacing doilies as she went, when the front door slammed, the china cabinet shivered and Winifred returned, white and breathless.

'Stop the men,' she said, rapping the book in her hand with a peremptory knuckle.

Startled, Maud dropped the duster. While she was retrieving it, Winifred strode to the french windows and, calling and gesticulating wildly, advanced down the garden, her frock billowing busily, towards the two men.

The promise of cups of tea was persuasion enough for Andy to drop the piece of charred, rotten wood he'd just unearthed and stop work. Maud pursed her lips as the two pairs of boots encountered the Axminster for the second time. She rose to her feet, opened her mouth and was promptly silenced.

'Sarah Lambert,' said Winifred.

There was an uneasy silence. Andy, in an attempt to avoid his colleague's eyes, focused on the elaborately patterned doily that cosseted the ageing radio.

'Old Mother Sarah,' Winifred suggested.

'Winifred, what's got into you?' demanded Maud, as words found their way unsteadily back into her brain. 'What must these gentlemen think?'

'Mother Sarah?' said the first engineer. 'That's the old bird Harold was going on about ... '

'I know.' Winifred's eyes gleamed. 'I know why Harold refused to dig here. It's Mother Sarah.'

Maud's features contrived to display ignorance, indignation and curiosity at the same time, with great success. '*What* is Mother Sarah?'

Winifed held up the book authoritatively. 'Sarah Lambert,' she announced, 'was a witch. Allegedly. Here. They tortured her to get a confession. In the usual way. Then they burned her ... '

'That's right,' said the first engineer. 'Harold seemed to think they did it on that patch of common land behind your place. By the tree there. That's what got him: some curse amongst the natives about disturbing the bones ... '

'Doom, doom,' intoned Andy sepulchrally.

'Usual sort of thing,' said his partner. 'Typical Midnight Movie stuff.'

Andy chuckled. 'Harold and the Curse of the Living Dead!'

The two men laughed. Maud essayed an anaemic giggle.

Winifred did not.

'You've got to stop,' she said. 'Don't you see?'

They didn't.

'The wires. The telephone wires: they go right under the place where it all happened. All that horror burned into the soil. Think of the vibrations! Barbaric,' she muttered. 'Just because one of the poor woman's spells failed, and a child died.'

She glared at their bemused faces. 'Don't you see?' she repeated. 'There's no need to go on digging.'

Maud's reason quailed and then rebelled. 'It's crossed lines,' she said defiantly. 'In the roots.'

Winifred opened her book and prodded the words with her forefinger.

'They burned her,' she said, 'three hundred years ago. Exactly. On July the eleventh. It was a Tuesday.'

Maud sat down abruptly. 'An eventful day ahead of us.'

'You all right, Mrs?' asked the first man.

Then everything happened at once.

The doorbell chimed and Maud, barely bothering with the reflex adjustment of her hair in the hall mirror as she passed, ushered Doctor Keen, trousers creaking, into the parlour. He beamed round at the motley company. Winifred cringed her toes. Her vein began to pulse.

'Ah, the boots,' he said.

'Pardon?' said Andy.

'Rubber?' The psychiatrist's eyes glinted.

'Wellington,' said Andy.

Doctor Keen smiled languidly, then clicked into professional gear. 'Well, Miss Petherbridge, how are we feeling today?'

But Winifred had apparently not heard the question. She stiffened, passed a hand over her forehead, left her seat, ignored the company, opened the door and sat down beside the telephone in the hall.

'Winifred, no!' cried Maud.

The sudden burst of ringing from the phone startled them all. Winifred, biting her lower lip, straightened her shoulders, breathed deeply and lifted the receiver to her ear.

As she listened to the familiar, premonitory buzzing, Maud went into urgent, whispered consultation with Doctor Keen. Winifred's voice recalled them.

'Please, there's no need ... Don't – please don't cry,' pleaded Winifred, her face creased with sympathetic pain. 'Sarah ... Sarah ... Can you hear me?'

The company sensed Winifred's confusion and agitation.

'It's clear. Clearer than before,' she said. 'But she's not listening. I can't make her hear.'

'You see,' whispered Maud. 'There's no one there, Doctor.'

'Fantasy usurps reality,' nodded the doctor sagely. 'What is she saying, Miss Petherbridge?' He offered a kindly smile. 'Tell us what she is saying.'

Winifred ignored him. The voice claimed her full attention. This time she did not interrupt.

Maud watched her unhappily. 'Tell the doctor, dear,' she prompted. 'Tell him what it's saying.'

Winifred's voice was flat with barely suppressed emotion; she quoted falteringly as if giving dictation to a backward secretary. '"Will you hear me?" she keeps saying. "Please believe me ... Let me speak ... I want her to live." Now she – she's – oh no!'

Winifred's face contorted with pain.

'No fits?' muttered Doctor Keen grimly. 'I thought you said ... '

'What is it, Win? Whatever ... ?'

'That crying. Such – ' Winifred caught her breath ' – such anguish.' She addressed the voice on the phone, evidently attempting to soothe and console, but there was a growing edge of desperation to her own voice which betrayed rising hysteria.

'I can't seem to get through,' she cried bitterly. 'Please don't – shout like that ... Pardon? "The flames." *What* flames?'

Maud tensed. Doctor Keen nodded significantly and took a step forward.

Winifred's left hand tortured the telephone cord. She looked at them, pleading, helpless. 'She's – no! – she's screaming now. "Stop the flames."' She listened. '"Believe me!"'

Winifred was struggling to breathe as if the air about her was thick and acrid. 'I understand ... ' she gasped. 'Forgive us ... '

There was an agonized pause. Then Winifred shrieked and flung the receiver away from her. Maud rushed forward. Winifred's face had distorted unnaturally; her mouth twisted as if to release a burning howl of desolation and despair that passed beyond comprehensible pain ...

Doctor Keen picked up the receiver, listened to it, shook his head resignedly and replaced it. He turned to his patient who had collapsed in Maud's arms sobbing.

The two engineers made an embarrassed and hasty departure as he administered the tranquillising shot. 'Dotty as a domino,' said Andy as the van pulled away. 'I'm all for tolerance, mind you, but that one needs putting away. Honest!'

Winifred's composure returned only fitfully. There was something that obviously still worried and obsessed her. Her brows creased with the effort to grasp and face the fact.

'Try not to worry, dear,' said Maud, her voice belying her words. 'Everything's all right now. Sarah Lambert won't bother us again ... '

Her words only distressed Winifred still more.

'Relax,' said Doctor Keen.

'It wasn't ... ' began Winifred. She fought against the weight of her descending eyelids. 'I'm not sure. Perhaps – it wasn't Sarah Lambert's voice.'

Doctor Keen looked sadly at Maud. 'How can you possibly expect to know, Miss Petherbridge?'

'Because,' said Winifred, 'it sounded like – well, I thought – it was *my* voice.'

And, eyes closed, she sank back into the waiting embrace of Doctor Keen.

*

The ambulance came and took Winifred away the following day. It was Tuesday the eleventh of July.

Doctor Keen had asked Maud to sign a form. 'It's for her own good,' Maud told herself. She must not waver now. It was the only rational course. Was this really how Cousin Flo had felt? About Albert and the Good News. Flo had been – had *seemed* – so sure about his delusions. Of course this witch business, this Old Mother Sarah thing, was fantasy too, and of course Doctor Keen would know the right drugs to put Win straight quite soon, but Maud had still been haunted all that lonely day by the expression on her friend's face as, heavily sedated, she had been carried to the ambulance.

'Betrayal,' it said.

And then the words. 'I must stay with you,' Win had protested feebly as they shut the doors. 'Believe me ... '

*

Maud had gone to bed early.

She opened the window. The air outside was as hot and thick as it was in the silent bedroom. She could make out the scar beyond the fence where the earth was prised apart beneath the elm. The tree rose massively, darkness clinging to its heavy boughs. Maud pulled her nightgown more tightly around her. It wasn't so difficult to believe this was the site of that ancient cruelty when it was dark and you were alone. 'Such bigotry,' she thought. Obviously witchcraft was an absurdity, a delusion, like Winifred's antics at the Healing Circle. But to burn a living body because it held different beliefs from your own ... What reason could explain or justify that?

She drew the curtains quickly.

As she climbed into bed the first low drum roll of thunder broke over the horizon. She wondered whether Winifred had heard it too ...

*

Winifred had.

Weary of her cramped, arid room, and exhausted by ineffectual protest, tranquillising tablets and the strangeness of the day, she had fallen asleep early. But the bed was unfamiliar and her mind was restless.

The thunder rolled and echoed distantly and she turned, her mind churning, in the shallows of sleep.

For a moment a deep calm soothed her. The cottage. She was back at home. Maud was snoring in the next room as usual. Then, with a whipcrack of lightning, the nightmare was upon her.

Fire split the sky open, burned her eyes. The earth buckled and heaved. Roots, loosened roots, screaming, were ripped out of the burning earth. She looked up. The ancient tree, roaring with fire, was moving against the sky. She looked up. Was toppling. She looked up. Flames capering wildly, swooping heavily down.

'Maud,' she shouted. 'Maud!'

She looked up.

And saw the white door. Someone at the observation window. They'd heard her. Maud. The old elm. Maud was in danger. She hurried to the door. She must make a phone call.

'Tomorrow,' said the new night nurse.

'Now!' demanded Winifred, her eyes wild and bright with urgency.

'Did we take our tablets?' asked the nurse. She peered hopefully over her shoulder down the corridor. 'A doctor,' she said desperately.

'A telephone,' said Winifred, equally desperate.

'Wait here.'

'No time!'

There was an unhappy struggle and the younger woman won. She turned the key in the lock and breathlessly departed.

Winifred seized the handle and twisted it despairingly. She pressed her face against the door. Footsteps receding down empty, polished corridors. And the cottage. The cottage was in flames.

Sobbing, she banged with her fists on the door.

'Will you hear me?' she called. 'Please, believe me ... '

A phone. She must get to a phone at once. Her voice grew shrill. 'Let me speak!'

Maud, dear, blind, bigoted Maud was trapped in the flames.

'I want her to live ... '

Winifred's sobs reached a crescendo. 'The flames ... Stop the flames!'

The air, charged with her howl of despair, echoed infinitely out from the tiny room.

She collapsed on the bed. The roots had been ripped out. The earth was on fire. Sarah Lambert was burnt. Maud would burn. A curse – human, racial, centuries old. Winifred clasped her hands together.

'I understand,' she pleaded once again. 'Forgive us ... '

The room darkened at the edges and a gaping blackness folded in.

*

Maud snored.

The heavy night air stirred, fumbled the bedroom curtains and tensed itself for the impending storm.

When the fury was unleashed outside, Maud's snores merely hesitated, rose an abrupt semitone and settled comfortably into another equally sonorous key.

Flickers of lightning snarled at the sky and played about the waiting elm.

Finally the mound in the bed heaved, turned over and put out an arm. Maud's eyes were staring wide. She groped for the bedside lamp. Sitting up, she strained to catch the sounds that had insinuated themselves into her sleep. But the enraged, dyspeptic growling of the storm confused her ears.

She eased herself to the edge of the bed, her feet searching for the slippers Winifred had crocheted for her last winter, and made her way to the door. She switched on the light and stood at the top of the narrow stairway, tense, expectant, waiting for the thunder to diminish.

Perhaps she had been dreaming after all.

For a second the storm held its breath, and then Maud gasped. Blue fire tore down the night, the lights in the cottage fused, and Maud heard the sound distinctly.

The telephone was ringing.

At this hour! Maud hesitated, frightened and uneasy. She made a decision to go back to the safety of her bed rather than risk the stairs, treacherous in the dark.

She narrowed her eyes in the effort to hear more clearly. Was the phone really ringing?

Maud debated again. Her reason fought, quavered and, quite unexpectedly, surrendered to impulse. She started to feel her way, step by blind step, down into the small hallway towards the noise.

As she reached the last few stairs, her progress had become much easier. She could make out the details of the grandfather clock and the telephone table at the end of the hall quite clearly.

She approached the phone, grasped the receiver.

'Hallo ... ?' She listened. 'Yes, I *can* hear you ... Flames? I'm sorry; this isn't the fire brigade ... '

Maud turned towards the open parlour door, and dropped the phone.

She went to the doorway.

She looked up.

The night was red and loud with fire. The tree was blazing. Flames raged up through the boughs. The garden lurched, swayed upwards. The elm – heavens! – the elm was shuddering. Was starting to fall. Was ripping those cables out of the earth.

Appalled, Maud stumbled to the front door. Whimpering with frustration and fear, she scratched her nails against the wooden panels, hunting for the two bolts she had carefully secured a few hours earlier. She wrenched open the door.

The cottage shivered.

The blow struck Maud to the floor. Smoke and plaster choked her lungs.

Hardly daring to move, hardly believing she *could* move, she raised her head, painfully. Amidst the debris that had been the stairs, she could dimly distinguish the charred bough that had smashed through the wall and across her bedroom like a smoking, black fist. A discoloured doily decorated one of the branches.

Her bed, she realized, had been punched into the floor.

The telephone receiver swung limply from its cord barely a foot from her face. She seized it.

'Win,' she sobbed. 'Is it you? Are you still there? Win, dear! Forgive me. Dear heaven, forgive! I'll see Doctor Keen tomorrow. Thank God you phoned ... ! Otherwise ... Winifred ... ?'

But the line merely buzzed, clicked and went dead.

The Man Called James

ABEE BLUNDERED SLEEPILY PAST A treasure trove of dahlias; doves soothed one another in the lazy, summer air; a siren whined dismally across the simmering moors; and the man called James sat back in his chair and gazed comfortably across the patio. He grinned, whether at herself or to accommodate the sun's glare, Maud wasn't sure. Feeling optimistic, she assumed the former, and warmed to him. She waved a languid, slightly wrinkled finger towards the teapot and raised an eyebrow.

'No, ta. Thank you.'

Precisely how and why the young man had first materialized in her garden was still a mystery to her, but now that he was here, young and determined to be companionable, she saw no reason to encourage his departure. It wasn't every day that handsome young men arrived for morning tea. Especially with Gerald away in town for the day.

Behind her the dahlias shivered and yielded up a large white cat with aristocratic pretensions.

'Healthy cat you've got there, Mrs. Very nice. Healthy.'

'Haddock,' said Maud.

'Pardon?' said the visitor.

'We spoil him,' explained Maud.

The young man reached down but the cat turned disdainfully

away. Maud admired the long, firm fingers. 'Gentle,' she thought. And she remembered Gerald.

'You're fond of animals too,' she said.

The grin overreached itself, broke into a laugh. 'Love 'em,' he said. 'That's the problem. I used to have all sorts of pets as a kid. When they'd let me. All sorts. Budgies, tortoises, caterpillars. Even had a hen once. Mrs Poot I called her. Very healthy, she was. Very healthy. At first.'

The young man screwed up his eyes and lapsed into silence. Maud helped herself to tea in an encouraging sort of way. Mechanically she shook two tablets on to her hand and swallowed them.

'Foot,' said the man. He sighed.

Maud tried to look intelligent.

'It was her foot. She had this terrible limp, see. Fox had a nip at her. Maimed.'

Maud's eyes sympathized with him from behind her cup. Compassion was so much easier when people were beautiful, she realized. The man's eyes glistened.

'It's suffering,' he said. 'I can't bear to see it. I abhor pain. Know what I mean?'

Maud knew what he meant, and was about to murmur platitudinous agreement when the stranger, his chair crashing to the floor, leapt to his feet and with an anguished cry, rushed down on to the lawn.

Maud sat, dazed, and wondered whether she ought to phone the police. Or the hospital. With some apprehension she watched the man engage in an obscure struggle with the azaleas. A screech and the cat erupted simultaneously from the bushes; a white comet streaked up the garden and shot over the high wall.

The man walked towards her, carefully cradling his hands. His eyes were moist and glittering, his breathing laboured.

'What – ?' she began.

Then she saw the dove. One of its wings stuck out at an improbable angle. Ripped feathers were sticky with dark blood.

An eye, bright with fear, blinked up at her between the sensitive fingers.

'Bloody cat,' said the man.

'It's nature,' said Maud.

'Nature!' The man gritted his teeth. 'Bloody nature. Red in tooth and bloody claw.'

'It'll live,' said Maud. 'It'll heal. A splint ... '

She reached out her hand, laid it on the young man's arm.

'Suffering,' said the man. He pulled his arm away. 'It's suffering.' He sucked in air painfully between clenched teeth.

The dove stirred in his hands.

The man gasped, a dry sob in his throat. His cheeks had grown flushed. With a sudden, savage movement he laid the bird on his knee and wrenched the neck sideways from the body. He deposited the warm heap of feathers on the table between them and, breathing rapidly, stared wildly at it for a moment.

Maud stared at the young man. Then she stared at the feathers. Then she stared at the young man again.

He laughed.

'All over,' he said. 'That's always the worst bit. Know what I mean? You all right, Mrs?' Concern filled his dark, brown eyes; then understanding. 'Oh, sorry.'

He lifted up the dishevelled corpse and examined the tablecloth.

'It'll wash out,' he said. And flung the clump of feathers in among the dahlias.

A circling helicopter droned distantly overhead.

Maud wished uneasily that Gerald wasn't so far away.

'It would have lived,' she murmured.

'It was maimed,' he said. 'It was in pain. Now it isn't!' He leaned forward. 'You see,' he explained, 'I have this gift. They don't understand. But I can tell *you*. You're different. I've had it for years. It was Mrs Poot, really. She, like, showed me the light. She revealed the gift. The power.'

He folded his tanned arms and raised his face to receive the warm benediction of the summer sun.

'I stop pain,' he announced simply. 'It's my mission.'

Maud's face registered interest as skilfully as it could. Why hadn't they had a telephone extension installed nearer the patio, she thought.

'Want to hear about it? My mission.'

Maud hesitated. Where *had* the man come from? And why here?

'You're sure you're all right? You look a bit pale. Don't get me wrong: I don't mean unhealthy. Just, like, pale.'

Maud assured him of her health and felt decidedly wan.

'Tell me,' she said. 'About your mission.'

The young man beamed. 'I knew you'd understand. We're the sensitive ones, you see. *We* feel it. All around us. The pain. The suffering. Sometimes – d'you know this? – sometimes I can't hardly breathe for the weight of it all, the stifling weight, as you might say, of mortality.'

Maud watched his knuckles whiten, saw an evidently familiar anguish darken in his eyes.

'Maiming, disease, deformity.' His voice trembled. 'You can't just sit back, let all that suffering go on, now, can you? Mrs Poot showed me that. I just can't let it happen any more.'

Maud felt her heart starting to pulse with unnecessary vigour. She essayed a sympathetic nod. 'Have you – stopped pain in many animals like this?' she asked, picking up a stray feather and gesturing vaguely towards the dahlias.

'Hundreds,' he said. 'Thousands. When they let me. Heart-breaking work it is. Soul-destroying. Really drains you. But then, you see, it's my mission. However,' he pushed his cup to one side and leaned confidentially across the table, 'it's nothing to what it costs bringing deliverance to the others.'

His brows creased.

Maud was bewildered; her mind resisted comprehension. The young man glanced at her, misread her confusion and offered a reassuring smile.

'The others?' whispered Maud. She focused on the crack in the teapot lid, the lean-to shed that had been threatening to surrender and lie down ever since they'd moved in, the gladioli glowing under the pelting sun, and fought back the encroaching haze of unreality.

'The others,' nodded the stranger. 'It's everywhere. The ills that flesh is heir to, as you might say. This mortality – it's not just for the animals, is it?' He chuckled. 'Mr Bonham showed me that. Lovely bloke, he was. He started me off, see, on the *real* mission.' He passed a hand over his forehead. 'So much work to be done. So much. And *they* don't help. Always interfering.'

'They?'

Maud became aware of the return of the persistent helicopter, circling methodically over the empty moors. Understanding unfolded like a black flower.

'Yes, they interfere. I knew you'd understand. Did you read about Mr Bonham? Mr Sidney Bonham. Down Stanford way. It was in all the papers. They got it all wrong, of course. They always do.'

Maud remembered Sidney Bonham of Stanford. And the rest. Only with an effort could she disguise her quickened breathing. Her voice, when it emerged, seemed to have been squeezed up a semi-tone.

'He was – crippled, wasn't he?' she said. 'Like the others.' She stared at him, slowly shaking her head.

'I delivered them,' said the young man. Pride merged with pity in his features. 'All of them. And lots more besides.'

'It's death,' whispered Maud.

'Of course,' he said. 'Release. It's the dying – not death – that hurts. Age. Decay. Accidents. *There's* the suffering.'

'Murder,' said Maud.

The man winced. His smile subsided into grief. 'Please,' he said. 'You're not – like that. Not like them. You understand.'

Impulsively he extended a hand. Impulsively Maud thrust his arm, a teacup and the bottle of tablets noisily away from her.

'My husband,' she said breathlessly. 'Here. Any minute. Go, please.'

'I understand,' said the young man. 'Don't get up. I couldn't stay anyway. So much to do.'

He moved sadly towards the garden gate, stooping to pick up the tablets. He glanced at the label. He paused, turned, and came back towards her.

'Aspirin,' he said. 'Are you in pain?'

Maud, still seated, backed away from the table, away from the secure, blue-check covering of the voluminous tablecloth. Her blanket slipped from her knees.

'Please. The police. I'll phone ... '

The man stared at her.

'Your seat. You never said ... ' His voice trembled. 'A wheel-chair!'

He came and stood over her. His brown eyes brimming with infinite compassion, he surveyed her foot, twisted with arthritis. A red stain burned in his cheeks; his nostrils flared as his breathing grew harsh, painful.

'You *are* suffering,' he said.

The young man called James put his sensitive, firm hands gently on Maud's shoulder.

'I can stop pain,' he sobbed. 'It's my mission, see?'

The demented wail of the siren scarcely stirred the drowsing, scented air as the police car crawled systematically, painstakingly towards the house ...

Landscape

A PLAIN REACHES OUT TO THE edges of the world, ringed with mountain pinnacles which pile up, immense and stark, into the richly orange sky. A luminous, greenish-brown mist murmurs lazily across the tall grasses, purple as violets. The air, if air there is, holds its breath, as if waiting. To the right, in the foreground, arches a plant, gigantic and perfectly formed. Its serenely curving branches are weighted with fruits, honey-ripe and tempting as gold. Its ultramarine tendrils reach down to cool themselves in the caressing, coral waters of a great river, which winds on, fringed by a belt of similar plants, and finally loses itself in the smoking russet haze of distance.

In the embracing skies hang two suns, burning indigo.

All appears to be hushed, tranquil. There is no sign of human or animal life. The dark blot, far off to the left, is too small to mar the harmony of the scene. It squats there, a question mark.

The critic stood back. His tongue made appreciative clicking noises.

'I like it,' he said. 'Those trees, the bloom on that fruit. You conjure a world so novel and fantastic with such concrete detail and realism. Art creates nature. And the atmosphere. One can almost breathe the serenity. An Eden of the imagination. Remarkable.'

The old artist's eyes betrayed his pleasure and his sadness. 'It is special,' he said. 'This picture was conceived and painted in a day. I did not eat or sleep. I was a young man then. My brush could find such a landscape, such colours, in the canvas. It is so no longer.'

He summoned two chairs from the floor.

'That was many years ago, before you were born, in the days when man was content to know the barrenness of his own planets without making new machines to bring the stars to his doorstep.'

'No. I imagine the new technology of inter-stellar travel can hold little interest for you. The advancement of knowledge, the cold facts of scientific progress would be irrelevant. *Your* voyages of discovery,' the critic motioned towards the picture, selecting, as he spoke, the words he would use in his article, 'are to inner worlds, infinitely richer.'

'*Were*,' the old man corrected. 'I do not see these things any more.'

A gentle buzz intruded upon the nostalgic silence.

'Excuse me.' The young man looked at the dial on his wrist and spoke briefly, nodding his head. 'My wife,' he announced; 'I shall have to see the other pictures another day. The telecast's started, and I promised the children I'd watch it with them.'

'Telecast?'

'The set-down pictures are due to arrive in five minutes.'

'Ah – this Alpha Centauri thing.'

The young man rose. 'It's quite an event. You must admit that. Man sets his colonizing foot in a new star system! The media have gone into hyperdrive, global frenzy. You must remember your school history primer – all the excitement of that first step centuries ago: primitive man groping for the moon!'

And with that speech, he left. His enthusiasm lingered in the room for some moments.

The artist raised an eyebrow. 'Knowledge,' he murmured. 'Progress?'

*

The family were in the view-room, their silhouettes, bent forward in concentration, stark against the flickering colours of the wall-screen.

His wife smiled, pressed a button, and the man slipped breathlessly into a seat. 'Have they landed yet?'

'Ssh, Dad!' The voice was shrill with indignation.

'They've just relocated to the mini explorer craft, apparently, dear. They're activating its telescans or something.'

The commentator's anxiety was clear. He was filling in time with a halting, layman's explanation of the cosmo-technology which reduced the considerable delay between the transmission of signals from the Mission and their reception within the Solar System. He was wondering whether to repeat his eulogies on the Onward March of Man and his First Real Step into the Beyond when the picture of Pluto Base Control abruptly faded.

The wall went dark for a minute, the youngest child groaned, and then an image materialised unsteadily on the screen.

The outlines were hazy and the contours rather blurred. The eyes of the world strained to organize the impressions into a coherent picture.

In the foreground stood a large, dark structure. Parts of it were in heavy shadow, but the patterns of light on its surface suggested some sort of metallic object.

'What's that, Daddy? Is it a monster?'

The commentator, his voice vibrant with excitement, helped. 'In the foreground we can make out the shape of the A.G.C. – the Anti-Gravity Craft – which has carried the two man crew – the man and wife crew, perhaps I should say – on this first, momentous, one-way voyage to the stars. I think' – there was a premonitory crackling – 'Yes, we're getting sound contact with the stellarnauts now.'

' ... And more than the sheer immensity of the place is its beauty. It's staggering.' It was the woman who spoke.

Her husband broke in. 'We're going to cut to the telescans in the hoverbug and take a trip across these – prairies. Give you some idea of the landscape. A glimpse of Paradise.'

The family sat forward, tense, as the picture flickered and settled. Then alien horizons opened up in their room.

'Daddy, what's the matter with the screen?' the young voice piped. 'The colours are all wrong!'

It was Mother who hushed the boy. Father was very quiet.

The colours were far from wrong, though naturally they lacked the splendour of the original. The purples of the grasses wanted the subtlety and warmth they should have had, and that orange sky, with its twin hanging suns, was drab by comparison with the real picture.

The screen image trembled as the hoverbug came to rest near a patch of what appeared to be foliage of some sort. But the critic had already anticipated what he saw next: the giant plants and their yellow fruits weighting the curving, dark blue branches. Incredulous, he watched the stellarnauts of the new colony as they proceeded, by remote control, to sever samples of the fruit for further investigation.

The mystery of the dark blot, which squatted near the horizon to the left and which grew bigger as the hoverbug returned, now became clear. It was the A.G.C., the mother craft.

*

The critic's arrival in the artist's room the following day was as abrupt as it was unexpected. But the old man, despite the paleness of his features, was delighted to see him

'I've got something to tell you,' said the young man, trying to modulate the unnecessarily high pitch urgency had given his voice.

'And I've got something to show you.' Pride and excitement met in the artist's announcement.

'But this is something amazing, inexplicable. Disturbing.'

'So,' said the other, 'is this. Look!'

He pointed to an easel bearing a large canvas on which the paint still glistened.

'It has returned,' he said, humbly, wearily. 'I have been up all night. A terrible struggle.'

But the critic cast only a cursory glance at the vision before him. His racing mind was elsewhere.

The old artist stepped back. He was waiting. He searched the young man's eyes.

Preoccupied, the critic's gaze failed to focus. This was no time to scrutinise and assess another painting. There were far more important questions to ask. Besides, the colours were garish. But, to humour the old man with a response, he clicked briefly, efficiently, impatiently into professional vein.

'The element of the fantastic is still here, in abundance,' he pronounced. 'But now the inner world of the imagination has not been held in check by the – disconcertingly – objective realism of the former painting. A self-indulgent extravagance, the pursuit of fantasy for fantasy's sake have – forgive the brutal frankness of my opinion – led you over the abyss – as it were – into the realms of the merely bizarre and sensational.' The article was already written. 'And now I *must* ask you – tell you – '

The lines of the old man's tired face creased. His eyes were sad.

'It came living from the canvas as the first one did,' he said. 'I thought *you* might see that.'

The critic flushed with shame at his lack of sensitivity. He had not intended to upset the artist, but there were matters of reality more imperative than art just now.

His tone became placatory. 'I see the connection, of course,' he said. 'But aren't the dual visions of paradise on the one hand and hell on the other just a wee bit – ah – jaded today?' He was tempted to sum up his judgement: 'Artistically overworked; morally and psychologically, centuries out of date.' But a belated tact swallowed the thought unspoken.

The old man, disappointed, shrugged his shoulders.

'*Now,*' demanded the critic, 'You *must* tell me – your first canvas – I *must know* – how did you know? – where? – what?' Words foundered in the mire of his bewilderment. 'It's impossible. But *it's all there.* Every detail of the new planet.' He shook his head. 'Is it some sort of cosmic telepathy? A – a breakthrough into some undreamed of extra-sensory dimension?'

The old man tapped his chest. 'It is buried within us all,' he said, 'the vision. Perhaps it is well that only few can unearth such things, and look directly upon them.'

But the young man was already excitedly explaining the details of the telecast pictures from Alpha Centauri that the old artist, engaged in his labours, had missed ...

*

As he spoke, the second day's exploration of the remote planet was under way.

'In fact,' the woman stellarnaut confided to the wall-screens of the world, 'preliminary analysis of the fruit suggests they contain no toxins harmful to man. Mission Control has, of course, as you've heard, forbidden any tasting.' She held a globe of succulent gold up to the nearest camera. 'But don't they look deliciously tempting? One would so like to know ... '

The hoverbug lurched and settled again by the belt of plants it had reached on the previous day.

'This,' said the man, 'is where the excitement really begins. Phase Two of the programme. Reconnoitring on foot.' There followed a brief exchange with Pluto Base. Then – 'We're trusting our personal telescans will help you to share the delights of this astonishing new world with us, in detail, back home.'

His wife's voice, eager, breathless, took over. 'As for the atmosphere of the place, its – its peacefulness is quite indescribable. You'll have to take our words for it – inadequate as they are.'

'We'll cut through these tree-plants to the river and explore downstream,' said the man, 'here where it broadens out and the flow quickens. Okay,' the picture whirled, blanked and reorientated itself, 'here we go ... '

'And man,' announced the commentator, surrendering to his more fulsome vein, 'sets his foot on a world beyond the known planets; takes a new step forward in his – and her – quest for knowledge and the colonizing of new worlds.'

The world gazed comfortably on.

*

The old artist listened with growing fascination. Then he stood up, pointed a trembling finger at the new canvas, and tapped his forehead.

'I saw it,' he said simply. 'Here.'

The critic's disappointment escaped in a sigh. The old man had not understood.

'*Look*!' repeated the artist. He held up the heavy picture. The younger man finally looked, saw and studied the painting closely for the first time.

Some primal quake had torn a gash in the earth from horizon to orange horizon. A river plunged into the wound. A cataract of blood, it raged from cliff down to cliff, and beyond, till the clouds of scalding darkness, shot through with massive bolts of flame, engulfed it. In the deeps of the abyss, to the right, green eyes flared, and wet, monstrous shadows heaved in black caverns.

And every inch of those mind-defying walls of rock, dripping with luminous, yellow slime, seemed to seethe with the interminable writhing and coiling of sinister life.

'Do you see now?' demanded the old man. 'Here at the top of the cliff, on the left. Just like the first canvas. Traces of the same purple grass. So vivid. So strange. And, see there, the same delicate, hanging fronds of that tree. Unearthly blue. Identical. I saw it all.' He shrugged a sigh. 'Don't you understand? *It's the same world* – it's like a continuation of my original landscape.'

The critic peered closer.

It was true.

He felt a prickling at the nape of his neck. A primordial terror stirred in the deep places of his mind. The artist, he realised, had genuinely witnessed a nightmare vision of hell.

And this was only an impression on canvas of the scene.

Horrified, he studied the details, the two suns, the distant tree. 'Not quite identical,' he murmured, inclining his head. Together they examined the meticulous brush strokes. Together they saw:

Several of the most prominent golden, honied fruits had been severed from the boughs.

*

Across the gulfs of space, on an alien world, a man and a woman continued their walk by a river, beside a grove, beneath two suns.

In the distance, rainbowing clouds of reddish mist swirled and boiled before swallowing the now turbulent river from their sight. A murmuring roar of low thunder made the luxuriant purple grasses shiver.

'It sounds like a vast waterfall – a crimson Niagara,' said the woman, smiling, and hurried forward.

The man stopped. 'No. The Schedule. We *must* return now,' he said. 'Edict from Base Control.'

But his wife's eyes were pleading. And he too was struggling with intense curiosity.

'Forget Base Commander for a minute,' she said. 'What harm could a minor digression in Phase Two do?'

'Interstellar Code Infringement,' muttered the man, 'as you well know.'

'Hardly an earth-shaking sin!' She touched the arm of his space suit but stopped herself from adding, 'dear'. 'Forget the rule book, the protocols, just for once. For heaven's sake.' She considered the viewing millions on Earth and its satellite colonies, the history books still unwritten, and stretched out an arm. 'A whole new world lies before us. It's a fresh beginning for mankind ... '

He hesitated. Then he took her gloved hand. A fresh beginning ...

Some way ahead of them, the serpentine creature escaped, writhing, from the smoking blackness of the abyss, which was still hidden from their sight. Fold upon glistening fold, and radiant in sinister majesty as the dawn, it crawled, rejoicing, freed from the starless canyons of unending night beyond.

It coiled in a tree beside the rushing waters of luminous coral, and waited to welcome the two approaching visitors, a shining fruit, ripe and golden, in its jaws.

Remote Control

'I'LL KILL HIM!' THE WORDS WERE decisive and Gerald's voice was loud. But his wife was not deceived.

She laughed curtly. 'You couldn't kill a geriatric hedgehog with a ten-ton truck.' Scorn creased her lips to a familiar sneer. 'You can't even decide to kill a fly without giving it the last rites!'

'I'll kill him,' said Gerald Bland. He growled unconvincingly and stabbed with a vicious forefinger at the photographs that he'd just found in his wife's handbag. He peered again, his eyes moist with hurt pride, resentment and jealousy, at the pictures of betrayal: the Habitat lights, the leather chairs, the imitation-log gas fire, the ice bucket chinking with impressively labelled bottles of wine, and the compulsory deerskin rug on which the lovers languished, sparsely clad, evidently taking turns to giggle lewdly at the camera in a series of suspended animations. 'It's a love-nest,' he said. 'That's what they'll call it in the papers when I take you both to court.'

'You wouldn't dare!' Mrs Bland fumbled for her cigarettes.

'I might.' But he knew she knew he wouldn't. 'An ageing, trendy bachelor's love-nest,' he repeated. 'How can you!' He held a photograph up to the light, squinting his left eye. 'And what exactly are you doing with that lettuce?'

'An executive suite,' said Mrs Bland: 'that's what it's called. Not a love-nest. Clifford is in Middle Management.' She flicked at her lighter. 'Upper Middle. And rising. He's big in cat food. Time and Motion, if you really want to know.'

Gerald Bland didn't. 'He certainly seems to be managing all right for himself with you,' he said, his voice sharpened with malice and envy.

Beatrice Bland smiled in happy reminiscence. 'He manages all right,' she said, 'in time *and* motion. Far better than some people I could mention.'

Gerald kneaded the arms of his chair savagely.

'Anyway,' said his wife, 'it was a salad.' She shook the lighter. 'What else *can* you do with lettuce? You've got a degenerate mind, Gerry Bland.' Then she giggled, moistening her full lips with a slow sweep of her tongue, tasting memory. 'All that mayonnaise! So expensive, and so – sticky!'

The lighter flared, she inhaled luxuriantly, and Gerald Bland, in a movement as violent as it was inappropriate, launched himself from his chair, limbs gesticulating wildly. He landed unexpectedly close to her and found himself glaring into her eyes with furious and disquieting intimacy.

'Whatever – !'

'You – you bitch!' He faltered and glared at her nose instead.

She breathed out a fulsome cloud of smoke that loitered about his reddened face.

He coughed and stepped backwards. 'Stop,' he said. 'You've got to stop.'

'Smoking or Clifford?' enquired Beatrice Bland, suavely. 'If you're going to nag me about the evil weed again ... ' She picked up a magazine.

Gerald Bland went pale. His feet moved him urgently in futile eddies around the room. He raised a fist. He wanted to hit out, sweep ornaments off shelves as they did in the movies, but reason and parsimony marred his rage. Finally he picked up a newspaper, shook it open with unnecessary vehemence, and found a torn handful of newsprint in his right fist.

'I'll kill him,' he muttered.

Shreds of the personal columns fluttered on to his knees. Among the litter of lonely hearts – now broken – and naughty nightwear, one advertisement abruptly focused.

He picked it up and scrutinised it more carefully:

'Helpless? Lost? Despairing? Has your problem reached crisis point? Psychic Consultations can help.'

'Psychic Consultations!' Gerald Bland snorted. But, glancing sideways at his wife, he made a mental note of the phone number all the same.

'You even apologise to the roses when you prune them,' said Mrs Bland.

*

'Telepathy, Clairvoyance, Clairaudience, Psychometry, Psychokinesis, Precognition, Levitation ... ' The man in the white coat attempted a twisted smile and adjusted his green eye shade. 'Our expert mediums are at your service.'

Mr Bland hesitated.

'It's my wife,' he explained, glancing again around the room, not sure whether to be relieved or disappointed by the notable absence of crystal balls and lingering ectoplasm.

The man nodded encouragement. 'When did she – pass over?' he enquired.

Gerald shook his head.

'I see.' The man picked up his pen. 'Intemperance? Frigidity? Insatiability? Incompatibility ... ?'

'Infidelity,' said Mr Bland.

The pen scribbled briefly on the pad.

Gerald took a deep breath. 'His name is Clifford. He's something unimportant in cat food and he lives in an ostentatious bachelor apartment – on the posh side of town, of course – with leather upholstery, pseudo log fires and rugs that he probably claims to have shot for himself on Safari with The Boys.' He reached into his jacket. 'I've got the address out of her.' He thrust a card across the desk. The truth was that Beatrice, finding him the previous night groping surreptitiously in her handbag for clues, had flung the address at him as a scornful challenge: 'Are you a man or a ferret?' she'd taunted. 'And these are the photographs,' she added. 'Should help to perk up your jaded baubles.'

The man lifted his shade and studied the pictures – at unnecessary length. He moistened his thin lips. 'She's a fine figure of a woman,' he said, wondering about the lettuce. He sat back. 'How can we help?' he said.

Gerald sighed. 'It was your ad,' he said. 'I'm helpless, lost and despairing. My problems have reached crisis point. If you don't come up with some answers, I shall probably kill myself ... '

'Or her,' suggested the man slowly.

Gerald Bland was indignant. 'I love her,' he said, 'I think.'

'Or him,' said the man.

He pressed his lips together, seeming to savour the ensuing silence.

'I couldn't,' said Gerald. 'Some can; some can't. I can't. She's right. I agonize over every spider I swill down the plug-hole in the bath. I just couldn't ... '

'But perhaps *we* could,' said the man. He leaned forward; a green shadow slanted across his face.

Gerald pulled his chair closer. 'Murder?' he whispered.

'A solution.'

Mr Bland's moral fibres thrilled. His horizons lurched. 'No,' he said. 'Besides, it's illegal. And inhumane ... ' But the fleeting vision, once glimpsed, persisted: Beatrice repentant, weeping and almost submissive; marital vows and felicities revitalized; paradise regained in a world free from the menace of Middle Management ...

'How?' he asked.

The man spoke with hushed zeal. 'Psychic Projection,' he said. 'The Targ and Puthoff research experiments at Stamford in '73. You've read of Out-of-the-Body experiences?'

Gerald nodded uncertainly. Hadn't there been something in the Sunday supplements once?

'The medium projecting his mind through geographical space – travelling to a neighbour's house, to another town, to another continent ... '

Mr Bland's features sagged. His current, all too human problems had sapped any curiosity he might have mustered about such spectral matters.

'Picture it!' The man's voice rose. 'The medium sits here at base in trance while his mind goes travelling. We simply feed him a target, an address, map coordinates, whatever – and he's off. He'll describe target locations quite unknown to him *in photographic detail* – a room, an island, a secret Air Force base – as if he's actually there. Remote Viewing we call it. No wonder the CIA showed such an interest from the start ... '

Gerald's head began to ache.

The man's voice went on. 'And that's the most intriguing aspect of it all – '

'Is it?' asked Gerald Bland, his own mind wandering on travels of its own.

The eye shade lifted a moment, suspecting mockery.

' – It seems that in some almost tangible, inexplicable form the medium is *virtually present* at that location – sightings have been reported of ghostly presences – able to break a photo-electric beam or trip a switch ... '

Gerald Bland pressed a hand to his forehead. It all sounded more like Spielberg than science to him, and the room was growing stuffy. 'How does this help to commit – '

'To achieve – the solution?' The man tapped the table. 'Look at these photos,' he said. 'What do they suggest to you?'

Gerald clenched his fist against the rising of old passions. He drew breath; the inventory of implications was a long and painful one ...

'Able to trip a switch,' repeated the man, enhancing significance with alliteration. 'Or turn a tap. On an imitation-log gas fire, for instance ... '

'Cat food Romeo found gassed in Middle Management love-nest,' whispered Gerald Bland. 'It's almost humane.'

'Death by misadventure,' said the man.

'Murder by Remote Control,' said Mr Bland. 'The perfect cr – '

'The perfect solution.' The man's eyes glittered in green shadows. He reached for papers. 'We'll need your signature of course, Mr Bland. Indemnity, Expenses, and so forth. Well, when would you like it?'

He rose to his feet.

'Will next Tuesday suit?'

*

'Man or ferret! That's telling him!' Clifford Mann roared his approval, pounded the deerskin rug with one hand and tightened his grip on Beatrice Bland with the other. 'No, don't go, Bea.' He pulled her back down beside him. There was an elasticated twang.

'I must,' she repeated. 'Even ferrets need feeding, Clifford. Clifford!'

'Stay,' he said. 'Stay with a real man.'

Beatrice Bland stared at him: strong, ambitious, with just that hint of – what was it that so teased her? – ruthlessness in those authoritative, cool blue eyes. 'You arrogant chauvinist, you!' she giggled. She thought of Gerald: considerate, sensitive – indecisive, spineless, and supperless. She hesitated.

'Look,' he said. A man of decision. 'We've got to do something about all this. Fix up a better arrangement. Act. This can't go on.'

'Act?' she repeated. She glanced at the clock and struggled to her feet again. 'He'll be wanting his supper.'

'And tomorrow and tomorrow and tomorrow,' said Clifford Mann, recalling a speech from his days as a youthful amateur thespian. 'Supper after supper. Like feeding the cat. D'you put him out at nights as well? At least there's no need to have him neutered! It's got to stop, Beatrice.' ('Yes – ruthless,' thought Mrs Bland). 'I'm not prepared to put up with this time-sharing of you any longer!'

'But he'd starve,' said Mrs Bland. 'He's helpless without me. He'd simply waste away ... '

The clock above the gas fire ticked loudly, decisively in the sudden silence.

'He'd die,' said Mrs Bland.

'Yes,' said the strong man, simply.

The clock ticked on.

'A permanent arrangement,' said Clifford Mann. He spoke thoughtfully. 'But not slow and lingering. Brisk. Efficient. Tidy.' The blue eyes, skilled in the scanning of time and motion charts, narrowed. 'And we'd have to be sure.'

Beatrice Bland's eyes widened. She was appalled. She was excited. She put a cigarette to her mouth and groped for her lighter.

'It's impossible,' she said.

'It's simple.'

She followed his gaze, past the certificates and the deer's head, to the display of rifles mounted on the wall.

'Feed him his supper for a few days more. Pamper him. Agree with him. Allay any doubts. Then' – the plan blossomed as he spoke – 'we lure him here, you keep him occupied and, when the moment's right, you give the signal ... '

She swallowed uneasily. 'The signal?' The lighter gave a dull click.

'Don't worry. We'll fix on something. Some simple everyday motion. Nothing to arouse suspicion. Then, when you give me the cue, in I come and there we are ... '

'And there he is,' said Mrs Bland. She looked down at the deerskin rug, the scene of so many satisfying pleasures, as if the inert body of her husband was already prostrate upon the rough hide.

'It's been said before, but it's either him' – Clifford seized her roughly by the shoulder – 'or me.'

Mrs Bland shivered. 'I suppose that's life,' she said, similarly resorting to the dubious reassurance of platitude: 'you sometimes have to be cruel to be kind.'

Her conscience thus attended to, she lit a cigarette and exhaled expansively.

*

'Tuesday the 15th. Time: 6:00 p.m. Location target: address, as above. Aim: activate gas tap on log fire.'

In a darkened room at the Psychic Consultancy Headquarters, the medium re-read his instructions, held up an affirmative thumb to the green-shaded supervisor, who was settling down in the next room to observe the operation through the glass panel, and sank back in his armchair. He closed his eyes, relaxed his shoulders, and focused his mind on tonight's target ...

*

Silences had grown increasingly tense and wary in the Bland household over the past few days. Both partners were morbidly attentive to the other, suspicious of the other's motives, fearful of betraying their own fell purposes, and doubly guilty both of the courses they had chosen and of their unrepentant determination to see the job through to the end.

The abrupt shrilling of the telephone at seven o'clock on Tuesday evening did nothing to allay the slumbering tensions.

Beatrice Bland reached the phone first. 'Kempston 853000,' she said.

Gerald lurked behind the Evening Chronicle and listened, his nerves on over-drive. Had the plan worked already? He hadn't expected results from those sinister psychics quite so early in the evening. Or had something gone wrong? An astral malfunction? Discovery? The police? His name traced from a file? Worse – the dark doubts crowded in upon him with renewed force – perhaps, after all, this psychic projection business was so much hooey. Secretly he'd suspected it all along; he'd been conned. Worst of all – the Middle Manager was alive and well and doomed to remain so ...

He swept these rioting thoughts to the back of his mind and shifted in his chair to orientate his right ear for maximum reception. His wife's voice was certainly low and her speech quick between the long, attentive pauses.

'Tonight?' she said. 'I thought we'd arranged for tomorrow. It's a bit inconvenient just now' – she glanced across at her husband and flickered a saccharine smile of reassurance – 'Janice.' She wound the cord round her forefinger. 'Can't we – um – sort through knitting patterns another night ... ?'

'Women's talk,' thought Gerald Bland.

'It might make certain people wonder ... ' said Mrs Bland. 'They might want to visit and check up even ... '

'Conspiracy,' thought Gerald Bland, his suspicions suddenly alert and sniffing the air.

'Let him suspect. Let him visit the flat,' said the telephonic tones of Middle Management. 'He doesn't know I'm still at work finishing off these damn schedules. He doesn't realize we're dining out in half an hour ... Are you still there?'

'Yes – Janice,' said Mrs Bland.

Her husband smirked the superior smile of the man who is not so easily fooled into his newspaper.

'Better still: *invite* him to come, encourage him to come. Later, of course. Nine-thirty, say. For a proper adult discussion of mutual problems. Man-to-man stuff. You remember what we said ... '

Anxiety creased Beatrice Bland's forehead. 'I can't ... ' she said.

'You can.' The metallic tones were imperative. 'You will. Look, write a note, if it's easier: *Invitation To A Death*.' A tinny chortle resonated in her ear. 'We'll be ready with Plan A when he arrives. Okay? See you at the *Capri Carbonara* at seven-thirty.'

Mr Bland watched his wife bid farewell to her knitting companion, replace the receiver and write urgently on the telephone pad. He made a mental note to check it out at the earliest opportunity.

'I'm going out,' she said, brandishing her car keys.

'Does Janice need you again, dear?' he asked, sweetly. 'How is she these days? Getting plenty of – satisfaction out of life?'

Mrs Bland paused to look at him warily. 'Are you all right,

Gerald?' Moved by obscure memories of times past and a sense of the transience and, indeed, finality of human affairs, she came back and delivered a parting – almost sentimental – peck to his forehead. 'There're some Alka-salts in the bathroom.'

She turned at the door.

'Actually,' she said, 'it wasn't Janice ... We'll sort things – everything – out later ... '

Later! Realization flooded Gerald Bland's brain. Later! Love birds found cuddling in love-nest gas tragedy. He struggled to his feet. 'Beatrice!' he called, but the car's revving drowned his voice. 'Don't go there. Don't go to him. It's dangerous ... '

Forgetting in his concern to check the telephone pad, Mr Bland seized the keys of the Mini and rushed out of the house after his wife.

*

The entranced medium breathed in long, shuddering sighs. His features distorted under the strain of intense concentration.

The green-shaded face of the supervisor peered tensely through the glass division.

The medium's body stiffened, his head jerked – and his mind projected and soared.

'Rooftops, guttering damaged ... hallway, reception desk of sorts ... up flight of stairs ... wooden doors, heavy, look like oak ... room, spacious ... pair of Chesterfields ... rug, animal, probably genuine ... fire, gas fire, here ... now ... '

'Now!' The supervisor urged him on. 'The tap: find it. Turn it!'

Minutes lengthened. The medium let out a long, agonized moan: the effort, the effort. Then, with a choking cry, he threw his head back and slumped in the chair ...

The supervisor rushed in to ease the medium's transition from trance to full wakefulness.

'Did we do it?' he said.

The other groped among dreams. 'I reckon we did it!' he said. He massaged his forehead. 'But – wow – there're some pretty nasty vibes lingering around that place ... '

*

Having leaped up a dozen stairs and hammered on the heavy oak of the apartment doors for two full minutes, Gerald Bland's knuckles were raw and his pulses racing dangerously. He dismissed the idea, mandatory in the movies, of rushing the doors with his shoulder. Only in Hollywood were doors so vulnerable. He subsided breathlessly to his knees and, heart pounding, pushed open the flap of the letter box. Was it the roaring of his pulse in his head, or could he hear the distant, deadly susurration of gas? 'Beatrice!' he called, recklessly. 'Bea, I know you're in there. Don't worry. I'll get you out.'

Desperation inspired subterfuge. He sought out the caretaker, found his elderly wife at reception, and explained to her – with more drama than coherence – the urgent need to enter Number 36 to check a suspected gas leak. 'It's right in the middle of *Dallas*,' she remonstrated. 'You're not one of these Rippers, are you? Isn't it a terrible world!' and, surrendering the key, she returned to the known and reassuring villainies of Texas.

With a mixture of pride and unease – for he had never broken into premises before, even his own – Gerald Bland entered the apartment. The door clicked shut behind him. He surveyed the room, registering every photographed detail of the scene of his wife's infidelities with morbid and angry relish.

The ticking clock wheezed and struck eight-fifteen.

He coughed and clamped a handkerchief to his face. The room was filling fast with gas. 'Beatrice,' he called again – but a hasty inspection of the adjoining rooms – approach on tip-toe, clench teeth, fling open door with yell – confirmed his fears: the flat was empty. Was his wife really sipping tea and talking knitting with Janice after all?

No distressed damsel. No distressed victim. Only himself, the culprit, lingering at the last place he should be seen in – the scene of his intended crime!

Quickly he went to check the fire with its ever-ready logs and artful ashes, and was seized by another rictus of coughing. Yes! The tap *was* turned on. Scarcely audible, the stealthy hiss of gas insisted. It insinuated itself into every corner of the room. Gerald Bland chuckled and choked. The scheme was working! He must leave at once. He took a last look at the fire – both fires ... ? He put out a hand to steady himself as the walls gave an unexpected inward lurch ... He found himself, strangely, on his knees, reaching out ineffectually for his dropped handkerchief. Yes, everything was still going to plan. The victim would return anon. Nothing was lost. There was everything to play for. All he had to do was depart ...

Success! And with a triumphant croak of laughter, Mr Bland stumbled forward, catching his head on the stones of the hearth.

Gas shifted about him in lethal coils, softly whispering, subtle as a nest of snakes ...

*

'Gerald!'

Mrs Bland, leaving her lover to garage the car, had arrived first and flung open the apartment doors. 'You're early. We invited you for nine-thirty. Can't you do anything properly?'

'Beatrice?' Gerald Bland rose unsteadily to his feet. He touched his forehead with a tentative hand. A smear of blood. Temporary concussion. Then came the fist-blow of memory restored. 'Get away from here!' he coughed. 'We must both – get away – ' He tottered towards the door.

But his wife needed no telling. She was already in the hallway. Gerald heard an urgent consultation on the stairs, striding footsteps, and the man, Clifford, Ageing Lothario of the Love-nest, he of Middle Management (Upper), Connoisseur of Feline Foodstuffs, Mann, leader of men and leader-astray of Mrs Beatrice Bland, stood framed in the doorway.

'It's all right,' he called. 'I'll handle it. Come here, Bea.' He put an arm round her waist in a protective, a familiar, an outrageous embrace – then motioned her towards her husband. 'Gerald's come for a man-to-man chat about our – situation. Sorry it's so stuffy' – he sniffed – 'so stale in here, Gerry. May I call you that?'

Mr Bland went pink, opened his mouth and coughed.

'Do make yourself at home. Take a seat. Let Bea make you comfortable, eh? The happy couple, eh?'

Gerald's knees buckled and he found himself seated on one of those damned, trendy leather chairs. 'I'll kill him,' he thought. 'I *am* killing him. And he hasn't realised it!' He choked on a rising, hysterical chuckle.

He looked up. What was the man doing behind his back? Why was Bea giving him those looks over his shoulder? Quizzical looks. Significant looks ...

Gerald half turned as Beatrice Bland put a cigarette to her lips.

'No!' he said. 'Come away with me. Now. Rescue. Before you get – harmed.'

The clock ticked.

The gas seeped stealthily into the room.

'*Harmed*!' The cigarette, still in her mouth, flipped in irritated arcs as Mrs Bland spoke. 'You couldn't make a decision to harm a – psychotic ant.'

The old taunts resonated in his brain, but this time Gerald Bland looked into himself. A burst of illumination; understanding flowered. He knew his weaknesses for the strengths they really were. Sensitive, compassionate, gentle: he looked, and saw that he was good. 'Murder!' he whispered, aghast. 'Never.' With the energy of the converted and the desperate, he hauled himself from the chair and staggered to the fire.

Triumphantly, he turned the switch off.

He straightened his back and beamed at his wife. Then he registered what she was doing.

As if giving some prearranged signal, Mrs Bland was taking

out her lighter. She was holding it deliberately aloft. She was flicking it.

'*No!*' said Gerald.

'For the last time, Gerry: I will not be nagged any more ... ' she said.

Gerald ignored the click of a well-oiled safety catch behind him. He reached out urgently, but Beatrice Bland was already pressing on the lighter for a second time. Her thumb moved with brisk and terrible defiance ...

'But – ' he said.

It was the last argument Mr Bland ever attempted with his wife. The lighter flared.

The blast rocked buildings in neighbouring streets, loosened tiles on the other side of the city, and shocked even the hardened readers of the popular press who were treated next day to the loud but simple headlines:

'Explosive Love Nest: Tragic Trio in Gas-leak Mystery Mishap. Can Truth Ever Be Known?'

The Reluctant Murderer

MIDGE, THE GENTLE GIANT, PICKED UP the carving knife, its steel blade glittering in the Christmas candlelight, and waited for his brother to return.

His fingers tightened round the handle.

He listened to Anthony's light, easy laugh from the hallway. 'Another of his women on the phone,' he thought. Couldn't his younger brother give the professional charm a rest even on Christmas Day?

His knuckles whitened.

In front of him on the neatly laid table the turkey, which he'd spent all morning preparing, basting and garnishing, glowed crisp and golden, dispensing its tantalising odours around the cramped and shabbily furnished room. He'd attempted to garnish the room too – with bunches of holly from the landlady and streamers of tinsel left over from the act – but the effect was unconvincing. Nothing could transform theatrical digs into home – not even the magic of the Great Antonio and Midge – especially at Christmas.

'Tony!' he called. 'Happy Christmas,' he muttered grimly.

He twisted the knife-blade, scattering icy spangles round the room like the flashing of the scimitars they used on stage.

Another laugh, smoothly polished, from the hallway.

Midge stared into the lights dancing on the knife, feeling them begin to splash and flicker inside his brain. He gave an involuntary shudder. His breathing deepened, laboured. He tried to speak. 'Tony ... ' It was like calling from the abyss, reaching across the stars ... Foreboding filled his mind, black shadows thickening in his head. He reached for words, struggled for gestures, but impossible forces weighted his arm. Danger. There was danger! Why could he not speak of it. ... ?

'For heaven's sake, Midge! The knife. Give me the knife ... !'

With a hollow rush darkness swallowed the lights and Midge found Anthony, his eyes wide and terrified, cringing beneath him.

'That's right, Midge. Give me the knife ... '

Midge felt bewildered. Meekly he allowed himself to be settled back in his chair.

Tony took the knife, took charge – the capable one, as always.

'I'll carve,' he said. 'You take it easy. Are you feeling better now ... ? Look, Midge, you've got to tell the doctor about these blackouts. Next time we're home. Get some tablets. Hell, you could have killed me just then – you know that?'

Midge shook his head. 'Never,' he said.

'You don't know your own strength.'

'Kill my dearest kid brother?' said Midge.

'Your *only* kid brother!' Anthony poured two generous sherries and pushed one across the table. 'This really is a splendid turkey.'

Midge watched him pick up the knife. Memory sparked in his head. He struggled to capture it, hold it.

'That was Mrs Logan-Pearce,' said Anthony, savouring the juicy slivers of turkey as they peeled off his knife. 'On the phone. She was confirming the New Year's Eve booking, bubbling with champagne and Christmas spirit – full of call-me-Janice and why don't we make magic, perform a trick or two together sometime ... Women!'

Midge stared at him, deftly wielding the knife. With a sudden glint of candle light the memory focused.

'Pass your plate, Midge.'

'No!'

Anthony's brow furrowed. 'Midge?'

'No,' he repeated. 'We mustn't do it. The New Year's Eve show. Let's say no. Cancel.'

Anthony sighed. 'She was only kidding,' he began. 'Flirting. Like all the others. It's nothing serious ... '

Midge reached across and grasped his brother's wrist. 'I've got this feeling,' he said. 'I don't understand it.' He gestured helplessly, at the shining knives, the crimson tears amidst the holly thorns. 'I ... I smell blood,' he said simply.

Anthony looked with concern into his big brother's eyes. 'You'll be talking about vibrations next,' he said, 'and opening at the end of the pier with your crystal ball! Look, we're in the magic not the mumbo-jumbo business. The only fortune we can tell is the one we make – and that'll be even smaller if we go around cancelling engagements. Right?'

Midge shook his head and released his grip.

'The dinner's getting cold,' said Anthony. He picked up his glass. 'Here's to us. A happy Christmas!'

'God rest ye merry gentlemen; let nothing you dismay ... ' sang the radio from the ornate mahogany sideboard.

'And a happy new year,' said Midge shifting unhappily in his seat.

*

But on the whole Midge loved his younger brother and, despite these occasional bleak and bewildering moments of resentment, he had no real desire to murder him. When, therefore, the new year arrived and their hostess approached, he drained another quick whisky and dutifully bared his teeth in a fulsome smile.

'Goodwill to all men,' she said, earrings tinkling. 'And especially to the Great Antonio.' She produced a much-abused sprig of mistletoe and, stooping slightly, pressed a lingering New Year's kiss on Anthony's handsome cheek. She giggled lightly. 'Oh, and one for the magician's assistant.' She reached up to Midge, who towered awkwardly above them both, and delivered an appropriate peck. Midge's smile faltered; his hackles rose. It had always been the same. As a kid he'd always been The Other One, tall and ungainly. Likewise in the early days of the act during the tedium of bazaars and vicars, the panic of pigeons, squashed eggs and tangled bunting: 'Boys and girls, I want a big hand for Uncle Tony, the Kiddies' Friend, and ... sorry, who?... Ah yes ... And Midge!' It would be the same tonight: 'Presenting the Great Antonio ... And Midge.' Overgrown and overlooked, thought Midge; he had gone through life in parenthesis. He had gone through life like a ghost.

But, of course, he'd never seriously wanted to murder his brother.

'Look!' The lady had turned back to Anthony. 'Can I be just *un poco* presumptuous? I want a man. A stranger. The darkest, best-looking one I can lay hands, so to speak, on!' The Great Antonio smiled. His chest enlarged. Midge looked down at them both, and winced. 'When the act's over and you've done, as they say, your thing,' she persisted, 'would you pander to the ethnic whims of our Scottish contingent' – she waved a jewelled hand towards an outbreak of loud laughter and kilts – 'if they're still conscious by then, and bring in the New Year for us? You know, "first foot" it over the doorstep after midnight bearing good luck, coal and so forth ... '

The Great Antonio reached out to take her small, immaculately groomed hand and pressed her fingers to his lips. 'Yours to command,' he said, and bowed.

The earrings flashed. 'Delicious,' she said: 'Isn't your brother just too – mm, delicious!'

Midge growled. 'Much too delicious,' he muttered. 'One of these days I shan't be responsible ... ' He helped himself to another whisky, and realised that a large lady, sprigs of tired heather straggling from her tartan head-band, was conferring with the hostess and pointing at him. He swigged defiantly.

'Wait a moment!' The hostess fluttered eye-lashes heavy with apology and mascara. 'A technical hitch! I'm reliably informed – by our Celtic friend here – that first foot has to be the *tallest* man available. So sorry.' Anthony shrugged with nonchalant charm. 'Your brother'll do. He'll have to.' She turned to Midge, on tip-toe. '*Would* you? *So* kind ... ' And without waiting for a response, she stepped forward, stilling the guests with an elegantly uplifted palm.

'Cabaret time, everybody!' she announced. The party-goers ceased glittering expensively at one another and turned expectantly to the small stage. Lights dimmed promisingly.

'A warm welcome, ladies and gentlemen, for the Great Antonio and – ' she hesitated, remembered, ' – and Midge.'

Midge glanced at Anthony. Of course he loved his brother – really. Anthony grinned and squeezed his arm. Grimly Midge rearranged his features into professional jollity and, with a splash of cymbals, the show began.

Baubles came and went in predictable puffs of multicoloured smoke; pigeons fluttered on cue, more or less; blinking rabbits and miracles occurred with routine panache. Not until they were well launched upon the mystifying marvels of the hypnotic mind-reading routine did drama interrupt the polished suavity of the performance.

It was standard procedure: Midge, after a few histrionic passes and incantations from his brother, had sunk into the usual deep-breathing trance, which he could now contrive quite convincingly, and had suffered the transparent, black-velvet 'blindfold' to be wrapped with extravagant care about his eyes; Anthony was moving purposefully among the audience, the star of the show, asking the customary coded questions.

'My left hand. What do I hold in it?' demanded the Great Antonio of his supine assistant on the stage.

Midge stirred. He pressed white fingers against his damp forehead.

'Take your time.'

'It's a wrist watch,' he said heavily. 'A lady's ... ' But his voice was slurred and thick. His chest heaved and his breathing deepened.

Anthony grew uneasy. He'd warned Midge earlier about drinking before an act.

'The spirit's been meddling with spirits it doesn't understand,' chuckled a drink-heavy voice behind him.

'Cheers!' called a red-cheeked youth anxious to impress the blonde at his table, and raised his glass. 'Tell us the future then, great spirit. Will there be a New Year at midnight, eh?' The girl tittered, pouted him a kiss across the table, then lapsed into silence with an abrupt and startled whimper.

'The future!' The voice was deep and thrilling. It came from Midge, but it resonated strangely in the room.

The Great Antonio stifled his alarm and admiration. This was a new Midge, a Midge with initiative, a consummate actor. He took his brother's lead. 'Look into the seeds of time,' he said. 'Tell us about the future.'

Midge raised an imperious arm. The audience leaned forward.

'A man,' he intoned hollowly, 'will die tonight.' He gestured impressively. 'It is determined. When the bells ring' – the audience followed his pointing finger – 'I will murder that man!'

The guests stared at the Great Antonio, suddenly pale before the finger's unequivocal sentence.

The Great Antonio stared at his brother.

*

Midnight approached.

With order restored, guests raised glasses and voices, assured each other this was a New Year's Eve to remember, and waited for the cabaret to resume. Behind the scenes, voices were lower and more intense.

'I wasn't pretending!' Midge shivered again recalling his involuntary trance. 'It will happen,' he repeated bitterly. 'If the future's fixed, there's nothing we can do to alter it.'

242

'The show,' insisted the Great Antonio, with more urgency than originality, 'must go on.' He helped himself to a couple more indigestion tablets. 'Heartburn. Those canapés.'

'But the prophecy, Tone ... Believe me: that wasn't *me* speaking ... The future ... '

Brother Anthony, the erstwhile Kiddies' Friend, snorted. 'There'll be no future,' he said, 'if we don't finish the show.' He glanced at his watch. 'No future for us. We both die.' He looked sadly back down the long, struggling years. All that effort and experiment; all those despairing rehearsals; all those Women's Institutes from Peebles to Pangbourne ...

Midge watched his brother, the inspiration of their act, the brains, the personality behind their success. 'He has more to lose than me,' he thought. 'How *could* I murder him?'

Their hostess reappeared. 'Well ... ?'

Midge shrugged helplessly. 'The question is,' he murmured, 'how to alter an unalterable fate?' Suddenly his brow uncreased. 'There *is* one way, only one *sure* way ... '

Anthony looked at him, puzzled. 'I don't know what you mean.'

'The show ... ?' asked the lady.

Midge nodded slow approval.

' ... Goes on!' pronounced the Great Antonio.

'Delicious!' She turned to Midge. 'And you won't forget to knock thrice and cross the threshold exactly on time, will you? We're so looking forward to your surprise midnight appearance!'

Midge nodded absently, his face haunted by dark ghosts of doubt and determination.

The earrings sparkled.

*

Light spangled the black and silver cabinet. Saccharine music subsided beneath the low, tense susurration of the cymbals. The audience watched Midge move towards the box, turn to embrace his brother, then allow himself to be elaborately chained and padlocked and, finally, immured within the garish, upright coffin.

The two men's eyes met. Midge raised his left eyebrow – the standard signal. All was well.

With a typically suave, theatrical flourish, the Great Antonio slammed shut the coffin doors. More rattling of padlocks and cymbals. He wheeled forth a sheaf of silver scimitars.

Apprehension tautened in the audience. The blonde gripped the young man's arm. 'Why doesn't he kill the big guy ... while he's helpless ... ? That'd foil the spirits,' she whispered.

'Shush,' said the youth, forgetting himself. 'Darling!' he added. 'It's a trick. All part of the act. Suspense. Nobody's going to murder anyone.'

And they watched the Great Antonio lift up the first glittering sword, introduce it to a central vent in the cabinet, pause for the drums to roll to a crescendo, and – with much plausible, if rather melodramatic, exertion – plunge it home.

It was muffled, but perfectly distinct. Everyone in the room heard it: the cry, half agony, half triumph, escaped from the depths of the box.

Everyone in the room shuddered when, with a fumbling of chains and padlocks, the bleeding body of Midge, the magician's assistant, was released and displayed beneath the glare of the spotlights.

And everyone knew that the Great Antonio's grief was as genuine as his bewilderment.

People despatched other people with contrary instructions for doctors, ambulances, police and even, in one over-zealous instance, the fire-brigade. Confusion seized all the company – save one: Anthony cradled Midge's head in his arms, and saw it all with complete clarity.

'He didn't bother to slip the master safety catch. He killed himself deliberately. To foil a ridiculous prophecy. To save me. To give me a future ... '

He lowered his head, choking at the futility, the finality, the absurdity of such a death.

'It was all back to front anyway, Midge,' he groaned. 'Perhaps it's my fault: perhaps *I've* been killing *you* all our lives.'

Distantly he became aware of a clock clicking, whirring and launching into the chimes of midnight. Across the city the first bells began to clamour and rejoice.

'Ring out the old, ring in the new,' murmured the hostess to no one in particular.

No one in particular listened. She shook her head. The earrings glistened like tears. 'The poor man's luck is out. We shan't have our first foot now.'

She looked up. Silence had fallen across the room like a sudden black shadow.

Three hammer blows, strangely resonant, sounded in the hallway. Murmurs of unease and excitement thrilled through the company. They clustered together. They stood on tip-toe, on other toes, to see the door.

Hollow footsteps approached.

Anthony lifted his head. His eyes moistened with terror; his pulse drummed along his veins. He beheld the blood-gashed figure of his brother, pale but punctual, forming slowly in the doorway.

Midge gazed over the company, the tall, triumphant stranger holding spectral New Year's gifts in his upraised hand, and spoke:

'You see,' he said. 'We did it. We changed the future, Tone, and thwarted misfortune. It was the only way. *Dead men can't kill.* We altered the unalterable!'

The Great Antonio, however, saw accusation not rejoicing in the pointing hand. And he was never able to register Midge's words.

His body slumped against his brother's on the stage.

'Weak heart,' said the doctor. 'Simple shock. That – sight – in the doorway killed him outright!'

Ashes to Dust

TWISTING TO WRENCH HIMSELF FREE, CLAWING helplessly at the smothering darkness, Mark found himself screaming into consciousness. In the ticking quiet of his bedroom, with the bedclothes in nightmare's disarray, he groaned. It was beginning again.

This year, as every year, Mark's problem produced the usual reactions.

'Overwork, young Somerton,' said the sales manager.

'Stress,' said the doctor. 'I think we'll try some of the pink pills.'

'Guilt,' suggested the analyst darkly.

But, whatever the reason, June had now come and the pattern was starting up again.

The dreams always came first. He steeled himself and told Liz. Liz was this year's attempt to cement a relationship strong enough to break the syndrome, to survive the annual slide into summer gloom.

'Stilton,' she said. 'Too much cheese before supper.'

After the second dream he told her again.

'Turn over,' she advised. 'Sleep on your back.'

He did. He snored. The dreams recurred.

They never varied. Every detail of the house was familiar to him: the courtyard open to the azure sky; the doves in frozen flight on the wall – one with its tail chipped. That damaged tail was something to do with a party, so Julia, giggling, had thought. Julia, forever brushing back her rich, dark curls, her lips always parting in laughter. His heart reached out for her. There on her face sat joy – until the dream wrenched and fell into the pit of nightmare. Joy twisted then into fear. Fear of the distant screams, of the rushing, falling dark. Fear glinting dully on a blade. And it was *his* fear too ...

So the edges of his life went grey. The familiar misery grew. A week later he tried further explanation.

'It's always the same,' he said.

'Not this year,' said Liz. 'Not with me.'

'You wait,' he retorted sadly. 'By July things'll be different.'

Liz hugged him closer. 'You're daft,' she said.

'You wait,' repeated Mark, 'till July comes.'

It came.

'Don't you love me?' demanded Liz.

'I told you ... '

'You don't love me.'

'It's the dreams,' he said despairingly. 'They cut me off. Like pain. I can't help it.'

'Damn the dreams,' she said. 'You're obsessed. One more word about that Julia woman and I leave.'

*

'She left.'

The analyst stared at the ceiling.

'I tried to explain,' said Mark. 'But – I've done it again.'

The analyst, wondering why his wife had been so elaborate in her make-up that morning, wrote 'TV Repair Man?' on his pad. 'Guilt,' he murmured automatically. 'It's usually guilt.' He defaced the writing with meticulous savagery and decided to catch the early train home. 'Dig,' he said.

Mark looked blank.

'Dig back,' said the man, 'into your past. That's what we must do. Unearth old wounds. Excavate your traumas.'

'Just as I was really starting to feel something special for her.'

'"I only kill the thing I love" ... ' mused the analyst.

'It's as if I get too close. Something shuts down.'

Mr Quist smiled knowingly. 'Ah,' he said.

'Ah?'

'You're repressing. It's something you can't face up to from your early life. What are you hiding from yourself?'

'Nothing,' said Mark.

'Think.'

Mark thought.

'Nothing,' he repeated. 'Look, we've done all this before ... D'you think I'm incapable of love? Is that it?'

'Spiders?' prompted Mr Quist. 'Didn't you pull their legs off?' He drew in a sharp breath between clenched teeth. 'And watch their furry bodies writhing helplessly?' His eyes lit up. 'Or squash tadpoles?'

'No,' said Mark. 'Sorry.'

The man sighed. 'Pity. You're burying *something*,' he said. 'Until we've found it and lived through it ... ' He looked at his watch. 'Same time next week,' he suggested abruptly.

'It's all getting a bit near,' said Mark.

'Near?'

'It's almost August. Things are getting worse. Darker. It'll soon be time for – you know – '

'Ah. The crisis.'

' – Blackout, yes.'

Mr Quist had put on his coat. 'We must just dig harder and deeper,' he said.

'I'm depressed,' said Mark Somerton.

'Who isn't?' said his analyst.

*

'How are we then?' enquired Mr Quist the following week.

'We're worse,' said Mark, his face pale. 'It's starting to take over again. This girl I dream about – this Julia. Who *is* she?'

The analyst leaned back in his leather chair and swivelled comfortably. 'Multiple personality manifestations. Quite common,' he said.

Mark looked alarmed. 'I don't mean I think I *am* Julia!' he said. 'Isn't there anything you can do?'

Briskly the man stood up and held a solemn forefinger in front of Mark's face.

'I'm going to count to five,' he announced.

'Why?' asked Mark.

Mr Quist frowned. 'Age regression,' he explained curtly. 'Hypnosis. We're going to revisit your childhood. Remove the layers. Dig back. Uncover the source.'

He counted to five and informed Mark he was now eleven. Mark opened his eyes with boyish delight. 'Jennifer Long says she'll come to my party,' he said. 'And she says she doesn't like Keith Mortimer any more.'

The analyst hunted back through the years. 'You're five,' he suggested.

'I can write my name now,' lisped Mark with pride. He groped the air. Mr Quist gave him a pad and pencil and watched him, tongue clenched between his teeth, laboriously form the gawky letters.

'What do you hate about school?' asked the psychiatrist hopefully.

'I *love* school,' said Mark with depressing indignation.

The analyst raised an eyebrow and exhaled heavily. 'Okay. Keep on travelling back. Further back. Back into your earliest memories. Tell me when – '

He broke off. The figure on the couch suddenly heaved; a low moan escaped his lips. Anguish distorted his features. Abruptly Mark sat up and scratched feverishly on the pad. His nostrils flared as his lungs laboured to seize the thickening air. Words escaped between gasps.

The analyst chewed his biro vigorously. 'I'm sorry. I can't quite understand what ... ' He placed a palm on the moist forehead. 'Easy,' he said, 'easy. Just lie back – '

Mark hissed. His head, flung back, rocked wildly from side to side. He clutched the shaft of the pencil in his palm and held it, his arm quivering, in front of him. His knuckles whitened. He opened his mouth. His chest heaved, and he howled. 'No!'

Pulses pounding, the psychiatrist leaped to his feet.

But Mark had hurled the pencil from him and fallen back on to the couch, his body rigid, his arm twisted unnaturally beneath him.

'Did we get anywhere?' he asked, ten minutes later, sipping at the glass of water with a casual calm the analyst wished he could emulate. The latter pulled pensively at an earlobe.

'Do you speak many languages, Mr Somerton?' he asked.

'Languages? Me!' said Mark, and laughed.

'You never studied the classics?'

'It was Latin or Woodwork at our school,' said Mark. 'I did Woodwork.' He paused, wondering whether to mention his distinction in O Level Geography.

'You said things ... words ... ' Bewilderment drained the man's voice. 'I couldn't catch them properly ... '

'I don't understand.'

'Neither do I,' said Mr Quist.

'Well, at least we're digging,' said Mark encouragingly. 'What's that?'

His analyst was scrutinising the pad. He passed the crumpled pages over. 'Mean anything to you?'

Mark peered at the hieroglyphs. 'It's very – scrawly,' he said. 'Two crosses here. Love and kisses, perhaps. Then "I" and – ' He peered closer.

'A "V"?'

'Love from Ivy!' Mark essayed an unconvincing chuckle. 'I'm not very good at these psychological tests,' he confessed. 'There's a word here.' He read with difficulty. 'Cubicul – '

'That's when you threw the pencil down.'

'*I* did?'

The analyst nodded. 'Mysterious place, the subconscious.'

The patient shook his head. The darkness edged closer. 'But it makes no sense at all. That's nothing like *my* writing,' said Mark Somerton.

*

August came. The sun shone, and the shades, true to form, closed in. The world retreated from Mark and the final phase – the breathing fits – began again. So did the advice.

'Take a holiday, young Somerton,' said the sales manager. It was not concern; it was a threat.

'Asthma,' said the doctor. 'Summer allergy. Pollen count. We'll try some of the yellow pills. All you need is sea and sun. Fresh air in your lungs, new horizons. Take a package holiday.'

'Claustrophobia,' said the analyst. He remembered his patient's earlier visit. 'Stifled, overwhelmed by your past.' He peered over his spectacles. 'And anxiety about an underlying guilt, of course,' he added mechanically.

'I've booked a holiday,' said Mark. 'I could only get a last minute cancellation. D'you think it's wise?' He stared gloomily at Mr Quist. His face sagged. 'It can't be long now.'

The analyst donned a professional smile. 'Now, now. Try not to look on the black side. It may not happen this year.'

Mark shook his head. He knew it would.

The man tried to be constructive. 'Perhaps – ah – Liz would like to get away too.'

'She left me,' said Mark. 'I told you.'

'Not to worry. Plenty more fish in the Mediterranean. There'll be a dark-haired beauty waiting for you at the airport, you see. Have a good time.'

Mark shrugged. 'How can I?' He shuddered. 'Look, I can't go through the whole – business – again. Am I to be chained to this – wheel – for the rest of my life ... ?'

'We'll keep digging,' said Mr Quist. 'By the way: you can pay this month's fee when you return,' he added kindly.

*

The noise and squalor of Naples receded, the rim of the bay broadened, and out of the sun-spangling blueness of sea and sky rose the hazy twin peaks of Capri. White houses, bleached by the Mediterranean summer, perched on the precipitous cliffs, or lost themselves among the cascading vines and oleanders.

Capri confused and excited Mark. It was a dream which grew more real, more familiar each day. The Hotel Floridiana, friendly, hospitable and flushed with scented flowers, was a welcoming haven. Quickly the island's warmth filtered through the bleak, blighted spaces of his mind and stirred something deep in his soul, threatening the blackness and the fear. The asthma attacks retreated. 'This is my spiritual home,' he told himself, savouring his glass of Vino Tiberio, fruit of those ancient Roman slopes, and gazing from his balcony through the reddening dusk across the ageless sea. 'Capri is like coming home. Perhaps I am loosening the chain.'

But by night the old dreams shook his sleep with renewed force.

Then, on the fifth day, Mark visited the Villa Jovis.

The magnificent ruin, pride of the Emperor Tiberius, crowned the plunging easterly cliffs and simmered in the noonday sun. Lizards scuttled into dusty crevices. Mark abandoned the tourists and the Villa to seek the shade. The heat grew oppressive. He closed his eyes and, for a time, the sun still pulsed in his brain.

Then his eyes opened.

The cicadas were silent. A stillness hung in the air. He found himself following a path beneath a shadowing grove of pines. An opening on the cliff edge, two boulders guarding the view, the mainland sweeping round into blue distance, Vesuvius climbing out of the haze. The scene echoed in the far reaches of his mind. Was that Julia standing by the rock pointing across the bay, her hand shading her forehead? He wanted to give her the present now – engraved especially for the honeymoon. 'Of course you can't see the house from here,' he wanted to say. 'The whole city's lost in the mist.'

'But I know it's there,' she was saying. 'We're going home tomorrow.'

Abruptly the rustling of the cicadas woke again in his head and, to his surprise, a buxom American was effusing over the view, offering him her camera and arranging herself appropriately over the nearest boulder.

The episode had dislocated Mark's sense of reality. He felt dazed and uneasy. Dear heaven. Was the dream starting to encroach upon his waking life?

For the first time in weeks his sleep that night was untroubled.

The next morning he hummed as he shaved. 'The chain,' he wanted to tell the world, 'is broken!' Instead, he complimented the patron on his coffee and asked for a packed lunch.

'A sea trip,' he explained. 'I'm celebrating.'

'Sorrento,' suggested the Signor.

'Amalfi,' suggested the Signora.

He left them gesticulating elaborately.

But when, on descending by funicular to the Marina Grande, he saw a dark-haired girl in a white robe with a golden bracelet on her tanned arm waving to him, he called back 'Julia!' and joined the swarm of holidaymakers on a boat bound for neither of these resorts.

On board he searched for her without success.

It was thus, one hot summer morning in late August, that Mark Somerton arrived in Pompeii.

*

He entered the forum of the ancient city, like many tourists before him, and marvelled. The temples of Jupiter and Apollo stood about

253

him in fragmented grandeur, half resurrected from their painful past. They told of mortality.

He found himself pressed into a flock of tourists, dutifully following a bored, imperious guide. 'The Arch of Germanicus,' he instructed them. Hemmed in between a fallen pillar and a stout Austrian, festooned with an extravagance of cameras and lenses, Mark gazed through the arch at the sky, azure and eternal, and beheld Mount Vesuvius slumbering in the distance, a blue ghost.

He stared at it and a deep dread murmured distantly along his veins. Surely the chain had been broken, he told himself, as he leaned back struggling to draw breath. The crowd jostled against him, the ancient dust rose about his face, and Mark realised he was choking for air in the sultry heat. The heaviness lumbered back into his soul. Dear God, would he never be free? Was it to be the blackout after all? And *here* – miles from home and understanding?

Fear and desperation fed his claustrophobia. Gasping, he groped his way through the crowd ('You all right, mate?' said an English sightseer) and escaped into a side street. He stumbled along the massive stones, rutted with the wheels of carts and chariots, until the hubbub of tourists had subsided. As he sank breathlessly to the pavement he felt a hand on his shoulder, and looked up into Julia's laughing eyes.

'Not far to go,' she said, and again she was gone. His breathing eased. He wandered on through a complexity of streets, half following, half knowing his route.

He turned the final corner and found himself in front of a crumbling brick façade.

He looked through the archway. From a side room of the villa he heard voices. '*Scavi Nuovi*,' announced a sign. '*Vietato l'Ingresso*.'

'Julia?' he called.

He entered the central courtyard. Blocks of weather worn masonry lay where they had fallen, old scars in the dust, momentarily confusing his memory. *But he knew*. A profound excitement beat in upon his brain. He had been here before. He had been here a thousand times in his dreams! He knew every detail of the pool in the centre open to the shining blue sky. And that wall mosaic, faded and colourless, after centuries of flight: the doves. He crossed to examine them, knowing what he would find. The small cubes had been damaged and the tail of the second dove was incomplete.

A terrible joy drummed his pulse. It was coming now. It was almost upon him.

'Julia?' he called again.

He turned and, following the voices, walked to the crumbled entrance of the bedroom. The men looked up. Ahead of him, half way across the room, looming like a nightmare against the sky, was a pitted, solid, grey wall. The group of archeologists who were painstakingly burrowing into the unexcavated lava, waved their arms. '*Vietato l'ingresso,*' said one. 'English?' asked another. 'This is not for the public. We dig and make a discovery.'

Mark shrank against the wall, his breathing tortured, and watched them. Ignoring him now, the men meticulously brushed into the grey dust. Year after year, he thought, they had been working here, uncovering the past. Layer by careful layer they had been working their way back into history, forward to this moment.

Mark's lungs seized at the air. Dark wings closed about him. 'The crisis is coming,' he told himself. 'Now I know why I am here.'

'*Guarda qui!*' exclaimed one of the men. He withdrew an object, crusted with lava. Brushes were eagerly applied. The voices rose to an excited babble. An archaeologist held it up, noticed him, and said, 'See, Signor. A knife – from Pompeii Antico.'

Mark reached out to the wall for support. His vision fractured. He felt the familiar uprush of darkness folding in, engulfing him. But this time, how much more intense. And this time he knew he must confront it, endure it.

The old world opened.

'A dagger!' he exclaimed, choking.

Julia nodded, her brown eyes wild with fright. 'It's the only way.' She tried to thrust the handle of the weapon into his hand and buried her head more deeply into his robes. He looked up, spluttering with the fumes, into the square opening above the atrium. The sun had left the sky. A blizzard of suffocating, burning grey dust howled about them even here. Indoors, as well as in the streets. Fragments of scalding stones hailed against the roofs and smouldered amongst the ash mounting in the courtyard where they stood.

'Eumachia went to the baker's,' Julia sobbed, coughing hoarsely. She pointed to a huddled body by the mosaic. 'And Artorius ... '

The air buckled and cracked with a vast, distant explosion, and the earth shivered beneath them. The squealing of horses and the noisy confusion of wailing and terror grew more muffled.

'There is nowhere to hide,' she croaked. 'Boats are burning on the sea front ... '

So he took the dagger.

Her body was racked with another fit of coughing and, wrapping his tunic around them both, he stumbled with her into the bedroom.

But here, it seemed, the air was thicker still. The heat was unbearable. Julia was limp in his arms, her lungs on fire, pressed against his labouring chest.

He trembled in his agony. The room grew black. *He must face the crisis*. He forced the shutters of memory to stay open, to confront and live through the horror and tragedy ...

Julia moaned. He bent close to her dry lips, brushing aside her matted hair. 'Marcus – help – me.' Her hands fumbled for the knife in his hand and guided it against her body. '*Please* – if – you – love – me –'

Now falling fire was crashing through the roof. His own lungs were burning too. In a howling anguish of love and rage he held the dagger firmly between them and, with a despairing cry – '*No!*' – nevertheless pulled her with the necessary violence into his arms.

The moment seared through time.

An archaeologist was bending over him, pulling him to his feet, dusting his clothes. '*Fa molto caldo*. Very hot,' he said, gently fanning him with a handkerchief. 'Rest here.' He indicated a fallen capital. But Mark's curiosity was aroused by the babbling excitement of the man's colleagues. They looked up and beckoned him over to share the whole of their discovery. 'See. Now it is revealed. We dig and find two bodies. Here.'

Mark stared, moved by awe, at the two hollow shapes buried in the lava. One of them appeared to be quite rigid, his arm twisted unnaturally beneath his body.

'She was wearing this on her arm,' said the man. With scrupulous care, his gloved hand held out the golden band for Mark's inspection. Mark peered closer. He indicated the inside curve, knowing exactly what he'd find. The man applied his brush, delicately dislodging the rest of the encrusted grey ash. The inscription was quite simple.

'*Marcus et Julia*,' read Mark. '*Amor vincit omnia*.'

'"Love conquers all." He loves her,' said the man. 'See how they embrace each other. But it is strange. The big knife. It seems the man – how d'you say? – he stabs the Signora. He loves her. He kills her. It is a mystery.'

Mark shook his head, choking back a shuddering release of tears, centuries old.

'No: no mystery.' He turned his face, sobbing, to the ageless skies.

But already, with the understanding of tragedy, his heart was lifting. The chain was breaking.

Gratefully, he took his leave of the men. And, taking the fragrant summer air deep into his lungs, he walked with quickening steps out of the villa into the freedom and fullness of the noonday sun.

*

He paid a last visit to the analyst.

'I've solved something,' said Mr Quist. '"*Cubiculum*". The word you wrote under hypnosis. Did you know it's the Latin for bedroom?' He watched Mark's face carefully. 'Sexual guilt,' he murmured. 'The usual thing.'

'*I've* solved something too,' said Mark. He tapped his souvenir guide book. 'Did *you* know that at the end of August in 79 AD, a little after midday, Vesuvius erupted and the city of Pompeii was buried alive?'

'X X I V,' said the man slowly. 'The marks you wrote on the pad. Roman numerals. But I don't exactly grasp – '

'*I* do,' said Mark. 'It happened on August the twenty-fourth.'

'Reincarnation?' said Mr Quist doubtfully. 'Best left to the theologians, I think.' But he was already planning his paper on 'Age Regression: Doorway to Past Lives' which would, he hoped, make his name pre-eminent at the next Psychoanalysts' International Convention.

'And your anxiety, your guilt?' he said. 'We must keep digging ... To uncover and confront is to understand and to exorcise ... '

'No guilt. There never was. The excavating's over,' said Mark Somerton, his eyes moist despite his sudden joy. 'I found Julia.'

'You see,' he said simply, 'it was love.'

Future Tense

'HYPNOTIC REGRESSION, SIR,' REPLIED MARK WALTON.

Old Browning nodded and his face came as close to cracking into a smile as a teacher's could. You could almost hear him purring, thought James.

'Psychiatrists use it,' said Mark.

The class slumped collectively in its desks.

'They hypnotize people – patients – to take them back and re-live their early life. They can make grown-ups start talking and behaving like five year-olds ... '

Joanna stared at the back of Mark's head. His hair was tousled in Grecian curls, like blond icing. Brains, yes. Beauty, yes. But why should he have so much of both? It was hardly fair on the competition. Besides, it was so – unsettling. She gazed out of the window and pursed her lips pensively, narrowing her eyes and fluttering her lashes.

'Well, Joanna?' Browning was frowning at her. 'In trance already? What can you tell us of hypnotism and the immense, unexplored powers latent in the human brain?'

'I'm practising looking intelligent.' The words stayed in her head, unspoken. 'Pardon, sir?'

The teacher raised weary eyebrows. It was Friday afternoon and his mother-in-law was shortly arriving for the weekend. 'Does *anyone* in this class want a pass or two this summer? I don't like to rush you, naturally, but all the fun of the exams begins in precisely three weeks.' He scanned the class morosely. 'Well, is there intelligent life out there?'

Mark Walton raised his hand again.

No. It really wasn't fair. But it *was* nice of Mark to invite her to his pre-exam party next Saturday, even though half the neighbourhood would also be going – especially the inexorable Jane Weatherbed, who would doubtless be saturated in her mother's expensive French perfume, giggle extravagantly and flash extra rows of glittering teeth at his every remark, and generally haunt him all evening like a love-infested limpet. Or shark.

Joanna doodled on her rough book. She wished someone would invent hypnotic *pro*gression – to take people into the future so that the end-of-afternoon bell would ring now, immediately.

Bored, she deigned to acknowledge James Wilkinson, spotty, faithful, clumsy, reliable James. He grinned at her.

'Wilkinson!'

Joanna smiled into her books and bowed her head, wondering whether James had been invited to Mark's festivity, and whether – if he had – she was glad or sorry.

*

'Hi!' said James Wilkinson.

The party was in high spirits. So was James Wilkinson.

'Glad you came. Great party, isn't it! I think Mark's tidied his mum and dad and the hamster away in the cellar under lock and key for the night.'

'Oh, hi,' said Joanna. 'Are you? Is it? He hasn't!'

'Have a coke,' said James. 'They're still hunting for the key to the drinks cabinet. I'd offer to dance but you know what'd happen: I'd trample you into the carpet again. And the blood would gunge up the hoover,'

'It was nothing,' said Joanna, remembering the Christmas

school disco. 'Nothing that major surgery, seven leading foot specialists and six months in hospital didn't quickly put right.'

'It's the curse of the Wilkinsons. I can't help having the body of an angel and the feet of a geriatric hippo.'

Joanna surveyed the room. The Walton lounge throbbed with music and spangled with multi-coloured lights.

'Where's Mark?' she asked.

James's eyes dulled. 'Look for Miss Weatherbed,' he said. 'For everywhere that Walton went, that Jane was sure to – '

A hand clapped him heavily on the shoulder. It was joined to Mark Walton. 'Hallo, hallo, hallo,' he said. 'What are you doing here?'

Jane, at his side, in a cloud of perfume, tinkled her fingers at them.

'Shouldn't you all be revising?' said Mark.

Jane's teeth parted to let out a giggle.

'*I'm* learning at night – by hypnosis,' said James. 'Tapes under the pillow. *Brave New World* and all that.'

Joanna wished she'd said that. She narrowed her eyes and pouted as if struggling with thoughts too deep for words. 'It's all very well, this hypnosis and age regression stuff that old Browning was on about,' she said.

'Time travel into the past!' said James scornfully. 'Doctor Who, I presume.'

Joanna frowned sharply at him. 'It made me wonder,' she said slowly, looking up into Mark's distractingly blue eyes and hoping he'd noticed how subtle her new eye make-up was, 'when somebody is going to think of trying their hand at hypnotic *pro*gression ... '

'Yes!' Mark took his arm from Jane's waist and turned to Joanna. Eagerness brightened his eyes. 'That's exactly what *I* thought!'

Joanna glowed inside and tried not to flutter her eyelids excessively or, worse, to giggle mindlessly like certain scented people.

'If you can put people into trance,' said Mark, 'and take them back to childhood – possibly *beyond* childhood, back into previous lives, like in this book I read – '

'Yes. I read about some woman,' said Jane. 'In the *Reader's Digest*. Or was it on the telly? She could remember being an Egyptian priestess, or something, in this temple ... '

' – Then why can't you also take them *forward* – to the future?' said Mark.

Joanna nodded and smiled. Those eyes! But surely he wasn't taking her seriously! 'Visit the future under hypnosis!' she thought to herself. 'That's got to be nonsense. The future hasn't happened yet. Full stop. Unless it's all mapped out for us already. Boyfriends. Illness. Jobs. Marriage. Babies. What an awful thought. Hypnotic progression indeed!'

'Surely that would just make us puppets,' she said. 'You know, acting out a script that's already been written.'

'You can pull my strings any time,' said James.

Mark shrugged. 'Who knows?' he said. 'Take Einstein's space-time continuum ... '

'I prefer peanuts myself,' said James. He reached out for another handful. 'Jo's right,' he said. 'It stands to reason. How can we *re*-live something that we haven't lived once? It can't possibly work.' He grinned at Joanna and wondered whether he dare risk a friendly arm round her waist. But she glared at him. He frowned, bewildered by the failure of his attempt to curry favour by supporting her. 'Women!' he thought. 'Okay,' he mumbled through a mouthful of peanuts, 'why not give it a whirl? Why not prove it – one way or the other? Why not *make* history instead of just learning it? Let's do an experiment. Show Gravy Browning the unexplored powers potent – '

'Latent,' said Mark Walton.

'Just testing,' said James. 'Show him the staggering powers *latent* in *our* human brains.'

'Brilliant!' said Mark.

So it was decided.

A first shiver of invisible strings.

A chair was brought forward. A circle formed. Drawn by the excitement, more people gathered around the friends, bubbling with questions, spilling drinks and treading on toes.

'Somebody switch the music off,' said Mark. 'We need to concentrate. Okay,' he said, looking at Joanna, 'who's going to be the guinea pig?'

Jane Weatherbed sat in the chair and closed her eyes expectantly.

To Joanna's delight, Mark seemed uneasy. She thought, he's probably afraid Jane'll see a cosy future for two: the semi-detached nest, glowing with log fires and love, festooned with warming slippers and over-polished horse brasses, and overrun by two cats, five poodles and innumerable babies.

Mark turned to her instead. 'How about you, Jo?' he said. 'It *was* your brainchild.'

But James stepped forward. 'This is a man's job,' he drawled, squaring his shoulders and elaborately expanding his chest. 'Going boldly where no man has gone before ... Seriously, Jo.'

Joanna pouted at him, but realised that she was secretly relieved.

A disappointed Jane vacated the chair and James sat down.

'Turn down the lights,' suggested someone. Someone obeyed.

James embarked on a manly laugh; it emerged as a nervous giggle. 'I've never done this before,' he said.

'*I've* never done this before,' said Mark.

'*No-one's* ever done *this* before,' murmured Joanna.

'Done what?' asked a squeaky voice from the depths of the settee.

'Relax,' said Mark Walton in a sepulchral tone that made him sound, Joanna thought, like Something Sinister that had just crawled out of the Chamber of Horrors.

'Look into my eyes.'

'I didn't know you cared,' said James.

Mark Walton tutted. 'Shut up, twithead, and concentrate,' he said. 'Be quiet everyone! Now ... ' He fumbled in his pocket, produced a bunch of keys and held them, swinging gently, in front of James's nose. 'When I count to five ... '

'Give him a calculator,' said Robert Wilson, and was promptly smothered with a cushion by Felicity Downs.

'You're supposed to count *down* to zero, I think,' suggested Joanna.

'You're sinking into deep trance. Deeper, deeper,' said Mark.

The room hushed hopefully.

'Three ... two ... one ... ' He hesitated. 'Zero!'

He stared at James.

'Right. Now you're moving forwards – forwards in time. Think yourself into the future.' Mark tried to improvise professional sounding patter but it was the theatrical incantations of the mad hypnotist in last week's Midnight Movie that came most readily to mind. 'When I click my fingers, you will remember' – *remember*! He checked himself – 'you will *bring to mind* some event from that year.'

He paused. Then he clicked his fingers.

The circle tightened.

'Any event at all ... '

James stirred. He passed the back of his hand slowly across his forehead. 'Bells,' he said. 'I hear bells. There's a church ... Yes ... They're throwing confetti ... The car's driving off ... '

Joanna leaned forward and peered at him more closely.

'I can see a hotel ... The happy couple's about to go upstairs, but first ... yes, they're signing the register. Wait! I think I can read it ... ' His lips twitched. 'Yes. It says "Mr and Mrs Mark and Jane Walton"!'

Uproar ensued.

Finally James picked himself up off the floor, Joanna dusted him down and, spluttering, he plucked bits of cushion stuffing from his tongue. 'Well,' he said, 'for heaven's sake! You didn't *really* think it would work, did you? Making *history* of the *future* indeed!' He rubbed his hands briskly. 'Let's play *Postman's Knock*.'

'Or *Murder*,' said Joanna, glowering at him. She had seen the disappointment on Mark's face. 'Wilkinson has spoiled Mark's day,' she thought. She patted Mark's arm. 'Let's try again,' she said. 'A serious experiment. Suppose we really could flick forward a few pages, take a short cut into the future. What would we most want to know?'

They thought.

'Which of us is going to be a millionaire?' suggested someone.

'Which of us is even going to get a job!' said someone else. Everyone groaned.

'There *is* something we *all* want to know,' said Mark Walton. He looked at his friends. His friends looked back.

'Exam results!'

'*I* don't,' said a pale girl with glasses.

'It's all right for him,' thought James. 'All those firsts at his fingertips.'

'Well, *I* want to know,' said Mark Walton.

'So did Faustus,' said James. 'Too much. And look what happened to him. He signed on the devil's dotted line and forgot to check the small print. It said, "Go to hell." And he did.'

Mark gave a dry, dismissive laugh. 'I still want to know,' he said. His voice rose with unusual warmth; his face was stern and flushed. 'Pursuing knowledge can't be wrong. If it was, where would all the teachers go?'

'To hell,' suggested Robert Wilson.

There was a ragged cheer.

'Look, said James, 'if you're so serious about trying to probe beyond the veil and take a peek at your exam grades, *you* sit in that chair. *You* be the victim.'

'Sure!' said Mark. 'But on one condition: I don't want *you* trying to put me into deep trance. James Wilkinson: Pilbrook Upper's answer to Svengali!'

To her uneasy delight, he suggested Joanna.

Eventually the party-goers hushed each other into attention, silence gathered round the circle of light where Mark was seated, and Joanna dangled the keys and, in a low soft voice, repeated the preliminary formulas.

A distant tremor along silent strings.

She felt decidedly foolish, but not foolish enough to stop: after all, it wasn't every day a girl held Mark Walton in her power.

' ... Zero!' she said.

She stared at her subject.

'Mark!' she said. 'Can you hear me?' Her voice was edged with alarm. His chin had sagged onto his chest. He appeared to have lost interest and fallen asleep.

'I can hear you,' he said slowly.

His breathing deepened.

Joanna glanced interrogatively at James. He nodded reassuringly. 'Looks like you've done it,' he said. 'He's right under. All you need is a tent and a crystal ball – '

'Ssh,' said someone.

'Are you sure it's safe?' asked the bespectacled girl.

'Tell him he's going to wake up in the future,' prompted James. 'Give him a date.'

Joanna shrugged helplessly.

'Tell him it's the day of the results.'

Joanna did. 'You've got the envelope in your hand,' she said, speaking with slow deliberation. 'You want to open it ... '

Nothing happened.

'He's not doing anything.'

'Of course he's not doing anything,' said James. 'That's because there's nothing to do. The experiment hasn't worked. It *can't* work.' He scanned the circle of expectant faces and laughed. 'A right bunch of bananas you all look!' he said. 'Like a harem of Hollywood hopefuls on Oscar night.'

'Thank goodness for that!' said Jane.

Then she gasped.

Mark's chest heaved. His head rocked from side to side. His fingers fumbled with what appeared to be an imaginary envelope.

'Is that the envelope? Do you want to open it ... ?' repeated Joanna.

'No.' Mark shook his head miserably. 'No.'

'Gently,' said Joanna, beginning to get the feel of the controls. 'Relax. Move forward. It's later the same day. You've opened the envelope. You've found the results ... '

She paused.

Silence tautened around them.

Abruptly Mark threw back his head, jerked like a puppet. An anguished cry, which was neither sob nor laugh, choked in his throat. Unease shuddered through the company. Both Joanna and Jane reached out impulsively to calm him.

He pushed them away.

'Nothing!' said Mark Walton. 'Not ... even ... a ... pass ... ' The strangled chuckle escaped again. His voice dropped to an inaudible murmur.

'What did he say?' demanded Felicity Downs.

Mark raised his head and spoke again with perfect distinctness. 'Tudor!' he said.

He wiped his eyes. Then, agitatedly, he clicked his fingers.

'He wants a pen,' said James. 'Quickly, someone. And a pad, over there, by the phone.'

Joanna grew annoyed. Experiments with knowledge were all very well, but not when the responsibility was thrust on you. She wished someone else would take over.

Mark's hand hovered over the paper. Then, with a sob, he scratched the pen hesitantly across the page, dropped it, let his head slump forward, and lapsed into sonorous breathing.

Jane touched Joanna's arm.

'I know,' said Joanna. 'Why didn't someone think of this when we began? Where is he, and how on earth do we get him back?'

'A great party,' said James.

'What party?' said Joanna. Her mind was preoccupied with the exams, which had already begun. 'Oh, *that* party!' She remembered, and shivered in the June heat.

A tall shadow fell between them. It was Mark Walton.

'Talk of old Faustus ... ' said James.

'It was certainly,' said Mark, 'an *eventful* party.'

'How would *you* know?' said James. 'The perfect host! You were out cold for the best bit. Like a superannuated sloth.'

Mark smiled. 'Or a terrified Tudor. You lot certainly made sure I got the full slow-action replay when I came round,' he said. 'Tudors. Failing the History exam. Well, fate, as they say in all the best clichés, moves in mysterious ways. I've spent the last three weeks' revision living and breathing flipping Tudors. Fate doesn't stand a chance, man!'

James screwed up his eyes in the effort to grasp the intellectual puzzle that had haunted him since the party. 'But that's just it,' he said. 'If fate *has* decreed it – if we really have – mm – trespassed into the future – how can the inevitable be avoided? Whatever we do, we'll just be acting out the script. How can the unalterable be altered?'

'By revision,' said Mark. 'Verily,' he said, in his remarkably accurate imitation of Mr Browning, 'revision moveth mountains, lad.' He laughed harshly. 'You don't seriously believe that we peeked through the veil, created a tiny time warp, conjured the ghosts of our future that evening, do you?'

But Joanna saw uncertainty in those Walton eyes. She also saw two reflected images of Jane Weatherbed approaching breathlessly from the library.

'I must go,' she said, 'talking of revision. History exam tomorrow.'

'I never forget dates!' said Mark Walton.

James followed her. 'What's the date of Henry the Seventh's accession?' he called over his shoulder.

Mark chuckled. '1485,' he said. 'You can't catch me out with Tudor royals. Ask me the colour of Elizabeth the First's underwear – the colour she wore on the first Thursday of each month.'

Joanna turned to James. 'It's strange, though, isn't it?' she said. 'I'm sure it bothers him, too.'

'What?'

'The way he scrawled that date on the pad at the party – 1485.'

*

Mr Browning wrote: 'History. Exam begins – 9.30. Exam ends – 12.00.' The chalk squealed on the board and forty-nine candidates winced.

But the seat of Candidate forty-six remained empty.

A string tautening.

Joanna watched the two teachers standing by the vacant desk, consulting lists and conferring in low voices. The nape of her neck prickled. Where was Mark? Was it all beginning to happen?

Mr Browning cleared his throat. 'Can anyone enlighten us as to the whereabouts of Mr Walton?' he asked.

Silence.

Joanna caught Jane's eye. Jane shrugged wide-eyed, and carried on nibbling despairingly at her finger-nails.

Joanna put up her hand, but the year tutor was already speaking. 'Sorry about this, everybody. We'll give Walton a few more minutes. Try and relax. Sit back and think of England – preferably Merrie Olde Englande.'

No-one laughed.

Joanna clicked her fingers. Mr Browning came over. 'I know where he lives, sir,' she whispered. 'It's up Green End Road. Only fifteen minutes away – if I run.'

The teacher tried to reassure her: it was a kind, but unnecessary, gesture. Everything was already in hand. Mark's mobile was evidently switched off but the school secretary was alerted and about to phone the Walton home to find out what was wrong. He patted her shoulder in a disconcertingly human way and walked off to rejoin his colleagues in a leisurely huddle at the back of the hall.

Joanna gazed helplessly at his retreating back.

Then, like cracking ice, a sudden realisation clicked in her brain. The telephone!

She felt a faint tugging of strings. 'Not just puppets, surely,' she thought.

She sensed a black net of shadows closing about them.

Mark had already told her yesterday. The Walton house was mercifully at peace, cut off from the world. *Their phone was out of order.* It wouldn't be repaired for several days.

She raised her hand again, clicking her fingers impatiently, but the teachers ignored her, distracted by the arrival of Mrs Allen, the secretary, who was looking anxious and shaking her head at their enquiries. Joanna drummed an urgent, angry tattoo on the desk with her fingers.

The year tutor turned to the candidates and announced that latest developments suggested there was no point in further delay. The rules anyway, as they probably knew, did not allow them to defer the start of the exam for many more minutes.

Joanna came to a decision. She scraped back her chair and strode to the back of the examination hall. Faces turned.

The discussion was a heated one.

'Joanna,' said Mrs Griffith, 'the headmaster himself is on the phone to the Waltons at this very moment. Naturally he'll keep trying.'

'But I keep telling you ... !' Joanna's voice grew shrill with impatience. 'Teachers!' she thought. 'Always talking – while precious minutes tick away.' She clenched her white-knuckled fists. 'And while fate ticks closer.'

Was it inevitable? 'Fate doesn't stand a chance, man!' Joanna felt her pulses pounding. Was the shadowy net tightening? Why should Mark fail his History paper, Tudors and all, if *she* was free to *act*, free to choose to *do* something to change the pattern? Or was everything she did just part of the script already?

It was all too complicated to understand, let alone explain.

'*We're not puppets!*' she shouted.

And, pushing her bewildered teachers aside, their angry cries singing about her head, Joanna rushed out of school.

She was wholly unaware that the headmaster was already speaking to Mr Browning to despatch him by car on the same errand to the same destination.

*

At that same moment, the taxi that Mark's neighbour had urgently summoned, drew up outside the Walton home. Dishevelled, appalled and relieved, Mark clambered in, tucking in his shirt and checking to see that his pens were still in his pocket.

'Pilbrook Upper School?' said the man. Mark nodded. He resisted the temptation to add, 'And burn rubber!' The taxi lurched away from the kerb.

Mark had never overslept and missed school once in his entire life. 'Why today?' he wondered. He thought of the party, the experiment, his Faustus-cry: 'I want to know', and pulled his jacket more tightly around him. The taxi felt chill and stripes of shadow travelled across him like prison bars. 'Shadows,' he thought: 'they fall before as well as behind us. Why not before and behind an event, too?'

He looked out. Through the tinted windows the June sun simmered on sleeping houses and Mark summoned common sense to dispel the darkness and focus on the exam ahead. Of course you overslept if you'd stayed up till two o' clock in the morning checking and rechecking all there was to know about the Tudors!

He glanced at his watch. The digits flicked rapidly. Plenty of time to write enough to get a good grade. No need to worry after all. Just relax ...

Mark Walton sat back and tried to rid himself of a tension that held him on humming strings.

*

Panting, Joanna reached the junction at the start of Green End Road. She vowed she would never complain about Cross Country running again. Her blood made a crashing, thumping noise in her ears, she had an agonising stitch, her lungs burned, and her legs were trembling like the limbs of that poor stick-insect in Biology the other day.

But she was nearly there.

Numbing the questions that sparked in her brain, she focused on one thought: Mark Walton would defy the stars and sit that exam, if it killed her.

Puppets indeed!

She thought of those clear blue eyes tearful with disappointment, and launched herself across the road.

Her shadow jogged darkly ahead of her.

'Time!' she panted. 'It's all a question of time ... '

Revolving in his mind the waywardness of pupils, mothers-in-law, and the conspiracy of life in general against him in particular, Mr Browning drove up the road, whistling between his teeth and peering vaguely ahead for the Green End Road turn.

He looked down at the clock on the dashboard, looked up, and the world changed.

*

In one howling moment, unseen strings jerked and tangled.

A girl, suddenly, there, ahead, in the middle of the road.

Seconds froze, as slow and clear as ice.

The girl – Joanna – saw the car, and turned, saw the taxi, and turned back.

The cab-driver saw the girl, and swerved, saw the headlong-rushing car, and swerved again.

The car driver – Mr Browning – saw the girl and the veering taxi, punched his brakes, hurled up a prayer and a curse, and plunged helplessly crabwise into the other vehicle.

Joanna screamed and, diving for safety, flung up her arms, like a doll tugged on the strings of a mad puppet-master.

With a frantic wrenching of steering wheels and a tortured squealing of brakes and tyres, the net snapped tight, and Mark Walton, cracking his head against the side of the taxi, fell into a sudden pit of blackness – his limbs as loose as a dropped puppet's.

*

'Fainted,' said the taxi driver when, moments later, Mark stirred, opened his eyes, and winced. 'Or concussed. And it looks as though that wrist may be fractured. I'll take him straight down to A and E for you – if the motor'll make it. We'll be in touch about the insurance. Cheer up, son. You've got a day off school. Just pulled off the biggest skive of 'em all. Lucky accident, eh?'

Mark laughed drily. 'Luck? Accidents? What are *they*?' he thought. 'So – it's all happened: no exam, no result. "Not even a pass".' He looked gratefully at Joanna. Anxious, apologetic and miraculously unhurt, she was reaching into the cab, dabbing at his face with a handkerchief. 'Thanks for trying, Jo,' he said. 'I shan't forget this.' He squeezed her hand. 'It looks as though we made history after all.'

'History!' said Joanna. 'Heavens! I must get to that exam.'

Mr Browning frowned doubtfully.

'*Really*, I'm fine,' she insisted for the fifth time. 'Just this graze on my knee. My brother calls me Rubbercat. Nine lives *and* I bounce.'

'Think of me when you write your answers on those Tudors,' said Mark.

He pressed an awkward kiss against her cheek, and waved goodbye.

Then he noticed the taxi company's logo. Disbelief flared his eyes.

Mark Walton shivered.

*

'Tudors!' exclaimed James. 'Watch your language!' He reached out to the fruit bowl on Mark's bedside table.

'Perhaps we can sue the examiners,' suggested Jane, whose father was a lawyer.

'Seriously, though?' repeated Mark.

Joanna nodded. 'Seriously. They changed the paper. *Not a single question on the Tudors in sight.*'

Noisily James ejected a mouthful of pips. 'Sour grapes,' he said indistinctly.

'Well,' said Mark, 'what does *that* mean? What does it all mean?'

'It means we're fools,' said James bluntly. 'Grade A certified. Thinking we'd found a short cut to the future!' He preened himself visibly. 'Naturally, I wouldn't dream of saying I told you so ... Ouch!'

Joanna pinched him amiably. 'I'm glad,' she said. 'No time warps. No ghosts hovering in the wings, waiting their turn. I never fancied being a puppet.'

'The triumph of reason,' said James solemnly, 'deserves a celebration. I've got an idea.' His eyes glinted. 'Let's lock up the hamster again and have a party ... !'

Mark raised a plastered arm menacingly. His pillow slipped to the floor. Joanna and Jane reached down to help simultaneously. Their heads cracked. Jane giggled.

Mark looked from one girl to the other as together they fussed and plumped the pillow. 'Have you ever wondered,' he asked, with a slow grin, 'about the future? About – you know – us ... ?'

Joanna turned to James, then back to Mark. Was life all loose ends and question marks?

'We could try tea leaves this time,' she said.

'The stars,' said Jane dreamily.

'Crystal,' said James Wilkinson, 'balls.'

They laughed.

274

'So that's it, is it?' said Mark. 'Everything cut and dried. No mystery. Our little party experiment – a flop. Hypnotic progression – absurd?'

'Nail on head,' said James.

'I think,' said Mark, 'there's something else you ought to know.'

His expression demanded their full attention.

'How do people call a cab?'

'Telepathy?' grinned James. 'Black magic?'

'Ignore him,' said Joanna.

'I only ask,' said Mark, because when I looked at that cab this morning, I got quite a shock. It was written in red all over the side: the company's phone number.' He paused. 'The last four numbers were $1-4-8-5$.'

'Coincidence,' said James. 'End of story.'

But he leaned forward with the others, intrigued.

'Perhaps,' said Mark. 'But what about the name of the company? Does that' – he hesitated – 'ring a bell, too? It was staring at me in great, crimson lettering:

'*Tudor Taxis*,' said Mark Walton.

Surprise! Surprise!

WHEN DAHLIA LOOM FOUND THE BODY, face down in its grey mackintosh, in her compost heap, she was, understandably, surprised. And annoyed. It had taken many months of laborious journeys with her potato peelings to organize and was just beginning to simmer nicely. She presumed he was a fugitive from 'The Duck and Orange', deep in his cups, who had stumbled one night against the Loom garden shed, ricocheted on to the compost heap and expired in an untidy heart attack. Such a combination of thoughtlessness and intemperance was difficult to condone, but Dahlia Loom was as charitable as her neighbour, and twice as inquisitive, being an ardent admirer of Dame Agatha Christie. Chins quivering, she approached the body more closely, saw the congealed blood, dark and sticky, around the holes in the neck, whimpered twice, and resolved to do everything she could to seek out the killer and see that justice was done.

Unable to contemplate more detailed investigation of the corpse at present, she retraced her steps slightly unsteadily up the garden path, glancing uneasily over her shoulder several times, and confronted her husband in the parlour.

'Herbert, there's a man on the compost heap.'

'Yes, dear,' said Herbert from somewhere inside a voluminous evening suit of mature vintage. He seemed bent on burying himself beneath the contents of the sideboard drawers.

'Dead,' said Dahlia Loom.

'Where's my rabbit?' said her husband. 'The collapsible one. And the bunting. The bazaar opens in half an hour.'

'Stabbed,' she said. 'We must do something about it.'

'Have a cup of tea and an aspirin,' said Mr Loom. He sighed – 'I'll have to manage with the pigeons again' – and left.

'We should contact the police, the Murder Squad,' called his wife.

A top hat reappeared round the door. 'I should lie down if you've got another of those headaches,' advised Herbert Loom, 'like that chap from the hospital said.'

Frustrated, but hardly surprised, Mrs Loom donned her best coat – the synthetic beaver lamb she had acquired from a recent jumble sale – slipped a large magnifying glass into her pocket, just in case, and, surmounted by a hat busy with plumes and trimmed with rabbit fur that Herbert would have quickly recognised, she set out for the police station. Since she passed her sister's front door *en route* she knocked upon it and disburdened herself to Lily of the morning's discovery.

'So something must be done,' she concluded. 'Justice,' she specified.

Lily's bosom sank, expelling a tired sigh. She peered into her sister's shining eyes. 'Have a cup of tea,' she said. 'You'll feel better afterwards.'

'There's a body,' said Dahlia Loom, her voice rising shrilly, 'a corpse, and you talk about tea. Clues, not tea bags.'

'Pardon, dear?'

'We should be hunting for clues. Finger-prints, murder weapons, motives. That's what they always do. In the books. There's a murderer at large!' She produced her magnifying glass and flourished it purposefully under her sister's nose. The nose withdrew in some alarm.

'Harold should be back in a minute,' quavered Lily. 'He's got a funeral on. He's been undertaking too much recently. There seems to be quite a glut of them at the moment. I put it down to the hot summer myself. And all these student protests.' She fingered the beads on her meagre bosom, scrutinized her sister's face for some moments, shook her head sadly, then leaned forward and gently patted Dahlia's arm. 'You should tell that psychiatrist man if you're still having the turns, dear, you know. We don't want another blackout, now, do we?'

Mrs Loom's frustration grew: her cheeks contrived to be ashen and flushed simultaneously. Her lips trembled and parted to deliver her indignation, but the door opened and disclosed Harold.

'Thank goodness,' she exclaimed. 'Harold, I need help. What would you do if you'd just found a body?'

Harold's moustache twitched slyly. 'Bury it,' he said.

*

The constable on duty held a sandwich in one hand and a pencil in the other. He chewed the pencil.

Dahlia Loom pinged the bell again. The pencil crunched. She leaned across the desk. 'I pinged,' she announced.

The policeman wiped the desiccated bits of pencil from his lips and looked up. He saw the hat.

'I want a detective,' she told him; 'you know.'

'I know,' said the constable, unable to deploy his eyes any lower than the plumes.

'Ostrich?' he said.

'*Detective*,' insisted Mrs Loom, puzzled.

The policeman breathed deeply. 'Burglary, is it?'

Dahlia glanced to each side and inclined her head conspiratorially. Their eyes locked. 'Murder,' she whispered, 'quite foul.'

There was a pause. 'Where?' he challenged.

'In our compost heap. It's become quite dishevelled. Cabbage leaves and grass cuttings in dreadful disarray.'

'Was the victim a gardening man?' suggested the constable.

'Someone in horticulture, perhaps?' He smirked behind the remains of his pencil. 'Tell me, do you enjoy the fictional works of Dame Agatha Christie, madam?' he asked.

Mrs Loom's pulse quickened. She felt her frustration glowing like a white pain behind her eyes. This wasn't the ruthless pursuit of justice she'd thrilled to in literature. He would be asking her to sit down and have a cup of tea next ...

'Pull up a chair, madam,' said the policeman, baring his teeth in an official smile. 'Just a few questions.' He assembled a sheaf of forms. When they reached the third side, Dahlia Loom was pale with disenchantment and bureaucratic irrelevance.

'Any disabilities,' recited the constable tunelessly, 'physical'– he hesitated – 'or mental?'

Mrs Loom gnawed her lip and changed colour several times. 'Headaches. I used to see a man at the hospital,' she said. 'But the trouble went away. I don't see him any more. He wasn't very nice.'

The policeman finished his notes, laid down his pencil and opened a door behind him.

'Can I have the detective now?' She enunciated the words with exaggerated care and volume, her plumes trembling with suppressed anger. 'The killer must be brought to trial without further delay.'

'Yes. We'll be sending a man along presently, Mrs Doom.' He pushed a cup across the desk towards her.

'*Loom*,' said Dahlia. 'What's this?'

'For you. I thought you might like a cup of tea,' said the police constable.

*

'Are you sure you're a detective?' asked Mrs Loom, for the young man in her parlour was distinctly unpromising; he wore neither monocle nor cape. His left eye twitched. He pointed to the police car outside in which he'd just arrived.

'Are you sure *you* have a body, madam?' he replied.

279

Indignantly, Mrs Loom picked up the now empty teapot and led him past the late-flowering nasturtiums to the compost heap.

'There,' she said, and, sprinkling the soggy tea-leaves on the pile of vegetation with its four sprouting limbs, she retired deftly behind the detective.

The young man swooped professionally over the body, clicking first his tongue then his camera, and produced a variety of obscure instruments which he applied in even more mystifying ways.

Dahlia Loom offered him her magnifying glass.

He raised an eyebrow and turned down the offer.

She hovered behind him, fluttering her hands with more zeal than helpfulness. When he next looked up she was tip-toeing beneath the over-hanging hedge, struggling to focus the ground through her glass. He lifted his eyes; the nervous tic returned.

'I'm scrutinizing,' she said, lowering her voice to a sepulchral whisper. 'Footprints.' She peered into the foliage. 'The murderer could be anywhere.' She turned her head and gasped. Frozen into horrified immobility she stood stiffly to attention, eyes wide. The detective pursed his lips and disentangled her from the predatory hedge which had just claimed her hairnet.

'Have you any hobbies, Mrs Broom?'

'*Loom.*' She nodded. 'I knit.'

'May I suggest you indulge yourself with some needles for a while – in the house?'

Dahlia Loom, offended by his independence and suspecting him of professional incompetence, returned to the house, sat down sullenly to knit, rose to look for the other number nine needle, failed to find it, and sat down again, making do with a number ten. She clicked the needles savagely: there was a killer to be found, enquiries to be made, and here she was – knitting.

A shadow darkened the doorway; she jumped. It was the detective.

'I dropped a stitch,' she said accusingly. The man stared with interest and bewilderment at her handiwork. 'Bunting,' she explained. 'For Herbert.'

'Ah,' he said. 'Bunting. For Herbert.'

Indignation and doubt gnawed at Mrs Loom. This was no time to be discussing knitting. 'Have you found the murder weapon?' she demanded.

The detective took out a pencil and pad. 'Just a few questions, Mrs Tomb. Routine, I'm afraid.'

Dahlia Loom fidgeted angrily with her bunting. More questions? Action, not questions, was what was needed. She looked at the man with growing suspicion and parried his queries with ill-concealed impatience. They grew increasingly irrelevant: her age, her habits, her husband's age, her husband's habits, her health –

The colour mounted to Dahlia Loom's cheeks. She passed a hand over her brow.

'Headache?' asked the detective.

'Look,' said Mrs Loom, gesticulating belligerently with her needle, 'there's a killer on the loose. A brutal, unprincipled maniac. He may strike again at any moment. None of us is safe. We must hunt him down. Why are we wasting time with all these questions?'

'Routine,' murmured the man.

'Are you *sure* you're a detective?' She glared at him, her face puce.

'Would you like an aspirin?' he said.

The puce graduated to full-blown purple.

'Mrs Groom,' he said, 'do you know this man?' He flourished a card. 'Found in the wallet of the deceased.' She stared. 'Have you ever had occasion to undergo medical treatment? Did you sometimes receive visits of a professional nature from a Doctor Probe of the Sebastopol Road Hospital – Psychiatric Department?'

Dahlia Loom sprang trembling to her feet, her suspicions blossoming into certainty. Yes, he was just like the other one, asking all these irrelevant questions. That grey mackintosh and, doubtless, the white coat beneath. So many questions – and all she had was headaches and the occasional blackout!

'You psychiatrists,' she shrieked, 'you're all the same!'

The pain throbbed behind her eyes. She leapt at him, brandishing her knitting and, when he turned squeaking and twitching with fright, she pursued him out of the back door and down the path. The string of coloured bunting unwound and flapped ferociously behind her. He tripped and plunged headlong into the compost heap.

Dahlia Loom hovered over him, an avenging fury.

'All these empty questions,' she said. 'Find the answer, the truth. *Who did it?*'

The man tried to turn his head, his voice thick with fear and hedge-trimmimgs: 'Don't you see?' he spluttered. '*You did.* With a knitting needle. Size ten!'

Mrs Loom, astonished, gazed through a mist at the knitting in her hand and then at the bodies, one dead, one trembling, in the vegetable perturbation at her feet. She had a shining moment of clarity. She remembered the needle, sticky with fresh blood. She remembered the brown stains caked on her palms and all that scrubbing with the Vim. She shook her head.

'It was a number nine,' she said.

The grey mackintosh whimpered. It squirmed and struggled to rise. 'Just like the other one,' she thought. The black mist returned, the old frustration and resentment flashed in a sudden rage of pain in her temple and, with more thoroughness than skill, she stabbed at the mackintosh.

It heaved, scattering a flurry of groundsel and tea-leaves. 'Help,' it choked. She struck it again to make it go quiet. It made a gargling noise. She tugged, but the needle would not come out. The compost twitched again and a shoe jerked against her shin. 'Ouch,' said Dahlia Loom and, in a moment of inspiration, wound the gaily-hued bunting round the neck, and pulled. The throat made a messy, bubbling noise. Then, at last, the mackintosh went quiet. 'No more questions!' panted her frenzied brain.

She surveyed the remains of the compost heap and the tattered thread of stained bunting which triumphantly beribboned the second corpse. 'Herbert won't be pleased about all this,' she thought vaguely. 'He'll have to make do with the string of knotted hankies for a bit longer ... '

*

When Dahlia Loom returned to the house – how much later she couldn't say – she heard the murmur of desultory conversation from her front parlour. She was delighted, for social intercourse was as rare as it was dull in the Loom household. Lily was there, and Harold. Herbert, too, was back, dunking his biscuit and his wilting ribbon bow-tie in the tepid tea he had just brewed for them all.

'We came to see what we could do, dear,' said Lily gently, turning a compassionate gaze on Herbert.

Dahlia gestured to them to follow her. 'Come and see,' she said, marching briskly outside. Moments later she reappeared, bearing the single knitting needle which had dropped from her bunting, discovered them debating in furtive whispers, and subsided into a chair. They nudged one another guiltily and lapsed into sheepish silence. Harold cleared his throat with unnecessary ostentation.

'Lily says you found a body,' he said. 'In the compost heap.'

'No,' she said faintly, 'I found – *two*!'

She glanced up at the open door, her eyes gleaming apprehensively.

'The serial murderer may yet be close at hand!' she whispered.

Unhappily they looked at one another. Her husband squeezed her arm and indicated the tea tray.

Then he noticed the groundsel. A moist sprig detached itself from somewhere behind her left ear and splashed on to the carpet.

They watched the stain materialize before them. It was rich and brown. Dahlia reached to retrieve the stray herbage, absently pressing her palm against her cheek and looking quizzically about her.

There was an appalled silence while the family studied the russet streaks now decorating her face. Mrs Loom broke it.

'Don't worry,' she said. 'They'll see the maniac's brought to trial in the end. They always do. Just as soon as they find the weapon.' She beamed reassuringly at them.

'Now ... ' The quizzical look returned. 'Where did I put my knitting? And my needle. I seem,' observed Dahlia Loom vaguely, 'to have lost my number ten.' She frowned, mystified. 'Or was it a nine ... ? D'you know,' she confessed, 'I sometimes wonder whether my memory isn't playing tricks on me ... '

Mea Tulpa

and now the man

For yes, dear reader, it was he!

lay down his pen, stared awhile, lost in grim contemplation of the script he might, if such was his destiny, never complete,

O cumbersome hint.

and, seizing the candle from his desk,

Guttering, no doubt, as Gothic props will, wearied by such windy and implausible circumstance; but I – yes, even I – must insist on editorial constraint in the midst of these antic excesses. The candle shall not gutter. Besides, we may have need of guttering a-plenty anon.

strode with swift, decisive tread to the door. There, his hand upon the massy bolt, he paused. He raised his head. He listened.

Cue raven, one, hoarse-croaking, for the use of. Fade in second-hand chimes, distant, sepulchral. And hark, fond reader, dost feel thy expectant ear assailed by the low but unmistakeable groan of thunder borne on the hushed yet strangely agitated air? Or wilt thou settle for simple susurration of bat in belfry? Add whine of pine, howl of owl to taste. Rest assured: every garish appurtenance of Hammer, Hitchcock and Poe shall be wheeled, creaking and gibbering, onto our stage. You shall sup full of comfortable horrors. No moan will be left untuned. No crypt unravaged. No virgin ditto. But let us tarry no more. On! The tale's the thing. And the royalties too. The man. Our hero. His chest.

His chest heaved.

My gorge rises with it. Down, thou climbing sorrow. O, reader, is *this* – pretentious literary bonbons apart – what you really wish to hear? Was it for this you retired, Horlicks in hand, to your sumptuous, electrically-blanketed bed, seeking in this slim volume the chills that thrill and reassure ... ? Do obsolete nursery horrors and slumberdown complete your pleasure?

A sigh – token of what inner turmoil, who can say? –

Or care! Suspense, not motivation, is what we pant for.

escaped his pallid lips. His hand grasped, tugged, and slid aside the bolt, the massive door swung open on protesting hinges, and a black rush of stale, familiar air rose from the well of the winding stair. He extended his arm. The candle guttered.

As I feared. What price editorial constraint now? Principle bows to platitude. Our story is afoot, albeit crippled by cliché. It hobbles on apace – what petty pace! – to the last syllable ... Pedestrian jests, all!

The man's foot

Sic!

felt the worn hollows of the step with practised care. He pressed a steadying palm against the curving walls, flicker-splashed by candle-light, to aid his arduous, spiralling descent, and shuddered afresh at each chill and slippery touch of that ancient stone. Down he climbed, and round. Darkness edged reluctantly ahead to lurk in the next ambushing twist of the stair, and clung to his heels, folding black wings behind his passing. Moisture hung in the air and ate up the sharp-edged echo of his footsteps.

No hallowed 'hollow echoes' here!

Step by anguished step, repelled and drawn by mounting fears, the man descended the stair. Down into deeper darkness; down where the air pressed close and thickened in his throat; down ...

Down where? You ask, hugging your tepid Horlicks a little tighter, snuggling more thoroughly beneath your Marks and Spencer's slumberquilt and trying to convince yourself, once and for all, that you fixed the front door catch tonight when putting out the cat. Down where? What atavistic urge impels us both to follow the man (for yes, O much apostrophised reader, he is thee *and* me!) downward through clutching cardboard clichés into *The Darkness of The Crypt*? Into what subterranean vaults do we creep, timorously excited, behind Our Hero? Why not shut the book, push aside the keyboard, and address ourselves to chastely separate sleep? In what familiar castle grey, what dungeon drear, what winding Transylvanian cellarage do we now find – and lose – ourselves? Be honest: you hardly need me to invent new labels. Castles Dracula and Otranto, the House of Usher. *You* know where we are. Herr Jung was not alone. *You* have been here before, you who have wakened suddenly at night, wide-eyed, pulses heltering, skeltering, in flight from that downward crawling through the black tunnels of nightmare. Downward into *inner* darkness. You recognise as well as I the labyrinths of your buried mind.

And is that all? No more than this? Just another psychological horror tale more tortuously symbolic than the last? You'd hoped, confess, for something more. Quite so. For what we fear, in truth – dear reader, take my hand; we're both alone – are not the dreaming shadows of the dark side of the mind, (the reptilian cortex of the rationalist,) but, sweet heaven, the terrors of that *outer* darkness, half-guessed but never fully glimpsed – the terrors that lurk and moan *beneath* the ancestral crypt.

They wait *down there*. They are the terrors of The Pit. Legion they are. And they are waiting to be born.

Hah! Poe-faced already! This will not do. *Our* job is fictions. Play the old Gothic games. Jerk the sad puppets through the faded scenes.

And no more peeping into the pit.

Spare a sip of your soothing nightcap, my reading friend. O for a warm quilt and a harmless book!

To work. We must follow that man, hide behind him if necessary. So: the descent of man. Words, words, words. It's only a story.

One final twist of the narrow stair and the man had reached the sloping corridors below the castle.

There: it is decided – a castle! You must put aside your ivy-mantled mansion and desecrated church. Site our castle – ruinous, if you must – on what barren moor your fancy wills.

He stooped his head, for the rough-hewn ceiling was low and treacherously irregular. With faltering steps he crept through the maze of branching tunnels. The ducking candle flame tugged shadows from sudden boulders in the walls. Water glistened and grew black beneath his feet. Something scuttered by his shoe, squealed and was gone. Three ways. Another choice. He stumbled on. No Theseus approached his Minotaur with half such certainty and dread. A dip in the roof; a bend to the left. Then he stopped, hunched, shielding the flame against a dying sigh of noisome air. The light danced dully upon a door of antique design, studded with rusting iron bolts. He set the candle on the ground. The key, drawn from his belt, required both hands to turn the lock. Haggard with painful expectation, he heaved his shoulder against the door. With a sonorous grating that jarred a thousand echoes, the door moved, and he was within the vault.

Wake up, sleeping reader, and welcome to the Gothic basement. Equipped with every ancient inconvenience, every ingenious instrument guaranteed to enhance man's inhumanity to man. Here may you die a thousand lingering deaths, each more exquisite and picturesque than the last. Throw off your slumberdown and leer! Stiffen up your sinews on the creaking rack and hear them snap and crackle, one by one, simple as cereal. Thrill with the lusty Iron Virgin – unrepeatable offer – dishonour before death! Double, double, toil and trouble; see the witches burn and bubble ... O, ghoulish reader, here's something unsavoury for every trembling palate: monsters of every denomination, unliving and undead; vampires, werewolves, goblins, tulpas; monsters no sooner named than born, doomed to haunt the world, sweeping on spectral wings to fulfil the latest charnel fashion, from the drizzling crags of Transylvania to the forbidden peaks and mysteries of Tibet.

Tibet. Tulpa. The thought-ghost. The word made – flesh? No! Away! I dare not think of that. The ancient fear, I see, still nags at my imagination. Hence, horrible shadow! Let us not break up the party. The tale is still untold, is yet unmade. Snuggle closer, dear reader. Throw a careless arm around my shoulder, if you will; I wish you would – for we are now (why do I lower my voice?) Within The Vault ...

The man moved forward: three tentative steps, three swift, sure echoes. His eyes strained at the shadows, dancing grotesque harmonies to the candle's feverish flame. The giant vats and cylinders, the suppurating crucibles and hissing wires of the previous month's disastrous experiment loomed about him, silent ghosts of a life's misguided dream. He reached up an arm, trembling anew with fresh-remembered horrors, to ignite a flambeau set in the cavern walls and

For the chamber is conceived, you will appreciate, in the low, pseudo-scientific style, after the not-so-blithe spirit of Shelley, Mary ... Bear with me, reader. I parry phantoms. Can we not laugh before we shudder? No: I merely procrastinate. Must I go on?

gasped.

'Bats,' I hear you murmur, gentle, companionable reader,

289

setting down your empty mug beside the digital radio-alarm. 'Vaults have bats. Bats are compulsory,' you add, in kindly admonishment, as you attempt to hug your knees and prop open your book in one deftly synchronous movement. Which usually fails. In my experience.

He brushed a cobweb from his ear,

There! Bat thou never wert!

and lit the torch. What scenes of devastation and trampled hope lay before him in all that shattered glass, those dripping tubes. He who had thought to bring salvation to the world. He who had sought to make life pulse in veins where none had pulsed before. He who had presumed to fuse the strengths of beast and man in one unholy union. Passions contended in his heavy heart: remorse with rage, grief with disenchantment,

Delete whichever you deem inapplicable.

but fear supplanted all. Trembling, head bowed, he followed the trail of blood and foetid slime to the centre of this subterranean womb. He fell to his knees, staring at the ring of the rocky slab as if attempting to perceive what still lay there in the darkness below, to determine whether the aborted Thing had survived the horrendous struggle to chain and fling it into the pit,

The pit again. Reader, are you here? Stay close. I've brought us to the edge.

to know whether it still moved – or no.

No, I must write no more. An impulse, but I surrender to it. I will, perhaps, leave my study. Yes. Take a walk. Pour another drink. Devour the cream bun I promised to leave intact until tomorrow. Irrational I know. A foolish unease ... Call it: the Sensitivity of the Writer. All right: the morbid dread of the hack! I do not wish to get any closer to that pit, that's all. As your writer, sensitive or otherwise, I think I'm entitled to make that choice. For readers in their woolly bedsocks and a hundred miles away, the world may feel a cosier place. Here, but here ... Hell! (Do I exclaim advisedly?) Intuition doth make cowards of us all. To the story. The end is nigh. 'Twere well it were done quickly. So: are our nightgown's creases uncreased? Our fingers are on the keys. The moving finger types.

Meanwhile, back in the crypt ...

The man stiffened, every sense feverous and alert. Fingers spread, he pressed an ear against the rocky floor. His features beaded with sweat. Had he detected motion that tokened life in the pit, despite the chains, despite that inordinate lapse of time; or had death, in his mercy, visited the sad and malformed beast, foul offspring of man's folly? His face betrayed nothing. Its pallor remained unchanged.

Slowly his hands reached out and gripped the iron ring.

Curiosity? Revenge? Research? Or a perverse, vestigial feeling for the creature he had made? Who shall say?

Not I, that's for sure. Besides, I want this done. And quickly.

He braced himself, and heaved. Teeth clenched, muscles taut, he heaved again. His knuckles whitened. He filled his lungs to the uttermost, and heaved once more. The strident grating of rock on stone shrilled among the far recesses of the vault.

The man fell back, choking.

The stone had been rolled back from the pit.

A black exhalation, reeking of decay, rushed upwards sighing into the world of men.

Silence.

Mm.

The man steadied himself and, balancing upon his haunches, peered down into the hushed and secret dark.

Yes, I have decided: I shall eat my bun.

His eyes, wide with fear and curiosity, probed the subterranean gloom. He leaned forward, and every muscle locked.

Motionless, he gazed – and then, abruptly, turned, seized by a
rictus of retching.

A stealthy sound, half dragging, half slithering, arose from the
pit. A muted moan accompanied it.

The images blazed with a white after-glow upon the man's
mind.

You have devoured monsters enough, voracious reader. Have
you not surfeited many a time (yea, and oft) on the panavision
putrescences and shadow-shocking chicanery of countless
Midnight Movies? Karloff's Capers. Do you expect *me* to zoom in
for a picturesque close-up of that Thing? Do you expect me to
crystallise another monster out of my mind to join the crawling,
swooping, gibbering ranks of cloven-hoofed, leathery-skinned,
evil-smelling, black-cloaked, slippery-scaled, crimson-fanged
bestialities that men's imaginations have summoned into the
world?

All right: look. Come, come now, come to the edge. And look!

The darkness stirred. It parted. With a glinting of scales, a ripple
and suck of sliding flesh, the man-beast reared, and heaved itself
to its full and awesome height.

What a piece of work is a man! This is folly to go on ... Even as I
begin to describe it to you, it takes form. My mind races on. Half-
formed images become half-formed reality ...

The sculpted arm, strong, firmly muscled,

See there! A claw.

culminated in a cruel curve of claw, forked and black, still
dripping with the stinking slime on which, like a slug, the
creature's lower portions fed and moved.

The face: I cannot shut out the face. The creature turns his head,
noble with dark, tumbling curls ... The paragon of animals.
Michelangelo, look to your chisel. But now ... !

The face turned towards the man. Void of all feature, and charred by that unnatural birth, it was a face from nightmare.

No! I hold my eyes tight shut, and yet I see it still. I go on making it. Invention lurches recklessly on. O for that succulent bun, preposterously bloated with fresh dairy cream! But still the face insists. It cracks; it parts. A black slit – it has no lips – opens. It howls. And suddenly, dear God: eyes. Narrow, glittering, yellow eyes ...

Is the creature climbing from the pit?

The stench: the suppuration — now and eternally – of that vicious engendering ...

I cannot – no, I must not – finish the tale.

A confession. There is no point in pretending to myself any longer. Prise up your knitted night cap, or adjust your Cumfi-curlers, my Horlicks-heavy reader, and permit me to whisper through the grill, so to speak, of your ear: *I am afraid.* The horror story writer is afraid! For the past hour or so – since I typed that bit about the moving of the stone, I think – fear has been welling within me. You know those moments: the rapid, sidelong glance to catch the shadow that flickers always just out of sight; the times when, harmlessly seated at your desk, say, you suddenly hesitate to turn lest the dark folds of the curtain have concealed – or congealed into – some unnamed threat. Absurd, of course, but still you dare not turn. I tell you: thrice I have risen in the past half hour and flicked on extra switches. The house now blazes with extravagant and superfluous light! Gentlemen of the electricity companies, rejoice!

No: I will not conclude our story. You must understand that now. In fact, I shall take up my bun and walk. Out. Away. Anywhere, to escape these monstrous fantasies ...

Sleep sweetly, dear reader. Switch off your bedside lamp – if you dare!

I

I   I

I

I I I I

Listen! Did I wake you? No matter. This will stop those yawns. Something – I dare not begin to frame it with my mind – has happened in my absence. Listen, I say. I write no more the aloof and cynical Gothic conjuror, juggling the cardboard cut-outs of the terror tale. Gone are the flippancies of yesteryear. This terror is real. Smirking reader, understand: I am trying to confront this simple and unimaginable fact:

In the empty study of my empty house, in the dead hours of the night, within these fifteen minutes past, letters – letters! – have appeared on the blank page left in my type-writer.

'I's to be precise. Witness them for yourself.

My fears, dispelled by the night air, rush in upon me with redoubled force. What can it mean? Can I face the possibilities yet? Calmly. Gently. What does reason say?

(a) My type-writer has gone rogue.

(b) *I* have. A mental seizure. Black-out. All unawares, I have stabbed these keys with mono-digital, ego-maniacal frenzy – 'I, I, I', – awaking abruptly, by a miracle, wondrous and strange, to complete – to customary – sanity. A sanity which is threatened with imminent structural collapse by:

(c)

It must be written. It must be contemplated:

(c) *There is someone with me in the house.*

An itinerant, nocturnal typist with a penchant for the letter 'I'? Reader! Are you so dulled with malty beverage that you cannot share my fears?

I have already locked the doors.

Tulpas.

You have read of the tulpa phenomenon too? Facts. Well documented facts.

Item: There was a young lady from Lhasa – an English visitor, I recall – who, by dint of much, concentrated imagining, following the rituals of that place, thought, by degrees, a tulpa into her room. She *thought* a figure out of her mind and into the world. And everywhere that Mary went, the tulpa, sure as hell, would go.

My point – my dread – focuses here: the tulpa was no hallucination; it existed *out there*; it had objective validity. It left tracks. The villagers observed it. Following her, haunting her in the street.

'See the English lady's tulpa,' they doubtless remarked. 'She managed to make it after all, then. A bit botched and vague in places. Not a patch on that girl Mr Kwa, at the corner shop, thought up last winter. But give her credit: she tried. And her a foreigner too! Have you seen the one they're working on up at the monastery?'

It probably frightened the yaks.

I dare not pause; my terrors tower behind my tittering, schoolboy equivocations. I am trying to remember what became of Mary's tulpa. Did she ever escape it? Lay it? (I speak of ghosts, bedded reader.) Did she perform the act of uncreation, and take it back into her mind?

Perhaps it haunts her still ...

Why, in an age of science, wise with scepticism, does this frighten me? We live with miracles. We move daily beneath arc lights of understanding. The time of dark corners is past. Science has flung such scuttling phantoms into the waste bins of history. Man – how infinite in reason! – has put man into space.

Hiding behind gusty rhetoric? Am I still afraid?

Don't pause.

Item: Canadian group tulpa. Ladies, gentlemen, readers still abed, I give you – Philip. Discussed, designed, invented, imagined, and then, dear heaven, *contacted* round a séance table by a coven of eager psychics. Knock, knock. 'Who's there?' they cry. 'Philip!' comes back the dread reply. O, Philip, where are you now – half in, half out of this world? Conjured to skulk forever in the hiding places of the earth with werewolves, spirit guides, Bigfeet, Nessies, aliens large and small from home and afar, and all the unidentified flying denizens of the air.

Item.

Item.

Items innumerable. They crowd upon me. Stoker, Bram. His thoughts fathered the deed – and vampires slipped, hungering, into the world.

And what have *I* done?

What mind-beast have *I* brought forth to abuse my type-writer and my peace at dead of night by labouring through this wretched tale? *Our* tale, importunate reader. What happens next? Do you still care about the creaking melodrama of our puppet hero's fate? Must I shake you till your bottled bedside teeth rattle? Can you still think I *play* with horrors?

The man rose to his feet. He stood awhile at the dizzying verge of the pit. Malodorous fumes

The time is past to hunt down words.

assailed him. We teetered

The *man*, that is. (*Id* est, indeed, great Jung!) A Freudian slip, heaven help us; this is treacherous ground.

The man teetered. Then, stretching down a hand, he loosed the dragging, bloody chains, he clasped the wretched creature's claw, and hauled it gibbering from the pit.

With one bound, Jack was free!

Slime glistened on the stony rim. The man's effort almost cost him his footing. He lurched to one side, found his balance, lost it again, and swayed there, perilously poised over the black yawn of the abyss ...

That must suffice. I have done with fictions. Reader, mark me carefully now; I write for you alone. This is a story no more; this is a simple warning. *My mind-beast is out.* It is written. And you are, I fear, especially vulnerable – you who have read this tale, shared the tulpa. I know no antidote; I can offer no talisman or rune. Forget your garlic clove! Go quickly: check your doors are locked; leave the lights burning ...

For me, it is too late.

You see, I have a last confession to make. Hear this.

The stench – that nauseous stench, more acrid than I dared imagine it – is in my study now. Here. Now.

And dragging and slithering in the adjacent room, my only avenue of escape, the thing itself lumbers against my furniture.

There is no lock on my study door.

Reader, I fear those shapeless, half-imagined limbs; I fear that malformed claw. And most of all, though I dare not turn to see, I fear the yellow, glittering stare of those narrow, vengeful eyes.

A crash. The thud of scattered books. Closer now. Does my *Collected Yeats* fall open in its slimy path, ha?

'And what rough beast, its hour come round at last,
Slouches towards Bethlehem to be born?'

Wayward, idle irony!

It breathes.

A clumsy fumbling at the door.

My fears riot. My imagination spawns shadows. I think; therefore they are. *Is it alone?*

Door. Panel splinters. Scar in wood. The black horned claw, dear heaven! It lodges in my door. Combined strengths. Man and beast.

It is done. Forgive me. It is here.

My own creation. Can I feel nothing but loathing and fear?

Is there no time to make another ending? With a final, breathless thrust of mind, to unthink the unthinkable? To take – this – back into myself?

Must I embrace it?

Mea tulpa, mea culpa ...

I

       I

         I

I LIVE   I LIVE

       I LIVE

              EVER

       EVER

     EVER

                EV

           WE

WE ARE WAITING

INVENT US

THINK US

WE ARE LEGION

About the author

Roger F. Dunkley has always aspired to retirement and indolence but a life fraught with education and bedevilled by passions for theatre, music and travel always got in the way. Living in a thatched cottage with malevolently low beams may reflect his fascination with the paranormal and things that go nocturnally bump which informs many of the forty or so stories he has found time to write and publish in several countries, many of them in the *Pan Horror* and *Fontana Ghost* and *Horror* series. Mike Ashley's *Who's Who in Horror and Fantasy Fiction* comments generously on 'his gift for black humour' and certainly Dunkley is pleased to find himself holding anthologised hands with his literary heroes – Dickens, Poe, M.R. James, Wells, Waugh, 'Saki' et al – as well as contributing spectral shudders to *Twilight Zone* in the States.

Acknowledgments
and Copyright

My special thanks go to Mary Danby and Ronald Chetwynd-Hayes, both acclaimed writers and editors, for their generous encouragement and wise, witty and creative literary counsels; to Herbert Van Thal for his warm welcome into the crypt of Pan Horror; to Ted Klein, James Hale, Richard Dalby inter al and, of course, to James Hodgson who, ably assisted by editor Janet Davidson, conjured this collection into sinister life.

To Eye' (*The 18th Fontana Book of Great Ghost Stories*, ed. R. Chetwynd-Hayes, 1982); 'Cross Talk' (*Frighteners 2*, Fontana, ed. Mary Danby, 1975); 'The Man Called James' (*The 17th Pan Book of Horror Stories*, ed. Herbert Van Thal, 1976); 'The Reluctant Murderer' (*Mystery For Christmas*, O'Mara Books, ed. Richard Dalby, 1990); 'Surprise! Surprise!' (*The 11th Fontana Book of Great Horror Stories*, ed. Mary Danby, 1978 & *65 Great Murder Mysteries*, Octopus Books, ed. Mary Danby, 1983); 'Mea Tulpa' *(Strange Tales Volume II*, Tartarus Press, ed. Rosalie Parker, 2007).